# AMERICAN LOVE SONG

## BRITT MIDDLETON

BRITT MIDDLETON PRESS, NEW YORK CITY

*To all the girls who dared to love, again and again.*

It's you and me, there's nothing like this.

— TAYLOR SWIFT

# AUTHOR'S NOTE

Dearest reader,

AMERICAN LOVE SONG is a joyous celebration of love, courage, and self-acceptance. It also explores themes of racism, anxiety disorder, depression and grief following the death of a parent. I hope you find that I've handled these tender subjects with the utmost of care and compassion. I also hope this story heals your heart in same way that it's healed mine.

Big hugs,
   Britt

# CHAPTER ONE

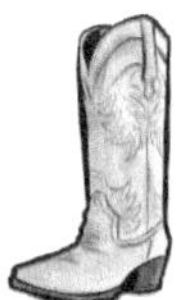

*B*rinton Shaw succumbed to the inevitable: she wasn't getting out of this hellhole alive. Figuratively speaking, anyway.

She tightened her grip on the cold metal railing in vain. Beneath her, the red carpet stretched another ten feet longer each time she exhaled.

Crowds were her biggest trigger. Yet, there she was, one of hundreds of journalists tightly packed like sardines inside a bullpen.

Brinton couldn't remember when the electric pulses started shooting up her arms and down her legs. Or, when she could no longer hear her own thoughts over the barricade of screeching fans.

She was, however, certain about this: the Grammy Awards were the absolute worst fucking place to have a panic attack.

Usually, she fought like hell to hide hers from everyone—and especially at work. But as the flashing cameras and swinging microphones gave her tunnel vision, there was nowhere to run.

Brinton's videographer, Lucero, was positioned with his camera and tripod four feet away. "You don't look so good," he offered, tilting his bald head.

Built like a pro wrestler, he almost exclusively scowled unless asked about his new favorite K Pop group. "Kinda like…a hunk of wilting brie in a heatwave."

Coincidentally, Brinton's insides felt the same way.

Shifting in her black-heeled combat boots, she forced a laugh. "I'm good."

*You have worked so hard to get here, just—please. Hold it together.*

She had to. In mere moments, she needed to smile and competently deliver the first of the night's red carpet interviews. There was zero margin for error.

When Rich, her *Landmark* editor, assigned Brinton to cover the Grammys red carpet, it was the biggest opportunity of her career. It got her closer to finally writing a cover story for *Landmark*, the pretentious but respected magazine she worked for in New York City.

In four years, she was the only *Landmark* staff writer who hadn't been asked to pitch a cover story. To her, this wouldn't have stood out so prominently if, year after year, she hadn't been the only Black person on staff.

The subtext popped out like a fresh BBL: in corporate America, diversity and inclusion were only valuable on paper. This was kindling for Brinton's imposter syndrome. Hot and husky on the back of her neck, it admonished that she should be *grateful* to be *chosen.*

She was one of the *good* ones.

Brinton had no choice but to keep her head down and work harder. Eventually, she would prove herself. Today was that day.

"You got Jamie Crawford Jr. headed straight to you," Lucero said, now behind the camera.

"Country music guy—I got it," Brinton answered, dragging her sticky palms down her silky gold wrap dress.

She swished her waist-length knotless braids off her right shoulder. Heat spread across her cocoa-brown cheeks. "This one will be easy."

If her brain didn't feel like a raw egg cracked onto a hot skillet, this might have been true. For days, she had memorized a dictionary's worth of facts about artists she expected to interview. This included Jamie Crawford Jr. and dozens of DJs with stage names inspired by exotic fruits.

But right now? All that preparation was meaningless. What if she flubbed a word? Or, if she had pit stains on her dress? Or, if she failed so spectacularly that Rich demoted her to reviewing *Kidz Bop* albums for all of eternity?

"What's the signal before we go live?" Brinton choked out, suddenly dizzy. She steadied herself against the railing behind her. The shock of cold felt like a relief on her sticky lower back.

"4...3...2..."

The light on Lucero's camera flashed red as Jamie Crawford Jr. approached. He was that square-jawed, *Varsity Blues* kind of attractive. In fact, he looked even *better* than in the pictures. It was actually quite rude.

Jamie's sandy blond waves were boyishly mused and kissed his ears. Brinton guessed he had earned his coppery tan from playing shirts-versus-skins football with buddies in a field. Or, driving a tractor for fun.

His midnight blue suit was impeccably tailored to his well-over six-foot-frame and drew out the shimmer highlights of his aquamarine eyes. The whole effect was effortlessly cool, like James Bond's twin brother, separated at birth and raised in a honky-tonk.

"Hey," Brinton said, hoping to sound more confident than she felt.

"Hey, yourself," Jamie answered.

He stretched each letter like he had swirled his tongue in molasses. God, why was she thinking about his *tongue*?

She was there to work, not hit on the talent. Why would he look twice at her? His options were probably like Olive Garden breadsticks: never-ending and hot.

Brinton, meanwhile, saw herself as more like a cute librarian than an Instagram baddie. At least she was blessed with enough curves that she needed to jump when pulling on jeans.

Jamie outstretched his catcher's mitt-sized palm. When she took it, he squeezed.

*God, his hands were huge.*

Brinton's belly clenched. Was it the thrill of unexpected warmth from his touch? Or, the triple shot of espresso that she had downed on an empty stomach?

It didn't matter. She had to get herself *together*. First priority: stop staring at this man. Brinton dropped Jamie's hand and pushed out a shallow breath. Her eyes shifted to Lucero's camera.

It was showtime.

"If you're just joining the live stream, I'm Brinton Shaw," she said. Immediately, she regretted how tinny her voice sounded. "I have a special guest with me, country music superstar Jamie Crawford Jr."

Without missing a beat, he flashed that glimmering, for-the-cameras grin. "I'm a huge fan of the magazine. Believe me, the pleasure is all mine, Ms. Shaw."

*Ms. Shaw.* A white-hot flash zipped up her spine as his smoldering baritone warmed her ears. For some reason, it anchored her enough so she could focus.

*Keep your thoughts on the sound of his voice.*

"Just wait until I've asked my questions," Brinton

answered. Her voice felt a hint steadier. Richer. Jamie's eyes flickered. Did he notice too?

"Maybe you'll go easy on me, since you've got home field advantage?" he asked, dragging those perfectly white teeth over his pillowy bottom lip. She had to stop looking at his *lips*.

"Um, we should get into tonight's nominations. You're up for Best New Artist," she stammered. "You must be ecstatic."

"I..." His voice trailed off. Jamie's eyes fell to his black cowboy boots. "I'm grateful to be here, but I don't always feel like I deserve such fortune."

Brinton raised her eyebrows. "I think your fans would disagree. Your song 'Table for One' shot to the top of the Hot 100 chart. It was the first country single to do so since, well..."

"My father," Jamie answered flatly. He frowned, then gazed back down at the ground. "Yeah, I couldn't believe it either."

Was he embarrassed? Who knew that was a prerequisite to Nepo Baby fame?

"I think you made the heartbreak anthem your own," Brinton volleyed back. "The facets of humor beneath the sadness were so unexpected."

He softly smiled, then leaned closer to her microphone. "Oh yeah? What were you expecting?"

Was he flirting with her? And did she like it? Or rather, *should* she like it?

Brinton wet her lips. Her thoughts raced quicker than her mouth could move.

"I wasn't expecting that any woman could make *you* cry into your whiskey. I mean, you're the Heartbreak Prince. You don't earn that nickname lightly."

"Well, I'm full of surprises," he quipped, as if egging her on.

Brinton took the bait. "Okay, then I have to ask, who was the lucky lady? You sing about so many women in that song. First crush, maybe?"

Technically, Rich had pushed Brinton to ask this. She wasn't angling to dig into Jamie's personal life. Even if he probably had an industrial storage unit full of women's panties fans had flung on stage. But Brinton was on a mission. She had to land this plane.

"Oh, honey, I don't kiss and tell." Jamie chuckled through a slow, easy smile. "Though, now I'm wondering if it might be you?"

He was definitely flirting with her. Famous people did this all the time to seem more relatable. So why did her mouth feel like she had licked a roll of sandpaper?

"Let's, um, stay on track," Brinton countered. Suddenly, she was burning up. It must be Lucero's lighting rig. Obviously.

"Hardball it is." Jamie laughed. "Shame, I bet you could make a grown man cry. That ain't a bad thing, by the way."

He was trying to be a good sport and make her comfortable. She needed that. Her ears had started to ring as the crowd's cheers swelled.

"I like to be thorough with my questions," Brinton said. "I hope that's not a problem."

"No, ma'am."

*No, ma'am.*

Without permission, her lips tugged upward into a soft smile. Brinton didn't even know this man, and he didn't know her. But she couldn't deny the spark of familiarity between them. It flared each time he spoke. Or when she breathed.

When Jamie smiled back, it seemed like a real one that reached his eyes. It should be locked away at the Pentagon.

Unfortunately, the moment was fleeting. Another

surprise wave of nausea thrashed in Brinton's gut. Her microphone slipped from her clammy grip.

Mercifully, Jamie's open palm shot out before it tumbled to the ground.

When he pressed it back into her hand, he didn't say a word. He was helping her, and she was grateful. Behind him, Jamie's entourage—an older white man with a salt-and-pepper goatee and a pageant-worthy brunette—whispered conspiratorially.

Brinton was running out of time. She still needed an exclusive angle that *Landmark* could run on the website's front page. Rich warned that she had to drive clicks.

Lucero circled his wrist in a "wrap it up" motion. This was her last shot.

"Does being a musician, and playing for thousands of fans, help you express yourself more authentically in your real life?" she asked. "Or does that ever hold you back?"

It was her favorite question of the bunch. She was surprised to have pieced it together, given how the circuit breaker in her brain was officially fried.

Jamie cocked his head like she had asked for the universe's deepest secret.

"My *real* life?" he started. Jamie spoke even slower than his Tennessean accent deemed possible.

"Nobody's ever asked me a question quite like that before, so thank you. I guess I believe music is where artists lay themselves bare—what keeps them up at night, and what gets their boots on the floor in the morning. In my real life, I wanna be that kind of person. No ego, just…honesty. That's why, I hope one day—"

Jamie glanced over his shoulder to the brunette and goateed man. Their expressions were tight and silently expressed something Brinton couldn't decode.

The goateed man shook his head.

For the first time, Jamie's broad shoulders stiffened. "Um, that's why I'm proud to share, for my forthcoming second album, my father once again took the reins as producer. And he's as authentic as it gets."

Beneath Jamie's lukewarm smile, there was a hint of something that felt like reservation. He seemed to bristle with every word that formed next. Why was that?

"You're hearing it here first," Jamie continued. "The album will be out this summer."

That was it—she'd landed an exclusive quote *and* a new album announcement. She had done it. There was no way Rich could deny her a cover story now.

Yes, she was close enough to *taste* it—

Then, a wave of stale coffee crested in her stomach. She swallowed a burp.

*Oh God.*

Jamie's brow creased. "You all right?"

Brinton jumped as his fingertips grazed her elbow. "Mm-hm."

Her lips twisted into a grimace. As her shoulders dipped backward, Jamie's palm spread over the small of her back.

She gripped his shoulders as one of his hands inched up to cradle her neck. A thin gasp escaped her lips when his calloused fingertips teased the springy baby hairs at her nape.

As she looked up at him, her nose brushed against his soft, freshly shaven neck. She wondered how it would feel against fingertips.

Or, a pair of lips.

He smelled divine, like honeyed whiskey spiked with cloves.

It was only a few seconds. However, all around them, the screaming fans and barking reporters flattened into a whisper. Jamie's breath hitched as his eyes searched hers.

*What was he looking for?*

Jamie brought Brinton back to level. "Sweetheart, why don't you sit—"

*Just try to focus*, she begged herself. *Just keep him talking.*

"What else can you tell us about the new album?" Brinton sputtered as her stomach throbbed.

For the second time, Lucero circled his wrist to signal Brinton to sign off. They needed to reset for the next interview.

"Can I get you some water?" Jamie asked, ignoring Lucero's pantomiming.

*Oh God. Oh God!*

It was too late.

Watery, hot bile tinged the back of Brinton's throat. She couldn't stop the rush. Seconds later, she was doubled over and spewing her sins onto Jamie's very expensive-looking cowboy boots.

"Woah," Jamie gasped, jolted by surprise.

Lucero dry-heaved. The brunette behind Jamie shrieked.

"Good Lord, that smell," the goateed man croaked. He jostled Jamie down the red carpet.

Presumably to burn his cowboy boots.

Brinton prayed to every deity that her exorcism had gone unnoticed, but as she stood and straightened, every bystander's phone was a sniper's scope trained on her.

"Um—we're on a commercial break," Lucero stuttered. Disgust streaked his hardened face. "But I heard from Rich. The live stream has over five million viewers. A new record."

Brinton didn't watch as her microphone splashed into the fresh puddle at her feet. She had gotten her interview, her big moment. But it had cost something she couldn't afford to lose.

INSIDE THE CRYPTO.COM Arena's bustling auditorium, Jamie sat in his dress socks. Regretfully, he'd stashed his favorite boots inside a VIP bathroom.

On stage, a willowy pop star wore yellow pasties and a skirt fashioned from matching caution tape. As she announced the nominees for Best New Artist, Jamie tried to mentally check-out.

Industry tastemakers had predicted that Jamie would win, but that was the last thing he wanted. Not after what he had done.

Jamie's stomach rumbled. They never served enough food at these events. When he got back to the fancy hotel his team had booked, he'd grab a cheeseburger, crispy shoestring fries, and a double whiskey on the rocks. He'd cap off the night in bed, watching *Sports Center*.

It would be a rare reprieve from the circus he called life.

His mind wandered back to Brinton, the *Landmark* reporter. Lordy, he felt for her. His team informed him that the red-carpet interview had gone viral. Great for the album, they said. Jamie knew that was far worse for Brinton.

Should he have someone send her a fruit basket? What was the protocol for "sorry you became a meme"?

He didn't know.

With all the cameras and shouting, Jamie understood why Brinton had seemed stressed. But he wouldn't wish what happened to her on anyone. In fact, he admired her grit.

Had he done something to trip her up? He wasn't trying to, but he kept getting distracted by her shy little smile. And how she squinted hard when searching for the right words. It was cute.

Hell, *cute* was an understatement. She was gorgeous. But

gorgeous women were a dime-a-dozen in his world. Brinton had something *else*.

She asked one hell of a good question about being authentic in his own life. It was rare that someone in Jamie's orbit cared what *he* thought, let alone encouraged him to say it aloud.

His team only cared about building his *legacy*.

Of course, Brinton couldn't have known that. Still, for a few moments, her question almost prompted Jamie to tell her the truth about his life.

It would have detonated his entire career, but at least he would have a clear conscience.

Would Brinton have wanted to help make that happen? The question yanked at something buried deeply in Jamie's chest. Then again, he probably wouldn't see her again.

Breaking his reverie, "Table for One" blared over the speakers. That was when Jamie noticed everyone was staring at him. Their faces were stretched with excitement, and they cheered like he had won a Grammy.

*Did I just win a damn Grammy?*

Enveloped by a roar of cheers, Jamie slowly stood and stumbled down the crowded aisle. He wanted to run away, but the congratulatory slaps on his back propelled him forward.

When the caution-taped pop star handed him his trophy, he kept his eyes glued to hers, despite the magnetic pull of those pasties.

"Holy sh—" Jamie breathed into the microphone, catching himself.

So much for mentally checking out.

Dread tightened the muscles at the base of his neck. He rubbed the warm spot with his free hand, but it didn't help. He was so damn overwhelmed.

"I—um—can't believe this," he began.

This was a nightmare.

"I want to sincerely thank the fans," Jamie continued. "You know, my father won this same award in nineteen eighty. When I was writing these songs, under his guidance…"

The words soured and clung to Jamie's tongue. What if he broke the cycle of lies? He could scrape up the dignity he had left. He could tell the world the truth.

He exhaled deeply. His chest ached as his heartbeat quickened. Suddenly, the air was too thick.

No—the Grammys stage wasn't the right place. It would be too easy for his intentions to be misconstrued. He had to find another way.

"I'm so grateful that the fans love these songs as much as I do," Jamie said, submitting to his team's approved talking points.

Extending more obligatory thank-yous, Jamie backed away from the mic stand. But as the spotlight—or, the light of inspiration—beamed down, he doubled back.

When he glanced down to his socked feet, the crowd exploded with cheers. Right.

How to explain that?

"I'd also like to thank Brinton Shaw. You might be my good luck charm. Though, you owe me a new pair of boots."

It was no Edible Arrangement, but it was something. He wanted Brinton to know he was thinking of her, and that he hoped she was all right. For now, it was the best he could do.

Jamie hoisted the gilded gramophone into the air and gave a practiced smile. It should have been the best night of his career. This was his father's plan.

But Jamie was a fraud. Soon, everybody else would know too.

*D*espite the cold pool of drool beneath her cheek, Brinton intended to enjoy the last forty minutes before her alarm sounded. Since becoming an internet sensation, deep sleep was increasingly rare. Instead, she spent nights googling herself, a search and rescue mission for her self-worth.

She'd seen thousands of posts these last three months. Some shipped her and Jamie Crawford Jr. as a post-racial poster couple for "changing hearts and minds." Many more ran the gamut of creatively repulsive racist and sexist insults. The resulting dread made her avoid mirrors most days.

Brinton hated herself for letting the poisonous seeds sprout. And yet she also wondered if her full-time critics were somehow right. By doing the Grammys interview, had she brought all of this attention—no, this shame—on herself?

As her eyelids dropped, pulsating bass and needling synth spilled from the Bluetooth speaker on her nightstand. Beyoncé's husky-smooth vocals did figure-eights through her body. Only one person was so sinister.

Shayla whipped her hips in the doorway, gripping her

phone like a makeshift mic and belting "Alien Superstar" so off-key it was actually impressive.

"Shay, what the—"

Shay tapped a button, ceasing her assault. "Mom wanted me to help get your raggedy butt up."

Brinton slapped the speaker into her nightstand drawer and slammed it shut. "*This* is helping?"

"It's Beyoncé," she purred, arms crossed over her flouncy chartreuse mini-dress. "I cleansed your aura, balanced your chakras, and re-upped your Bad Bitch Energy. You're welcome."

Brinton lifted her torso, body rebelling in a fit of rigor mortis. She was only twenty-seven but felt as vital as an expired prune. "Right, my mistake." Even she knew better than to downplay a Beyoncé dance break.

Shay, two years Brinton's junior, was a real-life Alien Superstar. A successful physical therapist specializing in women's pelvic floor dysfunction, she lived in a slick Harlem loft. Her bleached mini 'fro was striking against her maple-brown complexion, and through certain sorcery, her signature strawberry lipstick was always intact. Sometimes, Brinton felt guilty envying her little sister as much as she loved her.

Shay snatched back the heavy gray blackout curtain from the bay window opposite her bed, releasing a surge of white sunlight into the glorified shoebox. Brinton hissed like Nosferatu.

"Oh good, you're up." Brinton's mother, Athena, breezed in carrying a tray of flaky croissants from their favorite bakery, Biscuit Wench; a steaming carafe of coffee; and mugs for the three of them. She pushed aside the graveyard of half-empty glasses, granola bar wrappers, and unread books to set the tray on Brinton's nightstand.

As usual, Athena wore one of her favorite cream linen

lounge sets. This one was short-sleeved and showed off her Michelle Obama–worthy biceps. She and Brinton had the same rich complexion, but Athena always looked lit-from-within. Her corkscrew coils were perpetually buoyant.

By this point in the morning, her mom had likely done her reading, taken a yoga class, made celery juice, and seen a patient for a therapy session. Five years ago, Athena amicably divorced Brinton's father, a curator for the National Museum of African-American History and Culture in Washington, D.C., and her glow-up had been next-level.

Brinton fantasized about how much easier her life would be if she had inherited her mom's executive function. But, fine. Getting her high cheekbones was still a win.

"Baby, I know things have been difficult, but it's not good for you to…languish," Athena said. "And would it hurt to change into some pj's before bed?"

Brinton appraised herself: yesterday's jeans and a white T-shirt with a stoic portrait of Maya Angelou on the front. She gestured down the length of her body.

"Mm, not nearly as efficient. See? I'm already dressed. Technically, I'm ahead."

Shay poured a gleaming stream of coffee into a mug. "They teach you that girl-math at Columbia, or did you think of it yourself?"

She glugged in half-and-half and passed it to Brinton. It smelled like chocolate, caramel, and life itself, rendering her useless at conjuring a witty retort.

"You aren't still worried about that little video, are you?" Athena asked. "The world has moved on. I think you should too. And I can't help but beg you to consider that, if you took care of yourself, these panic attacks wouldn't stand in the way of what you really want."

Having a licensed psychologist as a mother probably should have done wonders for Brinton's mental health.

However, her father, whose discipline she admired, was ruthlessly pragmatic, encouraging her to see logic as far more reliable than emotions. It was a protective measure, she understood. His attempt to buffer a world where her naked otherness didn't fit into prescribed contours. Inevitably, she never felt equipped to process the maelstrom inside, and feared she never would.

"Yeah? Even without the panic attacks, I'm still the struggling, failed artist of the family," she said. "So, what do you make of that?"

When Brinton first graduated from college, she tried and failed to get her short story manuscripts published. Journalism was the easiest pivot, and now, working at *Landmark*, she at least had the status of writing for a legacy publication in New York City. That made her *somebody*.

Brinton groaned as her mother frowned. It wasn't yet nine a.m., and she was exhausted. "I appreciate what you're trying to do, Mom, but in the worst moment of my life, millions of people decided who I was. I'm reminded of it every day. And that's including the people I work with, who barely look me in the eyes."

Ultimately, her interview with Jamie drove millions of hits to the website, which saved her job. That and blaming her sickness on eating bad shrimp. Still, she felt the pang of isolation from her co-workers—from her sense of self— marrow-deep.

"Just because people think they know you as one thing doesn't mean you can't change," Shay said, ripping off a hunk of croissant. She pinched the golden dough between her glossy, black-manicured fingers. "Like this perfect French pastry, you got layers, baby."

Truthfully, Brinton's life stalled well before she'd moved back in with her mom a year ago, right after Eli dumped and then not-so-politely evicted her from his Financial District high-rise.

Athena squeezed Brinton's foot through the baby blue quilt she'd had since seventh grade. "What if the magazine isn't the right fit? You've been so miserable. What about creative writing, like you studied in school?"

The best thing about attending Columbia University was learning from a decorated faculty of literary creatives. The worst thing was that in doing so, Brinton owed more in student loans than she made annually as an actual writer in New York City.

Saving for an apartment was a Sisyphean feat, and she refused her mother's persistent requests to help. Brinton's confidence couldn't survive another hit.

"Or you could sell pictures of your ears?" Shay mused. "Make an app and call it something sexy like…'Only Lobes'?"

Athena and Brinton exchanged perplexed looks.

"I've seen your feet. Nobody deserves that." Shay cackled, drunk off her own wit.

Brinton launched a throw pillow at Shay's head. "Ha-ha. You should take this routine on the road, like back to your apartment."

She turned to her mother and softened. "If I quit now, the last four years were a waste. I'll figure it out."

"Girl, wake up!" Shay waved her withering croissant in the air. "Don't you get the sense that they're using you? They've had four years to promote you but haven't. Why? Because as long as they have one Black person on the masthead, they can pretend to be this forward-thinking company that"—she made air quotes with her index fingers—"values diversity. You're a melanated bargaining chip."

Deep down, though excruciating to admit, Brinton knew this. Even with her recent post-Grammys slump, her work was solid, and while she wasn't particularly close with her colleagues, she'd never received a single disciplinary action that would warrant being benched as an entry-level staff writer for so long.

"Remember your first day?" Shay tutted. "Rich talked all that mess about being your 'authentic self'? But we know what he really meant was, be 'authentic' to his expectations. Approachable, but not ditzy. Savvy, but not a know-it-all. Malleable enough to notch into both obvious and covert perceptions about you: where you were from, where you went to school, if that was your real hair."

"Whether or not I grew up with a father," Brinton put in, shaking her head. "I thought *Landmark* was going to be my big break. I wanted to leave my mark."

When she first started at *Landmark*, Brinton spoke up in meetings, questioning problematic story pitches that leaned heavily on racial stereotypes. There were only so many "hip-hop's unlikely white savior" discussions Brinton could stomach. She was always met with a chorus of groans and calls that she was being "too literal" or "too sensitive" or "too much."

She offered to help with brainstorming for future issues. This, of course, only led to her own burnout. Eventually she was doing the work of three different people for the same title and meager pay.

The last straw came on her one-year anniversary, when Brinton finally had the courage to demand Rich change the office-wide playlists to only feature versions of songs that edited out the N-word, which none of her colleagues bothered to omit when singing along off-key.

"It makes me uncomfortable to hear it, for hours on end, being the only person in the office who identifies as African-American," Brinton had told him. "I'm just asking to make an effort, because I'm on this team too. Shouldn't we make it a safe space for everyone?"

Rich, however, felt that it was their job—*as a team*—to be "dialed into" the cultural zeitgeist. "That means appreciating music in its original form. It shouldn't feel political or like a personal attack," he reasoned.

Later, at the team editorial meeting, the entire staff found her guilty of "killing the vibe."

"See, everyone else *loves* the playlists," Rich had said. Then, brightly, "Have you considered wearing headphones?"

It was clear then that Brinton was never going to get the support she needed from Rich, or anyone else at *Landmark*, and that being a "team player" meant accepting the poison with a smile.

But she couldn't quit, not until she'd gotten a cover story she could be proud of. So she stopped asking so many questions and stopped advocating to deaf ears, because bemoaning it all felt like a self-inflicted wound. Because Brinton was living the new American Dream: blessed with an Ivy League education and a *Black Job* countless others would never experience. So, she did what she had to.

"That's why I'll write an amazing cover story. I'll leverage it to get my reputation back," Brinton told Shay, peeling back her croissant's tender center. "I'm not going to let a thirty-second Grammys interview screw me over forever. I'll figure something out."

"That's a lot to manage, baby," Athena started. "Have you given more thought to—"

"Therapy?" Brinton edged in. She slumped down, dragging the quilt over her head. "I'm fine, Mom. Really."

Brinton had tried seeing a psychologist a few times over the years, always at her mother's behest, but it never stuck. Eventually, every doctor had expected her to have made some progress with the various coping techniques for intrusive thoughts. But Brinton's fears were too overwhelming to outrun. They engulfed her before she could catch her breath.

"I'm worried that you're letting life happen to you," Athena reasoned. "And you deserve so much more."

Shay stood and crossed to Brinton's open closet door. She swiped through a few hangers before landing on a slinky black midi dress. It still had the tags. "Mom's right. It's been three months. You're in a rut."

"You can't borrow that," Brinton droned. She poked one eye out from beneath the quilt.

"Why not? It's not like you ever go out anymore."

"Okay, that's enough," Athena interjected, waving a shea butter–anointed hand.

"Sorry," Shay said, extending her vowels like a petulant teenager. She marveled at the dress, as if it hid the Holy Grail in its halter neckline. "This dress is a masterpiece. It deserves to be peeled off slowly by a stupid-hot man. Preferably when pressed against his bedroom wall…"

Athena hid her smile behind her coffee mug.

Shay returned the dress to its rightful tomb. "I'm the Pussy Whisperer. I know these things."

Athena loaded empty coffee cups, water glasses, and plates from Brinton's bookshelves onto the tray. "Honey, please don't say pussy before ten a.m.," she called out, gliding through the door.

Shay exhaled dramatically. "It's not my fault somebody started that hashtag for me. Anyway, as a Master of the Vaginal Arts, it's my job to help women feel safer in their bodies. And I know a little consensual humping can work wonders. Great for stress relief and helps you feel more connected to your body."

"Funny, on most days, I feel *too* connected to my body," Brinton said, still swaddled in cotton.

Shay's hands planted on her perfectly curved hips. "You, girl, need some fresh energy. When's the last time you went on a date? And please don't say that hemorrhoidal ex-boyfriend."

Eli was a software engineer. They worked in the same building—he was three floors up at a startup app that matched singles based on which subway line they hated most. He checked all the boxes: tall and attractive, with short brown hair and penetrating brown eyes. Midwestern-friendly, though he worked hard to ditch his accent now that he'd "escaped."

Eli was the first guy she dated who she told about her anxiety, and he seemed understanding at first. But after two years, he'd roll his eyes when she begged him to cancel plans if she needed to recover from a panic attack. They argued quietly in the darkened corners of rooftop parties and bars when she pleaded with him to leave early. He never went with her.

And when the lightning-hot stabs of an anxiety-induced migraine sliced through every nerve in her body, he said running out for Pedialyte drained him and that he didn't sign up to care for a sick child.

Brinton flipped the quilt off her face and eyed Shay. "I don't want a date. Or a booty call, a sneaky link, or a Netflix-and-chill."

"'Netflix and chill'? Ew, be more old. I dare you." Shay clicked her tongue as she rummaged through Brinton's closet.

It was pointless because a guy would find some reason to reject her once he saw her hideous emotional scars. Therefore, a relationship—or love—wasn't realistic for someone like her.

"What about the country singer? You still talk to him?" Athena asked, returning to the room with a stack of fluffy white towels. "I think he was flirting with you during that interview."

"Yes, the country singer," Shay squealed. "He caught you in his arms like the juicy-booty damsel you are. You should slide into his DMs and refresh his memory with a titty-gram."

One thing about Shay: she didn't waste time with subtlety. At sixteen, when she came out as a lesbian, she sat the family down for a PowerPoint presentation on why, in her experience, teenage boys were simply the worst. In summary, they possessed the emotional maturity of a walnut, wielded Axe body spray like a weapon, and didn't look at all like Rihanna.

"First off, they call him the Heartbreak Prince," Brinton said, counting on her outstretched fingers. "He's a walking red flag. And second, he used me as a punchline in his awkward-ass acceptance speech, like I'm not a real person with a life outside of our mortifying five minutes together. Nah, I'm good."

She scooted off the bed and met her mother at the door, grabbing the towels from Athena's hands. A cream business card with a name and phone number typed in neat serif font sat on top.

"Today's a new day, I can feel it," Brinton said. She wasn't quite convinced, but if it'd get her family off her back, she'd take it. "I just need the right opportunity."

Athena kissed her cheek. "If you change your mind about therapy, call her."

Brinton had the decency to wait for her mother to leave before she opened her top dresser drawer and dropped the card inside, beneath a dusty stack of pamphlets extolling the power of Cognitive Behavioral Therapy.

"Be for real. You're a little curious to see what he's packing in those Levi's," Shay trilled as she twerked against the edge of Brinton's mattress.

Brinton turned her back so she wouldn't laugh. "I'd rather walk naked through Times Square than ever see Jamie Crawford Jr. again."

# CHAPTER THREE

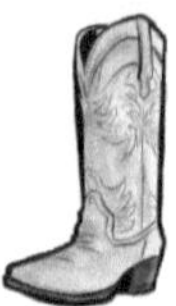

$\mathcal{A}$ few hours later, in Nashville, Jamie sat at a sterile conference room table with half a dozen record label executives. The cavalcade of batshit ideas had only gotten worse.

"Let's cut a deal with Chevy; for every new Silverado sold, we throw in a deluxe copy of the album for free," barked a man with a thick auburn mustache and ruddy cheeks.

"What, you wanna sell our boy like an economy pack of Costco socks?" asked another. His scraggly blond ponytail whipped as he shook his head. "I got a guy at an erectile dysfunction pill manufacturer who's dying to talk sponsorships. Check out the slogan."

Ponytail dragged his hand across the air wistfully, as if unveiling a Sunset Boulevard billboard. "Pop one for hours of fun."

"Forget brand deals," said a third man with sleep-deprived eyes. "Jamie Jr. ought to endorse a politician. Somebody who gets people fired up and engaged. Somebody like—"

Jamie held up a hand to stop him. "I'm not endorsing

anybody, or shilling trucks, or anything else." He didn't need to pop *anything* to have a good time. He excelled at falling into bed with the wrong person, at the wrong time.

"Well, son, we gotta go with something," Mustache grumbled. "We ran the numbers for the new album, and first-week sales projections are down two-percent compared to your debut."

"Is that bad?" Jamie asked. He was no mathematician, but a two-percent dip sounded trivial. Allegedly, his job was to focus on the music.

"It's not bad. It's fucking terrible," Mustache retorted.

Ponytail cleared his throat. The sound was thick with phlegm. "We agreed the Heartbreak Prince thing was working. The first album soared with the buzz around you and Kendall. Hell, we wrote a whole album around it."

Jamie's team had masterfully engineered the "Heartbreak Prince" persona amid his breakup with Kendall Chase two years ago, before his first album came out. Kendall was a gifted singer from Memphis. With her family connections in Jamie's tiny hometown of Iris, Tennessee, Jamie Sr. insisted they get acquainted.

Kendall was ambitious and spoke her mind, which Jamie admired. That took guts in an industry that fed on complacency. They dated off-and-on for a year, and much to Jamie's chagrin, the tabloids christened them as country's Justin and Britney.

Mustache's crooked smile widened. "Jamie and Kendall should get back together. Social media will eat that up, and—poof—our problem is solved."

Jamie's team didn't know that for Kendall, at least, the feelings were real. Six months in, she had told Jamie that she loved him, but he couldn't reciprocate. Not when love failed to keep his family from falling apart after his mother's death.

Love hadn't saved her from the abyss. Jamie knew it wouldn't be any different for him.

It was better to keep things light. Detached.

When Jamie finally broke things off, Kendall embarked on a scorching press tour, painting him as the "heartbreaker" who had strung her along and betrayed her trust. He hadn't done either of those things on purpose, but it didn't matter. He couldn't take any of it back.

"I'm just saying," Mustache threw in, "let's make lightning strike twice. It clinched us the eighteen-to-thirty-four women's demo. Though the cougars love you too."

What he meant was, they pushed Jamie as the serial bachelor. It was a perfect—and lucrative—contrast to Jamie Sr., whose personal brand in the '80s and '90s centered on traditional family values.

His team set him up with a stable of celebutantes and ensured all the right details about his "relationships" were leaked to the press. Jamie wasn't keen on building a fake public persona, but his father was on board.

Even as a thirty-year-old man, Jamie still yearned for his father's approval. It probably seemed crazy to anyone not from a small, Southern town, but there were rules for how sons and daughters honored their elders.

Respect for family legacy was at the root of everything.

Beneath the table, Jamie balled the frustration in his fists, offended by how little anyone actually believed in him. He should have told Mustache to screw himself.

"Kendall and I are not getting back together. We're just friends."

This was mostly true. While they weren't in a committed relationship, Jamie and Kendall met each other's basic needs on occasion. A scratch-my-back, I'll-sit-on-your-face kind of arrangement. Though it had been months since he'd last seen her.

"What we need is a media push, something fit for an icon in the making," said a man with a combover and sweaty brow. "We get you on a cover of *Landmark*, and the buzz is guaranteed. Six months after your daddy's first *Landmark* spot, his debut went platinum."

Combover's gaze flitted to Jamie. It was a fruitless gesture, considering everyone knew who would make the final call.

All eyes cut to Jamie Crawford Sr., seated opposite his son. Now in his late 60s, he was as rugged-handsome as ever, with short, salt-and-pepper hair neatly combed back and the right amount of stubble on his squared jaw. If Nashville was the mafia, then Jamie Sr. was Don Vito Corleone. Jamie was expected to leave the gun and take the cannoli.

Jamie Sr.'s low grunt tumbled out like loose gravel. "We'll set it up."

The Suits unleashed an obsequious chorus of "how genius" and "*Landmark*'s perfect" and "fit for an icon."

While Jamie had done press interviews with local and regional outlets, nothing came close to *Landmark*'s prestige. The reporters were often on Jamie Sr.'s short list of middle-aged white guys with coffee-stained teeth. They were all guaranteed to write something favorable.

*Landmark*'s journalism was deep and probing. It turned moderately famous artists like himself into household names. Jamie didn't want that if it was all based on a big, fat lie.

The Suits filed out as Jamie's father rose from his seat.

Hopeful, Jamie pushed back from his own chair. "Daddy, can we talk for a second?"

Jamie Sr. impatiently checked his gold Rolex. "We need to get back to the studio. Got some re-writes for the last few tracks."

"Actually, that's what I wanted to discuss," Jamie said,

shoving his hands into his jeans pockets. "You said if I let you handle the first album, you'd let me write my own songs on the second album. Then you said 'wait and see' after the Grammys, and if I won, I could write on the third album. If we keep pushing things back—"

Jamie Sr. rested a hand on his son's shoulder. He narrowed his eyes. "You know I'd never steer you wrong."

"But you said—"

"This ain't the right time to…experiment. You heard the team. This album needs to be a smash. Luckily, you've got the best songwriter on Music Row working for you."

Hesitantly, Jamie stepped forward. "We agreed to use a ghostwriter for my debut. You said I needed a competitive edge. But I don't want—I don't need that anymore."

It was a well-guarded secret with his label and management team. When Jamie's debut was an instant hit, his father convinced him that it would be crazy not to replicate the success. Jamie Sr. brokered his record deal, paid for the studio time, and had the country music industry in his back pocket.

Jamie, consequently, was trapped.

"I feel like there's still an opportunity to correct the narrative out there," Jamie pleaded. "If you let me write something now, that's a good faith start."

His father shot him a disapproving look, which made Jamie's shoulders jerk backward."Opportunity? Boy, let me tell you something about opportunity. Your generation is up against a different beast, with your little algorithms deciding what lands on the charts. You gotta use all the resources you've got. That includes me, and this team busting their hides for you."

"But that don't make up for…" Jamie started softly, the last drop of hope siphoned out of him. "I don't write any of these lyrics, yet we slap my name on them."

"Many of country's best don't write their own lyrics. This has been happening for years."

"But they don't lie about it," Jamie said thinly. His windpipe clenched tighter with each breath. "They gave me a Grammy, for God's sake."

On that stage, in front of the world, the industry rewarded him for compromising his integrity.

Could he ever become a legitimate artist? The question was a switchblade. It tortured him each night, when he lay his head down to rest.

Jamie Sr. drained the final whiff of whiskey from his crystal tumbler. Jamie flinched at the clanking of glass on the mahogany table.

"Best New Artist is awarded for performance, not just songwriting. Did you sing those songs?"

"Yes, sir."

"Then you earned that Grammy." His father tutted. "Not everyone can write and sing. Not everyone can be like Dolly, or Cash, or hell, like Taylor Swift."

"You wrote all twenty of your number-ones. I want the same chance to prove myself."

Jamie Sr. squeezed his son's shoulder hard enough to prove his point. "We're building your legacy. Let's get through this *Landmark* article, then you can make whatever album you want next," his father said. "Just trust me."

Paranoia and regret soured Jamie's stomach. For the first time, he couldn't see a future where he wasn't locked away in a cell of his father's making. If his father was willing to go on the record with this lie, with a reputable magazine like *Landmark*, there was no end.

There would always be another "trust me" if it led to pursuing *his* vision.

A sliver of hope pierced the darkness clouding Jamie's mind. What if he told his story, on his own terms?

What if he revealed himself as a fraud and rebuilt himself into the artist he longed to become?

What if Brinton helped him? They could work together in secret, like a mission. A calling.

She was damn perceptive with her questions. He couldn't hide from her, which made him nervous. Usually, women didn't affect him that way, but it was attractive. Really attractive.

It would also be nice to see her again, to make sure he pictured her face just right. He did this often as he lay awake in bed. Late on the night of their interview, he found her email address on *Landmark*'s website and wrote a message confessing his guilt. His cursor hovered over "send." But as his heart thudded in his ears, he lost his nerve.

Again, it wasn't the *right* time. He wanted Brinton's support, not her pity. Jamie had deleted the email, then poured his frustration into lyrics for a song no one would likely ever hear.

But this new plan…Goddamn, this was *it*.

Jamie Sr.'s eyes shifted toward the door.

"We need to get that *Landmark* reporter Brinton Shaw to write the story about me," Jamie blurted out. "The team loved the social media pop from the Grammys, so why not leverage that? Maybe that storyline is the ticket, because fans wanna see us…reunite?"

Jamie almost felt guilty for manipulating his father with recycled language he had heard in these team meetings, day in and day out. But manipulation seemed to be the only language his father spoke.

Jamie Sr. grunted, then thumbed his jawline.

Was he contemplating, or choosing his preferred weapon?

"It's like you said, the album's gotta be a smash," Jamie added. "The story'll write itself."

"We do need a smash," Jamie Sr. repeated. His expression was inscrutable as he swirled his right pointer finger in the air. "We'll also need advance approval before it's published, and—"

"I'll stick to the talking points," Jamie interjected. "I'll keep the story on the right track with her, make sure it goes down in history. For my legacy." That was one way to put it.

"Legacy is everything," Jamie Sr. said, nodding.

Jamie's heart hiccupped into his throat. Had he really pulled this off? "You won't regret it."

"Better see to it that I don't," his father answered, ducking through the doorway.

# LYRICS - "MIDNIGHT GOSPEL"

— JAMIE CRAWFORD JR. (2026)

<u>Verse #1</u>
I tried to bury that part of me
But you dug me up whole
Lying next to you,
My lies weren't no lighter
So I tried to hold you tighter
Than this whiskey in my glass
Hoped that darkness came to pass
Prayed it stayed hidden
At daybreak
But I knew it'd come to light

<u>Bridge</u>
Never trust a map if it leads
You to me
I'll only show you a dead end
Make you forget what's real

Darling, these scars on me
Ain't the kind that heal

Chorus
Do you know who I am now?
Am I the man you knew?
Am I worthy of
Your midnight gospel
Whispered in my room
I saw my reflection
In that broken mirror
Two faces I never knew

Verse #2
I tried to keep you like a vow
But you deserved
More than my word
Crying out for you
My lies weren't no lighter
I tried to hold you higher
Than my deepest regrets
That's the thing about secrets
The longer you try
The harder they are to keep

Bridge
Never trust a map if it leads
You to me
I'll only show you a dead end

Make you forget what's real
Darling, these scars on me
Ain't the kind that heal

<u>Chorus</u>
Do you know who I am now?
Am I the man you knew?
Am I worthy of
Your midnight gospel
Whispered in my room
I saw my reflection
In that broken mirror
Two faces I never knew

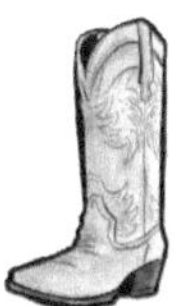

*B*rinton inched up her rolling chair. The lip of *Landmark*'s black lacquered conference table cut into her belly as she summoned the strength to do the seemingly impossible. Annoyingly, her mom and Shay were right: she needed to stop languishing and turn things around.

Between floors fifteen and twenty on the office elevator, she had cemented her grand plan to beg Rich for another shot at a cover story, even if it killed her. Which, honestly, it might.

Inside the all-glass conference room in Midtown, she watched her co-workers awkwardly pretend not to glare back at her. After the Grammys, Brinton learned about the office pool betting that she'd quit before the end of the year. The prize was up to a thousand dollars, which was offensive. She was worth at least twice as much. As Rich sat across from her, looking more than a little bored, she could guess how he had wagered.

Rich was in his early 40s and wore his short black hair perpetually tucked into a baseball cap. A Pittsburgh native, he considered himself a man of the people. Although, he wore limited-edition Jordans and dated influencers with names like Maddi and Ali and Charli.

Brinton met Rich through a Columbia University alumni mixer five years ago. He liked her portfolio from freelancing at a few Black women's lifestyle websites and took a chance on her when a music writer position opened up on staff. She assumed he had only hired her to assuage his guilt of being a rich white guy with upward mobility. Probably because there hadn't been another Black person on staff in over five years. She had checked.

Rich, already on the offensive, adjusted the bill of his orange Supreme hat. "Are you happy here?"

A foolish question for someone who'd told her she wasn't quite ready for a cover story, day after day, for four years.

"I could be," she offered, "but I feel like you've pushed me into a box."

He clasped his hands, unwilling to cede. "What kind of box?"

"Um, a Black Box, so to speak?"

At some point during her *Landmark* tenure, her colleagues had assumed she was the resident Black-spert. That meant doing sensitivity reads (i.e.: re-writing) on other people's work to fill gaps for articles featuring Black artists she hadn't already been assigned.

Of course, African-American artists didn't get *Landmark* covers nearly as frequently as their white counterparts, a fact no one did anything about despite public outcry that spiked on social media every few years.

Ironically, on the rare occasion that *Landmark* elevated a Black artist to a cover story, Brinton wasn't assigned those stories. Her value, it seemed, was adding telltale seasoning to staff photos the social media team posted to *Landmark*'s channels.

She'd become the hot sauce of workplace diversity.

Her stomach clenched. "I noticed a pattern with how you've assigned my stories and—"

His thin lips curled. "It's because you're so dialed into the culture."

Rich emphasized the word *culture*, as if doing her a favor. As if she liked being reduced to a catchphrase.

Being the spokesperson for all Black people who had ever lived was exhausting. She had whiplash from the code-switching. Brittle bones from contorting into the version of herself that earned her colleagues' acknowledgement.

"Look, you know I consider myself an ally," Rich added lightly.

Brinton's right eye twitched.

"And I think you should see this as a strength. I'm actually jealous."

Because she was the *Black-spert*. She opened her mouth again, but he cut her off.

"Brinton, I like you. I gave you a break over the whole Grammys thing. But I called you in here because you haven't pitched a banger since. And what you've written for the website isn't driving traffic."

"I know, Rich, but—"

He shook his head. "Media publishing has gone to shit—everyone's facing layoffs. My bosses are asking who I can let go. I don't want it to be you, but you haven't given me anything to work with."

She was proud of her recent articles: a PSA on the underrated genius of Tracy Chapman's "Fast Car"; a review of *Titles Ruin Everything*, Drake's poetry collection so petty it could have doubled as Regina George's *Burn Book*; and a think piece exploring SZA's unlikely parallels with Princess Diana after channeling the late royal in her *SOS* album artwork.

The latter was the most trafficked article on *Landmark's* website at the time, and it was the reason Rich gave her the Grammys red carpet opportunity in the first place.

But now, she had to grovel, because she couldn't start at the bottom somewhere else. Somewhere worse. "I want another chance to prove myself, because I've moved on from the whole Grammys…incident."

"Go on."

"I want to write something relevant and challenging. Something that could possibly be positioned as a cover story."

"All right, so pitch me something."

"When?"

"Now."

Her eyebrows shot into her hairline

*"Now?"*

She'd hope to have more time to prepare, like other writers did before pitching what could be a career-defining story. But, of course, this was her luck.

He crossed his arms. "I thought you said you were serious, Shaw. So, let's go."

Brinton's eyes darted to the massive dry erase board mounted behind Rich's desk. It had all the staff assignments for the next issue mapped out. Most spaces had been filled in, but there were two openings: the untold history of Kidz Bop, which sounded about as exciting as an ear infection and…

*Oh God.*

*No.*

There, written in red, within the clean lines of the outlined grid: Jamie Crawford Jr. album review. Next to it, an asterisk followed by the word "cover" and a giant question mark. It seemed to taunt her. Shay would have gotten a kick out of the irony. It's pretty fucking impossible to avoid a man you actually *need* to save your job.

Brinton picked at her thumb's cuticle bed. "The Crawford story," she started, the words forming at a glacial pace. "I can do it."

"Didn't you just say you'd moved on from the whole 'Grammys incident'?" He waggled his eyebrows. "What if you wrote something a little more…dialed into the *culture*?"

"Crawford and I already have an existing working relationship, and I think he's more likely to open up to me."

"It's the funniest thing," he said, cocking a brow conspiratorially. "About an hour ago, his camp called. They requested you write something about the new album. I said Agatha had more experience—"

"Not more than me. Not about this." Brinton's voice warbled, but she straightened her shoulders. This cycle of gaslighting couldn't persist. She refused to give up because if she did, she might as well pack up her desk right then.

"But we need something more than an album review. Anyone could do that," she added. "I say we do a character piece that pulls back the curtain, both on Crawford as an artist and the son of the most successful country music icon of our generation."

"Interesting," Rich said, studying her as if a rare species in an exhibit. "The second album comes out at the end of June. Crawford's team pitched sending a reporter down. Two weeks at his family compound in Tennessee. If I send you, you need to come back with something *juicy*. Frankly, I think his good-natured Southern boy act is tired. With a family like his, I wanna know where the bodies are buried. Get what I'm saying?"

Her palms were slick and her inner ears crackled. She needed to calm down. It probably would have helped to stimulate her vagus nerve, as her mother often suggested. She never bothered to look up what the hell it actually was. The last thing she needed was for a horrified Rich to watch her violently jab at each of her crevices while he dialed building security.

"Yeah, I get it."

She needed this job—she needed out of the proverbial Black Box.

"We're projecting big numbers for this story. It would also include a pay bump. Might even be a cover," he said.

Suddenly, her lungs swelled a few millimeters. "A cover story?" The elusive carrot dangled inches from her face. Validation she'd wanted for years tightly wrapped in a single answer. One moment.

"Might be a cover," he reiterated, his smile inscrutable. "If you can deliver something juicy."

*Juicy.* That word again.

Thrill snaked down her spine and she shuddered.

She considered herself an above-the-board kind of reporter, not a gossip monger or a user. Jamie was attractive; that was obvious. And even as there were a handful of nights she'd thought about his hands still pressed into the small of her back, there would be no *juice* to be squeezed. She couldn't let whatever repressed tension—she refused to call it chemistry—throw her off.

Rich's half smile faltered as he picked up on her apprehension. "I thought you said you wanted this?"

She nodded, but she wanted to say that she didn't do "juicy." She wrote pieces celebrating the humanity of her favorite artists, because they were people, like her, with hopes and dreams and fears. There had to be some way to make this work. Even if Jamie's tongue wrapped around his vowels in a way that made her suddenly very thirsty.

*Shit.*

"I'll do it," she said instead. Yes, she would do this and salvage the hangnail of honor she had left. She would get in, and get out unscathed. She would win.

Rich leaned back in his chair, its squeaking gears a serrated blade through the silence. "Good. Remember, this article has to kill. I can't give you another shot. Your future with this magazine is on the line, and possibly mine too. So, please, don't screw me."

# CHAPTER FIVE

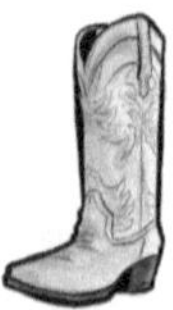

Two weeks later, early Monday morning, Brinton stretched her calves and wiggled her toes inside her Doc Martens. She felt like she'd cheated the system. Let the extra five inches of legroom tell it, she had.

Jamie's team had sprung for a first-class flight to his hometown of Iris, Tennessee, which she probably should have turned down. Brinton figured they wanted to buy her loyalty. She wouldn't compromise her journalistic integrity. But dammit, she wasn't passing up toasty hand towels and imported rosemary cashews served on a gold-plated dish.

Still, she was uneasy being so far outside her comfort zone—nearly nine hundred miles, to be exact. She'd never done an extended sit-down like this with a celebrity. Usually, she got her quotes from a phone interview. Efficient but impersonal. This article, conversely, was extremely personal.

She had a lot to prove; her article needed to be masterful or she was out of a job. Who would she be then?

Fishing out her phone from the seat-back pocket, Brinton connected to Wi-Fi and texted Shay.

Brinton: What if Jamie is worse than I already
know he is? What if I hate Tennessee?

She'd never been to Tennessee, but according to *Forbes*, Iris was America's Best City to Move To. Over the years, the Nashville suburb had become a bastion for country music royalty and Hollywood types hankering for farmland and small-town hospitality. Still, Brinton couldn't shake the creeping fear that Iris still employed the Brown Paper Bag Test. Southern hospitality didn't extend to people who looked like *her*. And she'd be trapped there for fourteen grueling days.

Thankfully, Shay responded immediately.

Shay: Girl, you'll live. If you get bored, play
Tic-Tac-Toe on his abs.

Brinton unleashed an unwieldy snort. Her seatmate, who looked like a cross between a russet potato and cranky seal, glared at her over *The New York Times* business section. She ignored him.

Brinton: You have to stop sending me
screenshots. It's getting creepy, even for you.

Shay: Be for real. I'm helping you prepare.
tbh, you should be paying me

Over the past two weeks, all Brinton had done was prepare. She was desperate to become fluent in all things Jamie Crawford Jr. Abs excluded.

His social media feed was a collage of mostly thirst traps, where the sun lapped bare shoulders as he wistfully strummed his acoustic guitar. In a few, he slung his arm around a shimmering blonde or dazzling brunette at a bar or football game. The pictures elicited a twinge of something Brinton refused to call jealousy but was equally uncomfortable.

Was he happy with those women? Why did she care?

Brinton had also read endless articles comparing Jamie to his father. She was insecure about her lack of accomplishments, but she'd excommunicate herself if her mother also sold a hundred million albums, like Jamie's father. How did Jamie handle that? She scoffed. It probably didn't bother him at all. Like his tan, his life was 24-karat golden.

As thin clouds tangled in the atmosphere outside her window, Brinton thought of journalist Joan Didion's iconic 1968 essay about interviewing a drugged-out Jim Morrison and his bandmates in Hollywood. Didion told the truth, revealing that even cultural icons could be vapid assholes. Would Jamie treat her that way? Possibly. He embarrassed her on that Grammys stage, which she was still pissed about. Would his antics amount to almost setting his own crotch on fire, like Morrison had? The jury was still out. Therefore, she refused to be caught with her pants down again.

Figuratively, obviously.

A flight attendant squawked over the intercom, and Brinton swallowed hard. They were making their descent into the Nashville area.

At the end of the long Arrivals hallway, Brinton saw him: an older white man, she guessed in his 60s, with broad shoulders and a smile that begged to know your life story. He held an iPad with her name typed on the screen.

When they met eyes, he rushed over, excitedly extending his bear claw of a palm. "The name's Michael Dooley. Glad to know you, Miss Brinton. I'll be your driver during your time at Crawford Ranch."

Her mother had given her a comfortable life in New York City, but they were miles from the kind of wealthy where she didn't take the subway every day. Now that she thought about it, her frame of reference for *that* kind of wealthy was Joe, Princess Mia's lovably gruff chauffeur-turned-confidant from *The Princess Diaries*. However, in his black cowboy boots and matching hat, grinning amid the airport melee, Michael more closely resembled a rancher who had made a wrong turn on his way to hand-deliver a calf.

He took her suitcase, smiling wider than Brinton thought humanly possible. "Welcome to Nashville."

Forty-five minutes later, the nondescript highway fell away to reveal lush, rolling green hills of the town of Iris. Brinton suctioned herself to the window as the storybook city center blurred by.

The wide streets were an unexpected patchwork of architecture dating back to the early 1800s. Victorian structures with inviting round towers flanked quaint storefronts—their flat facades holdovers from the Greek and Gothic Revival-favored palates of the Antebellum South—painted in cheery shades of blue, green, and white.

Shops boasted wholesome names like Sweet B's Bakery and Miller's Hardware. Lou Lou's, a '50s-inspired diner bathed in orange neon light, advertised homemade strawberry pie; *$1-a-slice* was scrawled in flourished cursive on its large bay windows.

An all-brick Baptist church with a steeple that pierced the cloudless blue sky presided over the town square. Iris was like a living soundstage for a '90s coming-of-age TV drama about a painfully aloof teenage boy and a creek, complete with astonishingly attractive locals in T-shirts and cut-offs, milling casually down pin oak–lined sidewalks.

Soon, the SUV idled before an imposing brick-and-iron gate emblazoned with an intricate crest that formed the letters *CR*. Brinton's heart faltered, but there was no turning back. The gates opened, and the SUV slowly crunched down the gravel driveway.

"Figured you'd wanna take in the view," Michael said. "Heck, I've been with the Crawfords for thirty years, and it never gets old."

She nodded at him, aiming to appear nonchalant, then gasped as the rural wonderland unfolded from every angle. They carved around the first turn, approaching the far edge of a shimmering lake, complete with an expensive-looking dock and a pair of gleaming white pontoon boats; wispy, pea tendril–green fields and shady trees; a horse stable; a pristine Padel ball court; and finally, the white stone–faced, two-story home. On either side, the main house was flanked by what looked like a smaller guest house and another structure. Probably a garage packed with rows of foreign cars, or a secret lair typical of the super-wealthy.

The SUV grounded to a stop in front of the main house. Before Brinton could protest, Michael opened her door and outstretched his hand to help her down.

"Oh—I can get my own door," she squeaked, more nervous than she expected.

He beamed up at her. "I know it, but that's not how we do things 'round here."

This would take some getting used to. Brinton half smirked as he deployed a roaring chuckle. "You're welcome."

The second her combat boots hit the glittering pavement, the door to the main house swung open. Sammi, the brunette on Jamie's team at the Grammys, fluttered over to the SUV, a vision in yellow and sky-high cork platform heels, glossy, expensive-looking waves fanning around her face. As Jamie's publicist, she had arranged Brinton's itinerary, and they spoke almost every day leading up to her arrival.

"Good to see you again," Brinton said, eyes wide and genuinely transfixed by her beauty. She couldn't do too much if she tried. That was rare in a world obsessed with filters and fillers. "Thank you for setting this all up." She outstretched her hand, but Sammi immediately slapped it away.

"Not how we do things 'round here," she said through snow-white teeth. She wrapped Brinton in a tight hug that left her unsteady.

This was *a lot*. This was also *day one*. Brinton tried not to bristle as her voice jumped two octaves. "Erm—I'm not really a hugger."

"Don't worry, we'll fix that," Sammi said, winking at her with glimmering emerald eyes.

Michael passed her luggage to a younger blond man, likely among the hundreds of staffers who maintained this palace.

"We have a lot to get to—Oh, honey…" Sammi's luminous smile dimmed as she eyed Brinton politely. "You wanna get changed?"

She used a cherry red–manicured nail to hone in on Brinton's all-black ensemble: cropped jeans, matching silk button-down, and her favorite heeled boots. Apparently, the look wasn't as chic as she initially imagined.

"Ah, no. My clothes are fine," Brinton said through a tight, forced smile.

"And you have more of…this in that suitcase?" Sammi nodded upward to the now red-faced guy dragging it up the flagstone steps.

"Yes."

"I see."

Looping her arm into Brinton's, Sammi guided them toward the main house and through the massive wood-and-etched-glass double doors. "I don't mean any harm. You look great—stunning even. It's only that, on a good day, it's gonna be a hundred degrees and steamier than a bayou brothel. I can carry you to a boutique or have some options sent over."

"I think I'll manage."

Sammi beamed, a true master of Southern passive-aggression. "No problem. If you change your mind, just holler. We'll get you set up at the guest house before the welcome party tonight. But for now, how about a tour?"

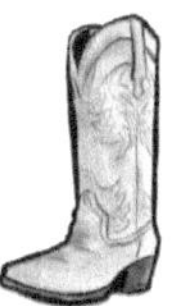

# CHAPTER SIX

*A*fter pleasantly roasting on a linen lounge chair by the pool, Jamie roughly ran a hand through his sopping wet hair and padded to the French doors leading into the kitchen. The space was bright and airy, with luscious white marble countertops, chocolatey hardwood floors, and a long bank of windows overlooking the glimmering pool.

It was usually quiet—his father took most meals in his office or the billiards room—but today, the kitchen hummed with staff tending to platters of sticky spare ribs, tangy collard greens, smoked chicken, baked macaroni and cheese, red rice, gooey butter cake, and whipped banana pudding for the cookout that night.

Liza, the family's head chef for the past twenty years, directed the troops like the pint-sized general she was. Pointing here and there, tasting a rotation of sauces on tiny spoons, and calling out intermittently "Needs more pepper, baby."

She did it all without getting a single drop on her crisp, white button-down. Liza was in her 60s, with a smooth, nutmeg complexion and a soul-soothing smile. Equal parts

Oprah Winfrey and Martha Stewart—wisdom, beauty, and grace. But don't dare trifle with her shit.

Liza painstakingly massaged two different linen napkins, one in each hand. "Mary, these are about as soft as a porcupine's backside," she told the twenty-something brunette with a severe ponytail beside her. Liza never raised her voice, but the entire room stood at attention when she spoke.

"Party's in three hours. I need you to run out to Tulia's and get the organic linen, but something dark. All this barbecue sauce, it's gonna look like an episode of *CSI*."

Mary nodded and followed Liza into the cavernous walk-in pantry.

Jamie loved watching her work. Even as a kid, and especially after his mother died, she always made sure he had what he needed. And all of the unspoken things his globe-trotting father couldn't provide. Jamie scooted past a man pushing a stocked cart of top-shelf liquor. He made a mental note to revisit that later.

He beelined for the long kitchen island in the center of the room, where someone had finished slicing a tray of Liza's famous cathead biscuits and cornbread.

Leaning against the kitchen island, Jamie grabbed one of each, savoring how every crumbly bite melted on his tongue. A familiar voice and the click-clack of multiple sets of heels on hardwood broke his carb-induced reverie.

"I thought I'd give you a sneak peek before the cookout tonight," Sammi told Brinton, who trailed behind her through the archway. Her head was on a swivel, and she took a beat here and there to scribble in the tiny black notebook in her hand.

Jamie figured he'd see Brinton at the party but didn't account for her catching him dripping from his gray swim trunks, a biscuit hanging from his mouth. The thought made his cheeks heat. Apparently, he cared about how she thought he looked?

Shoot, he did. But only because she could write about that, and he wanted to come across like the legitimate artist he longed to be? And, yes, he wanted her to like him. Maybe as much as he liked her. Maybe more?

Satisfied, he popped the last bite of biscuit into his mouth.

She wore one of those silky blouses that didn't make a lick of sense in the country and tight, black jeans that absolutely did. He scolded himself for clocking how they hugged her hips. No, Brinton was absolutely off-limits.

He wanted her to write about the *real* him, not the philandering Heartbreak Prince he paraded around as. Besides, he couldn't give a woman like her—driven, and most important, genuine—what she deserved: stability and true partnership. He didn't know the first thing about either, because his own heart was fractured.

It happened the night his mother died, before he slammed into that oak tree. His father had looked him in the eye and codified that runway emotions would be his downfall. Jamie replaced his heart—split like the front end of his father's truck—with a self-generating force field. It protected him from being too open, too willing to risk assured pain. Or to hurt someone else because of his shortcomings.

That settled it. He'd ignore whatever was percolating about Brinton and those jeans, and all the glorious ways she filled them, and focus on the job at hand. He needed to earn her support, not sleep with her.

It was a real challenge when you'd won every gold medal in the sport.

Once Brinton's eyes settled on him, they grew wide, as if she were embarrassed. They quickly retreated back into her notebook. Was he making her uncomfortable? A few thick beads of water rolled defiantly from his crotch and down his thigh, not unlike pee. Was she gonna think he pissed himself?

This was already off to a fantastic start.

"Great timing, Jamie's here. You remember Brinton?" Sammi asked as brightly as her yellow dress glowed in the sunlight.

"Sure, hard to forget," Jamie said, hearing his dry tone and wincing. He only meant it'd be hard to forget wearing her DNA on a livestream with millions watching, but he didn't want her to think he was still worried about it, because he wasn't. "I—yes. Of course I remember you."

"Though it seems you forgot you own at least one shirt," Sammi quipped. One of the things he loved about her: she never missed the opportunity to cut him down to size. It kept him humble.

He offered a cocky smile. "You know how I feel about tan lines."

Turning back to Brinton, he went in for a friendly hug. It seemed appropriate, since they'd met before, but she thrust her hand toward him. *Right,* he was soaking wet and half naked.

He took it, squeezing gently. "Sorry, I was out by the pool. But I'm so glad you could make it."

She looked flustered. Was *she* nervous? No. More likely it was some special separation anxiety Manhattanites experienced once they left their imposing skyscrapers and fancy espresso martinis behind.

"I'm wet to be here," Brinton said, apparently a little louder than she expected. Eyes like saucers, she flicked her waist-length braids off her shoulder and stifled what sounded like a scream. She was definitely nervous.

Jamie cracked an appropriately juvenile smile. It was... cute? No, endearing. That sounded more professional. She seemed like that kind of girl—er, woman.

"I mean—I'm happy. To be here," she mumbled, eyes dipping back to her notebook.

"Can I get you something? Water, peach tea? Something stronger?" Jamie asked.

"No, thank you."

"How was the flight?"

"Good."

"Enjoying the weather so far?"

"Yes," she said, finishing a few scribbled notes.

He gestured to her notebook, craned his neck to steal a peek. "You…planning to share with the class?"

Brinton snapped it shut, face stretched into an almost painful smile. "Sorry, no. That's not how this works."

Damn, getting right down to business. Pleasantries apparently weren't a thing with this woman. He respected it though.

"James Sawyer Crawford, Jr., I know you're not tracking water onto my clean floors," Liza admonished, her whisper-shout cutting through the awkward tension from the archway.

"I know, I know. And I'm sorry. Won't happen again." He went in to hug her, but she playfully swatted him with an oven mitt.

"Tell the truth and shame the devil," she said, casting a knowing grin.

Sammi crossed to Liza and wrapped her into a decidedly drier hug. "Liza, this is Brinton, the journalist I told you about."

"Charmed to meet you," Liza said, and braced Brinton so hard she almost tipped over. Liza pulled back, eyes wide with concern. "You okay, baby?"

"Yes," Brinton said, pantomiming an awkward hug. "I guess I'm not really…"

Jamie chuckled. She was a little uptight, but she probably meant well. Again, endearing.

"Oh, we'll fix that," Sammi said, crunching on a thinly sliced cucumber from a tray on the island. "Liza is head chef, and she's behind every sinfully delicious thing you'll put in your mouth."

"You hungry?" Liza asked Brinton. "Dinner's in a few hours, but let me know if I can fix you something. No trouble at all."

Brinton smiled, a shy but blinding one. Jamie's breath hitched. He wasn't sure what to make of that. "I'm good for now, thank you."

Liza nodded, and like some kind of textile genie, she produced a dark blue towel, which Jamie took. Her one flaw? She couldn't ever stay mad at him for too long.

He planted a soft kiss on her cheek. "You're an absolute angel, you know that?"

At the stove, Liza stirred a boiling pot of macaroni. "Uh-huh. Now, take that outside. I don't wanna see your handsome face until the party, you hear me?"

"Yes ma'am," he said, then glanced at Brinton. "Guess we'll have lots to catch up on at the party tonight?"

Sammi nodded, but her usual smile grew tight. She stepped a few paces closer to Brinton, lowering her voice. She was a heat-seeking missile, launching into PR mode.

"I want you to have the best experience. In fact, I'm here to ensure it. Some things you see and hear during your stay may be sensitive, so all I ask is that, when reasonable, we keep those moments off the record."

Brinton looked up from her notebook, her expression unreadable. Jamie wanted to interject, but there was no stopping Sammi once she'd locked in.

Brinton's eyes didn't leave hers. "I understand that, but

I'm a journalist. I'm here to write about what I see, hear, and experience. I won't sign an NDA."

At least she stood for something. For his plan to work, this was exactly the kind of thing he needed.

Sammi's expression softened. "I swear, I'm not trying to dictate how you do your job," she said, as earnest as he had ever heard her. "At the very least, give Jamie a fair shot." Her feline emerald eyes met his. "This interview means a lot for the new record."

Brinton tugged on the hem of her blouse. Damn, why was he studying her like a textbook? He averted his eyes to the bank of windows before he creeped her out more than he already had.

"I'm committed to writing this story with integrity," she added, unsmiling but warm. Like she meant it. It reminded him of their Grammys interview. She had a willingness to go beyond the surface level. Excellent.

"That's good enough for me," Sammi said. Her smile had returned to its former glory.

"Me too," he said, probably too eagerly. Sammi and Brinton's heads jerked his way, like they had forgotten he was standing there.

"How about we chat now on the patio?"

Jamie smiled his award-winning smile and poured two glasses of iced peach tea from the pitcher on the counter.

He handed one to Brinton, who grasped it hesitantly, as if it might have been spiked with cyanide. His grin faltered. All right, this might be a smidge harder than he had hoped, but he was up for the challenge.

Brinton looked to Sammi for some kind of affirmation and seemed to have gotten it in her sharp nod of approval.

"Okay," she mumbled.

Clearly, she was still getting her bearings. But he knew how to loosen her up.

# LANDMARK.COM: TRACY CHAPMAN'S 'FAST CAR' WAS JUST THE START

*By Brinton Shaw*

"I had a feeling that I belonged. I had a feeling that I could be someone."

That woman was pop-folk singer-songwriter Tracy Chapman. The song was her 1988 smash hit "Fast Car." The Grammy winner has asserted that she originally wrote the track, which explores maintaining hope amid an often bleak, blue-collar life, as a teen growing up in Cleveland, Ohio.

Despite mainstream radio largely overlooking Chapman's brilliance after her breakout success in the '90s, as tastes shifted to bubblegum pop and bravado-laced hip hop, Chapman was absolutely right. She belonged. And she always has.

With every defiant guitar lick, and every smokey note she sings, Chapman's music is not just to be heard, but *experienced*.

After country music star Luke Combs covered "Fast Car" in 2023, Chapman has enjoyed a well-deserved resurgence in popularity. With his entry, Combs--crediting Chapman as one of his favorite artists--introduced a new audience to Chapman's tender storytelling.

Both Chapman and Combs's renditions of "Fast Car" capture the precariousness of an unknown future, knowing something good is just beyond the bend, if you're brave enough to take the first step. Yet, Chapman's version feels imbued with a certain ache resonant with being an outsider. Chapman has said that "Fast Car" wasn't necessarily autobiographical, and yet its authenticity feels as fresh today as it did some forty years ago.

Through a contemporary lens, it's hard not to consider how Chapman's experiences as a Black female, in the largely white male-dominated folk genre, and as a Black woman in America, might have shaped her trajectory. However, to believe the best Chapman has to offer lies within the four minutes and fifty-seven seconds of "Fast Car," or even her bluesy 1995 coffeehouse staple "Give Me One Reason," is not just an understatement. It's a devaluing of a career spanning ten studio albums, four Grammys, and more than thirty-two million albums sold worldwide.

Not to mention, the countless people she has inspired along the way.

# CHAPTER SEVEN

Brinton cocked her head and studied the wooden contraption about twenty feet away. The slanted board sloped downward on one side and had a small hole at the top. Adding to her confusion, at Jamie's behest, she was now barefoot in the lush lawn nestling the patio, soft blades of grass tickling her toes.

Behind her, two bubbling jacuzzis and enough teak loungers for a football squad flanked the enormous swimming pool. Dotting the perimeter, an army of shady sugar maple trees.

It was proof that, if you were rich enough, heaven on Earth did exist.

"What's the point of this again?" Brinton asked.

Jamie, also barefoot, let out a playful, exaggerated groan, like this was the most natural thing in the world.

"The point of cornhole is to have fun. It's a game." He nodded to the small red and blue bean bags next to him, haphazardly piled beside their iced teas on a teakwood table. "You throw these bean bags into the hole in that board to score points. The first person to score twenty-one wins."

A *game* was not what she needed. She needed a *time machine*. She'd planned to come off in control when seeing Jamie for the first time in months, but back in that kitchen, it was like no time had passed. She was stuck in Grammys purgatory, paralyzed by fear and shame all over again. A snarled bundle of nerves. Soon enough, Jamie would see her flawed emotions, like Eli always did. She'd screw up this interview, and she'd get fired. Because she didn't belong here. Yet, there she was, barefoot with a still-shirtless Jamie Crawford Jr.

*Jeez, did everyone walk around flashing their gilded pecs all willy-nilly?*

He handed her a stack of four red bean bags. "I thought this could shake off the cobwebs. First interview and all." His lips curved into a broad smile that steadied her like a long, deep breath, which she also didn't need. She simply could not fall for his charms.

In fact, she'd spent days studying them from past interviews she had watched online. That smile wasn't genuine; it was a destabilizing weapon. When he bit his bottom lip, he was flirting. Sometimes, he did this twitchy thing, where he spun the chunky gold ring on his left pinky. She didn't know what it meant, but she would figure that out too.

Knowing all this, her pulse still raced. She needed to relax so she didn't scream. Or worse, project from a different hole in her body. Brinton breathed in deeply through her nose, held it for four counts, then let it go, as her mother had taught her. Sweet wildflowers and freshly cut grass filled her nostrils.

Yes, she could do this.

Brinton took the bean bags from him and, to her horror, a spark danced between their fingers as they briefly touched, just like at the Grammys.

It was probably static electricity. Happened all the time.

Didn't it? She flung the thought from her head. "Follow-up question, why aren't we wearing shoes?"

He offered a low chuckle, his glistening abs flexing from the force. You really could play Tic-Tac-Toe on them.

"Oh, that's 'cause it feels nice. Figured you don't touch grass much in New York City."

Who had time for Earthing when you were in a perpetual state of dread? She rolled her eyes, but her smile eked out.

*Oh, great, he's funny too?*

"No, but I've pet a lot of bodega cats, which I'd argue is better."

When she wiggled her toes, it *did* feel nice. Crap, if he was going to walk around being right all day, bronzed nipples out in triumph, she needed something stronger than iced tea to drink. "Are you still okay with me recording our conversation?"

"Go for it."

She crossed to the table, clicked on her digital recorder with her free hand, and turned back to him, expectant. "So, what next? These bags are getting heavy." And they were burning daylight.

He picked up his four blue bags, eyes twinkling despite the cool shade blanketing them. "By Crawford Rules—which is how we play—each bag in the hole is worth three points. A bag that lands on the face of the board but doesn't go in is worth one. We'll take turns. The real fun is that if either of our bags land on the board but don't go in the hole, the other person can knock it in with their own bag and steal the points."

Without permission, something warm bloomed in her chest. He looked genuinely excited, which was genuinely... sweet?

"That sounds like sabotage." She laughed.

He grinned back at her. "Only if you miss the hole. And honey, I never miss the hole."

He winked, and her stomach dipped. She'd never think of the word "hole" quite the same. Jamie stepped back so she could approach her starting point, which was on the right side of a second slanted board two feet ahead of them.

"Take all the time you need."

"Wow, somebody's cocky," she said, immediately blushing at her word choice.

He furrowed his brow and gripped his chest in mock offense. "Who, me? Never. But…why don't we make this more interesting. For every shot you make, I'll answer a question. Anything you want. And for any I make, you'll answer mine."

He bit his bottom lip as a sunbeam warmed her inner thighs. At least, she hoped it was the sun. She peered at him, taking in all his sharp edges, and considered shutting this right the hell down and rescheduling for a decidedly less *stimulating* location. A warehouse full of glue sticks?

His eyes grew soft and he smiled, all sugarcane-sweet and Southern boy congeniality. "Please?"

Brinton regarded him through a curtain of braids that had conveniently fallen into her face, a temporary reprieve from his magnetic gaze. Rich demanded a *juicy* angle, so maybe she had to let down her guard a tiny bit. She blinked away her discomfort at the thought.

"One question."

"I'll take it." He smiled wider, then gestured toward the target. "Try not to overthink it."

Through her side-eye, she caught him watching her. Taking her in like he wanted the memory tattooed on his brain. She'd never tell him, of course, but it felt good to be seen for once. Even momentarily. She sucked in a breath, cupped one bag under-handed, arm outstretched behind her, and launched it forward. Her eyes widened in disbelief. It sailed straight into the hole.

He rubbed the ghost of golden stubble on his chin, impressed. Frankly, she was too. "Damn, that's a nice shot."

She shrugged. "Beginner's luck."

He waved his pointer finger in the air, eyes raking over her body appreciatively. "Nuh-uh. I know when I'm being hustled. But hit me."

She inhaled. "Okay, let's start with the new album. Is there a title yet?"

He exhaled deeply, as if the question were an anvil he was pushing up a steep cliff. "It's called *The Heartbreak Prince*."

"You…don't seem too happy about it."

Staring down the infinite stretch of green ahead, he slapped together the stack of bean bags in each hand. "Let's say it wasn't my first choice."

She thought back to all the articles—and fine, gossip—from her research. "Is it because you feel like that's all people see? A guy who goes from woman to woman?" She knew from experience what it was like being forced into a box. Did he feel the same?

Facing her, he smiled through a glint of something else in his eyes. Was it shame, or maybe embarrassment? She couldn't put her finger on it, but she recognized it as what you did when you wanted to hide in plain sight.

"Technically, that's two questions, but I'll allow it. I guess, yeah, being a musician, people want you to fit into a specific hole, and you gotta stay in that hole or there's no place else for you."

He wound back and lobbed his bean bag over-hand, hitting his target with startling precision.

"Is there some part of you who wants to be in that hole? I mean, there are videos of you making out with dozens of women at Nashville bars. Not to mention your breakup with

Kendall Chase, which, ultimately, seemed to benefit you. You won a Grammy—"

His jaw set and his eyes cut away again, searching for what to say in the dense tree line but coming up short. He was uncomfortable.

"All right, it's my turn to ask you a question," he said, voice lower.

Should she press him to answer? At this point, things were going well enough, and she didn't want to risk him telling his team that she ambushed him. So, she let it go. "Fair is fair," she said, turning to face him.

He cocked his head. "You think I'm a bad guy or something? Because I know you just arrived, but it seems like you've already made up your mind about me. You can tell me, really."

She didn't think he was a bad guy per se, but she didn't know what his intention had been in calling her out in his acceptance speech. Brinton hadn't exactly expected him to reach out and explain, but it might have eased the roiling discomfort she felt as the internet picked her bones clean over many agonizing months.

She had to know if she wanted to survive these next two weeks. "I'm trying to understand you."

Brinton tossed another bean bag, this time overhand, which disappeared into the tiny abyss. Time to pull the trigger. "I vomited on you—I ate bad shrimp, for the record—but you embarrassed me in your Grammys speech. You called me your good-luck charm. Do you know how many weirdos messaged me online because of that, sending me photos of their puke boots or asking me to do the same to theirs? My name is still trending."

As she looked at him, her heartbeat ricocheted between her ears.

He stooped down, dropped his bean bags on the ground.

Stepping closer, he placed a hand on her shoulder, fingertips gently brushing against her blouse and making her shiver. "God, Brinton, no. I'd never—I'm so sorry I made you feel that way. On that stage, everything happened so quickly. I was caught up in the moment..." He trailed off, stepped closer. She shivered again. "Truthfully, you were the highlight of that night."

Her lips parted, releasing the breath she'd been holding. "I don't understand?"

Now he blew out a breath, his blue-green eyes a wellspring of sincerity. "But I didn't consider how you felt about what happened, what you'd gone through that day. I thought about you a lot though, all those months. I wanted to shoot you a DM. Hell—I even tried sending you an email, so I could tell you..."

He ran a free hand through his hair. "But, I—well, it's just that..."

She hurled another bean bag forward. It sank into the hole. "Why did you wait, Jamie? You could have sent me a DM. You could have said something."

He looked down at his bare feet, dragging one across the grass. "I know I could have. It's embarrassing, but I don't even control my social accounts. My team does. So, if I got the chance to tell you what I needed to say—or to see you again—I wanted it to be on my terms. Not theirs. And I was afraid..."

"Afraid of what?"

His eyes latched with hers, and the corners of his mouth upturned softly. "That no matter what I said, it wouldn't have come off as genuine, because I'm in the public eye. There's a lot of pressure when people know you. A lot of room to get this misconstrued. I hoped having you here for these next few weeks was my chance to tell you how glad I am that we met."

The massive knot in her stomach unfurled a bit. He hadn't been making fun of her. Shit, now she *felt* like a cornhole.

"Oh." She picked at the cottony fibers of the last bean bag in her hand. "I assumed you thought I was joke."

*Exactly like everyone else.*

He fervently shook his head. "Never crossed my mind. And for the record, I think you're an awesome writer. You ask thoughtful questions, you're smart as hell, and I can tell you care about doing things right. I admire that. And I was looking forward to having fun hanging out."

As her adrenaline leveled out, his words were a weighted blanket. She couldn't remember the last time a man—and certainly not a legitimate famous person—wanted to hang out with *her*. She could have fun with him too. Professional, sanctioned fun. This was how she would get the angle she needed and land a cover story.

"You really like my writing?"

He flashed a sheepish grin. "I may have read all your *Landmark* articles before you got here. I think the Tracy Chapman piece was my favorite. You really nailed how before-her-time she was, and how her raw, tender storytelling remains relevant."

No one ever mentioned that one, but she felt the same way. She grinned back at him, more than a little pleased. "A little recon, huh?"

"I remembered you were a sharp-shooter. I can tell you got a sweetness about you, but you also got a stinger. Like a honeybee."

He appraised her slowly, making her feel exposed and coveted all at once. She reached for her iced tea and took a hulking gulp. A feeble bid to cool the heat spilling across her chest. "Doesn't sound too bad."

"Not bad at all, Honeybee."

*Honeybee.* Outside of properly embarrassing pet names her family gave her, she'd only had one nickname. At thirteen, she got her first period *and* had her first panic attack at Carmen Bryant's sleepover. Carmen only used tampons because she refused to wear "a vag diaper." Brinton refused to wear a tampon because she was terrified it'd get stuck and sprout like a swallowed watermelon seed, its absorbent, cottony cover crushing her from the inside out. She cried at school for a year over her new nickname: vag diaper.

Honeybee was considerably better.

Eager for a distraction from the effervescent giddiness in her stomach, she looked down at her hands—she still had two bean bags left. "Should we keep playing?"

"Hell yeah," he said, brushing her shoulder with his and imbuing her whole body with strange tingles. "But it's my turn." He tossed one of his bags, which caught on the hole's lip but didn't fall in. He winced as his self-proclaimed winning streak ended.

"Tough break," she said, stifling a laugh.

"Mm. Well, you can't win 'em all. You're a worthy opponent." He eyed her softly, like he meant it. She gulped down a tennis-ball of tension and tossed another bag. It grazed Jamie's, the weight sending both tumbling into the hole.

Jamie whistled. "Now, I suppose, you earned two more questions."

Slowly, she crossed her arms in mock protest, daring him to argue. Against her better judgment, she was having a good time. "I kinda feel like you owe me four now."

He chuckled, nodding his head in surrender. "All right then. I'm just a man at your mercy."

Now, all the heat in her body rushed to the same place. She clenched her thighs, making it worse. What the fuck was happening to her?

At the same time, she was getting somewhere. She had to keep him talking…

Behind him, the clattering of boots on flagstone breached the charged energy between them. They both turned to find Tex, who Brinton had learned was Jamie's goateed manager from the Grammys, and Jamie's father waiting. Tex tipped his black cowboy hat to her, but Jamie Sr. looked straight at his son.

"Need you back in the studio," Tex chirped, ignoring Jamie's sullen expression. "Gotta polish up the tracks before the party tonight. A few folks from the label are coming."

Jamie was still watching her, some kind of yearning in his eyes. Like he wanted to stay. If he was serious about this interview, wouldn't he want to?

"We're in the middle of an interview," he said.

His father grunted. "That wasn't a request, son." His voice lowered as he stepped closer to Jamie. "Do I need to remind you how hard everybody else is working for *you*?"

Jamie flinched when his father said the word "you," and so did she. Why did Jamie Sr. have such a hold on his son?

Finally, Jamie turned to his father. "No, sir." His eyes bounded back to hers. A broken smile on his face. "We'll talk more at the party tonight, but you keep practicing. He placed his bags in her hands, then let his fingertips linger against his wrist. "Looking forward to our rematch, Bee."

Was this his game? Bring her to the *edge*, then yank the cord so she didn't get too *close*? She closed her eyes, disappointed at the realization that despite all her planning and pep talks, she fucking *liked* him. Despite what she should have felt: objectivity. Impartiality. A subtle "I-give-nary-a-fuck."

She was unceremoniously screwed. It was going to be a long night.

Inside Jamie's father's studio, the recording booth was cramped, but it had space for a stool, an easel for lyric sheets, and Jamie's favorite acoustic guitar. In the control room, through a massive window by the door, Tex, producer Tom Hathaway, and songwriter Melvin Scott huddled closely around Jamie's father, whispering conspiratorially.

Jamie was a puppet, and those four men pulled the strings.

Tom, a scrawny man in his 40s with a thin, brown mustache and sunken cheeks, pressed a button on the soundboard that filtered his voice from the control room and into Jamie's booth. "Why don't we retake the bridge?" Tom asked.

Jamie raked his hair from his weary eyes. "I think we got it. We did it at least twenty times already."

Even if Jamie wanted to retake that wretched bridge—which he didn't—he was spent. The interview with Brinton earlier that afternoon had thrown him for a loop. To learn how much distress he'd unintentionally caused her with his

Grammys speech snuffed out any goodwill he'd hoped to earn. Had he done enough to reassure her that he wasn't an asshole? That he was more than the reputation that preceded him?

Shit, what if he hadn't? He couldn't get a solid read on her, and she seemed to watch him like he'd grown another head. Was she the right person to reveal himself to? For his half-baked plan to work, at the very least, he needed her to *like* him. To trust him, and to *want* to help him. If their first interview was an indicator, it would take more than two weeks to earn her trust, and for good reason. She'd been through hell. Largely because of him.

Revealing himself to Brinton wouldn't work. He pinched the bridge of his nose as the realization sank in. He needed a new plan to come clean. But how?

Tom glanced at Jamie's father, who nodded. "It's not really flowin'. Let's try it again."

Melvin, a stocky Nashville veteran in his 50s with leathered skin, hadn't spoken directly to Jamie even once. He had worked with all the major players but rarely as a ghostwriter. That, apparently, was another string Jamie's father had pulled to ensure this album came together exactly as he wanted. He whispered something to Tom, who laughed dryly, which pissed Jamie off.

"If you ask me—and I know you didn't—what if it's the lyrics? This bridge feels inauthentic," Jamie said. Was there a diplomatic way to say *I'd rather my balls catch in a zipper than sing these words*? Cringing, he read aloud from the lyric sheet. "*You want love/But I need space/Baby my heart beats/At a different pace/I can love you right/But only for tonight.* I wouldn't say anything like this to a woman."

He didn't want a serious relationship, but he wasn't intentionally trying to be a dick either. "This is my chance to talk about my life and really say what I'm about, right? That's what all the best artists are doing now—peeling back the layers."

Before he released his debut, Jamie showed his father a few songs he'd written for the first time. They represented what he *thought* being in love felt like. Of course, he'd never experienced it himself, but he liked the idea of connecting with people over something universal. So many artists he admired did it seamlessly, including his father. He wanted that too.

But Jamie was devastated when his father laughed in his face, calling his lyrics "a dogfight of clichés." So, he stopped trying. Then he won the Grammy, which became an unexpected push to un-suck his life. He had no idea if his writing had improved—nobody had seen or heard it.

The men were quiet.

"Lyrics are fine and work with your personal brand," Jamie Sr. said, finally. "We did thirteen songs like this for your debut. Now, you got a Grammy."

At the reminder, Jamie's chest tightened. He closed his eyes, hoping to block out his inadequacy. "I've been working on something that feels more...like me." He held up the brown leather-bound notebook atop his stool. "How about we lay it down and see—"

His father didn't let him finish. "Dammit, Jamie. I'm not paying for studio time to 'lay it down and see.' Do it again, and let's move on."

Adrenaline snaked through Jamie's veins, and he wrung his hands to stop himself from slamming the easel against the wall.

"Why don't you take five? Rest your voice," Tex said with the skill of an FBI hostage negotiator. "Come back, and we'll lay it down again."

Usually, Jamie would have sucked it up and shut his mouth. But then he remembered what Brinton had said: he put himself in a specific hole, this damn early grave. He had to stay vigilant with his plan to break free and needed a platform with some credibility.

What if he leaked the news himself on a burner Instagram account his team couldn't access?

Gracious, that wasn't what he wanted at all.

It was egotistical to admit, but he wanted people to take this announcement seriously and for it to have some permanence beyond an algorithmic feed. He wanted to point back to it, years later, with pride. A *Landmark* article would've done it in spades, but now, that was out of the question.

Jamie exhaled, his breath acidic against raw vocal chords. At least this was the last album he had to make with his father's cronies. He'd get through this, then figure out a new, feasible way to start over.

"I'll miss working with you, Melvin," Jamie grumbled into the mic, hoping the sarcasm wasn't lost in translation.

His father chuckled, low and easy enough to make Jamie's spine straighten. "Actually, the label loves the early cuts we've sent, as I knew they would. And the *Landmark* article is icing on the cake. So I've extended Melvin and Tom's contracts for the next two albums. You'll have your new papers to sign tomorrow."

*Ain't that some shit.*

Jamie flexed his fist as his pulse jabbed his temples. "The next *two* albums?"

"Gotta strike while the iron's hot. You understand, son?"

Jamie shouldn't have been surprised. This was always the way with his father. He was the boss—the big man with big plans. Jamie spun his gold ring around his pinky, each revolution revving his agitation. "Yeah, I understand."

He understood, now, his father would never stop playing these games. He had two choices: do nothing or, for the first time, go against his father. And it had to happen that night.

BRINTON INHALED THROUGH HER NOSE, filling her belly with positivity, and exhaled negativity from her parted lips. Yet, somehow, there was no drowning out the nagging buzz filling the space between her ears.

Nerves. Butterflies.

Either way, she felt the vicious sting nearly every waking moment.

She inhaled positivity again but caught a glimpse of her puffed, reddened cheeks in the white wicker-framed bathroom mirror and felt ridiculous. Brinton paused the aggressively woo-woo meditation app on her phone and yanked out her earbuds.

The party started an hour ago and she was still at the guest house, sitting cross-legged on the cold marble floor. Not only was she forced to attend this party, with this crowd of strangers, but she had no viable angle for her article other than Jamie was sorry for embarrassing her. That wouldn't work.

Her mother would have said she was being too hard on herself, but Brinton knew what was on the line: her dignity. Earlier, she'd scoped out the patio, mapping out escape routes back to the guest house in case she got too overwhelmed. The absolute last thing she needed tonight was a panic attack.

She FaceTimed Shay, who answered on the first ring.

"Tell me I can still back out," Brinton whispered, knees pressed into her chest.

"Why are you whispering?" Shay asked casually, waving a banana in her free hand like a magic wand as she perched atop their mother's granite kitchen island. "Also, *where* are you? That all-white room is giving off hostage vibes."

"I'm at Jamie's house. Well, his dad's house." Brinton squeezed her knees tighter, trying to breathe through the invisible chisel needling her temples. "But I have to meet him at this party where I won't know anyone but *him*. And I'm scared I'm gonna screw it all up or embarrass myself again. So, tell me to quit and come home."

Shay leaned closer into the screen. "Why are you sitting like that? Did Jamie tie you up? Wait, that is kinda hot."

"Shayla, how do they let you out of the house?"

"Consensually, of course! Didn't think the man had it in him. But I like it."

"*No*, he didn't tie me up!" Brinton snapped, panning the screen down to her unbounded hands and feet. "Can you just agree with me for a minute?"

Shay paused to chew. "Depends. Are you trying to talk yourself out of interviewing the man who, as you believe, can fast track that career you keep griping about?"

"I mean, yes—"

"Then absolutely-fucking-not. You've already talked to him and survived, right?"

"Barely." Brinton still hadn't found a way to get the stain out from her Grammys dress. "Anyway, Rich says I need a juicy angle."

"Leave it to that clown to ruin the word juicy."

Against her might, Brinton giggled. "Yeah, and I probably won't get that from Jamie without pinning him down."

"Now, that's an idea I can get behind."

At Brinton's guttural groan, Shay rolled her eyes. "Look, you're brilliant, and you spend all day researching people, places, and things for *Landmark*. I also know you're anxious right now, so maybe it feels harder to summon that sexy sleuth inside. But just slow down, remember that you busted your ass to get there, and let this new world guide you.

There's a treasure trove at your disposal. Everything you need to know about the man is already there."

"Shit, you're right," Brinton breathed. She wiped her sticky free hand on her jeans. "He's gotta have some snaggle-toothed Little League photos lying around or something. I could start there, with a few easy questions about his past. Get him talking?"

"There she is! Now don't call me back until you do." Shay cocked a brow. "Or if he lets you tie *him* up. Then definitely call me back."

Twenty minutes later, after a quick shower, Brinton changed into a black tank top and matching belted midi skirt with pockets. It was the most casual outfit she had packed. Pushing her braids off her shoulder, she slipped in her favorite gold hoops and stepped into a pair of black platform Mary Janes. In the massive vanity mirror, she smiled. She looked better than she'd hoped. Plus, she was wearing her good bra.

*Yee-freaking-haw.*

On the marble countertop, a small framed silver photo caught her eye. A young Jamie Jr. and a supermodel-beautiful blonde, whose bright smile lit up the sun-faded image. She kissed his cheek as they posed in front of the spinning teacups ride at Walt Disney World.

It had to be Jamie's mother, judging by the uncanny likeness.

MaryBell Crawford died of natural causes when Jamie was a teenager. At least that's all Brinton could find online about her. Not much else had been published because she died long before social media's rise. She was also married to a notoriously private music icon.

In her research, Brinton hadn't found a single article where Jamie had mentioned his mother.

*Why is that?*

The question looped in Brinton's mind as she plodded downstairs and through the front door. It was obvious how Jamie's father had influenced his career. Was there something untapped about his mother? That was a hell of an exclusive—and something Jamie's Country Boy Charm couldn't evade.

Because Brinton wouldn't let him.

# CHAPTER NINE

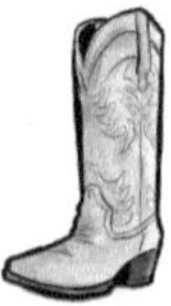

"Y ou really don't remember?" Stella Wrangler asked Jamie hopefully.

Jamie only vaguely remembered her from junior high. Stella was still petite, with a mess of wavy blond hair that overtook her small frame. She leaned in so close that the smoked chicken on her breath slapped him across the face.

"We necked outside the Piggly Wiggly at least twice."

At Stella's side, Abby Wrangler ceremoniously clinked wineglasses with her fraternal twin sister. Abby was curvy, with an auburn, cheekbone-grazing bob that made her look much older than she was. Jamie wouldn't have guessed they were related if not for their violent orange spray tans and identical, ear-piercing cackles.

"We both did," Abby squeaked.

No matter if it was a hometown concert or backyard cookout, Jamie was always cornered by a rotating cast of nosy neighbors and former classmates. They either treated him like a walking photo op or signpost for reliving the "good old days."

Case in point, he found himself caught in the Wrangler sisters' clutches, beneath a cabana festooned with twinkling fairy lights. The beaming women planned to drag him, kicking and screaming, down memory lane.

On a stage across from the pool, a local band played an enthusiastic cover of Tim McGraw's "I Like It, I Love It," sending the packed dance floor into a frenzy. Beneath the stately pinewood pavilion, long tables boasted Liza's never-ending feast.

Jamie looked to Cory, who stood across from them, for help. His best friend ran a hand over his low-cut fade and laughed into his beer. Oh, he'd pay for that later.

Jamie took a swig of his own beer, fishing for one of his go-to lines that usually worked. "Those were the good old days, right?"

In fairness, Jamie had blocked most of junior high from his mind. It was his darkest grieving period after his mother's sudden death when he was thirteen. Back then, he had done a lot of stupid things to avoid his feelings. Stolen beer from his father's mini fridge. Missed curfews. And, yes, his fair share of heavy petting in darkened parking lots.

The sisters prattled on about junior prom, but Jamie wasn't listening. He was scanning the crowd for Brinton. He needed to find an opening for them to talk. But each time he saw her, she was deep in conversation with someone else.

Doing the job he brought her there to do. Right.

Stella cupped one hand on his ass. She squeezed hard, ripping him from temporary solace.

"And if memory serves me right," she purred, "you were very good on the dance floor."

Jamie bristled, then quickly buried his annoyance beneath his practiced, for-the-cameras smile. Another thing he loathed about hometown parties: people thinking they could take a piece of him whenever they wanted because he was somewhat famous.

"Well, ladies, it was nice to catch up," Jamie said through gritted teeth. "I hope you enjoy the rest of the evening."

"You can't leave so soon," Stella whined.

"You just got here," Abby drawled.

"You know what? I see our dear friend Sherlock, who we haven't spoken to all night," Jamie said. He slapped Cory's bulging shoulder cap hard enough for him to get the hint.

Sherlock was the code name they'd used since sixth grade to escape any unpleasant scenario. "We can't be rude. So, if you'll excuse us."

"Oh, right. Sherlock's here. We couldn't be rude," Cory echoed, his Oscar-worthy acting skills coming in clutch.

They waved to the women, now with pronounced frowns on their faces, and retreated toward the pool. As they left, the sisters whispered in not-so hushed tones.

"He used to be better looking, don't you think?" Stella accused.

"Hairline's getting thin," Abby hissed. "But bless his heart."

Once they were out of earshot, Jamie and Cory busted out laughing.

BRINTON HAD KNOCKED out a few background interviews with other partygoers, quickly discovering that Iris locals were friendly, animated, and loved to gossip about their hometown hero. The standouts included Mrs. Hollyhand, Jamie's kindergarten teacher, with whom he regularly exchanged handwritten letters. And she still critiqued his penmanship.

Then there was Mr. Gilbert, who owned a convenience

store, where an eight-year-old Jamie once shoplifted chewing gum. Mr. Gilbert revealed that Jamie felt so guilty, he returned every chewed-up piece in a sticky ball. He volunteered to work off his debt in the storeroom after school.

Bob Lowell played JV football with Jamie and once walked in on him "jackin' the beanstalk" to an Angelina Jolie photo spread in *GQ*. This was surprising, because Brinton had pinned him as a Jennifer Aniston kind of guy.

Earlier that night, Brinton had caught sight of Jamie, wearing a white T-shirt that still managed to scandalize his body's rigid peaks and valleys. He was with a tall, handsome guy of even larger build. The men were close to the stage with two blondes, both in strappy white sundresses that made their natural-looking tans pop.

The group laughed heartily, and one of the women clasped Jamie's bicep. Against her wishes, Brinton's heart stuttered. The women were gorgeous, exactly the type she expected him to go for. Not that she had any kind of claim to him.

That was at least an hour ago. Where the hell was Jamie now? It was getting late, and Brinton needed to get her story back on track. She scanned the patio until her eyes landed on the fire pit.

"I CAN'T BELIEVE old Sherlock still works." Cory laughed through stretched breaths.

"No shit, Sherlock," Jamie said, doubled over and clutching his ribs. "Though, I ought to ream you out. You were gonna let them double-team me if I didn't call an audible."

"Sorry, I'm a happily married man," Cory said, his caramel cheeks stained pink with amusement. Slowly, he waved his gold wedding band in Jamie's face.

In return, Jamie held up his bare left hand before flipping him off.

Cory swatted Jamie's hand away as they approached the bar for another round. "You're right. I know you've been on a cold streak, but you didn't deserve that."

"What do you mean cold streak? I'm thirty years old, practically live at my father's house, and I get to binge all the bad reality TV I want. I'm livin' good."

They clinked their beer bottles, laughing.

Jamie took a sip. If tonight went the way he needed, there'd be plenty more beer in his future. He and Cory used to share tube socks and bunk beds. But now, he needed some honest-to-goodness advice.

"You ever needed to tell somebody something, but you didn't know how?"

Cory smirked. "No, I'm not available to end your cold streak, but I'm touched." He stopped laughing when Jamie's expression grew solemn. He clasped Jamie's shoulder. "What's going on?"

Jamie caught him up about Brinton's arrival and his father extending his "songwriting" deal. Outside of his team, Cory was the only person who knew about his father's control and the ensuing lies bundled with it. He'd supported him in spite of it, and Jamie was grateful.

"I want to tell Brinton my plans to go out on my own, and soon," Jamie said.

Cory knit his heavy brows together. "Shit, that's a hell of a landmine."

"This article might be my only shot to start over. But I need to do it in a way that I can still protect myself. In case…"

"Shit goes sideways? You know that's a real possibility, right? Telling a journalist the one secret that can destroy everything."

Jamie swallowed hard. He'd been avoiding that truth: that this article wouldn't be the redemption he yearned for. It could end up worse.

"Yeah, I know."

"But you trust her?"

"I want to. I think, if I talk to her, and show her I'm serious about this, I can trust her."

Cory scratched his stubble. "When?"

"Tonight."

"Lordy, Crawford," he exclaimed, hands flying out to his sides. He rested his chin against his knuckles. *The Thinker* sculpture in real life.

"Okay, take her somewhere so y'all can be alone. Too many bystanders here. Then, make her feel comfortable. Spin it like you can both benefit from working together."

Jamie nodded. "That's what I was thinking too."

"It'll help her see you as a person, not some celebrity she's writing about for a paycheck," Cory added. "Which you *need* for this to work. And when you tell her, ease into it. Wait for the right moment."

"How do I know when it's the right moment? I'm running out of runway."

"No clue, brother. But you'll know. It's sink or swim."

Jamie rolled his eyes. "Sure, that seems easy enough."

Cory grinned. "Because that's the easy part. The hard part? You gotta keep her away from your daddy. If he finds out what you're up to—"

"I know."

Cory nodded. "Good. Go find her. I'll cover for you here until Priyanka calls. I'm on diaper duty tonight. You got Sr.

to deal with, but I'm far more scared of what my wife will do if I turn up late."

Jamie pulled Cory in for a tight bro-hug. "Thank you, man."

As his friend disappeared into the crowded dance floor, Jamie finally spotted Brinton on the farthest side of the patio, behind the dance floor.

Thankfully, she was alone. Jamie drained his beer and took long strides to catch up with her. But then she beelined for the firepit, right toward his father.

*Shit.*

BRINTON COULDN'T BELIEVE her timing. Nobody could give more context on Jamie's journey than his father. She was relieved to knock out his interviews so early in her stay.

Tex tipped his wide-brimmed hat as they crossed paths, leaving Jamie Sr. alone. Her heart galloped in her chest as she approached.

Jamie Sr.'s long and lean silhouette was awash in a blaze of scarlet and saffron. He looked like a tableau from one of those old Westerns she used to watch with her own father.

From the cobalt Adirondack chair where he held court, Jamie Sr. offered a wry smile.

Brinton fidgeted with a few braids that had spilled over her shoulder. "I wanted to thank you again for hosting me and for the party. It's great," she said, trying to keep her tone even despite the stress drop-kicking her in the stomach.

"Mh-hmm," he said, eyes fixed on the crackling flames.

She held up her voice recorder in one hand. "I was hoping I could get a quote from you. You're one of the most successful country artists, well, ever. How do you feel about passing the torch to Jamie, who's not only an up-and-comer, but your son?"

"Passing the torch, huh? Didn't realize there was a name for it," Jamie Sr. said impartially. Slowly, he rose from his seat. "It feels like a lot of blood, sweat, and tears coming to fruition. It feels like something I would do anything to protect and nurture. Do you know how *that* feels, Ms. Shaw?"

She cleared her throat. "Sure. Legacies help people make sense of life and their place in it. Do you agree?"

"You mind if we speak candidly?" he asked, nodding toward her recorder. "Off the record."

She pressed the stop button. Jamie Sr.'s brown eyes glowed amber in the low light.

"I'm gonna protect my son's best interests, even when he can't do it himself. He can be impulsive, even reckless when he don't feel in control. Been that way since he was a kid when he..."

Jamie Sr. stopped himself, then rolled back his shoulders.

"I've seen it to know that he needs somebody to guide him, to keep him on the right track. So I'm not going to let him throw his life away. That means keeping a close eye on you and that article of yours. He's friendly with young women like yourself, as I know you've heard, but I didn't do all that I've done"—he motioned with his open palm to his surrounding kingdom—"to let him get distracted. Am I clear?"

Did he take her for some kind of notebook-wielding trollop? Brinton wanted to unleash the hot current of fury lighting up her every neuron. Throw that fancy Adirondack chair in the fire. But Black women rarely had the privilege to exist peacefully in the world, let alone the luxury of being angry. Or to cry.

"What do you think I'm here to do?" she asked Jamie Sr.

She was keenly aware that, this time, there wasn't a quick exit plan.

He rattled the ice and whiskey in his glass, clicked his tongue. "I suppose we'll find out eventually," he said, disappearing through a side door and into the darkened main house.

As Brinton stood there, too stunned to move and so much unsaid coursing through her veins, her eyes found Sammi's. Mid-twirl on the dance floor, she gave Brinton a thumbs-up. Lips formed into a half-baked smile, Brinton shot her one back.

*Yee-freaking-haw.*

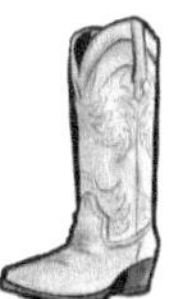

*J*amie's fingers drummed against the slatted wood tabletop. He'd been watching Brinton and his father from the pavilion. While he couldn't make out what they were talking about, predictably, it looked tense. What had he said to her? Jamie had to find out.

Brinton stalked toward the dessert table about twenty feet away, and he made his move.

A few moments later, Jamie tapped Brinton's shoulder. She turned, eyes wide and cheeks plump with whipped cream.

"Oof. Sorry, caught you at a bad time?" he asked, trying hard to ignore how endearing she looked. He needed to focus.

Brinton tried to talk with a full mouth but resigned to shake her head.

"Take your time. Liza makes the best banana pudding on Earth. It should be savored." His smile faded. There was no use in beating around the bush. "But I did wanna talk to you about something."

She raised her eyebrows and swallowed. "Actually, me

too. Let me grab my recorder," Brinton added. She nodded to her tote bag on a nearby bench.

"But not here," he whispered. Damn, his throat was dry and his nerves danced up his spine. "Can we go somewhere more...private?"

Eyes narrowed, she set her plate on the table. "That's not a good idea, Jamie. It might look like—"

"Like what?" His throat tightened, and he spun his ring tentatively. "Did my father say something to you?"

She stepped backward, arms crossed over her chest defensively. Jamie's heart dropped. This plan was going to hell in a handbasket.

"Were you spying on me?" Her accusation pierced him like a blade.

"I wasn't—well, I saw you two talking. He can be a little..."

"Intense?" A shadow of a smile crossed her lips.

Was it an opening? God, he hoped so.

He laughed, relief buoying him. "Yeah, that's putting it nicely."

Brinton's shoulders relaxed, her hands now loosely folded at her waist. "He's really hard on you, isn't he?"

He wasn't always that way. He was a businessman first, playing for sold-out crowds and making the family name shine bright. That meant missing his fair share of Friday night football games and class graduations. But Jamie knew his father loved him, in his own way.

Although Jamie still replayed the memory from the horrible night his mother died, when the quiet comfort between him and his father shattered. But *this* simply wasn't the time to dig up that grave. Or why it was all Jamie's fault.

"My father has his reasons," Jamie said instead. He prayed it was enough to talk her down from the invisible ledge. "But...are you okay?"

Brinton's arms were cinched around her chest. Her eyes bounded around the crowded pavilion, settling on anything but *him*. Whatever ground he'd gained while playing cornhole that afternoon had officially gone down the shitter.

"Thanks, but I can take care of myself," she countered evenly. "And I don't want anyone getting the wrong idea if we're sneaking around. I need to be taken seriously here. I know this article won't change much about your life, but it means everything to me. So, whatever you need to say, say it here."

Finally looking at him, her eyes brimmed with conviction layered with a pleading he knew all too well. Those captivating almond orbs, chocolaty brown and swirled with caramel in the center, enveloped him like a warm bath. He didn't know why they called to him, but they were getting harder to shake.

As if pulled by an invisible string, he stepped closer. "It means a lot to me too. And believe me, I take you as seriously as a heart attack. I say it here because…"

He couldn't find the words as insecurity set in. What if it was hopeless and high time he gave up? She searched his eyes, which made him inexplicably dizzy for a moment. His heart was a locomotive in his chest.

"Jamie, I really don't have time to waste, so please…"

He had no choice but to tell her, right then. Right now.

*Shit.*

He just needed to stop stalling and say it. Get this over with. He leaned in closer, a feeble attempt at being subtle when he felt like he was about to drop an atomic bomb into a kiddie pool.

As he opened his mouth, someone gripped his shoulder from behind. The long, watermelon-red nails and old-money-yet-faintly-old-lady perfume—jasmine and orchid and *privilege*—were dead giveaways. Jilted exes had a way of haunting you.

Jamie and Kendall Chase ended most parties at his father's compound inside the darkened pool house, her legs wrapped around his waist and a pool noodle jammed into his back. But he didn't want Brinton to think he was nothing more than his shitty public persona. He wanted her to get to know *him*. That couldn't happen if Kendall got her way. Or if she got wind of his plans.

"HEY, STRANGER," Kendall said, flipping her pin-straight, honeyed mane over her bare shoulder. She eyed Jamie like a marbled ribeye. She intended to devour him whole.

And why wouldn't he let her? Kendall Chase was beautiful. No, she was a beauty filter come to life. In her strapless black mini dress—designer, probably French—her bronzed, Pilates-toned legs stretched on for eons. Her hair—extensions, definitely expensive—fell like silk down her waist.

Brinton adjusted the square neckline of her Zara tank top, scoffing silently. Jamie was going to ditch their interview now that someone better—someone he had a very storied history with—came along. She'd been so quick to let down her guard and look where it got her.

Whatever, it wouldn't be the first time a man disappointed her.

"How're you doing?" he asked Kendall, sounding genuine, at least.

Kendall closed the gap between them with her gravity-defying chest. "Bored. You?"

Her Tennessean twang was decadent, as if dipped in tempered caramel, and potent, like it never failed to get her what she wanted. When Jamie stepped backward, her glossy, baby-pink lips flattened into a frown.

"I'm good," he said evenly. "But we're heading out."

Kendall cocked her head, appraising Brinton like she was for sale. Heavily discounted at the bottom of the bin. The humiliation worsened the longer she looked. "*We?*"

"Yeah. This is Brinton. She's here to interview me for *Landmark.*"

Kendall planted her hands on her waist, ready to blitzkrieg her way to victory. "Well, you and I haven't talked all night. You're the host. Can't ignore your guests. I know your daddy raised you better than that."

She leaned in. "In fact, I should ask him. You know that I love a spectacle."

Brinton took the apparent snub on the chin, but Jamie's eyes darted around nervously. She could feel him squirming under Kendall's laser. But she could help him this once. If nothing else, for the cover story?

"Jamie, we really should go. I'm on deadline, remember?"

Brinton raised her eyebrow for effect. They traded glances. Were they on the same team now?

Jamie turned back to Kendall. "You're right. I can't ignore my guests." He stepped around her and joined Brinton at her side. "Good night, Kendall. You need a ride home? I can have Michael scoop you up."

Kendall's hazel eyes singed holes into Jamie's for a moment. She clicked her tongue, perhaps a harbinger for the rematch to come.

"Are you serious right now?"

"I am."

She summoned a nice-nasty smile, something menacing and yet spellbinding. It was quite the secret talent. "You two have a good night," she spat, striding away with the grace of a vengeful gazelle.

As they watched Kendall go, Jamie's winning smile returned. "That…was pretty good. I don't think she's ever taken no for an answer."

"First time for everything." Brinton laughed. "Now you owe me one."

"Does that mean you trust me now?" he asked, voice low, the sound velvety and rich.

Her stomach folded into an origami swan. Why, she didn't know. Or at least, she wasn't ready to interrogate it. "It means I'll go with you."

He laughed. "A win's a win. C'mon, Honeybee. We got a lot to talk about."

# CHAPTER ELEVEN

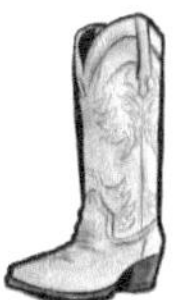

Twenty minutes later, Brinton cautiously shifted her feet on the dock and peered across the lake. It looked like darkened glass that threatened to crack beneath her. The dock stretched thirty feet from Crawford Lake's shore. On each side, two dozen pillars lit the way, casting an amber glow reminiscent of candlelight.

It would have been romantic if not for the lake's heady aroma. It was faintly sulfuric, reminding her of trash day in the city. The thick, ninety-percent humidity coated her lungs.

Already in the water, Jamie gazed up at her expectantly from a ten-foot row boat tied to the dock.

"Is that thing going to hold us? It looks like a death trap," she said, leaning over the dock's edge.

He chuckled, playfully rolling his eyes. Despite the darkness, they still sparkled.

How'd he do that?

"It's not a death trap," he said plainly. "It's a dinghy."

She crossed her arms. Clearly, he was fucking with her.

"What did you call me?"

Now, he was full-out laughing. "A dinghy—it's a type of boat."

She bit back a smile, but dragged her thumbnail against the edge of her pointer finger until she felt the centering sting of broken skin.

Lakes were murky and slimy. Then there were brain-eating amoebas and a menagerie of dead bodies lurking at the bottom.

Brinton didn't want to admit her fear. Namely because she was afraid of everything. Once Jamie knew that, why would he take her seriously?

"I live in New York City. I don't get out on boats much," she said instead.

His laughter softened, and he nodded to the long paddles affixed to the boat's sides. "This one has oars, so it'll be a nice, easy ride. We'll be back at the dock before you know it."

He unwound the thick knot securing the boat to the dock. "Can you swim?"

She nodded. Swimming used to be a beloved hobby. She'd even led her team to a state championship in high school, but it had been over a year since she set foot near a pool. As her panic disorder matured, Brinton realized almost everything she once enjoyed could potentially kill her. Including boats, lakes, and swimming.

This was where Jamie wanted to talk. Her choice was made. Brinton wrung her slick palms together, which, unfortunately, he zeroed in on.

His smile faltered. "I'm not gonna let anything happen to you. I'll help you in, paddle us out a bit, and we'll come back. Okay?"

When he looked at her so earnestly, the screeching doubt in her mind dampened. She liked that as much as she scrutinized what it meant.

"Okay," she answered.

Steadying herself, Brinton braced one hand on a metal ladder leading into the boat's inner shell. The other gripped Jamie's hand. His palm melted into hers, transferring an essential dose of assurance as she maneuvered.

Soon, they faced each other, knees touching. She tried to keep her breath steady and relax her death grip on the boat's low railings.

"Comfortable?" he asked, as if he knew the answer.

"Yep. This is great," she said, voice jumping an octave. Her breaths audibly zipped from her nostrils.

On the plus side, being out there—far from city lights, traffic, and interminable to-dos—was a nice change. Brinton surveyed the cloudless sky and appreciated the softly twinkling tapestry. She would have never experienced these stars back home.

Jamie slowly paddled them away from the dock. A wake of ripples trailed behind as the boat sliced through the lake's placid surface.

Brinton traced their path. She needed the distraction from his shoulders, chest, and forearms. Planes of lean muscle lazily, teasingly stretched and swelled beneath his white T-shirt with each rotation. How might they tense and release during more vigorous cardiovascular activity?

Brinton bit her lip, cataloguing his soft intake of breath and smooth exhalation.

In and out. Over and over again.

Close enough to feel Jamie's body heat, she'd realized how lonely she'd been. Adding further insult, he smelled so damn good. Sweet and smokey, like when they first met.

"You're good at this," Brinton said, snapping back into focus.

Surely, he was good at many things.

He smirked. "My dad taught me when I was a kid. Said a man should know how to steer his own boat."

"How's that working out for you?"

Jamie dragged his eyes to the night sky. "Some days there's a hole in the hull—that's the bottom of a boat, by the way—but I do all right." He sounded skeptical, like he didn't believe the words himself.

"How do you patch a hole in the hull?"

He laughed dryly. "I'll let you know when I figure it out. How's your boat?"

She ran a hand along the cool metal edge. If he had a hole in his boat, hers was the Titanic. She didn't have hobbies outside reading and music, which were inextricably tied to work, and the manuscript she had started and stopped writing dozens of times since graduating from undergrad.

Aside from her sister, she had no real friends, but not out of lack of desire. It was more that when the judgmental voice in her head told her that she was too awkward, too needy for anyone to want to be her friend, she believed it.

When she was dating Eli, there was a brief period when Brinton thought things were changing. She'd gotten to know Callie, the girlfriend of one of Eli's co-workers. Callie worked in fashion PR but was a true music aficionado, which Brinton appreciated.

While Brinton politely declined Callie's invites to various Instagrammable parties and late-night speakeasies that'd seemed too overwhelming at the time, it was comforting to feel like, maybe, one day, they'd go together. That, perhaps, they had found some easy kinship.

When Eli dumped Brinton, however, Callie ghosted her as if she had an expiration date. Brinton knew it wasn't personal, just the friendship politics. But it still hurt.

"I guess I'm built for dry land," she said, suddenly too aware of herself frowning over everything she couldn't change, so she forced her lips into a watery smile.

There was the weekend book club she ran for Gael, her

twelve-year-old neighbor, and other kids on her block. Children, she found, were far more accommodating of her particular brand of uptight. But a reading circle with preteens probably sounded pitiful to someone with millions of Instagram followers.

He nodded but didn't push her to explain. She appreciated it. Pulling her recorder from her skirt pocket, she placed it in her lap. "So, you wanted to tell me something?"

Jamie stopped rowing. They were about thirty feet out from the dock. He watched his ring flip around his pinky for a moment.

"Yeah, I guess I did." Then, he smiled. Not a real one, but the one she remembered at the Grammys.

"Please don't do that," she said faintly.

He laughed humorlessly. "Can't a man smile?"

"Not like that. That's your on-camera smile. When you're performing."

"Ah, been studying me?"

She chucked up her shoulder. "It's my job. And if this interview is going to work, I need you to be real with me. That's the man I came here to interview."

He laughed weakly, nodded to her voice recorder. "Sorry, it's a bad habit. I wanna be real, I wanna tell you something that's gonna change everything for me. But I need to work up to it, if that's cool?"

"That's fine."

For now.

"Thank you. So…you had something to ask me too?"

She clicked the record button. "Your father has had quite the Midas touch on your career. But I'd love to know more about your mother, how she's influenced your music. Like, have you ever written a song about her?"

Jamie clasped his hands tightly in his lap. "You sure got an interesting definition of going slow."

Brinton shrugged, then shifted her recorder to her knees so the audio was sharp. The recorder was reinforced with duct tape after many years of neglect, but she couldn't risk a blip. Not when she was this close to her goal.

"There's so little out there about her, so I thought…"

Her voice sank into the black expanse surrounding them.

"That it'd make for a good story?" he asked, eyes narrowed. The energy shifted to something undeniably tenuous. Tense. For the first time, Brinton couldn't tell what Jamie was thinking when she looked at his face. It worried her.

"I assumed she was important to you. I saw her picture at the guest house, and I felt like it was a good way to paint who you are. Beyond being a celebrity, or a Grammy winner, or heartthrob—"

He leaned back, but his posture was slightly less defensive. A smile—a real one—crept across his lips. Then, his teeth grazed his bottom lip, torturously slow.

"You think I'm a heartthrob?" he asked.

She rolled back her shoulders, suddenly tighter with each second his mouth worked over soft flesh. "Some people think you're a heartthrob. And stop flirting with me. I know the whole lip-biting thing too."

He chuckled to himself. "All right, that's fair. There's a lot people don't know about me…" He looked like he wanted to say more, but instead, his knee bumped hers. She twitched violently enough that her recorder slid dangerously close to the boat's low wall, only a few inches up from the waterline. Brinton's eyes rounded. An inhuman squeak spiraled from her diaphragm as Jamie snatched the recorder mid-tumble.

Her chest swelled with adrenaline as she tried to speak. "Shit—I can't even…thank you."

He nodded, then handed it back. "I appreciate you asking

about my mother, wanting to do right by me in that way. But that's not something I want out there publicly."

Brinton's heart sank, but she understood. And yet, she mourned the loss of her most viable story angle. It would have set her article apart from anything else published about him. It would have all but guaranteed a cover story.

She felt for Jamie's immense loss. She truly did. She couldn't imagine surviving her own growing pains without her chronically supportive mother.

However, Brinton simply couldn't afford to go home empty-handed.

"Then you have to give me something else," she said.

# CHAPTER TWELVE

"I will, just—ask me anything else," Jamie said earnestly. His pleading eyes made Brinton's heart jump into her throat.

She thumbed her recorder and exhaled. "Right, let's talk about your father. But I need something that's not out there. I wanna dig deep."

"What do you wanna know," he answered. His shoulders slumped as if anchored by an invisible weight.

She leaned back, summoning strength of her own. Committed to peeling back his layers. "When your dad was still performing, country music wasn't exactly an inclusive space. Some would argue that it still isn't. Is that something you've discussed with him?"

If she had a rare opportunity to mine Jamie's depths, in a way *Landmark* never would, she had to take it. It was then her new story angle crystalized beneath the silver moonlight: who was the *man* behind the *myth* of Jamie Crawford Jr.?

He let out a pained sigh, but his expression remained open. Head tilted, a faint smile on his lips, he laughed. "You wait until we're stuck in a boat to ask me that?"

She shrugged, smiling back. "I thought you liked my thoughtful questions?"

"I do. So, let's talk about it."

Brinton exhaled, bracing for this conversation to take a hard right turn, pun intended. "Country music in the American South wouldn't be what it is today without the influence and ingenuity of enslaved Black people," she started. "In fact, historians have traced the banjo—a staple in early country, bluegrass, and folk music—to origins in West and Central Africa before appearing in North America due to—"

"Slavery. Yes, I'm aware," he interjected. Remorse blanketed his tone.

Was he genuine or trying to win her over because he was, in fact, being recorded?

"I think there's an opportunity with artists of my generation and everybody who comes long after," he continued. "A chance to correct these mistakes and level the playing field for a lot of people who've been shut out."

She picked at a ragged cuticle on her thumb. She needed to be strategic without scaring him off.

"Right. Largely, Black country artists today are still fighting for financial parity with their white counterparts. Let alone for respect."

Brinton had discovered this in her own research. It filled her with despair for the stories she hadn't heard, and those no one ever would.

He nodded slowly. "You ever heard of Charlie Pride? He was one of the most influential country artists ever. He's also remembered as the first Black country superstar. Charlie was a friend of my father's. Meant a great deal to our family."

"I researched him. And his contributions are undeniable. Same with Linda Martell, the first Black woman to release a country album. And Beyoncé—the first Black woman to have a number one country album on Billboard. You and I both know there are countless more deserving of recognition, but who are denied a seat at the table because they were born with the wrong skin color and last name."

Brinton cleared her throat. "No offense."

Jamie ran a hand through a soft-looking thatch of waves that had fallen into his eyes. "You're absolutely right. I'm not going to argue with you, but—I guess—I'm still learning how to navigate this myself."

"Are you talking about that Instagram photo?"

He nodded. "Case in point why my team controls my social media accounts."

The previous summer, Cory posted a photo of him and Jamie in front of the Eiffel Tower and captioned it "N****s in Paris."

This was fine for Cory, a Black man. But when Jamie, a white man, hearted it on Instagram, the flogging was swift. The post was only up for a few minutes. Jamie donated tens of thousands to various civil rights organizations and apologized publicly, but the damage had been done.

"I would have apologized forever if I could. It sickens me to this day that I hurt any of my fans and gave the impression that I'd use that word so carelessly. Or that I supported people who did. Those people don't deserve to listen to my music."

She now regretted thinking he delighted in ridiculing her when he gutted himself over hurting countless people he'd never met. He had a heart of gold—probably too rich for this world. He deserved to know that.

"I believe you," she said. "And I think the people who love your music do too."

His grateful smile plowed through the last few barriers she had erected.

"Thank you, Brinton."

She nodded. "Since we're on the topic, would you ever consider writing a song about your political beliefs?"

Jamie's ring spun around his finger. This, she now understood, was his tell for when he was conflicted.

"My songs are about having a good time, not making political statements," he offered.

Her brows drew together. She needed to tread carefully. So far, Jamie's quotes were great, but she could go a little further with some luck and a teensy bit of tactful prodding.

"Well, you're a songwriter. I'm curious: how do you decide what parts of your life you share and don't?"

That easy comfort his body always carried went rigid. His eyes cut away from hers, like he was in the middle of an argument with himself about whether to say more or nothing at all.

"I don't get too political. Not my place," he said, finally.

"You don't think you're hiding behind that? It's more socially acceptable than ever for artists to speak out for what they believe in."

"Look, if you're listening to my music, enjoy it for what it is. Why should it matter who I voted for?" he said, his tone sharper than she expected.

"Who *did* you vote for?" she snapped, then swiftly clamped a hand over her mouth. She'd come in like a wrecking ball for a conversation that required surgical precision. But her anxious mind never kept pace with her words. It was one of several reasons why, at *Landmark*, she spoke only on an as-needed basis.

Eyes wide and lips parted in not-quite amusement, Jamie peered at her. He probably thought she'd set him up for a hot-mic gaffe for future exploitation. But she'd never do that to him—or anyone.

All too well, she knew the agony of having your self-worth sold for parts at public auction. She was fighting to salvage what was left.

"That wasn't—I didn't mean…" she stammered, clutching the sides of the boat.

"You're good," he said.

Somehow, his short, breathy laugh steadied her, despite the vessel's gentle sway. He tilted his head back. The moon's antique-white contoured his sharp collar bones like chiaroscuro. "We're having—what do they call it? A frank conversation."

When they both laughed, she simultaneously took respite in his kindness and envied how easily he doled it out. He seemed unafraid of being misinterpreted as weak. He lived so freely, while she was entombed in an Alcatraz of her own making.

Nonetheless, her shoulders melted from her ears and she exhaled. "Okay, tell me something else I should know."

His knee bumped hers again, triggering a zap that hopscotched up each of her vertebrae. "That's easy. The best party I ever threw was right here, on this lake. An eightieth birthday celebration for my Mamaw."

"I'm sorry, your *what?*" Brinton screeched.

He smiled again. This time, a teasing one. "Mamaw. My grandmother. I must forgive you Yankees for such willful ignorance."

"I was born in Virginia, if you must know," she volleyed back, grateful for their newfound familiarity but certain her cheeks would scald to the touch. "My family moved to New York when I was fifteen."

"Ah. I was wondering about your accent. Or, lack thereof."

She winked back. "We can't all be so charismatic."

He barked out a laugh. How did even that sound pitch-perfect?

"Can I ask you a question now?"

"I guess you've earned one," she said, smiling.

He leaned in, intrigue incandescent in his eyes. "What's your country song?"

She pursed her lips, unsure if this was a trap. "I like Beyoncé's country music."

"*Cowboy Carter* is a masterpiece," he nodded. "But respectfully, there's a whole lot more to discover too."

She scrunched her nose, mostly amused. But she didn't want to spoil the goodwill passing between them. For the story's sake, she reminded herself.

"I don't know. It's a lot of talking about shooting whiskey, having a jacked-up truck, and finding a good, God-fearing girl who worships the ground you walk on. And then drinking enough whiskey to forget her when she inevitably leaves you."

"Fair—some of the themes can be…" His voice trailed off as he tried to pull the words from the thick air around them. His gold ring orbited his pinky at lightning speed.

"Sexist and misogynistic?" she offered.

His brow creased in mock offense. "I was gonna say old-fashioned. You know, a lot of stuff about gender roles and putting a woman's worth in her looks, which I don't agree with."

Here he was again, a far cry from the honky-tonk lothario she had expected. That probably would have made for a better story. Yet, for reasons she wasn't ready to unpack, this revelation was far more compelling.

"So enlighten me," she said, instinctively leaning closer, luxuriating in his spicy-gourmand scent.

Smiling back at her, he looked as eager to submit to whatever was dragging them closer. Unless it was all in her head? Of course it was; famous people lived to be charming.

She pulled back.

"To me, country music is about telling the truth," he said. "It's about love, family, and maintaining faith in the future. And, for me, coming into my own as a man."

A few quiet moments passed as she relaxed into the boat's soothing rhythm. "'That Don't Impress Me Much' by Shania Twain,'" she said, finally.

His eyes narrowed atop his smirk.

"My favorite country song. Sophomore year of high school, during study hall, my English teacher blasted it daily from her CD player."

He looked impressed. His smile reached his eyes, which made the boat suddenly feel like it was levitating. "Shania's a saint. She's my godmom, if you ever wanna meet her."

Brinton gripped both sides of the boat in awe. "Wait—so your dad's a legend, along with your godmother?"

He bowed his head and chuckled. "Garth Brooks is my godfather, so yeah, I guess you could say I'm extra blessed."

They laughed again, an unnamed comfort passing between them. It felt like a warm, well-worn cardigan.

Was that how it'd feel to be wrapped in his arms?

"What's your country song?" she asked instead, determined not to submit to her ill-advised curiosity.

"'The Long Road' by my dad. It's about making a home on the road while your family moves on. It's so vulnerable, which is...unlike him." He paused. "Do you like my music?"

He looked nervous. It was surprising because she didn't expect a person so incontestably cool to care what she thought. After all, she was a grown woman who still ordered off the kids' menu.

She gnawed the soft flesh inside her cheek, eager to make the right words appear. Like it or not, she wanted him to *like* her, certainly enough to make the rest of her visit enjoyable. "'Table for One'...is catchy."

He laughed, but the sound came out strained. "Oh, you

mean that stellar chorus? 'I can't be tied down. 'Cause I need to go the distance. We've had our fun, but this table's for one.'"

Brinton scrunched her brows. "I guess I'm confused. I mean, you wrote it."

Was the song's message more than a little douchey? Yes, but she'd leave that part out.

He forced an uneasy but authentic smile. "Actually, that's what I wanted to talk to you about. My songs." He blew out a breath, then shook his head. "Shit, I'm freaking out. But I need to say this."

When he looked at her, she felt tingles all over.

"Brinton, I—"

The tingles turned into a sharp scrape. Then, there was a lingering hiss. Stiff, translucent wings crunched against her collarbone.

Brinton's shriek pierced the night air. A cockroach had burrowed into her top's neckline. Its spiny legs were caught in the fabric. Every hair on Brinton's body stood at attention.

"Holy sh—get it off." She screamed again.

"It's all right—probably a water bug," Jamie said, eyes wide. He tried to steady the boat, which now rocked as Brinton wildly flailed her arms. "Here, lemme—"

But she couldn't hear him anymore. Because now she'd reached over the side of the boat and into the cool depths, baptizing herself for dear life. The boat careened.

"Oh, fuck!" was the last thing she said before her feet flipped toward the sky, and her body plunged backward into the water.

# CHAPTER THIRTEEN

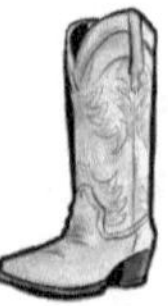

Jamie dove in after her. Her head popped back up to the surface, and he followed a few seconds later. "Are you okay?" he asked, panting.

"Oh my God. My recorder, I—it's gone." She blinked thick droplets from her eyes. Her voice was choppy as she trod water.

"That had everything I got from the party tonight. Shit. Shit. Shit!"

"I'll go down and look for it," Jamie said. "We'll get it back."

He plunged into the pitch-dark depths, again and again, but he couldn't even see his own hands in front of him. Once again, he'd been so unintentionally careless with her, like when he name-checked her in his Grammys speech with a poorly worded joke, only to find out how much that had hurt her. He hated himself for it.

He wouldn't repeat that mistake.

"Forget it—it's way too dark." Then, Brinton screamed. "Oh my God—something touched me."

"Try to keep calm," Jamie said, swimming closer.

Her eyes skirted across the water line. He had the urge to reach out for her, but she wasn't kidding about being a good swimmer and was already approaching the dock. When he caught up to her, she was trying—and failing—to hoist herself up the narrow ladder and onto the dock's wood-planked surface.

He didn't blame her; in the water, his clothes and boots added ten pounds, easy.

"Lemme help you up," he pleaded.

She nodded, breaths ragged and shoulders bobbing. He quickly scaled the ladder, then outstretched his arms. Jamie coiled his hands around the curve of her waist to lift her up.

Sheets of water slid down their bodies. Abdomens pressed together, the telltale heat from contact overfilled in his chest, along with the spike of something unnamable each time his hip bones grazed hers. When she gripped his back to steady herself, noses close enough to brush, he cradled her neck for the longest moment he'd had since the Grammys.

His heart pummeled his ribcage, but he remained cocooned in that moment, content to trace every plump bead of water streaking her lush cheeks. Then, he understood. She was crying.

"Honey, you're all right—I got you," he said, breaths tattered as her shoulders shook violently against his heaving chest.

He pulled her tighter. To his relief, she let him.

"If I don't ace this story, I'm going to get fired." Her voice came out singed. "And—because of-fucking-course—I lost my recorder and my interviews on my first day. I'm screwed."

Gently, he angled her chin upward, still gripping her tightly. "No, you're not. This was my fault. I brought you out here, so I'm gonna fix it. I'll get a new recorder and connect you with everybody you talked to tonight. And we can re-do all my interviews whenever you want. I'm gonna fix it, yeah?"

He meant every word. He should have been worried about how much he meant every word. He should have also been worried about the little spark that lingered in his chest whenever he was near her, but he wasn't. He liked her. She was brilliant and, sure, a little awkward, but he liked that too.

In the span of an hour on that lake, she had pushed him to examine his lot in life in a way he'd been terrified to confront. If he did anything to jeopardize her future, he'd never forgive himself.

Brinton loosened her grip on him and took a few steps back. He knew he shouldn't, but he instantly missed her body's warmth against his.

"Okay, yeah," she said. The fear in her eyes seemed to thaw. "Thank you—you're amazing."

Her words pierced his heart, filling it with a sweetness he didn't deserve. The tenderness reminded him of when Kendall first told him she loved him, and how he didn't have the courage to tell her the truth. He'd hurt her, which meant he was capable of hurting Brinton too, even if he wanted nothing more than to have her keep looking at him like the most capable man in the world.

He was a shell of man, reinforced by loneliness, lies, and secrets.

"No, Brinton, I'm not. Believe me," he whispered.

She shook her head emphatically, batting away his insecurities. "You're one of the good ones. And I've seen enough of the bad ones to know the difference."

For her, he could become one of the good ones. He let the faint pricks of hope imbue him. *This is the right moment.* He took the opening.

Jamie could barely hear himself think over his heavy breaths. "Brinton, I'm a fraud."

"You're a *what?*" Her inflection dulled to a croak, and her shoulders shook.

"I—my songs. Fuck, I don't want you to hate me. Or anyone to hate me, but…Brinton, I have a ghostwriter. My father hired him years ago, and he's written every song I've ever put out."

His head slumped at the wilting weight of his omission. Wasn't he supposed to feel better now?

Brinton stared at him for a long moment. Her expression was inscrutable. God, he needed her to say *something*.

"You lied to me? To everyone?"

"Yes," he said, chest on fire. "My father told me it was the only way to build my legacy, and I believed him. There was a contract and I couldn't get out. But now, I have a chance to start fresh. I need your help. I need you to break this story with your article so I can make music on my own, without my father. He wants me to sign a new contract tomorrow, so I need to know tonight if you'll do it."

She stumbled backward. A deep tremor overtook her entire body. He wanted to hug her, to steady her. To steady himself.

Her eyes, heavy with fatigue, cut to the water's edge behind him.

"No," she said, so quietly he barely heard her.

Jamie's stomach bottomed out. "Maybe you need a beat after falling into the lake? But I got you. We're good now."

"No," she repeated, a little steadier now.

"I just thought, at the Grammys—we had a moment."

"A moment?"

"Yes," he rushed out. "A moment. You asked me if being a musician—playing for thousands of fans and stuff—helped me express myself more authentically? Well, you, Brinton...I want you to help me do that. I don't wanna hold myself back anymore."

"No, Jamie," she repeated. "I'm sorry, but you want me to go up against your father, one of the most powerful men in the music business? Assuming you're telling the truth—"

"I am," he insisted.

"He'll want revenge," she continued. "Everyone's afraid of him and you know it. So whatever he's planned for you, it'll be even worse for me. I'll be blackballed. I probably won't get another writing gig."

Finally, he got the nerve to reach for her shoulders, which stilled under his touch. "You said you wanted an angle no one has seen before. Brinton, this is it. We could work together. I could protect you—"

"No, you can't," she said. She gently shrugged off his hands and buried her face in her own.

"It sounds like you can't even protect yourself from him." She dropped her hands. "For the record, I don't hate you, Jamie. And I'm sure you did this because you felt like you had to. I know what that's like. And I wish I were stronger, that I could pull this off for you. But I can't take this risk. I desperately need a fool-proof win."

His greatest fear had come true. Now he was completely out of options. But he couldn't hate her either. He respected her too much for that. "I understand," he said. "But would you be open to thinking about it? Please. If you decide otherwise, we can do the interview any way you want."

She closed her eyes and exhaled. The sound cut him to the bone.

"I'm sorry," she whispered.

He smiled despite his mounting despair. "Can I walk you back?"

Once she was safely inside the guest house, Jamie's body

crumpled on the porch steps. He rested his still-damp fore-head against the towering white column. Tonight, in revealing his secret, he regained a piece of his soul. Tomor-row, when he regretfully signed his new contract, he would give it all away.

# CHAPTER FOURTEEN

"Ohat's in the box?" Shay squealed on FaceTime the next morning.

Brinton's phone was propped against a coffee mug on the guest house kitchen's gray marble counter. Next to it, there was an expensive-looking lavender package, crowned with a huge iridescent bow.

Earlier, Brinton had discovered it on the doorstep. It was almost too gorgeous to open.

"What's in the *box*?" Shay repeated, louder now and dragging out her vowels for effect. In her own office at the clinic, she bounced in a furry fuchsia swing chair. The tiny but joyful space was decorated completely in "pussy-pleasing" shades of pink, from the pinstripe wallpaper behind her to the custom Lucite desk, where she gleefully rested her elbows.

"Did you watch *Seven* again last night?" Brinton laughed at the inevitable. Nobody should be simultaneously so well-adjusted and unhinged, but that was Shay to a T.

"You know grisly crime thrillers make me sleep like a baby," Shay cooed. She looked like a living, breathing Warhol painting in her peony denim jumpsuit and signature strawberry lipstick.

"Now, answer the damn question."

"It ain't Gwyneth Paltrow's head."

Shay cast a wicked smile. "Of course, that would be horrible." She paused. "Is it Agatha's? I'll pretend to act shocked."

Agatha was a more senior music writer at *Landmark*, despite only being there for a year. In fact, Brinton had helped onboard her. Back then, before the knives came out, they were cordial. They even ate lunch together a few times in the break room. That was, until Agatha picked up a nasty habit of saddling Brinton with tedious research and fact-checking that she couldn't be bothered to do herself. Agatha also claimed it as her own whenever Rich asked.

Brinton rolled her eyes, desperate to shuck off the Agatha-shaped albatross slung around her shoulders. "Look, there's a card."

Carefully, Brinton slid open the thick lavender envelope with a butterknife.

"'Bee, thank you for seeing me for more than the headlines. Hope we can put some miles on this one together. Yours, Jamie.'"

*Yours.*

The word melted into her subconscious. After the whirlwind of last night, her first in Iris, "yours" had taken on new meaning. His secret was certainly hers now, as unsettling as it was.

Shay shrieked, ripping Brinton from her Escherian mental maze. *"Bee?* He gave you a nickname? Okay, Lake Bae."

Brinton had filled Shay in on her eventful evening but purposely left out the endearing—and jeez, sexy—nickname. She was hoping to avoid this exact conversation.

"He was being nice. It's not that serious," Brinton said,

failing to snuff out her smile. Wasn't it serious though? The man put in a hell of a lot of effort. Effort that overwhelmed her with gratitude as much as it made her head spin.

Brinton gently peeled the wrapping paper from its matching box. Inside, there was a brand-new, high-end voice recorder with twenty different buttons, cloud-based storage, and Bluetooth features.

She gasped. "I have to give this back. It's way too much." Her last recorder was a budget find that met her requirements: it had an on button, off button, and complimentary next-day shipping.

Shay's eyes widened in disbelief. It was the same look their mother had when someone said they didn't like Tyler Perry's movies.

"You will not. You will march your cute little ass to his house and thank him. And while you're at it, tell him that yes, you'll avenge his daddy's misdeeds."

"I told you, I'm not doing it," Brinton answered.

"You told me that you'd think about it," Shay volleyed back.

"Well, I thought about it. I'll pick a new angle…Influences on his new album or something."

"Wow, that's so…uncharacteristically mid-tier. That's *not* a world-class exclusive, and you know it."

Brinton tugged her black mock-neck top's snug collar. She hated the idea too. Unfortunately, in five minutes, she was due to give a status update during her daily editorial meeting with the team in New York. She was as excited for it as an unmedicated root canal.

"I mean, it's fine."

Her frown betrayed how fine she was.

Shay crossed her arms, wading through the ruse. "Oh, really? You don't seem fine. You seem kinda sad. In fact, you seem like you're throwing away your chance to dunk on those schmucks. Temu-Hunter-S.-Thompson-looking-asses. And, wouldn't it be nice to legitimately help Jamie? He's shown nothing but trustworthiness."

She rolled her eyes and held up a preemptive hand. "Well, except for the lying about his entire career thing, but you know what I mean."

This was true. Jamie had made good on his promise and emailed contacts for the people she'd spoken to at the party whose interviews were lost in the lake. Brinton had already arranged new phone interviews with everyone that afternoon.

"So, what are you going to do?"

Brinton sighed. Jamie's mea culpa had gotten him off her shit list, but what he wanted from her demanded too heavy a toll. She could lose everything she had ever worked for.

"I gotta jump for a call."

"Let me know how it goes." Shay's frown lifted. "I also want a play-by-play if, along with that recorder, Jamie lets you put some miles on his—"

"Shay," Brinton hissed through a defiant smile.

Once they exchanged good-byes, Brinton lumbered to the long wooden dining table. She slumped into a chair with exactly enough time to fluff her braids and pick egg-and-spinach frittata from her teeth in her laptop's camera.

*Landmark* was an institution of excellence with an illustrious fifty-six-year history. It was also a hypercompetitive shitshow that made *Fight Club* look like *Sesame Street*. The staff writers who sold their ideas—and themselves—best in the daily editorial meeting were published in the prestigious monthly print issue. This left everyone else to jockey for daily bylines, considered secondary, on the website.

Brinton clicked into the video call, her smile stretched to The Joker–esque proportions. It matched her disillusion.

"Hey, everyone, happy Tuesday."

The whole team, about twelve reporters in all, stared back at her blankly from the long conference table. Waiting for her to stop taking up space.

Their constant jokes about her Grammys fiasco made going to work an infinite loop of abuse and alienation. She felt unmoored, forever questioning if it was her fault that she seemed at once so easy to pass over and ridicule when she made a mistake.

Before every editorial meeting, each of Brinton's muscles seized and stayed that way until she left *Landmark*'s offices.

She felt the same pang now, even a thousand miles away.

"Brinton, I decided to take reviewing Megan Thee Stallion's new album off your hands this week, since you're already on assignment," Agatha said, casually smoothing her platinum bob. She offered a doll-like smile.

"But since Megan is, you know…a Black woman—is that still the PC term?" She paused, then rolled her bottom lip between her teeth. "I don't want to be—well, I know how sensitive you are about these…things."

Brinton winced as Agatha pursed her lips. She had resorted to these subtle digs ever since Brinton had complained to Rich about her dumping her grunt work and calling it "collaboration." At the time, Rich reasoned that Brinton should pat herself on the back. A senior staffer had requested her input, because Brinton was so "dialed into the culture."

"Yeah, I think Megan Thee Stallion would prefer to be called a Black woman," Brinton said slowly. She was trying to discern if this conversation was real or a Tennessee humidity-induced fever dream.

"Great! I'd also love to leverage your *expertise* as a sensitivity reader."

What Agatha meant was that Brinton, without byline credit, would do all the nuanced "cultural reporting" *for* her.

Because, once again, Brinton was the Black-spert.

Agatha had already started clacking on her laptop. "So, can you review by EOD?"

"I think that's a great idea," Rich beamed. "Brinton, you're the best at finding problems no one else notices."

Brinton picked at her cuticles, the fresh sting ringing as loudly as her incredulity. She felt backed into a corner when she needed to project confidence. She just wanted to move on to her pitch and get the hell off this conference call.

"I'll see what I can do," Brinton said.

Triumphant, Agatha's smile returned. "You're the best."

"All right, enough stalling—let's get into pitch." Rich yawned. "Brinton, whatcha got on the Crawford piece?"

"I'm thinking of a legacy piece," she said evenly. "With the new album coming out, I'll make connections sonically to his blue-ribbon history. Obviously his father, but also his godparents—Garth Brooks and Shania Twain? I'm sure I can sit in on some listening sessions. Plus, I've been in touch with people who grew up with him and know him best, so it'll be an intimate character piece too."

She hoped it was adequate enough to secure the respect she'd coveted—no, that she had *earned*. Steadily, she had built her self-worth on a job that had produced diminishing returns. Brinton regretted this, but she was desperate to be defined by more than her anxiety.

Unfortunately, the room fell silent, quiet enough that Brinton could hear Agatha's nails clicking on her phone screen.

Rich pinched the bridge of his nose. "Brinton," he started, carefully drawing out the sharpest blade from its sheath. "I didn't send you to Iris for an intimate character piece. I sent you there for something that would sell copies and drive clicks to the website. Juicy, remember?"

"I know, Rich, but this is better than *juicy*. This is a generational look at a man poised to redefine country music."

"It's dry as fuck," Agatha squawked into her steepled fingers.

Laughter rippled through Brinton's laptop speakers. Her cheeks grew hot. Nervous stress made her top cling to her lower back.

"I could absolutely turn Crawford out," Agatha continued, licking her lips. "Journalistically, of course." She winked into the camera.

Brinton fantasized about rearranging Agatha's smug face like a Picasso.

"I think he's all hype," Agatha added listlessly. "Nothing inside that sun-kissed head of his. No real purpose. That's the story. A Nepo Baby Prince hand-delivered a kingdom."

"Can't say I disagree." Rich laughed.

Agatha typed on her laptop. A ding rang out. Rich looked down at his screen, smiled, and nodded to her.

Panic, sharp and acidic, flooded Brinton's stomach, but she couldn't let Agatha win. "Rich, I got this," she choked out. "What I've shared is only a start. You're going to love it."

"Doubtful," Agatha cooed.

Brinton grimaced.

Rich's expression shifted between skepticism and boredom. "Yeah, it's a pass for me. But Agatha, send me over a full pitch. It never hurts to have a backup in case…"

Not only did Brinton need this opportunity, but now she knew, in detail, the magazine wasn't only out for her blood. Jamie was as much of a target to be exploited. Especially if Agatha sank her Gel-X claws into him.

Initially, Brinton had turned Jamie down because she was afraid to break a story so controversial she'd be exposed to more backlash than with the Grammys. She was also afraid that somehow, she couldn't execute in the way Jamie needed. He'd resent her for it.

But nobody at *Landmark* would handle Jamie's truth with dignity. And Shay was right. So far, Jamie had been nothing but kind to her. Brinton wanted to extend that same kindness. He was an unlikely friend in a sea of sharks.

"I'm working on something else," Brinton put in, already piecing together a fail-safe plan to get her cover story *and* help Jamie. "I can update you soon."

"I know you will," Rich said, not bothering to mask his sneer. "Or I'm reassigning this story."

# CHAPTER FIFTEEN

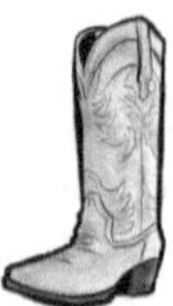

*L*ater that Tuesday afternoon, ear-splitting ticking grated Jamie's already frayed nerves. He rubbed his throbbing temples as his eyes settled on the taunting seconds hand of his father's antique clock.

*Tick-tock, jackass.*

Jamie wished to foil the impending trainwreck, but he couldn't. He shifted on the maroon leather couch inside his father's office, quite possibly his least favorite place on the planet. Here, Jamie Sr. courted ghostwriters, producers, and label executives. Jamie was never invited to those meetings, of course. Another signpost of his powerlessness.

Across from Jamie, Tex and Sammi sat on matching leather armchairs facing Jamie Sr., who presided from his imposing cherrywood desk. Its broad Queen Anne silhouette never failed to make everyone else in the room appear half their size.

The three of them were going on about logistics for the upcoming tour. Jamie had tuned it out, instead waiting for the ticking to stop, when he'd sign that God-awful contract binding him to another two albums.

Hell, who was he kidding? He was never getting out now.

"You hear me boy?" his father asked. He held a thick stack of papers in his hands. "I asked how the interview with Ms. Shaw was going?"

"Oh," Jamie mumbled. He hoped she'd gotten his package and wished to have seen her smile when she opened it. That smile would have cured him.

God, he wished she were there now. Jamie would apologize for asking her to jeopardize her career to save his. It was a bad hand all around. Brinton couldn't help him, and he didn't blame her.

"She's good at her job."

"How good?" his father asked sharply.

*Good enough to know not to get entangled in my mess.*

Jamie flicked his ring around his finger, but he didn't feel any more soothed.

"It'll be a great article. Got nothing to worry about."

Not that his father ever worried.

Jamie Sr. grunted. "Kendall called this morning. Said you snuck off early from the party with Ms. Shaw?"

Sammi straightened in her chair, hands tightly balling the skirt of her strapless peach maxi dress. "Oh, I'm sure they were talking about the article, like we agreed." Her eyes pleaded for him to take the bait. "Right, Jamie?"

"Um—yeah," Jamie stuttered. He'd owe Sammi a whole field of flowers for trying to cover for him. "I told Kendall good-night and walked Brinton home."

"That ain't what it looked like." Jamie Sr. slid his phone across the desk, revealing a photo of Jamie and Kendall at the party. Her chest pushed against his, their faces whisper-close. On the edge of the frame, Brinton looked decidedly uncomfortable.

Posted on Iris After Dark, an anonymous Instagram account devoted to hookups and gossip around town, the post claimed Jamie and Kendall were "canoodling over canapés" while Brinton was pegged as the sour-faced interloper.

Jamie was frequently the subject of conversation on the account's feed. He could handle that. But he rued implicating Brinton in this *Real Housewives of Bullshit*–level nonsense.

Jamie pointed down at the photo, which silently mocked him. "That's a bold-faced lie."

His father's scrutinizing look sucked the oxygen from the room. "I invited Kendall because it was good for people to see you together, get more mileage from that storyline."

Jamie Sr. was an expert at stirring the pot and torching everything inside.

"It'll be good for the album launch," Tex added, blissfully oblivious to Jamie's despair.

"I told you to be careful what you say around Ms. Shaw," Jamie Sr. said, glowering at his son. "She's a journalist, and when it comes down to it, she's loyal to that magazine. Not you."

The words lashed him. Jamie didn't demand Brinton's loyalty, and he respected her wishes. Yet, the hopelessness hacked at him. "I know, Daddy."

Jamie Sr. nudged the stack of papers toward Jamie and held out a pen. "I'm giving you a lot of slack here, doing this interview at all. Don't make me reconsider."

Fuck, here it was. His past and future. A spectacular collision, and he was trapped inside as the flames raged. Jamie rose from the couch and walked to his father's desk. He stared at the contract, where, at the bottom, a large *X* beckoned.

His eyes floated to the glossy fountain pen, still pinched between his father's fingers. Jamie willed it to combust. A smoke bomb, earthquake, or freak hail storm would have also worked. Anything to buy him more time.

"Let's get on with it," his father snapped.

Jamie took the pen and rolled it between his fingers. He brought it down to the blank space, primed to engulf him and his dreams.

Suddenly, Sammi shot up from her seat, clutching her phone. "Butter my butt and call me a biscuit."

Tex adjusted his black cowboy hat. "Well, don't hold us in suspense."

Characteristically, Jamie's father didn't say a word.

She grinned and spun on her cork heels. "Guess who's headlining Yeehaw Fest next Saturday?"

Jamie dropped the pen, more than a little confused what this had to do with him. "Mother Teresa?"

"God rest her soul," she volleyed back. "But no, my sweet little smart-ass. It's you."

Jamie's neck jerked back at the timing. The performance was in just over a week. "I thought we weren't playing until after the album launch?"

"That was until Luke Bennett had to pull out. On vocal rest for six weeks. Shame, I was looking forward to meeting him. Among other things," she said, smiling wistfully. "Anyway, I called in some favors, and it's all you, baby."

"Well, how about that?" Tex howled, slapping his hands together.

Jamie was stunned. Three years ago, he was playing to crowds of a thousand or less. Now, he was set to play for an audience of a hundred thousand. It was cruelly poetic: the deeper the lie about his music became, the bigger his career got. His shame swallowed him. It was an insatiable quicksand, no matter how hard he clawed.

Jamie rubbed his neck. The muscles had seized into one throbbing mass. He forced a smile from the dregs of his soul. "Wow, that's—thank you."

"You're welcome. However, we need to get things moving

with the promoters, including a photo shoot today. We gotta leave right now."

"Me and your daddy will finalize the set list," Tex said, rising to meet Jamie's father at his desk.

"Great," Jamie offered, still a little dazed as he started toward the door.

"Son—the contract," Jamie Sr. said. He tapped his pointer finger on the documents. Jamie froze. Regret pricked the back of his neck.

"He'll sign it tomorrow," Sammi called from the hallway, yanking Jamie's bicep. "We're gonna be late."

While prepping for a massive, last-minute show wasn't on his bingo card, he was grateful for the escape route.

Jamie followed and closed the double doors behind him. "Hey, thank you for helping me back there. I—"

Sammi practically floated down the grand wooden staircase. "Oh, I didn't do it for you. I don't want your daddy to start meddling, as he's wont to do. I like Brinton, and while you're trying to play your daddy like the radio, I know you do too. I know your tells."

She paused mid-step and narrowed her eyes. "Is something going on between you and Brinton? As your publicist, I wouldn't hate it, given how much attention y'all got after the Grammys. Could be good for the album. But also, as your publicist, if there is, I need to know so I can manage it. Or, at least, manage your daddy. I can't do that if you keep me in the dark."

There wasn't exactly *not* nothing going on. He'd revealed his deepest secret to Brinton. It hadn't gone as planned, but he believed Brinton wouldn't leak it.

And while he trusted Sammi, it'd be easier, for now, to keep her on a need-to-know basis. Right now, there was nothing to know. As for Brinton, he'd keep his promise and go for whatever story angle she wanted.

Then, he'd crawl back into his miserable hole.

"Nothing going on but the article," he said.

When Jamie slid into the back of Michael's waiting SUV, his phone buzzed. There were two new texts from Brinton.

> Brinton: We need to talk…
>
> Brinton: Somewhere we can be alone.
> Tomorrow?

She had made her decision. Yet, he needed the closure, even if it was a rusted shovel hollowing him bare.

A little nauseous with trepidation, he turned to Sammi, who watched him skeptically. "I got a favor to ask."

# CHAPTER SIXTEEN

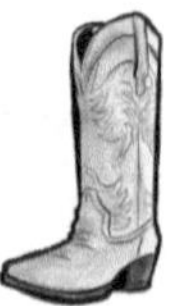

The next day, Brinton expected to meet Jamie in a darkened sports bar's corner booth. The kind of place with sawdust heaped on the floor, local beers on tap, and wall-to-wall TVs, each playing a different full-contact sport. She didn't expect to be riding shotgun inside a Polaris, idling at the bottom of a steep, rocky hill.

Off-roading was a package deal featuring three more of her anxiety triggers: heights, confined spaces, and, generally speaking, falling off a fucking cliff. Brinton still needed to survive another week-and-a-half in Iris.

Jamie convinced her that this was the perfect cover to speak candidly without intrusion from jilted ex-girlfriends or domineering fathers. Plus, it was great scene-setting for the article.

A fantastic idea until she was strapped inside a glorified Mario Kart.

Gleefully, Jamie revved the engine.

They were two hours outside of Nashville, in an area known as Turkey Bay. It was prized as an off-roader's paradise, offering some one-hundred miles of scenic trails and verdant brush. Jamie gripped the steering wheel with the ease of a man who could do this in his sleep.

"It looks way worse than it is," he assured. "Besides, Sammi will kill me if anything happens to you." Jamie revved the engine again. "You'll love it, you'll see."

She nodded, even though she could barely hear him through their helmets. She looked straight ahead, heart pounding like a war drum. Slowly accelerating, Jamie crept up the jagged, dusty path.

They traversed a slight dip in the terrain. The vehicle lurched and swayed, spitting up thick clouds of dust. Rocks crunched beneath the heavy tread as Brinton dug her fingers into her padded protective jacket.

Suddenly, she couldn't breathe. Was her jacket too tight, or was the helmet suffocating her? They hadn't even started the actual climb yet.

She gripped her knees with both hands.

Brinton tried visualizing herself floating on a cottony cumulus cloud, the sun warming her face. Sometimes, this worked to ease yapping panic, but she kept getting distracted by wayward branches whipping against her door.

As if he instinctively knew, Jamie squeezed one gloved hand over hers. "I promise, I'm gonna take care of you." The tension in her shoulders melted, his touch a panacea. It should have surprised her, but it didn't.

*Why didn't it?*

"You trust me?" he asked.

She wanted to trust Jamie, obviously for her safety, but maybe with something else she couldn't quite articulate yet. But trust always felt so confusingly intimate. Harrowing. One misread cue and her foundation crumbled.

It'd happened all the time with Eli. She'd feel him disengage, sighing at her from across the dinner table, turning away each time her veneer cracked and her undesirable core shone through. She feared she'd never deserve better.

But what if she could start down a new, albeit rocky, path with Jamie?

That frightened her too, but when he looked at her, all steeped in assurance, it felt different...Real. And maybe a little intoxicating. She could almost taste it, whatever was brewing between them.

Her heavy breaths fogged the helmet's visor. "Yeah, I do. Trust you."

"Good, because I wanna show you things you ain't seen before. But only when you're ready, okay?"

She nodded. Jamie initiated the climb.

Brinton allowed this newfound trust to steady her as the vehicle jerked forward.

Eventually, she laughed through the bumps and marveled at the dense canopy of cypress and sumacs blanketing the path.

Thirty minutes later, they reached the top, a vast clearing with sweeping views of the trees below. Out of the woods, they were in the clear. She shook with exhilaration.

Climbing out the vehicle, Brinton popped off her helmet. "That was awesome!"

"You did so good, Bee," Jamie cheered, flaxen waves wild and megawatt grin gleaming.

He wrapped his arms around her waist and lifted her a few feet off the ground. When his fingertips grazed the top edge of her jeans, teasing her exposed skin, a thrill reverberated through her entire body.

Jamie leaned close, filling the sacred air with his damn delicious honeyed whiskey scent. She briefly fantasized about sinking into his warmth, even as she knew she shouldn't. Jamie was still her interview subject. She was supposed to remain objective. Keep some distance.

Eyes stretched wide, his face was jolted with surprise as he lowered her to the ground. "Shit—I'm sorry. I should've asked to hug you."

"It's fine," she said earnestly, suddenly a little dizzy. "I guess I'm a hugger now." Despite the treacherous terrain, she felt safer in his arms than she had in years. "Oh my God, this view…"

Grinning sheepishly, he pulled the gloves from his hands and gestured at the picturesque expanse surrounding them. "They don't got hills like this in New York City, huh?"

"Definitely not."

"I love being out here. It's so freeing, surrendering to the elements. Probably the closest high to performing on stage."

Brinton pulled her notebook from her crossbody bag and jotted down his quote. Then, she caught a glimpse of the lake behind him. Given the elevation, it looked like glazed marble.

"I guess we should talk about that now…Your songs?" she asked, eyes dipping to her dusty combat boots.

She'd prepared all morning for this moment, and now it was slipping from her fingers as she struggled to grasp the words. "Jamie, about the article—"

"I shouldn't have put you in that position," he interjected. "This is my problem to solve, not yours."

"Jamie—"

"It was selfish of me," he continued. His eyes were glassy, likely from the dust. Or was it something else?

"I just—I want you to know that I understand that now," he stammered.

Brinton grabbed his shoulders. She gulped hard at the pronounced ridges of muscle and bone. Unadulterated beauty.

Finally, she found the words.

"No, I want to do it your way," she said. "Together, we can do this."

He stepped back and raked his hands through his hair. "Seriously?"

She nodded, smiling shyly. "I want to help you. I know for a fact that no one at *Landmark* will. I can't let those assholes ruin your life. I wouldn't even have this opportunity if it weren't for you. That Grammys interview was my lowest moment, but ultimately, we went through it together. And... you have so much to offer. Now that I know you—the real you—the world needs to know you too."

He shook his head in disbelief. "Brinton—I don't know what to say."

"Say you'll tell me the truth. I can't write this story if you leave anything off the table. You asked me to trust you, and now, I need you to trust me."

"Absolutely," he rasped. "You got more heart than anybody I know."

She laughed bitterly, remembering the footnotes of every past mistake and missed opportunity. "Well, my track record begs to differ."

He rested his hands on hers, which still gripped his shoulders. His warmth spiraled down her spine. She didn't want him to let go, even while touching him like this tugged at any objectivity she was supposed to maintain.

"I'm in awe of you," he whispered, sapphire eyes glowing. "Since the first time I saw you on that red carpet."

Gratitude scorched her cheeks with his admission, the weight of their secret alliance. "Thank you," Brinton said. "But...I also need to know that you understand what you're asking. Your record deal, your fans...could all go away if I write this story. You're effectively asking me to blow up your life as you know it. Do you want that?"

The sharpened line in his jaw ticked. "I have to. I know it won't be easy. I know some people won't accept it—or me. But I'd rather stand in the sun than cower in the shadows."

She dropped her hands from his shoulders. "What about your father?"

"I'm doing this for me," he said, fortified with a resolve that made his eyes dance like a lit fuse. "You won't regret the next week and a half, I swear."

She knew she wouldn't.

Brinton exhaled, then clicked on the recorder. "All right then, from the beginning. Tell me everything."

# CHAPTER SEVENTEEN

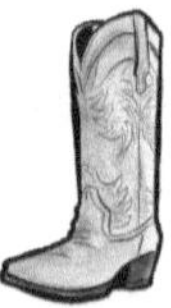

"Who's ready to learn a chord?" Jamie asked the six rambunctious eight-year-olds forming a semi-circle around him inside his father's recording studio on Thursday morning.

The main space was large enough to fit ten people comfortably. It was outfitted with light wood paneling on the walls and matching coffee tables, which made the cozy interior seem much larger.

One of the highlights of being a small-town celebrity was volunteering with his mother's favorite charity, Sacred Heart Home for Children, a locally run orphanage. Since he was eighteen, Jamie hosted a monthly guitar lesson with the kids. It was gratifying to bring some positivity to their lives.

And, it helped keep his mother's memory alive, even as some details about her—the sound of her laugh and the smell of her perfume—had begun to fade.

The kids smiled up at Jamie like he was a faultless hero, which he definitely wasn't. He could, at least, broaden their world in a way that music did for him.

Fingers pressed into the fretboard, Jamie held up his acoustic guitar, which gleamed like lacquered licorice.

"C Major is made up of three notes. You put your pointer finger on the first fret of the B string, middle finger on the second fret of the D string, and ring finger on the third fret of the A string. Then, strum from the A string down."

He strummed, and the pleasant harmony floated out from the hardwood frame. The kids erupted into *oohs* and *aahs*.

It seemed to make Brinton marvel too, which made Jamie smile even wider. They'd been exchanging amused glances as she and Sammi watched from a plush beige couch in the far corner.

After yesterday's Turkey Bay trip, Jamie had told Brinton everything about his songwriting deal. Now, it was like a weight had been lifted. They still had a little over a week of interviews left, but he could handle anything now. At least, he hoped he could.

"Mr. Jamie, show us again," shouted Freddie, a redhead with a bowl cut, through his gapped teeth.

Jamie had explained the same chord five different times, but he didn't care if it meant he'd get to see Brinton's eyes glinting with wonder.

Err, so long as the *kids* were happy.

Jamie passed Freddy the guitar. "Why don't you give it a try?"

He helped Freddie get positioned, genuinely sentimental as the curved body dwarfed the boy's slight frame.

"Looks great on you," Jamie said. He slipped the strap over Freddie's tiny shoulders, like his mother had once done for him. "Remember what I taught you?"

"Uh-huh," Freddie squawked. Jamie tenderly guided Freddie's slim fingers into place. Finally, he strummed, replicating the same harmony Jamie had moments before.

"Atta boy," Jamie said, laughing right along with Freddie.

When he flicked his eyes at Brinton, she was giggling and writing in her notebook. From above, shelves of his father's industry awards cast a golden aura around her. She was a rarity that belonged in the Louvre. He could admire her all—

"Mr. Jamie, look what I can do," Freddie squealed before strumming hard and fast across all six strings at once. Three popped instantly from the assault. Jamie winced, his heart a balloon pricked with a pin as the other children bellowed in unison.

"I'm so sorry," Freddy sobbed. "I didn't mean it."

"It's all right, buddy. Please don't cry," Jamie said, rubbing Freddie's back. He lifted the guitar from the child's shaking shoulders.

Shit happened, and these kids had been through enough in their lives. Scolding anyone did more harm than good. Jamie knew from experience.

"Sometimes, you gotta break things to learn something new," Jamie cooed.

Sammi sprung into crisis mode, crossing to where the kids sat. In her five-inch cork wedges, she crouched to their level. Her periwinkle sundress swished at her knees. "How about we go into the kitchen? I think Liza whipped up some ice-cream for y'all."

Freddie's tears magically dried. The children cheered as they leaped to their feet and followed her through the narrow door. Over her shoulder, Sammi winked at Jamie.

"You're welcome," she trilled.

Jamie nodded gratefully, then turned his attention to his guitar. He was a wartime doctor assessing a wounded soldier. Definitely on life support.

Brinton crossed to him slowly. "I'm sorry about your guitar."

Rising from the floor, he laughed to himself, shaking his

head. "Serves me right for bringing it out, but it's my favorite. A seventh birthday present from Cash."

"As in Johnny Cash?" Brinton asked, eyes darting between him and the mangled guitar.

"The very one."

He laid it on a table, then sat in a rolling chair at the expansive soundboard. "But nothing I can't fix."

He gestured to the matching chair at his side, and she eased onto it.

"I forgot to thank you for this during our drive yesterday," she said, holding up her voice recorder. "You're way too kind. I don't deserve it."

Her words wrapped around him like a blanket fresh from the dryer. "You're welcome, but I think you do."

*Shit, was that too much?*

"I mean, not that I can tell you what you deserve."

She smiled graciously, perhaps reading his mind. "I know what you mean. And I appreciate it." Flicking on her recorder, she pointed to the soundboard's infinite illuminated buttons and switches. "So, how does all this work?"

He exhaled, relieved that she wasn't freaked out by his bush-league flirting. Jamie wasn't *trying* to do it, but it kept happening. "Slide closer, and I'll show you."

As she rolled over, he felt a magnetic pull he knew didn't come from the wheels beneath him.

He cleared his throat, hoping to regain his bearings. "This is an audio mixer. Essentially, it controls the levels of different sounds you're recording. So, for example, vocals, guitars, and keyboards are recorded on separate channels and then routed through the mixer. An audio engineer uses these levers called faders to blend everything…It's called the optimal mix."

"Sounds complicated," she offered. Her eyes lingered on the tiny, ridged knobs.

"It is, but it's also fun, kind of like a puzzle." He pressed a button, and a melancholy acoustic guitar riff filled the room. He pressed another, and his vocal track followed. It sounded robust and a little charred on the edges.

"Can I show you?" he asked.

"Yeah, show me everything."

He placed one of her hands on a channel fader and put his on top. Jamie inched her fingers up gradually, until the guitar overpowered his vocals and electricity ricocheted where their skin touched. At some point, he stopped breathing.

He shot her a furtive glance. She was holding her breath too.

"Wow," she breathed.

*Did she feel that too?*

"Yeah, it sounds imbalanced," Jamie said, silently cataloging where his fingertips gripped hers. He savored the naked contact. "The vocals and guitar need each other, in the right proportions, to sound good."

Eyes on hers, their fingers still intertwined, he guided the faders back down, blending the outputs into soothing harmony.

"It's beautiful," she whispered.

*So are you, Bee.*

He'd keep that part to himself. He couldn't risk scaring her off, because she was there to help him. Professionally.

Then, that reflux-inducing chorus slithered through the speakers: *You want love/But I need space/Baby my heart beats/At a different pace/I can love you right/But only for tonight.*

When Brinton jerked her hand from beneath his, it felt like a piece of him had gone missing. His optimal mix.

"These lyrics are…" She let the words hang in the charged air between them for a few uncomfortable moments. "Did Melvin write this about anyone in particular? Like… Kendall?" She looked down at the floor. "It's for the article," she added quickly, but the mulberry flush on her cheeks betrayed her.

Lordy, she was adorable. He paused the recording.

"This song isn't about Kendall," he said.

"Or someone else? I guess with your 'Heartbreak Prince' nickname, there's probably plenty of…inspiration out there."

He breathed shakily. Time to unearth another truth. "I know you've heard all the stories, and, yeah, I've dated a lot of women. But those relationships weren't real. My team thought I needed the press after my breakup with Kendall."

She was quiet for a few moments, and his heart did a fifty-meter dash in his chest. What if she pushed him away, now that the latest lie had come to light? What if, upon further inspection, she decided that his dreams weren't worth saving?

But when she looked at him again, her expression was stripped of judgment. He didn't expect it, but he was grateful.

"Was it real with Kendall?" she asked.

"I didn't feel the same way about her. I wanted her to be happy, but I didn't—I couldn't love her, even though she loved me. The more I tried, the more I knew it wasn't there."

Brinton looked down at her hands, as if transported to a painful memory of her own. "How did you tell her?"

He tipped his head back and winced. Frankly, he'd been an asshole about it. But he didn't want to hide that from Brinton.

"I said I wasn't looking for love, which, at that time, was true. But I should have told her sooner, should have been kinder." Jamie sucked his teeth. "I never properly apologized. Hence, the legend of the Heartbreak Prince."

Her shoulders grazed her ears. She probably thought he was nothing but an industry himbo. Honestly, that was fair.

"Well, everyone has a chance at redemption, right?"

Jamie smiled weakly and nodded. She wasn't the type of

woman he deserved. She was honest, hardworking, and fearless. He struggled with all three, so why was he kidding himself?

"What are you looking for now?" she asked.

Was this an opening? He wanted to reassure her that he genuinely liked spending time with her, in whatever way she'd let him. But the part of him that feared truly baring his heart—and inevitably hurting her when he fucked it all up—throttled his confidence. He needed to ease into it.

"For the record, I'm not seeing anyone right now."

Her shoulders relaxed, giving him permission to do the same. "I'm sure a lot of women would be interested to know that," she said, but her smile was uneasy. The room dipped about twenty degrees as she knotted her fingers together.

It was risky. Technically, they were working together now. But the itch, he knew, demanded to be scratched. He had to slip through the cracked door.

"What if I wanna know what you think?"

He only slightly kicked himself for his lack of finesse.

Brinton eyed him inquisitively. "About what?"

"About anything."

A soft smile danced across her lips, daring him to do unspeakable things. Especially to her Cupid's bow. It was so damn deep, Jamie pictured teasing it with his thumb. Or sucking it between his own lips.

But he'd never cross that line, not unless she wanted him to. It was embarrassing how much he wanted to.

"I think…"

Her breath hitched, and his gut clenched in anticipation. As if cued by a bejeweled fairy godmother, a few errant braids tumbled down the front of her black blouse. He swept them over her shoulder, hand lingering against the warm slope of her neck.

It was long enough for him to inch closer. She smelled

amazing. Creamy vanilla with little hints of something herbal, and her lips looked so achingly ripe for contact.

He swallowed a groan.

They stared at each other, shallow breaths communicating secrets they didn't quite yet dare to say aloud.

Was it his imagination, or was *she* leaning in?

Slowly, she licked her lips, and he was immediately entranced by her tongue. Warm and wet and begging to be tasted. What he wouldn't give to taste her.

He angled his head. She tilted her chin closer.

"Jamie," she whispered. "We shouldn't…"

"I know," he breathed. "But I can't stop thinking about—"

"How it would feel?" she asked, still craning her neck. "Me too. I just—"

Gently, he cupped her jaw. "Brinton, do you want this? Just tell me you do. Tell me right now, and I'll—"

When she moaned, her warmth caressed his lips. Just another millimeter, and she'd be his.

Instead, the studio door flung open, snapping that invisible string between them. Jamie Sr. walked through first, followed by Tex.

Jamie's spine straightened, and he pushed his chair a good foot from Brinton's. She took the cue and did the same.

"Hey, y'all," Jamie said, voice cracking at the exertion. "I was showing Brinton how the mixer worked."

"That so?" Jamie Sr. asked, disapproval thick on his tongue. He crossed to the wet bar next to the couch, poured two whiskeys neat into etched crystal tumblers, and passed one to Tex. He set a beige folder on the counter.

"We should put in a few hours," Tex said, sucking his teeth after a hearty sip. "The guys'll be here in twenty."

Jamie's tense smile fell. "Oh, I thought today was an off day?"

"There are no off days." His father laughed dryly.

"That's what kills me about your generation. Nobody wants to do the work. Why don't you get in the booth and warm up?"

"Yeah, got it," Jamie said, head slung low. He needed his father to believe nothing had changed with Brinton. Even though he wanted nothing more than to rewind to sixty seconds earlier, when they were alone.

"Sorry, honey, this is a closed session," Jamie Sr. told Brinton.

Slowly, she rose from her seat. "Sure. I have plenty to transcribe anyway." She slipped on a brave face, but from the time they'd spent together, the waver in her voice meant she was hurt.

That explained the battering ram he felt in his chest. But his hands were tied.

"We can pick this up later," Jamie called out.

At the door, she offered him an unconvincing smile. "I got what I needed."

Once she was gone, Jamie was still at the soundboard, holding his head in his hands. He'd almost kissed Brinton merely minutes ago. He wished he had. Even as he knew that would be harder to hide from his father than his betrayal. That threat paled in comparison to the spark he felt the day he met Brinton.

That spark refused to be snuffed out. He was completely fucked.

His father loomed over him like a specter. "You tell her anything I should be concerned about?"

"I told you, I was showing her how the mixer worked," Jamie retorted, brows creased.

"Yeah, that's why I called a few friends at Highland."

Highland was *Landmark*'s publisher. It was a family business that had been around since nineteen-fifty.

"It seems they're lukewarm about Ms. Shaw carrying this

story. And that she hasn't been the highest performer in the past. It'd be a shame if I expressed my own concerns, don't you think?"

Reflexively, Jamie clenched his fists. It was one thing for his father to antagonize him, but Brinton was innocent. "Daddy, c'mon. That's not necessary."

"I think it's time you prove where your loyalty lies." Jamie Sr. reached for the folder and thrust it into Jamie's lap.

Inside, Jamie's new contract stared back at him. His chest tightened.

Tex wedged his stout body between him and his father. "It'll be good to tie up this loose end, son," he reasoned.

Tex held out a pen. This *loose end* was a lasso, signaling his father had won. But if signing this contract saved Brinton's job, Jamie would put his own happiness on hold. There was no other option.

So, he signed his name with a flourish, next to that stupid *X*.

He'd tell Brinton what he'd done before long. Once he figured out a new plan.

# CHAPTER EIGHTEEN

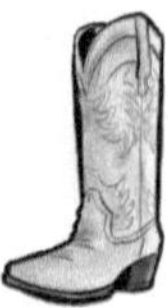

*Jamie Crawford Jr. is a man with a reputation that precedes him. But he's out to prove he's so much more than the rumors. In fact, he's nothing like them at all.*

Brinton had typed the same three sentences, in slightly different order, exactly six hundred times since plopping down to write at the guest house's sprawling kitchen table two hours ago. Nothing was sticking. She was mired in a wicked case of writer's block.

Fine, it wasn't writer's block. It was holy-crap-I-almost-kissed-Jamie-Crawford-Jr.-block.

Yesterday's lapse in judgment at his father's recording studio remained etched in her mind. Was it so wrong that she wanted to be both professional *and* desired? That she was slowly, against what she knew was convenient, starting to desire him too?

Being in Iris, she felt more open to not only expressing herself, but *being* herself. Perhaps because Jamie was one hell of a muse. In such close quarters, she got know him in ways that felt privileged. Rare. That filled her cup more than it should have, yet she couldn't stop herself from daydreaming about what could be.

Someone rapped three times on the front door. Brinton answered, revealing Sammi. She wore a mint green romper embellished with lace trim. Curved into a mischievous grin, her lips gleamed with a luscious apricot gloss.

"What's up?" Brinton asked, gesturing for Sammi to come inside. "I didn't see anything on the schedule for today. Did I miss something?"

Sammi perched like a songbird on the back of the enormous cloud of a couch. "Nope. I wanted to check in and see if you were free today?"

"Well, I'm writing," Brinton replied. She slipped back into her chair at the table. "Though I could use some more time with Jamie, if you can set something up?"

Sammi let an exasperated sigh fly. "Jamie's in the studio again." Then, a little brighter, "But I have an alternative."

Brinton lifted a brow. "You have to give me more than that."

"It's Friday night, and I'm taking you line dancing," she squealed, clapping her hands in time. "There's this great bar—"

Promptly, Brinton spun back to her laptop. "Ah, let me stop you there. I'm not a bar kind of person."

She was always self-conscious about taking up physical space, a requisite of socializing in public. Then, the task of striking up dreaded small talk with someone, only to feel them recoil when something—or someone—better came along.

Brinton would sooner put her head inside a Vitamix.

"Bars are not my vibe."

Sammi pulled up a dining chair across from her. This was now a negotiation.

"Well, you're gonna like this one. It's a locals-only kind of spot. More importantly, this counts as your cultural immersion program. You gotta cap off your first week right. You know, get out of this house and see the *real* Iris."

Sammi leaned in and cocked a brow. Brinton caught a whiff of her sugary perfume. "It was Jamie's idea. He thought you'd like it."

"Really?" Brinton couldn't beat back the smile bursting behind her lips.

Was *this* a date? No, that'd be crazy. *This* was work. So why was every single one of her senses firing at once?

Brinton shut her laptop screen. "So, he's going to be there?"

Somehow, when stress turned her blood acidic, Jamie was a constant, affirming presence.

Sammi smiled, basking in her victory. "I figured y'all can also squeeze in an interview."

"Yeah, okay then," Brinton said passively. She had to at least pretend that butterflies weren't currently throwing a rave in her belly.

Sammi rose and twirled on her heels. "Amazing. So, the last thing is getting you some boots."

"I'm not a cowboy boot kind of girl. I prefer combat boots." Brinton glanced down at said scuffed boots, stuck one out for effect. "They double as a weapon in a pinch."

Sammi fluttered her dark, miles-long lashes. "My goodness, New York City has hardened you, huh?"

Brinton smirked at the thought. "Sadly, my per diem doesn't cover cowboy boots."

Like a sassy sorcerer, Sammi produced a black American Express between her pointer and middle fingers. "Lucky for you, I got the company credit card. Consider it a welcome gift from James Sawyer Crawford, Jr."

Finally, Brinton let her simmering smile escape. "Should I text Michael to pick us up?"

"No need." Sammi beamed. "Mama's driving today."

Brinton followed Sammi to the driveway, where a custom, sky blue Mercedes SUV awaited.

Walking backward, Brinton circled the body appreciatively. "I pegged you as a quiet luxury kind of woman."

Sammi slid into the driver's seat, then flashed her signature grin. "In this town, men are either trying to hold you back or feel you up. But when I roll up in Jolene, they know my balls are just as big."

Twenty minutes later, Jolene rolled into an unassuming strip mall and parked beneath the chipping, hand-painted sign outside Ladybird's Boot Co.

"This place is the best. Don't let the chaos scare you," Sammi assured. She held open the creaky glass door, and Brinton stepped inside.

A cramped, dimly lit space that smelled faintly of leather and mothballs, Ladybird's was a time capsule of Iris's storied past. From the yellowing linoleum, to the '50s upholstered couches still in plastic, to the dusty shelves packed with tchotchkes, it was a charming relic to behold.

Brinton scanned the frame-covered walls of icons, including Elvis Presley, Dolly Parton, and a few U.S. presidents. They had all come to the same place to get "boots blessed by the best," as a battered tin sign above the cash register read.

"Sammi Smith, you better come here and hug my neck," someone chirped in a magnetic, Tennessean twang.

Brinton turned around to find a short, older woman embracing Sammi. She had the grip of a lumberjack.

"Birdie, this is my friend Brinton," Sammi said, a little breathless.

"Don't be shy, sweetheart," Birdie beckoned, arms outstretched. Sammi nodded enthusiastically, and Brinton obliged. It was one of the shades of "new" she'd embraced, surely thanks to Jamie's doing.

Truthfully, it felt good to be physically close to someone after months of self-isolation.

"Ladybird was my mama," Birdie offered, unclenching Brinton's ribs. "We ran this store together since I could reach the counter. She passed away last year. God rest her soul."

Sammi bounced on the yellow, paisley-print couch and patted the open seat beside her.

"This place is amazing," Brinton said, sinking into the cushion. It was as malleable as a warm gummy bear. "It seems like everybody who's anybody has been here. Did I see a picture of LeBron James on the wall?"

"Oh, yes. Did a custom pair for him. The man loves rhinestones. And feet as soft as a baby's bottom, would you believe it?"

"Oddly, I can." Brinton laughed.

"We're here on serious business," Sammi whispered in mock-secrecy. Her arm snaked around Brinton's shoulders. "Our girl needs some boots—her first."

Birdie grinned, making her deep smile dance across her sun-kissed skin.

"Oh, I know just the pair. Lemme measure you," she said, her short, chestnut ponytail bobbing jollily. She slipped a tattered roll of measuring tape from her apron pocket, pulled up a small stool, and sat before Brinton.

Carefully pulling off Brinton's boot from beneath her jeans, Birdie measured every conceivable angle, somehow committing each dimension to memory.

Brinton watched Birdie with rapt attention. "I'm usually a size nine. I know that's huge, and you probably don't—I could probably squeeze into an eight-and-a-half..."

She'd become so used to overcompensating so she

wouldn't be misperceived that she couldn't turn it off. Disappointment tugged her smile into a taut line.

"Darlin', ain't nothing wrong with having a larger boot. Woman's gotta have room to kick some tail, right?"

Birdie winked, and Brinton's heart warmed from the familiarity. That she could, possibly, belong here too.

"These boots gotta be custom-measured. Not like those out-of-the-box types. Like you, they're one of a kind."

Affirmatively, Sammi grinned. "Birdie's hands were touched by the divine. You'll see."

"How's my boy?" Birdie asked, still working with surgical precision.

"He's performing down at Yeehaw Fest next weekend," Sammi said. "I'll add you to the guest list."

"You're a peach," Birdie chirped. She rose from her stool and ambled to the ancient cash register. "Brinton, let me show you something. Look at this picture. Recognize anyone?"

She pointed to a cracked red plastic frame above her head.

Brinton slipped on her own boot, then met Birdie where she stood. Squinting hard, it suddenly hit her.

"Is that—"

"Mm-hm. My mama fit Jamie for his first pair when he was four years old. His daddy got his first pair here too, before he made it big."

In the photo, a young Jamie sat on that same yellow couch, legs splayed across his father's lap. He beamed up at Jamie Sr. like he was Superman and Captain America rolled into one. Jamie's mother sat next to his father, but her smile evoked shades of Jamie's for-the-cameras facade. Like she was holding something back.

Birdie's tone softened, and sadness clouded her amber eyes. "It's tragic what happened to MaryBell. So young. She struggled a lot, but that little boy was her whole world. I was praying she would get better."

"Birdie, we have a few more stops before we gotta get back," Sammi said softly, more solemn than Brinton had ever heard her.

Birdie's eyes fell to the scuffed linoleum. "Sure, sure, honey. Let me grab your boots from the back."

A few minutes later, she returned with a plain brown box, which she carried as if filled with the world's riches. In some ways, it was. When Brinton opened it, her mouth dropped.

The leather was buttery-soft, in a creamy eggshell shade with cognac stitching and matching block heels. Brinton slipped them on. They fit like a glove.

Her heart filled with something indescribable but surely close to hope. The simple gift of bespoke boots made her vibrate with happiness, and that happiness could dispel every shadow that seemed to follow her. She wanted to believe it.

"Birdie, these are incredible," Brinton said.

"Aren't they?"

"I didn't think I could pull them off."

Birdie came up behind her and placed calloused hands on her shoulders. "Well, you can't limit yourself. My mama always said you gotta try new things while the breath's still in your body."

Like most people Brinton had met in Iris, Birdie's kindness and warmth were like a safety net she never knew she needed.

She closed her eyes and smiled. "Thank you, Birdie."

Back in the car, Brinton couldn't stop thinking about Jamie's mother. She turned to Sammi.

"I don't want you to take this wrong, but I noticed you stopped Birdie when she brought up Jamie's mom," Brinton started. "When I asked him about her, he also shut down. Did…something happen to her?"

Sammi pursed her lips and squeezed her eyes shut, as if she'd been dreading this moment. "Publicly, there's not much out there about Jamie's mom," she said. "It's out of respect. She was beloved—a good woman who got dealt a bad hand. Understandably, Jamie is sensitive about her passing. I don't feel right getting into it, because it's his story to share. I can tell he's taken a shine to you though, so try talking to him tonight."

She smiled sincerely, then added, "The boots might bring you some luck."

They exchanged grateful smiles before Sammi pressed a button, igniting the engine's subtle whir. "Let's hit a few boutiques. I know you don't want new clothes, but—"

"That sounds great," Brinton cut in. "Honestly, I've been sweating my ass off since I got here."

She tugged on the collar of her black pin-striped top, which clung uncomfortably to her torso in the Tennessee humidity. "A pair of shorts won't kill me, and you've been trying to *Pretty Woman*-me all day. Congratulations, I concede."

Sammi smiled like the cat who got the Chanel No. 5. In her best Julia Roberts impression, she playfully snapped, "Big mistake. Big. Huge!"

# CHAPTER NINETEEN

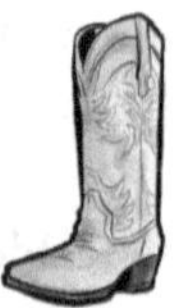

*A* few hours later, Brinton barely recognized her reflection in the full-length mirror. She wore a white tank top that was cropped above her navel and light-wash Levi's cut-offs. On her feet, her new boots.

It was a lot of skin for someone who typically used clothing as an invisibility cloak. But, damn. She felt like popping her shit.

So, she pulled her braids into a low ponytail, spritzed some vanilla perfume, and slicked a gilded peach gloss on her lips.

Makeup, sundresses, tank tops, shorts, flip-flops, and bikinis littered Brinton's bed. A "Southern-girl starter pack," as Sammi had coined it.

As Brinton fastened her gold hoops, the chime of an incoming FaceTime rang out, forcing her to dive into a heap of lacy thong underwear that she absolutely did not buy with Jamie in mind.

Brinton thumbed the green button and extended her arm so her body filled the frame.

"Do I look ready to line dance on a Friday night or nah?" she asked.

Poised atop their mom's gray quartz kitchen island, Shay shrieked. "Damn, girl. Zoom in—I wanna see everything. Wait, are those cowboy boots? My sister's in her Yeehaw Era."

Brinton rolled her eyes. "So, what I'm gathering is, I normally look busted?"

"Not busted," Shay volunteered. "The whole sad-chick uniform is your thing. But, bitch, you slicked your edges. And that cat-eye is a slay."

Brinton feigned offense, but she was proud as hell. She'd watched fifteen tutorials and nearly lost an eye before sharply carving the line just right.

Propping her phone on the white-washed wood dresser, Brinton smoothed a gold-flecked, tonka bean body oil on her legs.

"I guess I'm in the mood to try something new. Living while the breath's in my body."

"Amen, sis. Now, all you need is some toe-curling sex with a small-town country boy."

"Ha. Well, that's not going to happen."

Even if Brinton considered the possibility with each passing day, that was a colossal step. She hadn't slept with anyone since Eli. Even though Jamie absolutely spiked her desire, she had little confidence that she wouldn't disappoint a man like him, especially when it came to sex. There were simply too many moving parts, and too much that could go wrong.

"But he's so different from what I thought," Brinton admitted instead. "He's kind and thoughtful, sometimes to a fault. And patient. And he makes me want to try new things. Shay, he had me up on a mountain."

"Wilderness quickies are the best," Shay mused, waggling her machete-sharp eyebrows.

Brinton chuckled. "Sorry to disappoint you, but there were no quickies. Though, being here, I haven't been afraid to…exhale. I know it's corny, but he makes me feel like that's okay."

"Are you kidding me? Not trying to judge—"

"That sounds like judging—"

"But there's a perfectly good, caring man at your disposal. You have a chance to let him fold you in half and you're wasting it? Make it make sense," Shay said, clapping her hands so they punctuated each syllable.

"In case it slipped your lizard brain, he and I are working together. Sort of."

Right, there was that whole nagging ethical conundrum.

Shay guffawed. "Chile, F that job. Hasn't Rich swapped fluids with, like, half of the cast of *Vanderpump Rules*? And how many times has Agatha bragged about being in Kanye's DMs? Like it's a flex."

Brinton brushed through her thick eyebrows, which refused to act or arch right.

"They play by different rules, and you know that."

"And it's bullshit," Shay countered. "All the reason to enjoy yourself tonight. Better yet, let Jamie enjoy *you*. Deny it all you want, but Ray Charles could see that man is into you."

Like clockwork, Athena's head popped behind Shay. "If you're both single, carpe diem."

"Mom—" Brinton and Shay barked in unison.

"Well, Shayla, if you don't want me to hear your conversation, you have your own apartment."

"Yes, but you have all the good snacks," Shay said, snapping into an edamame chip.

Athena moved closer to the camera, and her expression hardened. "I have to ask this. Are those white people out there treating you right? Do I need to get on a plane tonight?"

"Yes, Mom, everything is fine. Everyone has been…great."

Especially Jamie, but she'd hold that a little closer to the vest, like a super-sexy secret. She blamed her new boots.

Athena's eyebrows unfurled, and she breathed a sigh of relief. "Oh, that's wonderful, Brinny. Well, I'm off to book club with the girls. We're reading *It Ends With Us*."

"Oh, nice, something light," Shay mused, giggling.

Athena kissed Shay on the forehead, sidestepping the sarcasm as always. Then, she leaned closer into the screen. "And remember, baby, if you have sex with this man, don't forget to pee right after. And wipe front to back—"

Brinton groaned. But honestly, it was a useful reminder. Nobody had time for a hypothetical UTI. She made a mental note to ask Liza for cranberry juice, just in case.

"Goodbye, Mom." Brinton laughed.

Athena waved, then disappeared through the kitchen archway.

"Okay, now that she's gone," Shay said conspiratorially. "How are you feeling for real?"

Brinton flung a lacy thong toward her pillows and flopped onto the edge of the bed. "No panic attacks yet. So, decent?"

What she couldn't say yet but couldn't deny? Everything was blooming in unexpected ways. Including her.

Shay popped a mini-pretzel into her mouth. "A little therapy would be a cute add-on… "

"I don't need therapy. I need to do my job," Brinton droned, eager to change the subject. "How are *you*?"

"I'm volunteering at an animal shelter tonight."

Brinton side-eyed her sister. "That's generous for someone allergic to practically every creature on Earth. I mean, who's allergic to snails?"

"It means God spent more time on me." Shay blew an air kiss and grinned. "But, if you must know, her name is Miley. She's a veterinarian technician, and Brinny, she's a saint. Afterward, I'll take her for boba, and then we'll do perfectly scandalous things on her futon. Truly, I can't wait to rub her feet while watching *Snapped*."

Brinton smiled, shaking her head. "Wow. Dramatic reenactments of horrific crimes and dessert. Really pulling out all the stops."

"What can I say? I'm a romantic. I even learned to trace her name with my tongue."

Brinton cracked up laughing. "If that's not love, I don't know what is."

Much later, while transcribing interviews at the kitchen table, Brinton demolished the plate of spaghetti and turkey meatballs Liza had sent over.

At eight p.m., right on time, the doorbell rang. She opened it to find Michael, smiling as usual and holding out his arm to help her down the front steps.

"Car's ready for you," he said. Michael looked her over and whistled. "Although, *those* boots are made for walkin'."

She couldn't help but smile.

# CHAPTER TWENTY

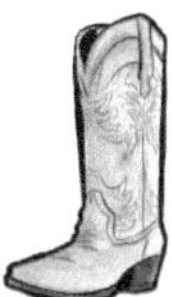

When Michael opened the SUV's back passenger door, Jamie's eyes practically popped out of his skull. He never questioned Brinton's beauty, and he liked her regular clothes. They were modest but fit her personality.

Now, she had on one of those tank tops with a deep scoop in the front, the material so thin he could tell she wasn't wearing a bra. As she climbed in, he caught a flash of butt cheek, the heavy curve jutting out from her shorts.

Did that mean she wasn't wearing panties?

He called it right then. Those shorts were going to be a fucking problem.

Worse yet, her skin was all glowy. The thick, black lines rimming her eyes made them even more penetrating. Sexier.

*Lord, help me.*

She caught him staring. Immediately, he felt like an ass. Jamie respected her, and she deserved to be respected, not ogled.

He shifted awkwardly in his seat and tried to think un-sexy thoughts.

*A Braves game on ESPN. Changing the oil in the truck. Building an Ikea shelf.*

"Hey," Jamie said. His voice was as coarse as sandpaper. "Sammi said she'd meet us there."

He braced his boots into the floorboards to physically ground himself. No woman had made him feel both so wildly turned on and straight-up giddy. A witchy spell he never wanted to end.

He still hadn't figured out when to tell Brinton about re-signing his contract, but that was a future Jamie problem. He'd find the right way to tell her soon. For now, he wanted to bask in everything she had to offer.

It was a hell of a bounty.

Brinton smiled, appraising him carefully. He liked that too.

"You look…nice," she said. "I like your hair."

It was embarrassing how long he'd spent on it, but he wanted to impress her. He also shaved and wore his favorite white Henley tee and dark-wash jeans.

"Unlike you, I have one look, and this is it," he said, gesturing down the length of his body, which gratefully, made her laugh.

"I like your chain too."

His grin spread wider. Jamie only wore the thick gold Cuban link when he wanted to add a little razzle dazzle. He absolutely wanted that tonight. In fact, he wanted Brinton to know he was game for whatever she wanted from him.

At the cookout, he was too in his own head to tell her how nice she looked, but he wouldn't make that mistake again. "You look gorgeous tonight. I mean—you always do."

When she blushed, the same heat spilled across his cheeks.

"Thank you," she said sweetly, fluttering her cosmically dark lashes. Was she flirting with him?

Mercy, he hoped so.

"Do you like my boots? At first, I wasn't sure I could pull them off…"

When she kicked her leg across the seat, her calf brushed against his knee, sending a bolt of shameless need straight to his crotch. His eyes traced the planes of her thighs. They were criminally thick in all the right places.

He didn't stop until he reached the soles of her boots. Frankly, he wanted to see her in those boots and nothing else. He'd probably combust on the spot, but he'd gladly bear every fiery lick.

Instead, with superhuman restraint, he rested his hands on his knees, even as he longed to inch up her sumptuous thighs.

"Bee, you can pull anything off. Ladybird's?"

She grinned and slid her leg off the seat. He stood corrected: her smile looked even better than those boots.

"Yeah, Birdie's a peach."

Jamie cocked his head, thoroughly amused. "Look at you, getting the lingo down."

"I'm very observant. You could say it's my job."

She winked at him, and he chuckled. Her sense of humor, her mind…There was so much to admire. A Rubik's cube he'd ferociously study until he cracked the code.

He was about to tell her that when she huffed out a breath, eyes filled with something he could only guess was trepidation.

What was she afraid of? At the thought, tension lashed Jamie's neck and shoulders.

"Birdie told me that she knew your mom. At the lake, you said you didn't want to talk about her for the article, and I understand that," Brinton began. "But…I guess, over these last few days, I've really liked getting to know you. And I realized that I want to know *all* of you, if that's on the table? And I want you to know me too."

It wasn't that he didn't want Brinton to know him. In fact, it was startling how natural it was telling her about every other part of his life, including his festering lie.

Even if they weren't working together on her article, he'd *want* to know someone like her. Someone dedicated to giving a voice to the voiceless, even if that person was undoubtedly privileged, like himself.

It'd been seventeen years, and yet talking about his mother brought him right back to the agonizing night he lost her. He felt powerless then, and still felt powerless now.

"Can we please talk about anything else?" he pleaded, eyes closed and head thudding against the headrest.

She leaned close enough that he breathed in her sweet scent. But even that couldn't quell the stinging micro-needles prickling his skin.

"I know this isn't easy to talk about, but I want to understand…"

He opened his eyes and met hers. They were steeped in earnestness.

"I hope you know that you can trust me with this, and anything else you want to tell me," she added.

Before he could think straight, the words gushed out. "I can't trust anyone with that part of my life."

This was another lesson Jamie learned from his father, who long discouraged any conversation about his mother's death. He claimed "living in the past" would make Jamie weak. Unfortunately, as a grieving young man, he'd believed him. Jamie wanted to be strong for his mother, even if he couldn't see her or touch her.

So he'd cauterized the wound, and tried to move on.

"Jamie, I know what it's like to be scared…"

Gently, she caressed his shoulder. For days, he'd craved her touch, but at this moment, he felt backed into a corner.

He flinched away.

"Then why are you pushing me? Unless you really wanna know for the article, but you don't wanna tell me straight up?"

Instantly, he regretted those words too. But that's what happened whenever he thought about his mother. His sense of reality morphed into pure survival instinct, like he was clinging, white-knuckled, from a jagged cliff, one breath from meeting a brutal end.

Brinton's lips parted, but she didn't speak. Instead, she angled her body toward the window, cast in an eerie glow as yellow and orange neon lights whizzed by.

God, had he gone too far? She probably thought he was a complete asshole. But he couldn't even articulate how painful ripping out those sutures would be.

He stayed quiet, hoping she'd sense how much he was struggling. Hoping she'd forgive him.

Jamie flicked his signet ring around his pinky.

"Brinton, I didn't mean…" he said, a few moments later.

"You think I'd lie to you?" All emotion had drained from her voice. Her eyes stayed fixed on her window.

"No." He exhaled shakily. "It's not something I can explain."

"I feel like I'm putting myself out there, for you. And you're…hiding."

He rubbed his brow. "I'm putting myself out there for you too. Brinton, I re-signed my contract. A two-album deal—for you."

*Fuck me.*

This was exactly the *wrong* way to tell her this development. He'd absolutely gone too far.

"What?" she screeched, eyes wide as she finally faced him. "Jamie, why—I don't understand. I thought you trusted me to tell your story?"

"I'm trying to protect you," he gritted out. His head was a hornet's nest. The harder he fought to find the words, the more viciously his thoughts swirled.

"Protect me from what?"

Jamie shook his head. He couldn't stand to upset her more than he already had. "Bee, please…"

"I thought we'd agreed to help each other?" She buried her face in her trembling hands. "There's no story if you signed a new contract. Shit, what am I supposed to tell my boss? I'm going to get fired. I should pack my bags tonight."

"No, I'll figure something out—"

"Please don't," she interjected, the sound grating against her throat. "You've done enough. And you won't even tell me why."

He wanted to squeeze her hand and reassure her, but she bawled hers in tight fists on her lap. Fully and completely detached from him.

It broke him.

The SUV rolled to a stop in an alley leading to a VIP entrance, away from downtown Iris's bustling main drag. Jamie stepped around to Brinton's side, opened the door, and held out his hand.

She accepted it, but her eyes stayed glued to the asphalt.

"Brinton…"

But he didn't finish. What else could he say? If he were her, he'd tell himself to fuck right on off. He'd blown his chance before he even told her how she made him feel, how he liked who he was when he was with her.

Was this for the best, before he could do irreparable harm?

"Well, you two have fun in there," Michael said, as if he'd watched Mom and Dad fight over a missed parking spot.

"Thanks, Michael. I'll call you soon," Jamie answered.

He held open the club's heavy back door. Once Brinton was safely inside, he beelined for a place, anywhere, where he couldn't make this night worse.

# CHAPTER TWENTY-ONE

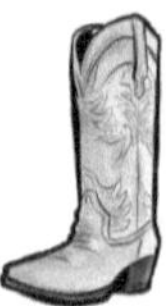

ccording to Sammi, at the Skylight, everybody belonged. The creaky barstools had lopsided cushions. Behind the dartboard, Polaroids captured years of Best Night Evers—sweaty and smiling faces, arms linked after more than a few rounds.

Sometimes, the draft beer was a little warm, but nobody complained because the bartenders never charged after the first one. Under the namesake skylight, throngs of women in tight jeans corkscrewed their hips as a seductive army. Their heeled boots tapped on battered hardwood to Alan Jackson's "Chattahoochee."

Brinton, however, wanted to crawl under a rock.

In a few breaths, Jamie had smothered every ounce of her glimmering optimism. He didn't trust her. Therefore, telling his story was pointless, because he'd re-entered into a shitty deal with his father.

It was yet another lie he'd told. But why would he lie to her? Had she been wrong to trust him?

She decided right then: tonight would be her last in Iris. This article had drained more from her than she had to give.

Could she get a new job writing appointment reminder emails at Shay's clinic? Brinton considered how many vagina euphemisms she'd have to memorize and sighed wistfully.

She needed a stiff drink. Were Long Island iced teas still cool?

The sting of a bare hand swatting her ass launched Brinton back into the present. Incensed, she spun around, instantly regretting not bringing her beloved combat boots.

Luckily, the homicidal rage behind her eyes cooled at the sight of Sammi. She was a honky-tonk angel in white denim shorts, a sleeveless black top cinched at her narrow waist, and cherry-red cowboy boots that matched her lipstick.

"Hey, sugar," Sammi called out. Her high ponytail whipping in time with the Danielle Bradbery song blaring overhead. "You look as good as sweet tea in a drought. I bet it's five seconds before somebody drags you onto the floor."

They embraced tightly like old friends—Brinton had slowly warmed to the idea that they were—but her enthusiasm was short lived.

While the Skylight was a place for the Everyman, Brinton was a Black woman. As she surveyed the room, as far as she could tell, she was the only one present.

Bewildered eyes had casually clocked her as she walked through the club. There was a framed Confederate flag over the DJ booth, for God's sake. Brinton's smile flattened.

A fiery lash of panic hit her at once. Was she moments from being called a slur? Or worse, being physically hurt?

"What's wrong?" Sammi asked, clocking the pretense etched across Brinton's face.

"Nothing," Brinton answered. Silently, she admonished herself for lying. Sammi had gone out of her way to make her feel welcomed.

However, being the only person who looked like her in a room meant being forced to shoulder unprovoked expectations the moment she opened her mouth. Judgements that sank her like boulders, grounding her so she didn't feel too empowered to speak up or levitate above the status quo.

And standing in that room, full of peering eyes, beneath *that* flag, felt equally suffocating.

Brinton's father's mantra slipped into her mind: *Swallow what hurts and move on.*

Sammi's eyes softened as she stepped closer, a bulldozer to the walls Brinton intended to erect around her heart.

"Hey, you can trust me."

Selfishly, Brinton wanted that too. But trusting someone still felt foreign. So did having friends. Sammi's eyes gleamed so earnestly that Brinton wanted to believe her. She sucked in a deep breath and dared to try.

"I'm worried that it's not exactly safe for people like me to be...here," Brinton confessed, the words tumbling out in a single rush. She pointed to the telltale flag.

"Oh, sweetheart," Sammi said, voice wavering. "I can't make up for the ugly in the world or the valid pain you feel, but I swear, I won't let anything happen to you."

Brinton started to pick at another sore patch on her thumb, but stopped herself. "Not to be all bleeding heart, but outside of my sister, I've never had anyone look out for me."

Sammi took Brinton's hands in hers and squeezed. "In this town, we look out for each other. If someone breathes too loudly near you, you tell me, got it?"

Brinton squeezed back.

Sammi nodded. "Now, let's get you lit like a firefly on the Fourth of July." Dragging Brinton by the hand, she led the way to the crowded bar, which parted like the Red Sea.

"First thing to know 'round here is how to shoot whiskey," Sammi said, a spirited twinkle in her eye.

A bartender with a dark, slicked-back man-bun, tight

black T-shirt, and footballs for shoulders appeared at the counter. He grinned wide. "What can I get y'all?"

"Two shots of Jack, please," Sammi said lightly. "And let's keep them coming all night." She handed him a hundred-dollar bill from her tiny red purse, but he shook his head.

"You ladies are far too pretty to be paying for your drinks."

Sammi shrugged, pleased with the proposition. "Well, if you're gonna twist my arm about it."

Man-Bun winked, then swiftly slid the shots before them. When they tipped them back, Brinton gasped at the burning sensation engulfing her throat. Sammi grinned like it was heaven's nectar.

"Second thing to know is how to line dance," Sammi said, swishing her hips in time to "Austin" by Dasha.

Brinton could feel the liquor's warmth in her marrow, but she wasn't crazy. The choreographed poetry happening on that dance floor was an entirely different level of dancing. What if she looked stupid? What if Jamie saw her and laughed?

"I can't do that," Brinton shouted over the music.

"You know the Electric Slide?"

"Yeah, but—"

"Then you can line dance."

Sammi leaned over the bar, immediately catching Man-Bun's attention.

"Honey, we need a couple more shots."

Another shot and many songs later, Brinton and Sammi were deep in the crowd. Brinton was a quick study, picking up the steps and howling gleefully as she kicked, spun, and two-stepped.

When she fumbled, the women around her cheered her on anyway, and the men hooted and hollered each time all the girls swiveled their hips in unison.

Apparently, Brinton was a line dancer now.

Her body hummed as the final notes of Luke Bryan's "Country Girl (Shake It For Me)" faded. An equally winded Sammi draped her arm around Brinton's shoulders and squeezed.

"Let's cool off a bit," she said, leading them to a roped-off VIP section at the back of the club.

The bouncer, whose full beard deserved an honorary spot in ZZ Top, nodded as he lifted the velvet rope. A hostess with short, auburn pigtails led them to a leather booth in the corner.

At their table, ice-cold water bottles, tequila, and all the fixings filled a fancy metal cooler.

"You were willing to pay that bartender a hundred bucks when you could have gotten bottle service for free?" Brinton asked.

"I only come back here to rest my feet," Sammi explained. "It's usually full of slimy A&R guys from the labels. The main bar—and the dance floor—are way more my speed," she said.

Despite Sammi's perfectly curated exterior, she didn't actively seek the others' approval. Brinton admired that.

The VIP crowd was a decidedly stuffy, less friendly mix of middle-aged men and their bored, twenty-something dates, who passed the time by snapping equally indifferent thirst traps on their phones.

"So, havin' fun yet?" Sammi asked, flopping dramatically into the booth.

Brinton gulped down her water, relieved not to be crying in a grimy bar bathroom right now. "I think I really needed this tonight."

She had prepared for the worst—looking like a fool on the dance floor or being accosted by people who meant her harm—but the exact opposite had happened. It didn't take away from Jamie's stinging betrayal, but it was a welcome distraction.

Sammi's emerald eyes flashed as she set down her water bottle. "That's what I wanna hear."

Brinton sank into the plush cushion and scanned the bar at the exact moment Jamie looked up from his untouched beer, meeting her eyes. Alone in a booth at the other side of the VIP section, he looked miserable as he peeled the label from his beer bottle.

She could go talk to him, but he'd effectively pushed her away, like Eli and every other guy she'd dared believe in.

So, that was that.

Sammi followed Brinton's gaze and exhaled dramatically. "What'd he do now?"

"We're not on the same page."

Brinton was used to metabolizing her feelings, sharp and punishing like vinegar. But now, with what felt like a trusted friend, she was hungry for closure.

Sammi's smile softened into something more solemn as she pressed her hand on top of Brinton's. "I'm going out on a limb to share this, but I really like you. It wouldn't sit right with me if I didn't."

They exchanged knowing glances across the table.

"Don't worry. This stays off the record," Brinton said, nodding. It was the least she could do.

Sammi exhaled, a rare shadow of trepidation in her eyes. "For as successful as Jamie is, his personal life don't come with much freedom. Given that you've met his father, I don't have to explain why. And I worry that sometimes, he's carrying too much on his shoulders."

"I don't think I can help with that," Brinton said flatly.

"I disagree. I think you've been a welcome relief for him. He won't talk to me about it, but his spirit seems...lighter."

Brinton's gut lurched as the realization sank in. Even as

she'd slowly gotten to know Jamie, she had taken for granted that despite the fame and women and whiskey, he was a person who hurt like anyone else. Perhaps then, she owed it to him to at least explain himself? Otherwise, the unspoken ease between them meant nothing.

Damn, she wanted it to mean *something*.

"I'll talk to him," Brinton said through a half smile. He'd convinced her to trust him, and in the process, she was starting to trust herself. She didn't want to give that up either.Sammi drained the rest of her water bottle, then screwed the top off the tequila. "This article is gonna be one for the books."

She arranged two shot glasses in front of her and poured the chilled potion into each. Sammi passed Brinton a lime wedge and nudged the shot toward her.

"Cheers," Sammi trilled, clinking her glass against Brinton's.

Brinton tipped it back. It was smokey and smooth, not unlike a certain man she couldn't extricate from her mind.

Sammi slid out from her side of the booth. "This is where I leave you, young grasshopper," she said.

She nodded toward the bar, where Man-Bun smiled back at her.

"I thought you wouldn't leave me to fend for myself?" Brinton asked, feigned outrage painted on thick.

Sammi craned her neck, scanning the room. "Oh, I'm not leaving you to fend for yourself. Let's not pretend Jamie hasn't been making eyes since you sat down. I'm sure he's bound to come find you and apologize for whatever charming thing he said earlier."

That would be ideal, but would it happen? Brinton peered longingly at his empty booth. What if he had gone home? Or worse, what if he went home with *someone*?

Kendall's frighteningly symmetrical face flashed behind

Brinton's eyes. Her heart plummeted into her boots. She was catastrophizing, her anxious mind's favorite pastime.

While, at home, Brinton couldn't stop herself from spiraling, she desperately wanted to stay in the moment now. To enjoy herself, as Shay had preached.

Sammi blew Brinton a kiss before spinning on her heels. "Have fun, text me if you need anything, and for all that is holy, don't puke on him again."

Brinton smirked, kicking her boots onto the bouncy leather seat. She would take advantage of this VIP section, even if she sat there mindlessly scrolling on her phone like the other women in her company.

She snapped a photo of the cornucopia of untouched booze and pulled up her text thread with Shay.

Brinton: Too much?

Shay replied a few seconds later.

Shay: NEVER ENOUGH, BOOKIE

Brinton snorted at her good fortune. This night had almost shaped up *too* well. For a woman expecting to be crushed when the other shoe dropped, she felt content to simply *be*, at least until she could figure out what to say to Jamie.

Wherever the hell he was.

"Can I join you?" asked a voice she didn't recognize a few moments later.

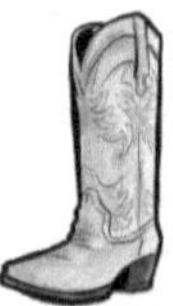

When Brinton looked up, she was disappointed to find one of the A&R clones leering down at her.

"Oh, um—" she stammered.

He slipped into her side of the booth, forcing her to slide her feet beneath the table. With Jamie and Sammi gone, she truly was alone. And a little uneasy about deflecting this man without him causing a scene that could ultimately end poorly for her.

That old, familiar feeling of dread hissed from the pit of her stomach.

"I'm Dane," he said, as if she'd asked. He was tall with rumpled brown hair combed forward to hide his receding hairline. He was probably in his late 30s and married, judging by the gold band on his ring finger.

He smelled like unearned confidence and Budweiser. A noxious mix.

"I couldn't help but notice you're the most beautiful woman here."

Back home, Brinton would have collapsed into herself.

But here, Sammi's no-BS policy propelled her.

Brinton stared straight into Dane's beady brown eyes. "This place is packed with beautiful women, who I'm sure are more interested in talking with you."

Dane balked and slid closer. "But you're the only one I'm curious about."

He dragged his sweaty palm mid-way up her thigh and leaned in so close hot spittle stung her cheek.

"In fact, I'm curious to know if your nipples look like Hershey's Kisses…"

"Don't touch me," she growled, thrusting herself backward until she collided with the brick wall.

There was nowhere to run. They were wedged deeply in the VIP section's shadows; she doubted anyone could see what was happening.

Dane squeezed Brinton's inner thigh. "Come on now, honey. I got a lot of time and money to spend…"

As Brinton opened her mouth to scream, Dane's face drained of color.

"Hey, Dane, having a good night?" Jamie asked. His signature grin had morphed into something distinctly sinister as he slid into the booth, facing them.

"Ah, yeah. I was—"

"Leaving?" Jamie asked. He propped one elbow on the table, knuckles grazing his chin. "That's good. I imagine Cheryl is waiting up with the baby?"

Dane checked his watch.

"How old is she now?"

"Um, she's—well, I guess it slipped my mind. Goes so fast, you know."

Jamie leaned back. "Now, that's no good. A man worth his salt should know, don't you think? I should call Cheryl right now, so we can get it straight."

"That's not necessary, Jamie. Loved the record, by the

way. Deserved to win ten more Grammys," Dane said, slinking out from the booth.

"You get home safe now," Jamie said in a razored tone she hadn't heard before. Its raw power was strangely comforting as dread curdled in her stomach.

"Because if I catch you even looking at her again," Jamie continued, stepping closer to Dane, "You and me are gonna do more than talk."

Brinton's parents didn't raise her to *need* a man to save her. She could have defended herself, if it came to it. But she was grateful that, for once, she didn't have to.

She was terrified, and Jamie had protected her.

Dane nodded, turned, and slithered away. Jamie dropped back into the booth, expression still tense.

"Are you okay? Did he hurt you?"

"Yes, I'm okay. No, he didn't—"

"Good."

Brinton clutched her chest. "I should have left with Sammi. It's my fault, I was here alone."

"It's not your fault," Jamie said, softer now. "A woman should be able to sit alone at a bar in peace."

"Thank you, Jamie. I mean it," she said, hands shaking as she pulled out a fresh water bottle. She realized how over-heated she was as her adrenaline dipped.

He nodded appreciatively as she slid a bottle to him.

"You don't gotta thank me. I saw him come over, and I knew his play. You remember hearing about the guy I had words with at my concert a few years back?"

She did. "Something about a punch thrown backstage? Was that him?"

Jamie placed his folded hands on the table, knitting his fingers together so tightly his knuckles paled.

"Yeah. I watched him repeatedly slip his hand under a

fan's skirt after she rejected him. So, I had to make sure he heard her."

She shook her head in disbelief. "The headlines made it seem like you got into a fight because he hit on your date."

The scandal made Jamie's song "Touch Me Like You Mean It" shoot to number one on the country charts.

Jamie tutted, and slowly unclenched his fist. "I wouldn't believe everything you read about me." That tender smile returned. "Unless it's something you wrote."

She set her hands on the table, close enough to touch his. But she didn't quite have the nerve.

He sighed. "Brinton, I'm sorry about what happened in the car. I signed the new contract because my father threatened to get you pulled from the story. He's got friends in high places. I couldn't—I refused to let that happen."

Brinton felt terrible for misreading Jamie's withdrawal and making it about herself. She was also unnerved to know his father would stoop as low as to sabotage her. And worse, that he'd punish Jamie in the process.

Jamie was willing to take it, for her.

"God, Jamie. Please know I appreciate you, but what about your plans to start fresh? You signed a binding contract."

He dragged his hand down his jaw. "I figure we double down. If we can get your article published, cover story or not, my father will cancel the contract. He'll have no choice once the truth is out there."

"That's a huge if."

The corners of his mouth lifted. "Go big or go home, right?"

She smiled, clinging to hope. For him.

"But if we do this, I want to go at your pace. Especially about your mother."

He pushed his hands closer, closing the gap between them

until their fingertips faintly touched. It was probably for the best; they were in public, and he was still extremely famous.

But it felt so good to be this close. Heat and intrigue sparked between their fingertips.

She couldn't speak, only drank him in. Her breath hitched. To her delight, his did too.

"Thank you, Brinton," he said. "I wanna tell you about my mom. I wanna tell you so many things, if you can bear with me. You make me feel like I've got a story to tell, and that what I want for my music—for my life—is in reach. Can you forgive me?"

She cracked a smile. "Only if you promise not to make insanely important decisions on my behalf."

He smiled back. "I'll see what I can do."

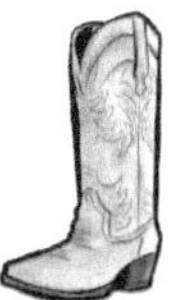

# CHAPTER TWENTY-THREE

The pigtailed hostess appeared at Brinton and Jamie's table. "Can I get y'all a drink?" she screeched over Florida Georgia Line's "Cruise."

Jamie winced but smiled politely. "Some more water for her, and—"

"Actually, I'll have what he's having," Brinton interjected, eyes lassoing him in. "It's part of my cultural immersion."

Jamie didn't fancy himself an adrenaline junkie. He preferred calculated risks within his grasp. However, the possibility in Brinton's smile flooded his head with endorphins. He was eager for the bungee cord's euphoric jerk.

Intrigued, he leaned back into his seat. "Two Bulleits on the rocks, please."

"Coming right up," the hostess said before bouncing to the bar.

"I normally go for whiskey, but bourbon is sweeter," he said.

Brinton waggled her eyebrows. "I like it sweet."

"I bet you do," he breathed. His tone sounded a little needier than intended.

But hell, he was. For anything she had to give.

Jamie traced feathery circles with his thumbs across the silky backs of her hands. "Is this…okay?"

It occurred to him that he may have moved too quickly, a Polaroid recklessly shaken before its beauty was revealed. "I know you're here to work—"

She nodded and smiled, seemingly equally relieved. "I like spending time with you."

He exhaled shakily at the unexpected intimacy, how it felt to lay himself bare without the fear of consequences. He'd never experienced that with his father or his team. Or even Kendall, because their relationship had a shelf life and an unspoken angle.

But with Brinton, it felt different. He was out of his depth but refused to get out of the pool.

"I like spending time with you too, Bee."

The hostess dropped off their drinks. Brinton lifted hers, examining the icy glacier poking through a burnt-orange sea.

"Tell me how you like it," she said.

Although he knew exactly what she meant, he could've cut the sexual tension between them with a knife.

Or, even better, his lips.

"First, two fingers of bourbon," he started. He leaned closer and rested his pointer and middle fingers horizontally against her glass.

"Only two, huh?" Her eyes flashed, completely as surprised—and charmed—as he was. "I'm sorry, that was—"

"Hilarious," he countered, laughing softly. "And, yeah, two fingers."

When her teeth sank into her plush bottom lip, desire scalded his cheeks.

"Better to ease into it." She laughed.

"Exactly," he answered, volleying the mischief in her eyes.

"Then, a fat cube of ice. Melts slow enough to cut the burn and make the flavors bloom. I like to taste everything."

They clinked their glasses and each took a sip.

"Mmm," she moaned, innocently enough. His mouth watered anyway.

"It's smooth as caramel."

He nodded, but not about the liquor. Jamie set down his glass, enchanted to watch Brinton continue. "Hey, you should slow down—"

She drained it in three gulps, then casually licked the lingering sweetness from her lips.

*Lordy.*

Did she want him to know how she'd like to be licked? Did she know he'd do it on command? The sheer fantasy of her tongue zigzagging across his sensitive, tingly skin made him shift in his seat.

The building pressure bit against his zippered fly.

"You should catch up," she said, laughing. It was gratifying to see her so carefree and to know he brought it out of her.

"Big words from a woman who's gonna feel that shot in about two seconds."

"I can handle my liquor. Can you?"

He cocked his head, then drained his glass. Jamie unleashed a hoot as he slammed it down on the table. "Darlin', you got no idea."

Flirting was fun—albeit, an understatement—but he also wanted *more*. She was a labyrinth, and he wanted to learn every blind curve. "Can I ask you something? If it's too personal, you don't gotta answer."

She nodded, expression so warm that his heart melted like butter in a hot skillet.

"Besides helping me, what do you wanna get out of this article?" he asked.

Her eyes dipped to her clasped hands. "I don't want to be the girl who vomited on the internet anymore. So, this article is the first step."

He understood the exhaustion she felt fighting a reputation she didn't ask for. It was inescapable, like swimming upstream with fifty-pound ankle weights.

"When Mom passed away, my father decided that I needed a more disciplined path. I just rebelled, with the sneaking out and the girls. After I dropped out of college, I spent the next few years whiskey-bent and hell-bound, floating between writing songs that went nowhere and too many bad choices along the way. Eventually, I felt so behind in life that I finally took my father's help. He swears I'd be twice as successful by now had I listened sooner."

Jamie spun his ring around his finger. "So, yeah…there's a lot on the line for me too."

Brinton took a deep breath, brushing her fingertips against his on the table and blanketing him in calmness.

"It must be a lot of pressure to live up to your father's legacy. But why do you feel like you can't say no to him? I'm sorry if that's out of line, but I guess, this is *your* life. He doesn't…own you, you know?"

Jamie sighed, then bowed his head.

"It's a fair question. It's sad to say, but before I met you, I couldn't recognize it as him controlling me. Where I come from, fathers create this lore about their families, and then that lore becomes law. It's about respecting them, and what they pass onto you. Loyalty…It's ingrained in Southern culture.

"My father, and his father before him, and so on, set the tone," Jamie continued. "Out of respect, or maybe humility, I listened. I'm sure that's hard for you to understand, but it's the truth. That's why I'm so taken by what you've accomplished on your own. It's a big deal to be where you are."

"I'm checking a box." She laughed bitterly. "My editor only hired me so that he and his bosses felt better about the bullshit *Landmark* perpetuates daily. In a year, only one Black artist covered the print issue. The story was written by a white writer with the audacity to debate the merits of Black-face with me, so I'll let you guess how that went. And I'm never surprised when, year after year, I'm the sole writer on-call during Juneteenth weekend. You know, in case some Black-ass news happens."

Brinton blew out a breath. "But it's a legacy publication anyone would kill to write for. I'm living The American Dream."

"God, Brinton, that is awful—I am so sorry," he said.

His heart splintered for her, and he was mortified spilling his petty problems when hers were so systemic they felt impossible to solve. He wanted to calm her fears and right every wrong in one fell swoop.

Ultimately, all he could do was tell her that he believed in her. It's what he'd want if he were in her situation.

He rose, then slid into her side of the booth. He sighed, grateful when she didn't push him away.

"They don't deserve you because you're not a box to be checked. You're not a Company Man. I mean that figura-tively, of course."

When she faced him, her smile was steeped in sadness. It pained him to see it.

"What am I then?" she asked.

That look of vulnerability on her face gave him courage to show some of his own. He smiled.

"You're an artist, like me. It's in how you talk and the way you genuinely want to connect with people. I do it on stage, but you—you do it on the page. And it's beautiful. So much that I think you're destined for more than *Landmark*. You could leave and do your own thing."

She slid her hands into her lap. "That's nice of you to say, but things move differently for us non-famous people. It can be really hard to start over."

When she looked back at him, the sparkle in her eyes had dimmed. He desperately wanted to get it back.

It was a bold move, but he gently clasped one of his hands over hers, testing the waters. She let him.

Breath shaky, he exhaled. "What if we're not so different?"

And bingo.

Slowly, she smiled. "I'm starting to believe that."

At the Skylight, everyone knew him, and people were respectful about not recording him on their phones. But it was still a risk, considering Brinton wasn't one of his team's hand-selected women whose social currency would boost his own.

Brinton didn't deserve to be used like that. He wouldn't kiss her so openly, despite the nagging urge that'd sparked when she slid into Michael's SUV.

But he needed to be *closer*.

"You wanna dance?" he asked.

That would be easier to pull off. He nodded to the much smaller VIP dance floor tucked into a darkened corner about ten feet away.

"It's a little more private than the main floor. People are generally cool here, but I don't want..."

He didn't want to scare Brinton off with another PR fiasco.

"You don't want me to school you on the dance floor? I've gotten very good in the last hour."

As Jamie slid out from the booth, relief rushed from his head to the soles of his boots. Brinton followed after him. Hands on her hips, and in those cut-offs, she was the sexiest little instigator he'd ever seen.

"I'll hold you to it," he said.

The winding, opening licks of "That Don't Impress Me Much" filled the room.

Brinton's face glowed, and her glossy lips formed into a perfect O.

"Oh my God." She laughed. "It's a sign."

Heaven help him.

# CHAPTER TWENTY-FOUR

*B*rinton and Jamie stood on the darkened edge of the floor, shielded by far tipsier couples swaying to Shania's sultry ad-libs.

There wasn't a camera in sight, which was comforting as Brinton stepped closer.

She couldn't remember the last time she slow danced with someone. Her aunt's wedding in Fort Lauderdale in ninth grade? What the hell was she supposed to do with her hands again?

They awkwardly hovered over Jamie's mountainous shoulders.

"Hey," he said softly, "I like you here like this, close to me."

He pulled her arms around his neck so their bodies melted into one another's. Jamie rested one hand on her upper back and one on the highest part of her hip. It was respectful and dignified, and yet the proximity to his tensed muscles, straining beneath his T-shirt and God knew where else, did things to her she never thought she'd feel.

"Okay?" he asked.

She nodded.

He spun her around gracefully, and they sidestepped to the left and right like a well-oiled machine.

Brinton let herself *let go.* It wasn't surprising because Jamie had that effect on her. When he spun her around again, she kept her back pressed against his chest, pushing her butt against him as her hips moved in time with the guitar's hypnotic whine.

Her body buzzed from the friction alone.

Did she hear him groan? She couldn't tell for sure over the music.

Jamie's hands slid lightly down her sides. Finally, one rested on each hip.

As Brinton rocked side to side, his palms pressed harder into her hips, deliciously grounding her.

Pulling her into him.

She didn't stop him, not when his touch felt so exactly right.

Craning his neck, he whispered in her ear. "If you keep grinding on me like that, I'm gonna stop behaving myself."

She leaned her head back against his chest and inhaled his clove-spiked scent, easily more potent than all the whiskey in the world.

"Don't threaten me with a good time."

"I knew you were trouble," he murmured against her ear.

On the inside, Brinton was a tornado of ecstasy. She couldn't believe that A) this was happening and B) that he felt the same way about her. First, their electric moment on the red carpet, and then at the lake. All the small, surprising, explosive moments in between.

Behind her, Brinton draped her arms over Jamie's shoulders. He took the hint, dragging his hands over her ribcage, down her waist, and across her stomach.

This time, she *felt* him groan into her ponytail. The little vibrations tickled the back of her neck before re-routing between her thighs. She was already swollen with pleasure.

Brinton unleashed body roll after tortuous body roll. Jamie's hands didn't miss a beat. Neither did his long, soft moans against her neck.

"You know I respect you, right?" he asked, breathless.

"Uh-huh."

"The way I want you—what I wanna do to you…"

"Tell me…" she panted.

Though she didn't need to ask. When she threw her ass back again, she felt the unmistakable answer in his jeans.

His breaths, satisfyingly hot and addictive, shattered against her neck. He spun her around to face him, paving the way for their hips to buck together freely.

She angled her face toward his. He cupped her jaw.

"I wanna run my tongue over you real slow, until you're slick and screaming for me," Jamie said. "I bet you taste so fucking sweet, Bee. Like pure honey."

What a coincidence—she couldn't stop thinking about how badly she wanted his mouth on her. Immediately.

"I'd lick up every single drop. Then, I'd fuck you six ways to Sunday." He paused. "Respectfully, of course."

Brinton swallowed hard.

"Of course," she said, a lust-hazy grin overtaking her lips, which, she decided, needed to be kissed. She needed his hands. She needed him.

Brinton pressed her chest against his, gripping his back to keep her balance.

"Sunday's my favorite day of the week."

"Follow me," he said, all smoke and lust, before taking her hand.

# CHAPTER TWENTY-FIVE

*J*amie led Brinton through a hallway she hadn't noticed before. A tattooed bouncer waved them through a narrow door. It dropped them off in the same empty alley where, a few hours ago, Brinton had considered punting Jamie through the SUV's passenger side window.

Now, she was desperate to relieve the pressure, intense as an unwatched kettle. Two-hundred-twelve degrees of canned heat between her thighs.

Considering how anxiety had whittled her sex drive toothpick-thin, this was almost inconceivable. The thought of sex with a man usually sent her spiraling, prompting a greatest hits reel of her imperfections: the heavy sag of her breasts and tiny spider veins creeping up her inner thighs, or the telltale slapping of her round belly in practically every position.

Sex had become a highly efficient solo sport, a short-lived distraction from the barrage of intrusive thoughts. Yet, beneath the electric blue haze spilling from the lanterns above, Jamie unlocked an urgency she refused to suppress.

And it was mutual.

When the heavy door shut behind them, a switch flipped. Jamie walked her backward until her shoulders brushed the brick wall behind her. He seemed to enjoy caging her body with his own so his eyes could skate over her freely.

It was warm, the air thick as gauze. But as he watched her, an undeniable flash of desire bolted up her spine. Her thighs clenched instinctively.

"You are so fucking beautiful," he said through shallow breaths that matched hers. "Can I kiss you?"

It was less of a question and more an urgent plea.

"Yes."

Jamie cupped her face. Massaging her jaw between his thumbs, he coaxed out a fractured whimper and everything else she'd felt since that red carpet.

His pressure was firmer than she expected, his lips velvety soft and so fucking warm as they glided against hers. Brinton sucked his tongue deeper into her open mouth until she swallowed his defiant groans.

Suddenly, he broke their kiss.

"You ever been fucked by a country boy?" Jamie asked, dragging his thumb from her jaw and down her throat.

She shook her head, whining in protest.

"Mm, I highly recommend it."

Slowly, Brinton traced the thin gold chain around his neck, which gleamed beneath the blue fluorescent lights. It felt cool between her fevered fingers. Something about it— the unabashed sluttiness, the inferred dominance—made her feral.

She wanted to grip it with her teeth.

"Come here," he growled, so low that the apex of her thighs flooded with warmth.

Brinton lifted her chin to meet his lips, but Jamie wrapped the length of her ponytail around his fist, giving it a gentle tug that cracked her open like an egg. It thrilled her. Almost as much as she liked him telling her what to do. Her body throbbed with need.

She raked her nails down his back, showing him how much she wanted him, even if it frightened her to say. She didn't want to wake up from the fantasy. Her cruel inner monologue reminded her daily that she wasn't quite good enough for anyone's time, care, or respect.

But Jamie, this living, breathing Adonis, saw something in her she didn't previously see in herself. Now, little by little, she could.

"I can't believe this is happening," she moaned instead. This didn't happen to women with baggage like hers.

His mouth claimed hers again, and her body vibrated.

His thick erection nudged her cleft. A wicked grin spread across his perfect lips. "Believe it now?"

"Fuck, Jamie…"

When he moaned in her mouth, she sucked his bottom lip, delighted to know he was as wrecked as her.

Brinton laced her hands through his hair, silken waves with earthy notes of sandalwood. She relished how his back and shoulders tensed each time she tugged. The power she felt was unmatched.

"I like that," he breathed against the shell of her ear.

"Show me."

He laughed, low and dark, then flooded each side of her neck with feathery kisses. "Tsk-tsk," he teased. "I told you, I'm gonna take my time."

Jamie's fingertips traversed the length of her arms, prompting her nipples to tighten so intensely that her eyes rolled backward. Her nails sank into his biceps.

He was barely even touching her and she was embarrassingly wet. Needy for him to do something.

*Touch me. Take me. Fold me in half.*

As if taking the cue, Jamie's hands found the hem of her cut-offs. He massaged the frayed denim, a few inches from where she wanted him most.

"These fucking little shorts," he said, voice as smokey as the añejo shots inside the bar. "Been driving me crazy all night. The way you move in them should be a crime."

"I can't be held liable for gravity." She laughed.

She wrapped her arms around his neck, pulling him closer. His sweet breaths coated her lips like nectar.

Jamie's hands slid to her ass. Brinton gasped, enthralled when he roughly massaged each cheek.

"I love your body." He grunted softly. "Every damn inch of you is perfect."

"I'm not"—another gasp—"perfect."

Jamie shook his head as his fingers gripped the back of her neck, gentle but firm pressure that forced her to lift her chin and look at him.

Her lips parted on a gasp.

"You are to me," he said, voice like iron.

Shifting to her breasts, Jamie's massive hands worked her until her head collapsed backward and she unleashed a low, rumbling moan. This only invigorated his tactics.

His thumbs slowly circled each nipple until they were pleasingly tender, and the strangled words coming out of her mouth sounded closer to the gibberish Missy Elliot perfected in "Work It." Dragging her higher, Jamie alternated between pulling and lightly twisting, based on what made her arch into him.

"That's it, Bee. Keep moaning for me. Do you know what you're doing to me? Fuck, I—"

Suddenly, her hands had a mind of their own, and it even took her by surprise when she found one massaging his crotch. The other squeezed his ass.

"I think I have an idea." She grinned.

Head bowed against her chest, Jamie shuddered as his thick erection rocketed into her palm, heavy and straining through his jeans. She couldn't wait to feel him inside her.

Brinton squeezed him there, hoping he'd take the hint.

"Such a good girl," Jamie groaned decadently. He tugged her ponytail again, and her belly clenched with satisfaction.

She was a feminist, dammit. But the way the words dripped off his tongue, viscous and *vital.* A new kink unlocked. Brinton made a note to unpack this when she wasn't preoccupied with such an excellent bulge.

"Always fucking surprising me," he murmured against her throat, hips still rocking. He steadied a hand against the cold brick. His other greedily squeezing her breast.

"Oh my God, Jamie," she whispered back, knotting her hands in his T-shirt. She slipped one beneath to explore his lean stomach, which she hadn't stopped obsessing over, and traced her fingers through the soft hair leading into his waistband.

"Say it again," he said. He nudged her legs apart with his broad thigh.

Brinton moaned his name as his palm settled between her thighs, which trembled on contact. He stroked her as if by memory, knowing exactly which strings to pluck, how long to hold each pulsating note.

"I'm desperate to feel how soft and wet you are," he gritted out. Through clipped breaths, he watched her buck against his palm, frantic enough that she now craved the bite of rough denim against her damp, sensitive skin. Anything to get her closer to *letting go*.

"So wet," she whispered, the last ounce of reservation leaving her body.

Jamie's lips parted into a satisfied smile. His eyes were heavy-lidded, like he was in a sensation-fueled daze. Like he could savor her like the smoothest Tennessee whiskey.

The whole scenario was a lucid dream: she, a hot mess, was about to have sex with a ruthlessly hot man. In a back alley that smelled faintly of Nashville hot chicken.

*Fuck it, it's fine!*

"Do you know how long I've wanted this?" Jamie slipped his hand from her thighs to cradle her face.

His kiss was so tender she almost forgot that she wanted him to yank off her clothes. Almost.

"Hmm," she hummed against his lips. "After I smoked you in cornhole?"

He laughed. "No, way before that." Jamie pulled back but still cupped her jaw with both hands. "The second I held you on that red carpet. Couldn't get you out of my head. Still can't."

"Ah, maybe you should talk to somebody about that," she said, grinning.

He reached for her shorts and popped the top button. "Yeah? Sounds like the best problem to me." His fingertips teased the open edge. Jamie's thumb traced across her navel, stopping at her lacy panty line.

There was a question in his eyes.

Yes, she could live in the moment. She could be a little reckless. She could let Jamie Crawford Jr. dick her down beneath the neon lights.

"Please," she said, so softly that she considered he had simply read her mind.

Jamie tugged down her zipper. "You ain't never gotta beg me, Bee. I'll gladly give you what you want."

His thumb dipped into her panties, pressing her open and gliding with gratifying ease.

Brinton's head lolled backward against the brick wall. Her knees buckled from his long, languid circles, but she'd be damned if she told him to stop.

He felt so fucking good. Too fucking good.

Equally satisfied, Jamie groaned. He pressed the rest of his fingers into her exposed belly, grounding her into place.

Way too soon, Jamie dragged his thumb away. He slipped it between his lips. Savoring her, his eyes closed, he sucked.

"I knew it," he said, voice strained thin. "Like pure fucking honey."

As usual, Brinton's anxious mind did somersaults. Her eyes squeezed shut.

*How does one fuck in shorts? Why is there not a manual on this?*

"You all right?" he asked, sensing her apparent agitation.

"Yeah," she replied earnestly. "Don't stop."

He eased two thick fingers inside her, bringing her back into her blissed-out body. She keened like a needy cat and clenched around him.

"So damn tight, honey," he murmured. "I fucking love it. You need more? I wanna—"

"Do it," she whined.

Jamie rewarded her with a third finger. Electricity propelled her hips forward as he massaged and thrusted and teased his way deeper, until she felt each of his knuckles strain inside her.

God, she needed more pressure, more of *him.*

Matching her frustration, Jamie threw his head back. His throaty groan spoke volumes.

"If we were in my bed—"

"Yes—"

"I'd make you ride me real slow." He hooked a thumb into her belt loop and tugged her hips forward. "I wanna watch you take me, Bee. 'Til we can't fucking talk straight. I want you all over me."

"You're an artist." She laughed, breathless. "Improvise."

"Yes ma'am."

Through a fiendish smile, he slipped his fingers from

inside her, then hoisted her thighs around his hips until her back scraped the brick wall.

She yelped.

His eyes, navy pools beneath the blue lantern, stretched with concern. "Baby, did I hurt you?"

Brinton shook her head. It felt fucking fantastic. Crossing her ankles, she let him kiss it better.

"Do you have a—"

"Yeah," he answered, teeth grazing her collarbone.

When Jamie pulled the foil packet from his wallet, it triggered that familiar onslaught of panic, which clouded her mind like smog.

*How many other people—and creatures—had pressed their bodies against this grimy wall? When was the last time I washed my fucking hands? What if I'm not good enough?*

"What if…someone sees us?" she asked, too self-aware for her own good.

"Don't worry, nobody'll come back here." With his free hand, he undid his belt and unzipped his fly. "This is my spot."

Of course.

This was as routine as tuning his guitar or cold beers with the boys on Fridays. This was routine for the Heartbreak Prince, a persona. And apparently, the man.

No, Brinton couldn't do this.

Her body went slack and she pressed her hands against his chest.

Immediately, he dropped his and set her back on the ground.

Jamie put a good three feet between them as she readjusted her shorts. When he looked down at her this time, worry clouded his eyes.

"Is everything okay?" He was still catching his breath. "Did I do something wrong?"

"This isn't something I do," she said, practically wheezing. Brinton circled her hands around the darkened alley. She was a fool to think she was somehow special, that they were each inching out onto a precarious limb for one another.

"I'm not just another girl you folded in half in a dark alley."

"Fold you in—slow down a second…"

"And you wouldn't know that because we barely know each other."

"But I want to know you—more than I can even say. I like you, Brinton," he said, gently cupping her jaw again. "Is this about the article?"

Brinton angled her face away. Now that he'd said it, she couldn't ignore it, as hard as she had tried all night.

It was one thing to be a number in his sisterhood of traveling groupies. That indignity lanced her heart.

It was worse that she was also putting her article at risk. Sleeping with a source was an ethical quagmire. While not illegal, it could slash the single thread of integrity holding her together, especially as a female journalist. As a Black woman fighting for opportunity.

What she *wanted* and what she *needed* had finally collided in spectacular fashion.

She didn't know what to say. Yet, she had to say something. "We're so wildly crossing a line, I can't even comprehend it."

He twisted that signet ring around his finger, then smoothed a few errant waves from his eyes. For the first time, they appeared dull.

"Okay."

"So what do we do now?" she asked, perhaps more to herself than him.

"Try to behave ourselves, I guess?" He laughed humorlessly, eyes cast down to the sticky asphalt.

A moment later, his eyes found hers again.

"I don't regret any of this, for what it's worth," he said.

She didn't either. But she couldn't tell him that, not when the wound was so fresh. "Thanks for the dance," she said.

Jamie nodded and texted Michael. Neither Brinton nor Jamie spoke a word the entire drive home.

# CHAPTER TWENTY-SIX

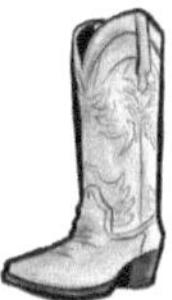

Michael dropped Jamie off at home hours ago, but he was as wired as he'd been in that alley, his hands on Brinton and his heart aching for her light.

Sitting on his porch and looking across the lake's glossy expanse, he still ached for her.

She'd blamed the article. Was that the truth? He wasn't sure.

Things had been going so perfectly. In truth, that also scared him. His attraction had grown beyond a superficial crush. Now, it was dangerously close to something that felt more permanent, like a searing tattoo.

Was this how it was supposed to feel?

Jamie certainly hadn't figured that out with Kendall. Or the Houston beauty queen. Or the daughter of his record label's CEO. She rightfully gave Jamie a purple-nurple when he broke up with her at the local drive-in, after they'd watched *Inside Out 2* together.

Or any of the other women he'd been with over the years.

Jamie's father never gave him "the talk" about the building blocks for a healthy relationship. His version of the birds and the bees involved a box of condoms on the kitchen counter the week before Jamie's eighteenth birthday.

"Make smart choices," he had said, sliding Jamie the Trojans. "Your future depends on it. The last thing you need is another dark night."

Jamie knew exactly what his father had meant: When the ambulance came, and the tears flowed, and both their lives crumbled into dust.

It was the last night Jamie had felt like a whole person.

But he had never stopped wondering how different things would have been if he'd felt safe enough to open up to his father about his feelings. Or his mother, who he believed loved his father, despite their troubles.

If he could, Jamie would have asked his mother so many questions about how love worked. Could it be fine-tuned like a song, or was it something more organic, wild and fleeting? With Brinton, deep down, he wanted to hold on to her, even as their circumstances kept tearing them apart.

Jamie leaned into his outdoor sofa's linen cushion as a slice of silver moonlight edged through the clouds. The candles he'd lit doused his notebook in an amber haze.

Jamie had been secretly coming out here to write, but it had been a while since he sat down to create something new. Five days ago, before Brinton arrived in Iris, he'd given up hope that any of it mattered.

Now Jamie wanted to name the entire scope of feelings he was exploring—the good, the exciting, the uncertain.

He wrote lyrics and worked out melodies on his acoustic guitar until his fingers cramped and the sun climbed over the horizon.

# LYRICS - "GUIDING LIGHT"

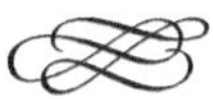

— JAMIE CRAWFORD JR. (2026)

<u>Verse #1</u>
Standing on that hill
You're holding on to me
Flowers at your feet
But the secrets that you keep
Hold you in the dark
A place I can't ever reach

<u>Bridge</u>
I'm looking for you now
Those flowers turned to ash
Buried somewhere in the past
I just wish I could go back

<u>Chorus</u>
I've got so many questions
You can't answer
Missed you so many days

I've lost count
Pieces I can't seem to mend
My heart breaking once again
But when I look
To the sky each night
You're my guiding light

Verse #3

I remember you now
The sun was on your face
I could barely keep upright
You kept your hand right on mine
I thought there was still time

Verse #4

I need you right now
Tell me how to know it's right
To lay down my heart or fight
I want to be the kind of man
That can walk in the light

Chorus

I've got too many questions
You can't answer
Missed you so many days
I've lost count
Pieces I can't seem to mend
My heart breaking once again
But when I look

To the sky each night
You're my guiding light

<u>Bridge</u>
That hill will never be the same
Lonely echoes of your name
I won't ever be the same
I won't be whole again

<u>Chorus #2</u>
I know you can't give
Me the answers
But your love burns
In the stars so bright
An eternal flame,
You make me whole once again
When I look to the sky each night
You're my guiding light
You're my guiding light
You're my guiding light

# CHAPTER TWENTY-SEVEN

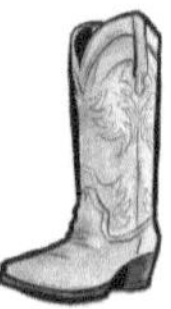

When Cory blew his coach's whistle the next day, Jamie rued not sleeping a few extra hours on a rare free Saturday morning. Yet, there he was, willingly torturing himself with sit-ups.

He dragged his bare torso from the grass, squeezing his fatigued abs and wringing out the last drop of oxygen from his lungs.

"That's one hundred," Cory barked, grinning as he leaned over Jamie's bent knees. "A little slow on the pump, and your speed drills are dogshit. But not bad for an old-timer."

Cory wailed on the whistle thrice more, the shrill peaks cleaving through Jamie's heaving breaths. "Let's go, round two."

Jamie fell against the turf, the pool of sweat from his forehead stinging his eyes worse than the mid-morning sun bearing down on the practice football field. When Jamie wasn't on tour, he and Cory worked out together at the Anderson Training Facility, where his friend's day job was to whip nineteen-year-olds into prime NFL picks.

Between Cory's masochistic drills and the physical cracks

and creaks of no longer being nineteen, it was grueling. But Jamie wouldn't trade this time with his oldest friend for anything.

Still, that whistle was as pleasant as sand wedged between every crack on a beach day.

"You blow that thing again, and I'm whooping your ass," Jamie said, once he got his breath back.

Cory outstretched a hand and peeled him from the ground. "I don't think you could catch me."

He tossed Jamie an icy water bottle from a cooler before they trudged down the sideline. "C'mon, let's walk it off."

Jamie simply nodded, still too winded to function. He drained the bottle in two gulps.

"So, we gonna talk about why you've been moping like when Liza fries okra, but you can only eat a sad plate of kale because of a photo shoot?"

Cory laughed, nudging Jamie's shoulder until he did too.

Jamie groaned. "If I tell you, you can't give me shit."

Cory rubbed the crop of stubble on his chin with his thumb and pointer finger. "Sorry, but that dog won't hunt. It's in the best friend handbook that I give you shit. I'm legally bound."

Jamie shoved his shoulder.

"But I promise to give you my honest advice, which you always need," Cory reasoned, nudging him back.

"Damn, I must be desperate."

Which, honestly, was true.

Cory howled, leaned back, and launched into high-knees. "And if you keep holding me in suspense, you're running laps till you puke."

Jamie gripped his hips and blew out a long breath. He hadn't told anyone about what had happened with Brinton at the Skylight last night. But Cory was his best friend, and Jamie needed someone to talk to so he didn't lose his mind.

Or worse, blow his chance if left to his own devices, which, frankly, he'd probably already done.

"Brinton and I…we've gotten pretty close."

Cory eased into a trot and narrowed his eyes, earnestly concerned. "How close?"

"We kissed at the bar last night."

Cory flung his hands skyward and ran circles around Jamie, who threw his own head back and laughed.

"Hallelujah! Judging by how y'all got on at the cookout, that's a good thing, right?"

He slowed to a walk, returning to Jamie's side.

Jamie shrugged. "I thought so. We were dancing and things got pretty…"

He let himself get tangled in the memory of her top-tier ass thumping against him and swallowed hard.

"Anyway, we both wanted some more"—he cleared his throat—"privacy, so I took her to my spot. Everything was going great until something set her off."

With his massive palm, Cory smacked Jamie upside the head.

"What the hell, man?" Jamie hissed.

Cory stopped walking. "I could ask you the same thing. You don't take a woman like *that* to a back alley."

"I take a lot of women back there," Jamie said, rubbing his throbbing skull.

"You told her that?"

"Yeah. It's quiet, so it's easier to…" Jamie circled his hand in the air, fairly certain there was no helping his case. "You know, have a conversation."

"And I bet you didn't consider that she might feel like she's no different than any other girl you've hooked up with? Not for nothing, but you've got a hell of a reputation. So of course she'd feel slighted."

*Shit.*

*Is that how she felt?* Because Brinton she *was* different. She was unlike any woman he'd ever met. Jamie shook his head, raking his hands through his sweat-slicked hair.

"I'm an idiot. I'm a fucking fool."

Laughing, Cory crossed his arms over his chest. "Glad you said it so I don't have to."

Jamie loosely hooked his arm into a headlock around Cory's neck, then released him. Once they both stopped laughing, Jamie continued. "I care about her, man. More than I ever have about anyone. She's so damn smart and kind, and she treats me like what I do and say matters. How do I fix this?"

Cory squeezed Jamie's shoulder. "You tell her that. Exactly that. And please don't wait because I've never seen you so smitten. You're blushing worse than a senator at a peep show."

Jamie grinned. "That's probably all the blood that rushed to my head."

And the fresh sunburn spilling across his collarbone.

Mercilessly, Cory blew into his whistle. "It looks good on you. Now, let's get some more pink in those cheeks."

He kicked Jamie in the ass, then bolted down the field.

"You're a dead man," Jamie yelled, sprinting after him.

At the guest house, Brinton awoke that morning in her bedroom feeling like a decadent shit sundae. Her throat burned as if she'd sipped the entire Sahara through a straw. Her joints popped like bubble wrap.

Brinton didn't remember when she crawled onto the floor last night. It must have been between her subconscious desires to be tucked and folded by a magnetic country music star.

Shay, of course, was no help when Brinton had texted her that morning. She wanted a play-by-play.

Worse yet, Brinton remembered everything. Jamie's hands on her body. His lips whispering ruinous praise against her fevered skin. Her fingertips were still raw from gripping his lightly stubbled cheeks.

But now, reality had set in: she'd read the whole situation wrong.

However, this was another time she'd crater her feelings. She'd get through the next week, her final seven days in Iris, and never bring up what happened in that alley with Jamie again.

Simple compartmentalization. Men did it all the time.

Brinton considered this as Rich, eyes expectantly glazed, stared back at her from her open laptop screen that afternoon.

Unannounced, he'd called to finalize her pitch. Rich was the embodiment of wearing cute white capris the day your period decided to show up early.

His slumped posture in his chair confirmed his low hopes for this meeting.

"So, whatcha got, Shaw?"

What she *got* was a world-class exclusive. But even then, she didn't trust Rich not to pass her hard work off to Agatha if she told him everything now. It'd be better that he read her finished article.

She needed to be vague enough to get him hooked and reaffirm her acuity.

"It's *juicy*," she said. Brinton tasted a faint wash of bile from parroting his own insincere words.

His eyes flickered beneath his fitted dad hat. "Yeah?"

She picked at a cottony white tuft from the eyelet quilt on

the bed. "Jamie is giving me unparalleled access into the agony and ecstasy of stardom."

*God, why did I say ecstasy?*

"I'm peeling back layers…"

*Of my clothes.*

"He's showing a side I didn't expect."

*His tongue strumming my tonsils!*

Brinton's cheeks heated. She was miserably, infuriatingly down bad. And way too fucking horny for this conversation.

Could Rich tell?

His obnoxious bark of laughter popped through her laptop speakers. "Peeling back layers, huh?"

Conspiratorially, he leaned forward and lowered his voice. "You aren't screwing him, are you?"

Just then, Brinton's phone buzzed with a new text from Shay.

> Shay: If you don't let that sweet-talking man butter that biscuit, I'm telling mom. Actually, I'm telling her anyway.

Brinton clenched her jaw until she heard a deafening pop. She was *so close* to getting what she wanted.

She hadn't *screwed* Jamie, but she almost had, not twenty-four hours ago. And while it stoked a long-dormant flame, her awoken desire had jeopardized her objectivity.

In more ways than one, she had gotten too close to the story. To Jamie.

"Because that would be a huge conflict of interest," Rich added, steepling his fingers. "And I can't have that."

She eyed her discarded cut-offs on the bedroom floor. Why did she feel guilty? Why couldn't she lie, like everyone else who'd sped past her to climb *Landmark*'s totem pole?

Brinton grasped for the words to save herself, but came up short. Because she wasn't a liar.

"Rich, I have to tell you something…"

Sneering, his hands flew up in mock defense. "I'm kidding. Jamie Crawford Jr.'s body count includes first- and second-generation supermodels. And you're a regular…No offense."

Brinton wiped her slick palms on her jeans. She didn't know whether to be incensed or amused that Rich had the social grace of an amoeba.

"Oh, in case Deb from HR is listening, I apologize for my spirited, off-the-cuff joke. I'll do better to temper my enthusiasm." Rich winked, one hand obsequiously over his heart. "Your generation's got no sense of humor."

Sighing, he continued. "You wanted to say something?"

The blood rushed back into her limbs. Brinton was safe, for now. But she had to cut off her budding relationship—if you could call it that—with Jamie.

She couldn't let the way every single muscle in her thighs clenched at the sound of his name derail her future with *Landmark*.

She smiled weakly. "It's nothing."

"Anyway," Rich went on, looking at his phone, "good work. When can I get a draft?"

"As soon as possible."

Satisfied, Rich nodded and ended the call.

Needing to channel her scattered energy, Brinton slipped on her headphones. She pressed play on her new favorite playlist of Black country music artists. She had started curating it when she first arrived in Iris.

Mickey Guyton, Shaboozey, Brittney Spencer, Breland, Reyna Roberts, and The War and Treaty were on repeat, and she found more each day. But not even Mickey's sweeping vocals could save Brinton from her free-falling thoughts.

Simple compartmentalization was not for anxious baddies after all.

# CHAPTER TWENTY-EIGHT

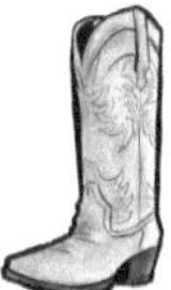

*L*ater that night, Brinton showered and slipped into a pink cotton camisole and matching shorts that unceremoniously rose up whenever she blinked. But she wasn't dressing up for anyone tonight.

Instead, she sat cross-legged in front of the floor-length mirror in her bedroom with a tiny squeeze bottle of hair oil she'd packed in her carry-on.

Doing her hair was a point of pride and one of the few self-care practices she could still manage. It made the heaviness of everyday life—the hulking weight of New York City and asphyxiating fear of the future—slightly lighter.

Section by section, Brinton meticulously gathered the braids at her temples, applied the golden elixir to the neat partings, and massaged it into her scalp. She was in a trance as she worked, fingertips gliding on auto-pilot.

Until the doorbell rang.

It was nine o'clock. Not exactly late, but she wasn't expecting company. Brinton quickly washed her hands and padded down the stairs.

When she opened the front door, she found Jamie, all

sun-kissed and sheepish grin, standing on the porch. He held a canvas tote bag in one hand.

His eyes widened, drinking her in as she wore next to nothing.

Self-conscious, she crossed her arms over her chest and wondered how quickly she could stealthily dislodge her wedgie.

"Sorry—were you heading to bed?" he stammered, eyes dragging up to hers.

"No, I'm up. What are you doing here?" she asked, tone harsher than intended. She regretted that when his smile faltered.

"I don't sleep much these days, so I'm kinda wired," he said, a little brighter. "Do you wanna hang out?"

She weighed her options: they could talk about last night. That had to happen eventually, even if she wished she had more time to get her story straight. But then, when he looked at her, with those disarming eyes, and dragged his teeth over his plump bottom lip...

It was hard not to fantasize about fitting their damp, naked bodies together like Jenga pieces.

Brinton shook the thought away, as tempting as it was. She stepped aside so he could enter.

She'd tell him that they had to set some boundaries, and that whatever was happening between them *couldn't* happen. Then, she'd send Jamie on his merry way.

Naturally, that plan didn't include watching the smooth curve of Jamie's ass flex in his jeans as he crossed into the kitchen.

*Shit, I will miss that.*

"I was also hungry, so I stole some rations from the main house," Jamie said, setting the canvas tote on the countertop. He pulled out a fresh loaf of bread wrapped in brown paper, a jar of homemade apple jelly, and a package of sharp cheddar.

"Want a taste?" he asked casually.

She wanted a lot of things.

"I'm not hungry, but feel free to make something for yourself," she answered.

Then her stomach—the traitorous tart—rumbled so loudly, it startled her. Jamie smirked and continued unpacking his bounty.

"Fine, I could eat," she said, joining him at the large kitchen island, but she stood on the opposite side. A feeble attempt to keep the sweaty Jenga at bay.

"What is all of this?" she asked, flicking her wrist across the counter.

He flashed a tempered grin. "You'll see."

After cutting four perfect slices from the soft loaf, Jamie spread a thin, golden layer of apple jelly on each and topped it with a generous slice of cheddar. He cut both sandwiches diagonally and slid one onto a plate.

"This, my dear, is the best sandwich you'll ever have," he said, handing her the plate. "My mom made it every day for me after school. She wasn't big on cooking, hence why Liza was a godsend, but this'll heal you like a prayer."

Brinton looked up in time to catch him slowly suck an errant swipe of jelly from his thumb. He was looking down at the counter, not even trying to entice her, but—damn.

*Like pure fucking honey.*

"One bite will change your life," Jamie mused, swallowing.

He could say that again.

When she took a bite, her eyes widened. "Oh my God..." she said, nodding at the explosions of sweetness and acid and salt on her tongue. It's exactly what kissing him tasted like.

"Right?" he asked, as if thinking the same thing.

*Is he thinking the same thing? Focus, girl.*

As they finished their last bites, they stared at each other, the weight of everything unsaid bearing down. The severing of the branch of possibility between them.

The seconds ticked on agonizingly slow.

She lifted her eyes from her empty plate and met his gaze. "Jamie, about last night—"

He didn't let her finish.

"I fucked up, Brinton." He looked to that impossibly high ceiling, laughing to himself. "And it's not the first time since you got here. I'm betting the house that it won't be the last. I guess…I don't know how to do this."

"Do what?" she asked, caught in a vortex of panic and uncertainty.

Would he tell her that none of what they'd shared had been real, like she'd feared? Would he plead temporary insanity by rancid whiskey?

*Crap, did whiskey even go rancid?*

She'd google it later. Not that it mattered. She was ending this—whatever it was—tonight. She had to.

But dammit, it *did* matter. So much that she'd already put her career, the very thing validating her and making her *worthy*, on the line.

He spread his hands wide, leaning against the counter.

"How to be with someone," he admitted. "I've never done it right, never thought I could. In that alley last night, I gave you the impression that these last few days haven't been exceptional. That you're like any other woman to me. But that couldn't be further from the truth. Because, Bee, I'm serious about you."

He exhaled, his laugh a nervous jumble. "I'm sorry, I've never said that to anyone before, and I'm scared shitless."

She couldn't believe this was happening again. Brinton had set herself up for disappointment. And yet Jamie was a rainstorm on a blinding sunny day. There was no choice but to dance until you were soaked to the bone.

"I'm serious about you too," she whispered, a lukewarm smile blooming across her lips. Sadly, that didn't solve the bigger problem.

Her eyes floated shut, as if she could shield herself from what was coming next. "But you're my interview subject. There can't be any doubts about how this story came together."

She shook her head as his smile dampened. "They'll think I fucked my way to a byline. And I don't want to lie about it, because that's not who I am. So we can't…"

Brinton couldn't place exactly when her hands started shaking, but Jamie crossed to her side of the kitchen island and took them into his. The warmth spread through her fingers, sheathing each fractured nerve.

"What if I'm not ready to let you go?" he pleaded, eyes wide and handily reeling her in.

"I don't think I'm ready either," she said before she could swallow the words. The tender truth. "But I don't know what else to do. Unless…"

Had Shay and her mother been right? Brinton had been miserable at *Landmark*. And who knew if this cover story would even change that?

"I could give the story to another reporter, and you can decide whether to share your secret."

As Brinton said the words, her stomach slicked with disappointment. She'd fought for this opportunity for years, but if she let herself actually be happy, that all disappeared.

Agatha's cacophonous snicker ransacked Brinton's mind.

Jamie tightened his grip on Brinton's hands. "I won't let you do that for me. And I don't trust anybody else but you to tell my story."

His hands circled her back as his lips pressed against her right temple.

"There's gotta be another way." He pulled back. Possibility

brewed in his eyes. "We're still getting to know each other, so what if we…" Adorably, he cocked his head. "Pump the brakes on…you know."

She eyed him, confused. No, she had no fucking clue.

He raised a brow. "Sleeping together?"

"Indefinitely?" Brinton's vagina wailed at the thought.

He grinned, then softly kissed her forehead. "Oh, sweetheart, I hope not. But how about until after the article is wrapped? Whatever you need to feel comfortable, because lying will consume you. I would know."

Hands inching down her lower back, Jamie thumbed her shorts' soft waistband.

She buried her face into his firm chest.

"So, you're suggesting we take things slow?" she asked, voice muffled by his soft cotton T-shirt. He smelled as good as ever.

Brinton feared cold turkey was the only option. Her mother had long warned her of All or Nothing Thinking, a cognitive distortion plaguing the anxious mind. The only way to counter it was to question it.

The question was clear: what if there was a universe where Brinton could be simultaneously successful *and* happy? She craved that so intensely.

Jamie flashed that real smile that made her knees go all soupy.

"Mh-hmm," he murmured. "Besides, there's plenty of other ways to…enjoy each other."

He nuzzled Brinton's cheek, wrapping her in his scent. His safety.

Jamie's hands hovered a millimeter above her butt. It was enough to make her press into him in anticipation.

"And there's a lot to enjoy," he said, laughing darkly. He pulled his hands back up to her mid-back.

The little scoundrel was teasing her. She soaked up every second.

Jamie's plan was also good. She trusted him because, unlike Eli, who cataloged her flaws with a magnifying glass angled beneath the sun, Jamie appreciated all the kinks and burrs that made her a work-in-progress.

In fact, she felt renewed each time they touched.

Suddenly, they seemed too far apart.

She licked her lips. "First order of business: you should kiss me now."

Smiling softly, Jamie's hands migrated to the hollows of her cheekbones. He angled her face up to meet his.

"Bee, you're reading my mind."

This time, their kiss was softer, sweeter. A physical manifestation of their sacred pact to each other, exhilarating and joyful and worth every hard-won ounce of yearning.

His fingertips firmly gripped the back of her neck, which she decided was a new favorite. Need tightened in her belly as his hands fisted her braids. The delicious tension sparked fireworks behind her eyes.

Unexpectedly, he pulled away. His eyes were shaded with curiosity.

"I think you got a little something on you," he said. "Can I—"

Still a little dizzy, she nodded.

Curling his hand behind the shell of her ear, he caressed her so tenderly. Morse code from his fingertips straight to her heart. After denying herself the security of intimacy and gift of pleasure for so long, she felt light enough to levitate.

He pulled his hand away, fingers glossy and perfumed with rosemary and peppermint.

Uneasiness rooted in Brinton's stomach. "Um—it's oil. I was doing my hair before you got here."

A Black woman's hair was sacred. The art of it didn't need

explanation or require an apology. But there was a critical point in a new relationship where a Black woman decided when it was safe to let that person see behind the curated veneer. Without criticism of her Amazon lace fronts, over-sized satin bonnets, or arsenal of oil sheen and edge control jammed into bloated bathroom cabinets.

When she was twenty-two, Brinton dated a guy—also Black, although that proved to be of little consequence—who asked her to sleep on a musty futon in his living room. So she wouldn't "grease up" his thousand-dollar Frette cotton percale sheets with "all the shit y'all pile in your hair."

Was Jamie part of the trusted few?

Brinton roughly blotted a wad of paper towels against the back of her neck as Jamie's fingertips glided together. She slid him a fresh sheet, but he shook his head.

Eyes on her, he slowly worked the slickness between folds of skin and across thick veins on the back of his hands, as if anointing himself with her essence. Like it fortified him.

The act was all at once unassuming and the hottest damn thing she'd ever seen.

"I like it. It smells really good," he said.

"Oh." She blew out a breath, relieved. "My sister makes it for me and my mom. It's like our family crest."

He held out his left hand and pointed to the chunky gold ring on his pinky.

"I suppose this is our crest. My mom gave it to me when I was seven. I couldn't even fit it then. She wanted me to have something I could grow into, carry with me long after she was gone. I didn't know what she meant back then, but I do now."

Brinton took his hand, her eyes following the wispy curves of the *C* carved into the bezel. Occasionally, she caught glimpses as he twisted it wistfully around his finger, but this was the first time she genuinely admired it.

Finally, Brinton understood why Jamie was so protective over his mother. He was fighting to keep those memories alive.

That nagging inner voice beckoned for Brinton to grab her phone, a few feet away on the counter, and turn on the voice recorder app. Ask him a few more questions. But her heart wanted to enjoy the hallowed intimacy between them.

So, she did.

"It's so beautiful," she said. When she released his hand, she dreaded the sudden emptiness.

"Do you need a hand with your hair?" he asked.

"You want to help me oil my scalp?"

"Yeah, I do."

She glanced at him skeptically, mining the depths of his eyes for some ulterior motive. She found none.

"Let me get the bottle upstairs."

# CHAPTER TWENTY-NINE

A few minutes later, Jamie sat on the couch. On the floor, Brinton rested between Jamie's spread thighs. She held the hair oil like a treasured artifact.

"Comfortable?" he asked.

"Hmm. If you're asking if I have ever let a white man touch my hair like this, the answer is no."

They both laughed at the culturally inclusive elephant in the room.

"This isn't weird for me, you know. I've done it before," Jamie said, taking the bottle from her hands.

Brinton cast him a sidelong glance.

"Is this some kind of weird Black lady kink?" she asked, a sugared sarcasm in her tone. "Do you lure unsuspecting, tender-headed women into your home and grease away their pain?"

He chuckled. "I wouldn't call it a kink. It's more like crushing on women hopelessly out of my league. But that wouldn't surprise you, would it?"

"I didn't think the Heartbreak Prince had to work that hard." She laughed, settling back between his legs.

Jamie sighed. He was ready to shuck off that persona once and for all.

"Before you came to Iris, Kendall and I would hook up sometimes. I thought I owed it to her, for hurting her. But I'm done with that. And after my new album comes out, I'm done with this Heartbreak Prince thing too. I guess I wanted you to know, since now we're…"

"A thing?" she asked, still facing away from him.

"A very good thing," he answered. He kissed her forehead.

She angled her body toward his. The caramel-gold flecks in her eyes glowed in the dimmed overhead lights.

"Jamie, in my wildest dreams, I never thought I'd be someone you'd want. I'm, like, a regular-ass girl with more neuroses than Larry David. And you're like—"

He clasped her shoulders with both hands.

"Honey, you're everything I want. You got courage, even when you're scared. You care about kindness, even when carrying your own weight. You got sense enough to know right from wrong, and you don't waver. I want all of that. Brinton, I want *you*."

Tipping her chin upward, he softly leaned his lips against hers. Tingly flashes of anticipation warmed his entire body as her tongue slowly looped around his.

She was the best fucking kiss of his life, and each time, it only got better.

Eventually, Brinton passed him a claw hair clip. "It'll be easier if you go in small sections, starting from the bottom up."

"Don't worry, Bee. I got this," he said, sectioning her hair like she asked. He squirted a rivulet of oil in the partings along her nape, then gently massaged it with his index finger.

"You got a bonnet or a scarf so I can tie it up later?"

Brinton giggled. "We'll see if you unlock that level of

Black Girl Magic after you're done. Now, stop stalling and tell me why I'm crazy enough to let you do this."

He couldn't see her face but almost *felt* her smile, warm and insistent in his chest. It made him smile.

Brinton letting him care for her in such an intimate way was a big deal. He wanted to take care of her because he recognized the signs: she was healing.

Hopefully, in the same way he was.

"Growing up, I had the biggest crush on Cory's sister, Callie," Jamie began, still diligently working.

"She's a year older. Of course, she wanted nothing to do with her kid brother's scrawny little friend. I was always at their house because my dad recorded most nights in Nashville. But one day, after football practice, I walked past her room while she did her hair. It was like this choreographed dance. She parted it with a long, skinny comb. She dipped her fingers into this little pot of stuff that smelled like herbs and flowers and coconuts, then quickly rubbed it in.

Callie asked me to help part the back so she could put that herb stuff in, so I did. She had cut off her straight hair and had all these soft curls. Every so often, when Cory was late getting home, and I was bored, she'd let me part her hair or massage everything in while we watched *Love & Basketball* or re-runs of *Living Single*. It felt nice to do that for her. Anyway, one night, a few weeks before she left for undergrad at Stanford, she took pity on me."

As he worked, Jamie laughed, thinking back to that simpler time. All it took was a stiff breeze to get him going.

With Brinton's shoulders nudging his groin, not much had changed.

Jamie cleared his throat for good measure.

"You can't leave me hanging," Brinton whined. "What happened next?"

"She…let me touch her boob."

"Excuse me?" Brinton shrieked.

He rolled his eyes and smiled. How was she this cute while giving him shit?

"Now, don't get carried away. I was sixteen. Her clothes were on, and it was five seconds, max. She had on one of those oversized T-shirts. But I could tell she wasn't wearing anything but cheer shorts underneath."

In a bit of déjà vu, from his vantage point, he could see right down Brinton's top. Her velvety skin and how her chest bounced when she laughed, talked, or breathed.

It'd be his undoing if he looked too long, so he forced his eyes back up and on the job. He cleared his throat again. A signal to his wild imagination to calm the fuck down.

They were taking it slow. It was *his* idea.

"It was the sexiest thing I'd ever seen. Well, until now." He bit his bottom lip, delighted to find her grinning up at him. "I think she caught me staring."

"Oh my God—what did you do?"

"What do you think? I was wound up so tight that, right then and there, I busted in my shorts. Perfect timing for Cory to walk by. We were all mortified. He didn't speak to me for a week."

Brinton howled with laughter.

"Isn't there an amendment to the bro code?" she asked once she regained her breath. "Something covering the consensual groping of a hot sibling's titty?"

"Not in his book." He laughed. "He still won't let me sit near her at holiday parties. She's a surgeon and married with three kids, by the way."

Jamie spread his fingertips wide, then massaged the back of Brinton's scalp in tight, slow circles.

"Oh," Brinton breathed. When she swallowed a moan, the stifled sound sent a shot of molten heat straight to his crotch.

Not ideal, given her head was inches away.

"Good?" he asked, inching toward her crown.

"Mm-hmm," she answered, practically hypnotized. "Shit..."

He circled her temples.

"Tell me what you want." The urgency in his voice refused to be tamped down.

"Could you get my neck?" She tipped her head backward. When he hit the spot she liked, her eyes closed and lips parted on a gasp.

He moved down the buttery slopes of her shoulders, to her sculpted collarbone.

"Keep going," she moaned.

"Shit, baby. You know I wanna, but—"

"I know. Just—*please.*"

Her boldness lured him into an intoxicating trance. Her shoulders dug into Jamie's inner thighs. The friction felt so glorious, if not taunting him to *release.* His need was almost punishing as his erection throbbed. Another nudge and he'd go off like a shot gun, but he had to hold on.

He wanted to *savor* this.

Slowly, Jamie's fingertips drifted down her chest, following the heavy curve of her breasts. Her back arched in invitation.

"Lemme hear you," he rasped, shamelessly squeezing her breasts. "Show off for me."

Brinton stopped trying to quiet those little noises that made him want to have her on the living room floor.

"There's my sweet girl," he murmured.

"I thought about you like this all day," Brinton whispered. Her head lolled backward into his lap. He pressed her breasts together, fantasizing about how they'd feel if Brinton were bouncing in his lap instead.

"Me too, baby. And every day since you got here. Every damn night too. That's why I came. I had to—"

His rumbling groan barreled through his chest.

"I had to touch you again. I want you in the worst fucking way."

In a flash, Brinton turned her torso, then angled her head closer. Fingers wrapped around the back of his neck, she tugged Jamie down until their lips collided.

Her wet, supple tongue whipped around his, as if claiming him as *hers*. At the thought, tingles reverberated from Jamie's scalp to his toes.

As they toppled onto the rug, Jamie's broad body eclipsed hers. Brinton was a panting mess. Much to her squealing delight, he pinned both wrists above her head. Slinking down her throat, he sucked here and nipped there, until he reached those breasts he craved so intensely. Brinton mewed each time his tongue flicked over her nipples. He did it over and over again, until her flimsy camisole was soaked through. He blew cool air over the twin splotches, enchanted as each tender peak pebbled beneath his lips.

Jamie sucked Brinton's right nipple, long and hard. "You like when I worship you like this?"

"Oh, *fuck.*"

"Yes or no, sweetheart? Tell me, or I'm gonna stop."

"Yes, Jamie—I like it. I fucking like it."

Her chest peeled from the floor. He latched one of his forearms across her ribs, grounding her.

"I wanna make you feel better than you ever have." Gently, his teeth nipped her left nipple.

"More," she said, practically vibrating.

He hissed, because he *needed* more too. His dick virtually screamed *Fuck this glorious woman, you big idiot!*

Jamie shifted to his knees, refocusing his efforts to her belly button, which poked out from her camisole's lifted hem. His thumb dipped into the silken crevice. It looked perfectly ripe for his tongue. He made good on that calculation, fervently darting in and out in time with her feathery moans.

Legs clamped around his waist, Brinton writhed against Jamie's aching erection. He watched their bodies notch perfectly into place, as if uniquely designed for each other. With every propulsive thrust, a heated jolt flared at the base of his spine. *Fuck*, it felt good.

"I love when you grind on me," he whispered, eyes heavy with desire.

Between her glorious thighs, the damp fabric was practically see-through. He could feel her sweetness through his jeans. With every fiber of his being, he ached to be buried deep inside her, until he saw flashing neon lights.

Jamie bowed his head to her chest, breathing in her honeyed scent and bargaining how easy it'd be to just *give in*. But he didn't want to be that guy anymore—the one who fast-forwarded into bed. Even as he was certain that Brinton would be the best he'd ever had. They were supposed to be taking it slow. It was *his* idea.

"I wish I could feel you," she said, in that exact way that chiseled at his resolve.

What if *he* didn't touch her? He could still satisfy her— and fuck, he *needed* to. It was high time he got creative. Jamie freed her wrists and rolled onto his side. Still on her back, she inched her head onto his outstretched arm.

Taking her right hand, Jamie sucked Brinton's middle finger into his mouth, then released it with a wet, satisfying *pop*.

"Touch yourself, Brinton, if I can't. Come for me."

Brinton's soft lips pressed into Jamie's throat. Her answering moan scorched him to the bone.

"I wanna see you undone, Bee. I bet you're so fucking sexy."

"Please," she answered. "God, I'm so—it's been so long."

Jamie guided her trembling hand between her spread thighs. She hastily pushed it into her pajama bottoms. Not content to be an idle viewer, Jamie slipped his own hand into her shorts, gently clasping it over hers. Damn creative, indeed.

She bent her knees and lifted her hips. A shudder ripped through Jamie's chest, his forearms reflexively tensed, as her finger slid easily inside her tender depths. She was so fucking warm. So slippery, her need was dripping into his palm.

Jamie's mouth watered. He caged his bottom lip between his teeth.

Their joined hands moved as one through each slow, determined pulse. Like a sensual duet, her elongated moans punctuated his ragged breaths.

"Put another finger in." Selfishly, he loved that she let him take charge. "If it were me, I'd fill you 'til you couldn't fit any more in that sweet, tight—"

Jamie groaned decadently. "So fucking perfect."

"Only for you."

"You're goddamn right." He squeezed her wrist. "How'd you want me to fuck you, baby?"

"Hard," she yelped, gasping her way through another powerful spasm. "I'd want you to fuck me hard."

"Do it then."

She pumped her fingers without reservation. His balls tightened greedily each time her knuckles plunged into her soft, glistening folds. He stood corrected: watching Brinton unspool, just for *him*, was the sexiest thing he'd ever seen.

"You take direction so good," he whispered against her ear. "Now, rub that pretty little clit. I want her good and hard. But don't stop fucking yourself."

Brinton obeyed. As both hands glided ruthlessly, her supple thighs squeezed and released—again and again and again. He longed to sink his teeth into them, or wrap them around his neck.

"I'm so close," she moaned, eyes rolling back into her head.

"Not yet," Jamie demanded. "Faster."

Again, to his delight, she obeyed. Her lips parted into a smile that grew with every passing second.

"This is how you deserve to be fucked, you know that? You deserve it all."

A thick, warm bead of her arousal ran from her center and into his palm. Jamie licked his lips. He was fucking ravenous.

His hand was so slick with Brinton's desire, he struggled to grip her twisting wrist. He was so turned on he felt the torque behind his eyes. But that had to wait until he was safely under his shower's steamy spray. Or, shit—in the driver's seat of his truck. That was more likely.

"Show me how much you want it, sweetheart. I bet not as much as me."

"I do—"

"You do *what?*" Jamie answered, pleased to watch her hips see-saw against the rug with diminished control.

When her brown eyes met his, they glowed as if powered by the sun itself. "I want it—"

"Then take it, Bee."

Her hips peeled from the floor. "I'm there. I'm—"

"Come for me."

Brinton's voice broke off sharply, a piercing cry that eventually smoothed into soft, rounded moans. Jamie squeezed her wrist through each cresting wave, until her shoulders stopped shaking and eyes floated shut. He could watch her like this until the end of time.

As her body went limp in his arms, Jamie kissed her hard, letting his tongue explore every inch his body couldn't yet.

"Woman, you are a revelation," Jamie murmured, breaking their kiss. He licked her damp fingertips clean, then collapsed onto his back. Still catching her breath, Brinton's head dropped onto his chest.

"I'm sorry, I must have sounded..." Brinton laughed, covering her eyes. "I warned you. It's been a long time since I..."

He thumbed her cheek and smiled. "Please don't apologize, baby. You earned that. And I can't wait for us to finish this article."

Jamie chuckled, adjusting the enormous bulge in his jeans. When she reached out to touch him there, he groaned dramatically.

"Aht-aht," he teased, intercepting her. He kissed her knuckles. "I'm trying very hard not to fuck you in my father's guest house, remember?"

Brinton smiled into his shirt. "I'm counting the days."

"Me too." He sighed. "But it's getting late. Let me help clean up here so you can get some sleep."

"How am I supposed to sleep after *that*?" she asked coyly. Exertion had stained her dewy cheeks mulberry, and her braids fanned out around her face like a halo. Absolutely breathtaking.

"Let me know when you find out." He laughed. "I'll come by tomorrow though, after the studio. Make you another sandwich."

Sated, and limbs lazily threaded through his, Brinton stared up at Jamie dreamily. "Is that what the kids are calling it?"

# CHAPTER THIRTY

The next morning, egg yolk–yellow sun spilled across Jamie's weary eyes. After leaving Brinton last night, he had stayed up late sketching lyric ideas about her—her laugh, her smile—and had neglected to set his alarm.

It was Monday, and he was due to finish the record on Friday. He would play Yeehaw Fest that Saturday, swiftly followed by the official album launch the following Friday. Brinton's article was due to come out that same day, but she'd be back in New York by then.

That meant she was leaving Iris in seven days. He already mourned this. Almost as much as when his lips left her smooth skin last night.

But right now, he needed to get out of bed and into the studio, where his father undoubtedly waited to chew him out for being late. Again. But at least now, Jamie knew he was closer to the finish line.

He didn't check his phone, despite it vibrating like a snake pit, so he could quickly shower and change into a gray T-shirt and dark-wash jeans. Hair still sopping wet, he hopped in his truck and carved down the tree-lined dirt road. By the time he arrived at the compound, he was completely winded and, if he were honest, nauseous from the adrenaline spike. Not even the hair of the dog could stop the volcanic eruption in his gut.

Shouldering open the studio door, he was surprised to find it empty. His phone buzzed three more times. Now he was straight-up afraid to check it.

*Where the hell is everyone?*

The last resort was his father's office.

Outside the shuttered double doors, Jamie mentally prepared for an ambush. His father's voice was muffled, and he couldn't make out the details, but it didn't matter. Whatever it was, it was already a done deal.

Jamie took a deep breath and rapped on the door.

"Come in," Jamie Sr. said.

Tex and Sammi sat opposite Jamie Sr. at his antique cherrywood desk.

"You look like hell," Jamie Sr. said lightly. He gave his son an up-down, then turned back to the stack of papers in his hands.

"Sorry I'm late, Daddy," Jamie told his father as he approached. "Won't happen again."

Jamie Sr. didn't look up. "Don't write checks your ass can't cash."

"Ready for the big day?" Tex chirped, attempting to cut through the tension with a butter knife. Jamie did a double take; Tex had traded his typical dress shirt and slacks for a yellow floral Hawaiian shirt and red swim trunks.

"Yeah, sure," Jamie said, eyeing Sammi, a question in his voice. Baby blue bikini strings poked through her white, off-the-shoulder sundress.

"Oh my stars. You forgot, didn't you?" she asked. Sammi shook her head, a mix of amusement and sympathy on her face. It wasn't the first time someone had given Jamie that look. But today, it scared the hell out of him.

"No, I didn't forget. But, you know, jog my memory. A lot's happening this week," Jamie answered. He whipped his ring around his pinky so fast there was a chance that he'd sever it.

"C'mon, now, son. It's your birthday," Tex exclaimed, rising from his seat. He wrapped Jamie into a bear hug, slapping his back three times. "And many more to you, you hear?"

A moment later, Sammi was at Jamie's side. "Happy thirty-first. May your good fortune be as enduring as your stubbornness." She smiled and quickly pecked him on the cheek.

*Ain't that some shit?*

Jamie pulled his buzzing phone from his pocket and found dozens of missed calls and happy birthday texts from what looked like his entire contacts list. Forgetting his birthday was a hell of a milestone. Or, his brain had finally given out after months of toiling for an album he wanted nothing to do with.

"Yeah, I guess it slipped my mind. That would explain why the studio is empty today."

"We figured you'd want the day off," Tex exclaimed. "And besides, you gotta get ready for the surprise party."

"Well, there goes the surprise," Sammi trilled, scooping her pastel blue purse from the chair. "Tex and I set everything up. I told the gang of hooligans you call friends to turn up at noon."

That was an hour from now.

"Oh, and figured I should invite Brinton?" Sammi asked. "I'm sure she'd like to come."

Jamie smothered a grin, hoping to downplay the internal fireworks at her name. He appreciated his team, but he didn't want to broadcast the thing that made him happiest these days. He shrugged his shoulders. "Yeah, that makes sense."

"You think it's a good idea to invite a journalist who's got an angle in mind to your birthday party?" Jamie Sr. asked, drawing everyone's eyes like a magnet. "She's probably champing at the bit."

"Hell's bells, she's not like that," Jamie barked.

His father quietly sidestepped the apparent insolence. For now.

Sammi eyed Jamie apprehensively but didn't miss his silent SOS.

"Yeah, she's been getting on great with everyone," she added. "I've been talking with her about the article, and it sounds like she and Jamie have a good flow." Her voice lifted. "And it's gonna be fun. You remember fun, right?"

Jamie Sr. grunted, flipping another page. "I remember we're days out from what will be his biggest album yet."

"If Sammi says we can trust her, I see no problem with it," Tex said. "All press is good press, ain't that right?"

"I'll vouch for her," Sammi said. Jamie cast her a grateful glance, and she nodded in solidarity.

"She should come," Jamie said, a little louder. His father eyed him like he was a talking dog on a tricycle.

"Great, I'll text her," Sammi said, already tapping on her phone.

Tex crashed his hands together like cymbals. "I can't wait to get out on the jet skis."

"And I can't wait to say I told you so when you wipe out," Sammi cracked.

Tex hooked his stout arm around her shoulders. "Don't worry, darlin'. I'm taking you down with me."

Sammi cackled as they ambled through the double doors.

Jamie shoved his hands in his pockets, ready to be anywhere but there. "All right, well, I guess I'll see you later."

Jamie Sr. shuffled his papers, then set them down. "One more thing. Anything you say, she's gonna use it if it'll serve her story."

Unbeknownst to him, that was the whole damn point.

"I know."

"Remember, she's not one of us."

That stopped Jamie cold. "Are you saying that because she's Black?" he asked, rage percolating despite keeping his tone even. "For goodness' sake—"

Jamie Sr. scoffed. "Boy, don't insult me. She's not one of us because she's looking for a weakness to exploit. Something that'll look good on a cover and sell copies."

"You don't know her like I do," Jamie said quietly, his nerves in a cage fight with his racing heart.

Jamie's father leaned back, a dark smile on his face. "I know you signed a contract." He rose from behind the desk and crossed to his son. "So, when you see Kendall, who I invited, take some photos together. It'll be great for the album."

Jamie clenched his fist as his father outstretched his hand. He shook it anyway.

His father turned back toward his desk, but not before twisting the knife a little deeper between Jamie's ribs. "Oh, and happy birthday, son."

# CHAPTER THIRTY-ONE

It was a sticky ninety degrees outside, not a cloud in sight. The kind of day that demanded as little clothing as possible to be worn, drinking copious amounts of frosty beer, and then plunging into the chilled depths until the last streak of sunlight left the sky.

Jamie's birthday party was lively inside the two-story boathouse, which was tucked along the shore. Crisp white linen daybeds anchored the wraparound porch on each level, ensuring that a bad view of the lake was impossible. Liza had catered Jamie's favorites: tangy hot chicken sliders on glossed honey butter biscuits, crispy steak and jalapeño quesadillas, chopped salad, and charcuterie and fruit standing at attention on rustic wooden platters.

The pièce de résistance, however, was a seven-layer caramel cake with homemade butter pecan ice-cream. Icy buckets of beer were parked every few feet and makeshift bar stations slung top-shelf hospitality at every turn. A fleet of jet skis and a pontoon boat beckoned like a mirage, and plump inner tubes towered on the slated swimming platform halfway across the lake.

Tex and Sammi had truly outdone themselves. Jamie always appreciated them, but this show of love drove home how much of a family they'd become. Even if that family had a trove of secrets. But he wouldn't dwell on that right now.

Jamie found Cory and his wife, Priyanka, perched on a daybed on the ground level. As Cory bounced their squealing daughter, Mia, on his knee, he looked so content. Priyanka laughed as Mia squished fistfuls of her thick, raven hair.

That kind of peace once seemed impossible. But that was before Brinton filled Jamie up with promise.

"Happy birthday," Cory and Priyanka shouted in unison as Jamie plunked down next to Cory.

"Thank you for coming. It means everything to me," Jamie said, beaming.

"Well, Sammi threatened to take a switch to my ass." Cory laughed.

Priyanka narrowed her big, amber eyes and smiled. "That's because you deserve it."

"Yeah, but I *like* it when you do it," Cory countered, quickly pecking Priyanka's sculpted cheek.

"We wouldn't miss this for the world," she said through an infectious giggle.

Jamie squeezed Priyanka's shoulder and playfully swatted Cory on the head. He tickled Mia's belly. She gurgled gleefully, outstretching her teeny arms so Jamie could scoop her up.

The three friends caught up on Jamie's album, upcoming tour, and the incoming freshman sure to be the next great University of Tennessee quarterback. Eventually, Cory and Priyanka said their good-byes, taking Mia inside the air-conditioned main house.

Thankfully, Jamie still hadn't seen Kendall, who he needed like a bad case of jock itch. If it happened, he'd deal with that too. For now, he was alone.

There was no sign of Brinton. He shouldn't have been worried, but he was eager to see her. Hopefully, she'd let him run his hands through her braids again later, which, good Lord, made him hotter than tailgate asphalt.

Jamie smiled at the thought and pulled out his phone to text her when she appeared on the path leading to the shore-side bar as Kacey Musgraves's "High Horse" blared.

She practically glowed in her orange mini-dress. The ruffled hem barely skimmed the top of those lush thighs he loved so much. She had piled her braids in a high bun, and her dark sunglasses made her look quietly commanding. Sexy and mysterious. Brinton trotted toward Sammi, who squeezed her then got her acquainted with a boisterous group at the bar.

Today was definitely looking up.

"WE NEED DRINKS," Sammi screeched, hooking one arm around Brinton's waist and raising the other to the sky. "Let's tie one on."

Brinton recognized Sammi's date, Man-Bun from the Skylight, who nodded and smiled before leaning across the bar to order. She'd been at this party for two minutes and already knew it would be miles apart from the cookout on her first night. That was decidedly Jamie Crawford Sr.'s crowd.

This party, however, was Jamie Jr. to a T. String bikini-clad girls balanced on the sturdy shoulders of men ripped from an Abercrombie & Fitch ad. There was an impeccable yet unexpected soundtrack of hip-hop and contemporary country music. The vibe encapsulated Iris's young elite letting their hair down, free from the watchful eyes of their conservative elders.

A few moments later, Man-Bun, whom Brinton later learned to call Rhett, returned with three icy mason jars of what looked like lemonade.

Brinton took a whiff. The telltale bite of whiskey, lemon, ginger, and honey was a suplex to her senses.

"It's called a Tennessee Beesting." Sammi beamed. "Something Jamie requested. Kinda cute, huh?"

It was really fucking cute. Another secret they got to share.

Brinton clinked glasses with her new friends. They tipped their jars back, then hooted together as the saccharine burn singed their throats.

Sammi flipped her chestnut mane over her shoulder and hugged Brinton again. "I'm so glad you're here."

"Me too. I'm trying to take some repeated advice to live a little. And I really like Iris."

"That's what I like to hear." Sammi demurely rested a hand on Rhett's bulging bicep. "Honey, would you mind fixin' me a slider?"

"Sure, baby," he said, moon-eyed as he softly kissed her cheek. "How about you, Brinton?"

She shook her head. Sammi waited until Rhett was out of earshot. Her effervescent smile slipped into a saucy smirk. "So listen, you and me. We're friends, right?"

"Yeah, absolutely."

"Then we need to get serious. What the hell is going on between you and Jamie?"

Suddenly, Brinton's throat felt entombed in dust. She took an avoidant gulp from her glass. Of course she was thrilled to bask in the newness of her relationship with Jamie, but what made it so good was that it was *theirs*. For now, at least. And she wanted to keep it that way.

Sammi wasn't buying it and narrowed her feline green eyes. "Mmm-hmm, that's what I thought," she said, hands perched on her hips.

Brinton cut her eyes back to the lake, where a petite blonde had lost her round of chicken-fight, landing with a resounding splash. She wished they could trade places right about now.

"The article is going great," Brinton offered, which was true. But the kissing? Oh, the kissing was even better.

"I know you're here to write this story, and I'm supposed to be impartial. But I feel like y'all have something special, so I'm gonna tell you what I told him. In the interest of the album, and his daddy, if y'all are gonna sneak around, be..." Sammi tilted her head. "Careful."

Brinton's cheeks flushed. "Oh...we haven't, like, slept together."

Not that her temporal lobe wasn't smoldering with impulse.

Sammi threw back her head and cackled. It still managed to sound pretty.

"Honey, I meant to be mindful in public." She casually swirled her pointer finger across the bobbing heads and gyrating bodies around them. "Eyes everywhere. So, you gotta be discreet." She winked for added measure.

"Noted," Brinton said, grinning.

They embraced again as Rhett approached with a plate of chicken sliders. Sammi's eyes lit up. She took a bite and groaned with delight. Bumping her hip against Brinton's, she whispered, "Don't look now, but here comes the birthday boy."

Their eyes locked as he approached, as they always seemed to.

Brinton couldn't tell if she was too warm from the sunshine or the liquor. Or was it Jamie himself?

He wore navy swim trunks and flip-flops but no shirt, daring her to trace the map of taut muscle and lightly sheened skin. He'd gotten some color, which brought out the ash highlights in his elegantly disheveled hair.

Too stunned to speak, she briefly considered the firmness of their no-sex policy. Then she considered the firm V carved into his hips and firm abdominals that flexed as he breathed. Her mouth went dry.

Clearly, she needed to ban the word firm from her vocabulary until this article was done.

"Hey," she said, breath as floaty as the butterflies in her belly.

"Hey yourself." He nodded upward at Sammi and Rhett. "Sammi, thank you for the party. I don't deserve such a beautiful day."

"Well, that's certainly true." She giggled.

He pulled her in for a hug and she squealed, lightly batting him away. Jamie's eyes settled on Brinton. Slowly, he scanned her body, appreciating things nobody else had. Things she'd never even thought to appreciate.

His teeth scraped over his bottom lip. Her core jumped another hundred degrees.

"You like the drink?" he asked.

She took a long, languid sip. "I like it a lot."

He smiled at that, picking up on what had become their silent code: *I want you. I see you.*

"Perfectly balanced," Rhett said, eyeing his now-empty glass. "That zip at the end"—he hooted again—"that'll put some hair on your chest. How'd you come up with it?"

Jamie laughed, then raked a hand through his hair. Brinton could watch his bicep jump from the motion all day.

His eyes latched to hers again. "Mother Nature's got a way of putting things together just right."

She sucked in a breath.

"He's a poet and a gentleman." Sammi laughed and took Rhett by the hand. "So, *we're* fixin' to head out. You two have fun though."

Sammi was, undoubtedly, the best wingwoman who ever lived.

Rhett drained his drink in about a millisecond before Sammi dragged him on the path to the main house.

"Nice seeing y'all again," he called out.

Jamie pointed out across the lake. "I could take us on the boat for another interview, by that swimming platform. It's a little quieter, so you can record it. Plus, the boat is covered, so it'll be nice to get some shade."

Brinton smirked. "Can I trust you not to throw me overboard?"

He smiled, blue and green pyrotechnics popping in his eyes. "Guess we'll find out, huh?"

Not long later, Jamie piloted the small pontoon boat away from the party's enthusiastic splashing and toward the lake's serene depths. The last time they'd been out this far, she ended up soaking wet and sobbing.

The memory made her grip the handrail on her seat a little tighter.

Jamie slowed the boat to a stop and flipped a few controls. He meticulously checked all the illuminated screens on his navigation panel. Opening a compartment on the bow, he pulled out an anchor, then dropped it overboard. He did it all like it was second nature. She couldn't stop staring at his hands as they moved, among other things.

When he finished, he turned to face her. "Can I fix you a drink? I grabbed water, beer, and Cokes."

He strode toward the large cooler opposite her seat.

"Water would be great," she said, taking the bottle from him. She was sweating through her cover-up but didn't dare to whip it off. She'd practically be naked in her bikini. Not that he'd judge her body, but that was still…a lot. For now.

He pulled a bottle out for himself, shut the cooler, and sat down across from her.

"You know, my jaw's still sore from kissing you last night," he said, smiling shyly. "But I'm more than willing to go a few more rounds."

Heat crept up her cheeks as she grinned back at him. "Tempting as that is, I told Sammi we'd be discreet."

"Well, lucky for us, we have all night."

"Lucky me." She squeezed his knee, and he bit his bottom lip. She wanted to do the same, but instead leaned back into her seat. "Before we start the interview, I wanted to give you something for your birthday. That's why I was late."

His eyes warmed, and her heart grew a few sizes. "Bee, you didn't have to get me anything."

"Oh, you needed this. Trust me." Brinton whipped out her phone from her purse and tapped a few buttons. "I'm texting it to you now."

Jamie's phone buzzed in his pocket. He pulled it out, then grinned at the screen.

"'Good Ass R&B'…you made me a playlist? Janet Jackson, SWV and Sade…Lots and lots of Sade." He beamed.

"'Cherish the Day' is my favorite song. It's life-changing," she offered. "Nineties R&B has all the elite hits."

Eyes drifting to the screen, his brows lifted. "And Paramore?"

"Everybody loves Paramore. It's a known fact."

He laughed, hands playfully raised in defense. "I love it, Brinton. Thank you."

Hearing him say *love* made her battered little heart flutter.

"Can I hug you?" he asked.

She nodded, transfixed by his eyes refracting the sun like turquoise glitter.

He pulled Brinton into his chest, engulfing her in his spicy-whiskey scent, which was now spiked with a sunblock chaser. She could get drunk on it.

Or do something incredibly foolish. Like lick him.

Gripping her shoulder with one hand, Jamie squeezed her hip with the other. It was so warm and familiar, especially now that she understood people in Iris hugged like it was their profession. He let her go, almost too soon for her liking, and they returned to their seats. Neither was in a rush, because they beheld each other. Eagerly awaiting the other's next move.

"Is there anything off-limits—for the interview, I mean," she stammered.

"Nope. Ask me whatever you want."

She pulled her recorder from her purse, turned it on, and set it on the cushion beside her. "What fulfills you as an artist?"

Jamie scanned the waterline. He looked back at her and nodded, as if giving her permission to meet him at his most vulnerable.

"I love talking about real life. The good, the bad—everything in between. I think that's why people fall in love with country music. Why I fell in love with it, anyway. My father is one of the great country songwriters of our time. A lot of his early hits were about his relationship with my mom. They got together when he first got signed."

"She was fresh out of high school and waiting tables at a diner in town," Jamie continued. "My dad wrote a lot about how lonely it was on the road and how he feared she would eventually leave him for somebody more...available. He feared I would forget him because he was gone so much. But that's the real shit, you know? What keeps me going is that, one day, I'll share something that helps someone else too. Even if it's the worst thing I've ever experienced."

"Like what?"

He looked down at the boat's sandy deck. "Like when my mom died."

Brinton held the space for him as he exhaled softly. "No one talks about this, but I wanna tell you because I trust you'll know how to use it. To get my story out there in a way that's authentic. Tell the truth."

His eyes drifted to hers. "Everyone thinks my mom died in an accident, that she'd fallen asleep in the tub. My mom had troubles, and with my father gone so often, life got dark for her. She tried to hide it, but I think she felt like she'd paused her whole life for him. One day, when I was thirteen, I came home late after football practice. But there was an ambulance outside. The police wouldn't let me see her, no matter how hard I screamed and fought. Tex just held me back."

"My father wasn't even supposed to be there, but he had come home early from the city to beat a storm that was rolling in. He was the one who found her. I overheard him tell Tex that paramedics saw her sleeping pills by the tub. Even then, as a kid, I didn't think it was an accident. Who takes sleeping pills in the middle of the day? But she was in a lot of pain. That night, I was too."

"Jamie," Brinton breathed, shaking her head. "If this is too hard—"

He shook his head. "I wanna tell you. I need to," Jamie added, roughly rubbing his fist against his lips, as if summoning the willpower to continue.

"Later that night, I stole my dad's truck keys. Had no idea where I was going. I just couldn't be *there*. It was so fucking reckless of me, but I didn't know what else to do. It'd started to rain hard, and I couldn't drive for shit, and it was so dark out. I slammed into a tree. Gave myself a nice little concussion. Thankfully, my dad found me, took me to the hospital.

But I saw something change in him. He'd lost all trust in me, I think. Couldn't blame him. I'd put him through hell, on the worst night of his life. We never recovered from that. A part of us died that night too."

"But everything happens for a reason, right?" he asked. Jamie's voice sounded hoarse, like a bitter pill had become lodged in his throat.

"I miss my mom every damn day, but I rest easier knowing she's not hurting anymore. And I thank God for my mamaw, who helped me process it all. That, and therapy."

"You go to therapy?"

"Briefly, after my mom died. Mamaw is big into looking after yourself and wanted to make sure I was coping. I probably should've kept up with it, but my dad…He thought telling strangers your problems was"—Jamie used air quotes—"self-indulgent. So, I found other ways to deal."

"What did you do?"

"Mostly whiskey and women." Jamie scoffed. "Clearly, I got more healing to do, because talking about her is agonizing. Sometimes, I feel guilty, like if I could have done more to protect my mom, she'd still be here. But I learned in therapy that guilt is a natural part of the healing process."

He smiled at her. It was pained, but she recognized that feeling.

"Do you think talking to your dad now might help?" Brinton asked.

Jamie tutted. "That would take a miracle. Or, another tragedy. But a few nights ago, I wrote a song about my mom for the first time. Kind of like this letter asking her all the questions I never could. If she were here, I'd want to learn everything she could teach me about being a better man."

"Oh, Jamie…" Brinton whispered, the sting of fresh tears swelling behind her eyes. He moved to sit next to her and squeezed her knee.

"Hey, it's okay—I'm okay. People in town pity me because I didn't have any siblings, and my father never remarried. It's probably why everyone around me felt like they needed to micromanage every detail of my life. But I think it would have been worse if my dad had moved on. It would have been this constant point of conversation with each new person who came into our lives."

He clicked his tongue, his gaze miles away. "Instead, we buried it. And I turned out fine, right?"

"I-I'm so deeply sorry," Brinton stuttered.

His gaze found hers again. "Please, don't feel sorry for me. That's not why I told you. I told you so you'd know why I do what I do."

In that moment, she understood what made Jamie tick, what he needed most but couldn't get from his father or his team. He needed someone to listen to him. Brinton's own mother always said that her empathy was her greatest strength. Brinton liked to think it also made her good at her job.

She was grateful for the opportunity to hear him now.

"Are you going to record the song about your mom?"

Jamie sighed and dragged a hand over his jaw. "I don't know if it will see the light of day. It doesn't fit the…" He looked again to the water, as if on an expedition for the right words. "It doesn't quite feel or sound like what most people expect from me. I'll need time to make something I know will land."

"Isn't that the point of starting over? Subverting those expectations? You could release the song as a demo, test the waters? A twelve-year-old Soundcloud rapper can do it. Why can't you?"

His body tensed, and the easy smile on his lips flattened. She recalled their first conversation on the lake, how he reacted the same way to her questioning his songwriting. But this time, she knew how easily triggered he could be when pushed. She didn't want that for him either.

"Darlin', it ain't that easy. I wish it were. What if the song is no good? What if I have to go crawling back to my father?"

She touched his knee, willing him to look at her. "You have to try, at least. Promise me that."

Jamie shot her a defeated look, raked both hands through his glistening waves.

"Brinton, I appreciate you, but please—could we drop it for now?"

"Of course."

It broke her heart to see him second-guess himself. Did he think she was projecting her own anxiety onto him? Just like she'd done with Eli, who blamed her for never leaving well enough alone? Brinton's spine stiffened at the memory.

She pulled out her phone and took videos of the lake to distract herself, convinced that in his next breath, Jamie would push her away too.

Yet, to her surprise, his warm hands circled her waist. She probably should have wriggled away. They were still in view of the shore. Instead, she melted into his chest, soothed by his warm, soft breaths against her cheek.

"Thank you for believing in me, Bee," he whispered.

"Thank you for giving me something to believe in," she answered. Brinton held out her arm, snapping a picture of them together.

When she checked the screen, she didn't care that the frame was lop-sided and her eyes were closed. He flashed a boundless smile, more at ease than she'd seen before. She felt the same way.

"You wanna go for a swim?" he asked. "I know last time we were on this lake, you were understandably freaked out, so—"

Brinton didn't even hesitate. "Yeah, I do."

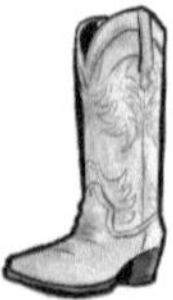

# CHAPTER THIRTY-TWO

On the wooden swimming platform, Jamie waited to help Brinton up the small set of stairs leading to the raft. He'd already swam from the boat and pulled himself out of the lake, which felt more like bathwater at this point in the day. But the combination of the water and the sun felt as good as a baptism on his skin.

"You comin' in, or am I gonna have to call the Coast Guard?" he shouted to her.

Brinton was still on the pontoon and fumbling with her purse. "I have to stow my recorder before you get any bright ideas," she called back, sticking out her tongue.

That wickedly sarcastic tongue was another thing he craved.

Then, she did something devastating. She reached down to the hem of her dress and peeled it over her head, revealing a white bikini. It had a small red print—flowers? It looked like a fitted bra on top with a sweet little bow detail in the center that begged to be nipped with his teeth. His eyes dragged down to the bottoms. They cut high on the sides, clinging to those heartbreaking hips, and kissed her belly button.

When she shook her braids loose from her top knot, they cascaded down her shoulders and back in slow motion.

*Have mercy.*

This woman was trying to kill him out here.

He swallowed hard, averting his eyes before he needed to cover his crotch with his hands. Jamie crouched down, with his back to her, and busied himself with smoothing the nonexistent wrinkles from the plush towels he'd laid out for them.

"When you're ready, swim over, and I'll help you up," he said.

A hearty splash. He turned around as her head poked through the surface. Her eyes sparkled, her smile blinding as she kicked and floated on her back like a mermaid. Jamie wasn't big on fairy tales, but Prince Eric had it pretty good.

"Thought you said we were going to swim? Are you a man of your word or not?" she asked, laughing.

"Rude of you to besmirch my honor. Gonna pay for that, Shaw," he said, diving in headfirst.

When he came up for air, he playfully splashed her, and she gave a generous splash back. They raced each other in laps, which she handily won, and competed to see who could hold their breath longer. Which she also won. Or did he let her win? At this point, he was too focused on how much he enjoyed the shrill peaks of her laughter.

Eventually, he hoisted her onto the swimming platform. They lay on their backs, letting the lazy afternoon sun heal what ailed them. Make them whole again. As her chest rose and fell gently, he wondered if she had fallen asleep. From this angle, he could finally make out the tiny cherries printed all over her bathing suit.

A Freudian slip was waiting to jump out of him, so he shut his eyes.

"Can I tell you something?" she asked, cutting through the stillness. "You've been so open with me today, and I need to clear this up."

"Yeah, of course," he said, swallowing his sudden uneasiness.

She sat up on her towel, and he followed.

"I didn't have the stomach flu when we met at the Grammys." She exhaled deeply. "I wasn't hungover or whatever else the internet said happened. Jamie, I was having a panic attack—a bad one. A lot of things have happened in the last few years. Unchecked shit I haven't dealt with. Plus, I was nervous to be there and interview you and all those wildly famous people. Anyway, it all came to a head that day. I've lived with anxiety and panic attacks for years. Sometimes, I can breathe and calm myself down. But other times, it feels like I'm dying. And being chronically on edge makes it hard for me to connect with new people."

She broke off with an uneasy laugh. "Hence why I have no friends. Well, except for my sister and twelve-year-old neighbor. Which, I know, is a big flex. And it's the reason my ex-boyfriend dumped me."

He rested a palm on her knee. "I'm so sorry you had to go through something so painful publicly. I want you to know that I'll be here for you in whatever way you need. And for the record, that ex of yours, he sounds like a Grade-A shithead."

Brinton laughed bitterly. "He was. So I try to be normal, because once people know…"

"You've been masking. I've heard of it while trying to understand my own shit."

She nodded. "There's a defined list of things I'm allowed

to be stressed about as a Black person—and especially as a Black woman." She counted on her fingers. "Police brutality. Hypothetical unplanned pregnancies. Struggle love with a dusty ex responsible for said unplanned pregnancy. And forget about it if I cry, because Black women are forbidden from expressing anything but anger."

She shook her head. "But I've got an entire spectrum of feelings. The real world, however, punishes you when you show that."

Jamie understood. He'd hid his pain since the day his mother died. "It must be exhausting. How do you—"

Jamie stopped himself and closed his eyes, choosing his words carefully. He owed her that.

"Would you be open to talking to somebody about it?" he asked. "Or medication? I tried antidepressants for a while after my mom passed. They helped."

"I don't want to be doped up to numb the pain. It seems so easy for everyone else. Why not for me?"

"Honey, if someone tells you it's easy for them, they're full of shit. One day, you might be ready to take that next step."

She tipped her head against his shoulder. "I think being here has been good for me in that way. Having time and space to think, breathe fresh air…Swim in murky lakes."

He smiled, then his lips grazed the back of her hand.

"Only my mom and sister knew the truth about the Grammys. And now you." A tear raced down her cheek, and she impeded it with a flick of her wrist.

But he wanted her to let herself cry.

"Sorry, I'm supposed to be interviewing you, not having another mental breakdown."

He wasn't surprised to hear what had been bothering her. He knew grief when he saw it. And he knew how devastating it was to exhume skeletons she'd rather keep buried.

"Thank you for telling me," he said, tracing her shoulder. It was as warm and soft as he remembered. "But you ain't ever gotta apologize to me for being who you are."

"Thank you, Jamie."

He leaned in and kissed her, softly and deliberately chaste. But satisfying.

"I'm not supposed to do that out here, but I decided I don't give a damn," he said, grinning.

"I'm glad you don't." Sighing, she wrinkled her nose. "I can't handle any more talk about feelings. Not good for my delicate constitution and all," she said with a laugh. "But...I do want to keep hanging out."

So they did. She told him about her lovably unhinged sister and her eternally optimistic mom, the women she loved and trusted more than anyone. He revealed that he and his father had become strangers, with the mixing of business and familial duty fracturing them like an ice pick. They talked about their favorite '90s nostalgic movies. She told him about Gael and the book club. Jamie told her about how, junior year, he and Cory got duped into buying dime bags of oregano from the resident burnout. Jamie's house smelled like lasagna for weeks.

A little later, the sun retreated behind the treeline and protracted shadows waltzed across the lake. From the boat, Jamie could make out a few party stragglers slurping beers on the shore. Yet, once again, he wasn't ready for the night to end. He hoped she wasn't either.

"Do you wanna come to my cottage?" he asked.

"Like a date?"

An inferno raged beneath his cheeks. It had been a long time since he'd been on a date without the handshake deal of no-strings sex. But what if she thought he was boring? *Sex* he was good at. But actual *courtship*? An entirely different world.

"You can say no though. You're probably busy with the article," he said, flipping his ring like it might conjure Aladdin's genie.

She cocked her head, then smiled. "I might be able to squeeze it in."

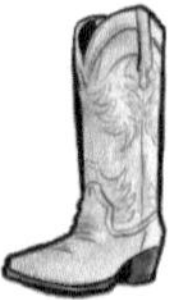

# CHAPTER THIRTY-THREE

As Jamie's Silverado crept down the asphalt, he was quiet. Brinton wondered if he knew what she was thinking. Because this house was certainly not giving cottage.

Sure, its footprint more resembled a bear cub compared to the compound's yeti, but make no mistake. The two-story, stone-front lake house was fit for a king. Or rather, a prince.

Jamie opened her door, but her eyes were transfixed on the house, which rested on a sprawling, impeccably manicured lawn that unfurled right up to Crawford Lake's edge.

She took his outstretched hand. "You said you lived in a cottage? I was thinking little-old-lady-with-ten-cats and a closet full of peppermints that expired in nineteen eighty-seven."

He laughed. "Well, it is a cottage. Or, it was. There used to be a sweet little house on this land that my mom fell in love with, so my dad bought it. They were supposed to retire here." He shut the door. "After she died, I think it broke his heart to look at it. So he tore it down and built this for me. Since then, I've done some renovations"—he rolled his eyes, amused—"Sammi ordered some renovations before we did this *Architectural Digest* video a few years back. But it's a real special property. I love it here."

"I can see why," she said.

Inside, the vibe was high-end frat-house, in a good way. In the living room, oversized leather couches in shades of weathered tobacco and pecan matched the exposed wood beams striping the vaulted ceiling. On the walls, contemporary abstract art mingled with portraits of his music idols, including Johnny Cash, Jimi Hendrix, and his father. A massive flatscreen TV crowned the stone mantle, along with a dozen framed, sun-bleached stills of his friends and family. At the far end, Jamie's gleaming Grammy.

"Make yourself at home. I'll only be a minute," Jamie called out from somewhere upstairs.

Brinton sank into the sumptuous leather and imagined him doing the same. Dreaming. Writing. Definitely playing video games, which she confirmed after plucking a rogue PS5 controller from beneath her back. A dog-eared copy of *Their Eyes Were Watching God* lounged on the mahogany coffee table, atop a crisp stack of papers.

A few days ago, on the drive home from their Turkey Bay trip, Brinton had told Jamie it was her favorite book. Still, she was touched to see that he'd read it. Knowing that he'd definitely read it for *her*. She opened it, admiring his sharp, all-caps handwriting in the margins, the blue and yellow highlights streaking the pages like watercolor.

Beneath it, there was a stack of equally graffitied lyric sheets, relics of his many months of dedication. As she thumbed the pages, admiration swelled between her ribs. She hoped her article gave him everything he wanted.

A moment later, Jamie bounded down the stairs, a cozy-looking blanket in one hand, a fancy-looking bottle of whiskey in the other, and an ear-splitting grin on his gorgeous face.

"You ready for the best date of your life?"

After Jamie built a roaring bonfire in the front yard, they shared the bottle of whiskey and leftover caramel cake Liza had graciously sent over. They took turns picking songs from Jamie's Spotify account on his phone. The music drifted out from his truck speakers, the low-beam headlights erecting a golden oasis around them.

As "Weak" by SWV faded out, Brinton softened against Jamie's chest. His arms draped protectively over her shoulders, she was content as his even, whiskey-sweet breaths warmed her cheek.

"My turn," he whispered, nuzzling against her neck. The prickles of stubble enlivened her insides like a shaken snow globe. She tipped her head back, thrilled to find his supple lips eagerly awaiting hers. His tongue teasingly circled hers as he traced his thumb along her collarbone. Her body buzzed with anticipation.

"But you're gonna need to stand for this one."

She whined in mock protest. Jamie pecked her on the lips once more and smiled, then pushed himself off the ground. He tapped play on his phone before pulling her to her feet.

Coiling one hand around her waist, he drew her into his chest, melting her into him. When his free hand found hers, she interlaced their fingers. The weeping guitar of "If Tomorrow Never Comes" by Garth Brooks enveloped them as they danced.

"This song is beautiful," she whispered. Even though they were dancing, it felt like she was floating.

As they gently rocked side to side, the fire painted his skin a burnished gold. Jamie's eyes glinted like gemstones.

"It was one of my mom's favorites," he said. "She would listen to it a lot when my dad was on the road, mostly crying alone in her room. I used to think it was such a sad song—this heartbreaking confession about how quickly life passes you by. But now, I see it as an emblem of cherishing every moment with someone while you got it. Now, when I hear it, I'm gonna think about you."

She leaned her forehead against his chest, breathing in his smokey-sweet scent. Her heart was full enough to burst. But that'd be beautiful too.

"You know, my mom would have loved you," Jamie said.

"I wish I could have met her," Brinton answered through the emotional lump in her throat. Her lips eagerly found his again.

Eventually, they settled down, content to watch the bonfire let out its final sigh.

"Did you get everything you wanted for your birthday?" Brinton asked.

He leaned down, then kissed her forehead. "I did now."

After Jamie took Brinton home, he sat on his couch, hunched over his notebook, reworking a verse for a new song. Something to crystalize his prismatic feelings for Brinton. He wanted to share a lot more with her. He wanted to be hers.

*Holy shit.*

Something unnamable but undeniable swirled in his gut and flooded him with endorphins. He felt it when he held her and every time he looked into her eyes. He felt it down to his bones. She'd wanted to take things slow, which he was more than happy to do, but he didn't want her to leave Iris next week without knowing that he wanted to be together. Like, *official.*

They still had to figure out how to do that strategically, of course, but he'd solve that too.

There was a knock at the door. For a moment, Jamie's excitement got the best of him; was it Brinton? He'd only left her an hour ago, but he wouldn't turn down a few more together. He opened the door to find Kendall smiling wryly, an open bottle of champagne in hand. She wore a crisp white denim corset top and matching mini skirt that only looked angelic.

"Happy birthday, Mr. Crawford," she purred in her best Marilyn Monroe homage. She pushed past him and beelined for the wet bar, which was built into a stone wall near the kitchen. The champagne bottle clanked on the distressed wood countertop as she rifled through cabinets.

He dragged a hand down his jaw. She always had a way with timing. "Ken, come on. It's late, and I've got an early morning."

Kendall ignored him and filled two champagne flutes, pouring until fizz gushed over the rim. "I thought I was being fashionably late, but I had to find out from Tucker Hayward —who you know I hate—that you'd already left your own birthday party. And without getting the very best gift of all?"

She met him at the front door, her black-heeled boots clomping across the hardwood, and pushed the glass into his chest. Jamie set it on an end table.

Kendall clicked her tongue, then drained her glass in a single swoop. "C'mon, Jamie. This is our tradition. We both know you're not one to change."

*Change.* Hadn't that been what all these months were about? He remembered what Brinton had said a few days ago in his father's recording studio.

*Everyone has a chance at redemption.*

Brinton believed in him, and he wanted to be a better version of himself, for *her.*

In this moment, he needed to own up that it was his own fault that he became known as the Heartbreak Prince. Not Kendall's, or his team's, or the media's, or whatever bullshit excuse he'd made over the years. Kendall had opened her heart to him, and he left her hollow.

He needed to make this right.

"Let's get to unwrapping your present, shall we?" As she

popped brass buttons down the front of her top, Jamie rested his hands on her shoulders to stop her.

"Kendall, this part of our lives…It's in the past."

He exhaled deeply, still holding her shoulders steady. "I've met someone who I really care about. So this can't happen anymore."

Jamie dropped his hands. She stumbled backward, clutching her chest like, once again, he'd hollowed her out.

Her eyes were wide and glassy. "The journalist?"

He nodded. "Brinton."

"Your daddy know?" Her typically syrupy voice sounded pinched, as if the oxygen couldn't come fast enough.

Jamie considered lying. Kendall and his father were clearly a united front. But like with the ghostwriting and the Heartbreak Prince persona, he was done carrying that weight.

"No," he admitted. "And I'd like the chance to tell him."

She slipped her phone from her back skirt pocket, then flipped the screen to show she'd highlighted Jamie Sr.'s number in her Contacts. She was one tap away from torching Jamie's fresh start. His redemption.

"It don't gotta be like this," Jamie pleaded, scrambling for a few spare moments to *think*.

"I'm sure he'd disagree," she snapped. But there was something more than anger in her eyes. A flicker of pain. It was probably always there, but he'd chosen to ignore it. Like the lies he'd told, it was *easier* in the moment than to do the right thing. He stepped toward her. "I owe you an apology. I've owed it to you for a long time. I thought, if we kept this casual thing going, somehow it'd make up for the fact that I wasn't brave enough to tell you the truth. I should've been more careful with your heart when we were together, and I regret that I wasn't."

She stared at him for a few tortuous seconds, thumb

hovering over the call button. Then, miraculously, she slipped the phone back into her pocket. Leaning on her heels, she roughly swiped a thick black mascara tear that streaked her reddened cheek.

"Why now?" she demanded. "All this time, you've been sitting on this revelation? You met somebody else, and then—"

"Look," he started. "I fucked up, and I'm trying to be better. About a lot of things. I've never *really* been with somebody, but I want to try. I need to. And I want that for you too."

"So why not me?" She laughed bitterly. "What didn't I do? Or say. Or give? We were so good together, things were—we could have made it, you know? The way I felt about you was real."

Jamie shook his head, unsure of what to say. "Do you really believe that though? With our teams telling us what to say, where to go. It wouldn't have...I couldn't give that to you."

Her lips parted like she wanted to speak, but she didn't.

"Kendall, I'm truly sorry."

Unexpectedly, she stepped forward, arms slipping beneath his. She gripped his shoulder blades. "Deep down, I knew it too," she rasped into his chest. "It's just that, I wanted it to be real. So fucking bad. And I've wanted to hear you say you're sorry for so long. It's been burning me up inside. I was so angry. But—I wanna move on. I think I needed to hear you say it."

He let her cry in his arms, let her feel what she needed to feel, until they said their good-byes and her waiting SUV's taillights faded into the dust.

# CHAPTER THIRTY-FIVE

*B*rinton bunched the spread towel between her knuckles. As the midday sun caressed her naked body, it was no match for the intensifying heat filling her belly and between her thighs. A familiar tightening that affirmed she was so, so close.

As her back pressed into the swimming platform, waves lazily lapping its edge,

Brinton's thighs trembled against the plush terry cloth. Her hips shot forward with the force of a bullet. Jamie's broad shoulders parted her legs while his greedy lips, tongue, and fingers performed sorcery. She didn't consider the top of a man's head especially beautiful, but how he moved—Jamie's was a damn masterpiece.

Teeth bruising her bottom lip, she grunted through each thrilling wave that crashed over her. Thankfully, he was steadfast in his delicious torture. Enough to take her *right to the edge,* then pulling back when she violently shuddered. Why didn't she let this man ruin her sooner?

*Clank.*

She couldn't place the sound's origin or speak coherently

as her orgasm barreled toward her with Tasmanian Devil–gusto.

*Clank. Clank. Clank.*

"Don't you hear—"

He glanced up with an appropriately devilish grin. "No, but this is the part where you wake up."

As endorphins threatened to rip her in two, she screeched, "Wait—what?"

Brinton opened her eyes, then bolted upright. She was safely in bed, inside the guest house's quiet confines on a still-dark Saturday morning. Five days had passed since Jamie's birthday, and she'd barely seen him. He'd been finalizing the album, shooting photos for his *Landmark* spread, and in marathon meetings with the label. This did, however, give her some much-needed time to write and join Sammi for surprisingly humbling Dolly Parton–themed Zumba classes.

Every night though, he'd stopped by to kiss her goodnight. Still, she'd missed him. So much that even her subconscious had conspired against her. She was desperate for skin-on-skin *contact*. Then she remembered their no-sex pact, simultaneously the smartest and stupidest thing she'd ever agreed to.

Worse yet, she was leaving Iris in two days.

The article was nearly done, meaning it was only a matter of time before they could allow themselves to explore every facet of their bodies. She wanted him, she was sure, but would he want her if he knew how fragile she really was?

Eli was the last person Brinton slept with. While it had been over a year ago, the memory still haunted her. That night, she had lain in bed for hours, nauseous from another spiraling migraine. Eli had gone to a friend's party in DUMBO. She couldn't stand upright without wanting to vomit, let alone have the energy to watch him and his trust fund posse debate whether Apple or Facebook was the bigger disrupter—the original chicken-or-the-egg conundrum.

At some point amid her fever dream, Eli had climbed into bed beside her, snaked an arm around her limp body, and pulled her close. He smelled like stale cigarettes and Baccarat Rouge 540. This wasn't the first time he had come home smelling like another woman. Brinton should have been furious, but did she have the right when she couldn't show up for him, like someone with fewer sensitivities?

"How are you feeling?" His breath scorched her clammy neck.

"I'm in a lot of pain. I can't sleep."

"Everyone asked about you. They're starting to think I made you up." Eli had dropped that line so frequently that it deserved a laugh track in the shit-com that was their relationship. He slowly stroked her waist with his free hand, which made her teeth clench. "I thought about you in the cab the whole way home…"

He dipped his hand into the waistband of her shorts, parting her thighs and rubbing against her. It should have felt good, but her body stiffened. She couldn't bear another ounce of sensation.

"I know it's been a while, but how about tomorrow?" she pleaded.

Roughly, he pulled his hand away. "Sure, fine." He flipped onto his side, his back now facing her. It wasn't fine. But he had known how bad things had gotten for her—she had been too ashamed to tell Shay or her mom at that point—and stayed with her anyway.

She felt like she owed him something.

"Hey," she said, her voice cracking at its peak. "It's okay. Come here."

He rolled over. "Yeah?"

She nodded.

He dragged her shorts down her thighs, pushed her on her back, and pressed his weight on top. His tongue was forceful and flooded her mouth with the aftertaste of espresso and pizza rolls. She fought the urge to gag and focused on proving to him that his invested time had been worth it. That she was worth it.

She wasn't nearly wet enough and didn't call his name as loudly as he wanted. She was too disoriented to twist into the positions he liked. But, curiously, when he finished, and she lay awake in the bed, the pain radiating from every cell stopped firing. It's when she had accepted that if she distracted herself well enough, she could escape almost any pain, even if only for a little while. Eli had ended things a week later, but not before telling her how bad it would make him look to his friends.

But that was in the past.

Rolling onto her side, she squeezed her pillow over her head, smothering her self-doubt. She couldn't imagine sex with Jamie being anything but spectacular. This was all such a surprise, even thinking of him this way, but as they grew closer, his smiling face had become a solid foundation for her runaway emotions.

Damn, she needed to see him.

At least she'd see him that night at Yeehaw Fest. Unfortunately, so would a gnashing crowd of a hundred thousand strong; the thought of which made her gut seize and stretch like saltwater taffy. But she could handle it, because Jamie would be there to ground her, as he always did.

*Clank. Clank. Clank.*

That unmistakable noise again. Bleary-eyed and more than a little annoyed that her fantastic sex dream had been interrupted, she snatched her phone from the nightstand. It was 6:03 a.m.

The sound was coming from a large side window overlooking the vegetable garden. She kicked the quilt off her legs and slipped out of bed. When she pulled back the curtains, a tiny pebble bounced off the glass. To her surprise —and absolute delight—she followed its trajectory and found Jamie standing in a patch of grass below. He wore his typical jeans and T-shirt, which, to her dismay, he always looked good in. But today, he added an orange baseball cap turned backward. One of those vicious things men did that made them look so lethally sexy despite requiring the same effort it took to blink.

She opened the window. "Are you crazy?" she shout-whispered.

He smiled, gripping something in his hand. "Lordy, woman, you sleep like the dead. I was fixin' to run out of pebbles."

She tried to hide the smile bursting behind her lips. "Do you know what time it is?"

"Foreday in the morning."

She cocked her head, amused. His little folk-isms had grown on her.

"It's early." He laughed. "And sorry about that. I was thinking you'd wanna go on a side-quest before my sound-check? I want you to meet a very special woman in my life."

"A woman?" Brinton's heart disintegrated in her chest. There'd been another woman this entire time?

He flicked up his shoulders. "I think she'd like you, and I figured it would add something to your article. You know, see the real people in my life?"

"The real people in your life?"

Un-fucking-believable. Brinton had half a mind to chuck pebbles—or something heavier—down at him.

"My mamaw lives in a retirement community down the road. Loves to watch me sing, but a music festival ain't ideal for an eighty-two-year-old with asthma. So, I'm gonna bring the show to her."

Brinton laughed, shucking off her panic. His mamaw—of course. "Give me ten minutes."

Jamie had parked his truck on a service entrance obscured by tall hedges.

"You look beautiful," he said, pulling her into one of his famous hugs. She'd changed into a blue seersucker dress with ties at the shoulders and brown sandals that felt meeting grandma–appropriate.

"Thank you." She cast him a suspicious look. "Are you sneaking us out of here?"

Jamie grinned. "Something like that."

Before he turned the key in the ignition, he typed something on his phone. Her phone dinged—a text message with a link to a playlist.

"'Yeehaw Summer,'" she said, reading from her screen. "You made this for me?"

"Mm-hmm. Required listening. Lots of my favorite artists and some others I figured you'd like too. If you want, we can throw it on now."

She nodded, then connected her phone to the Bluetooth speakers. They pulled off to "Wide Open Spaces" by The Chicks. Brinton smiled, grateful as the morning sun tiptoed up the horizon.

Twenty minutes later, Jamie pulled down the cinematically long driveway of Iris Grove Senior Estates. It led them to an impressive two-story building that had a *Gone with the Wind*–worthy balcony on the ground floor. Handsome English Ivy climbed up its brick facade. Nearby, a dozen cottages were nestled among the freshly cut lawn and mature magnolia trees.

Jamie inched into a parking spot. "Not bad, huh?"

"Not at all. She lives here alone?"

"Well, hardly alone. Pop-Pop—my grandfather—passed away about five years ago, but she's settled in nicely here. Has lots of friends, plays tennis every morning, and learned three languages since she moved in. She's an absolute firecracker."

His thumbs drummed on the steering wheel. "I've never introduced her to one of my…"

He cocked his head, clearly fishing for the right word.

Brinton wondered the same thing. "Friends?" she asked, hesitant, heart deflating a little at the thought. Though friends-who-canoodled-in-dark-alleys-and-other-venues didn't quite fit either.

Without hesitation, he shook his head, eyes cutting from the parking lot to meet hers. "Brinton, you're more than my friend."

As cool relief filled her chest, she smiled. "I can't wait to meet your mamaw."

That was mostly true. Often, Brinton was nervous to meet new people, and this felt like a metric ton of added pressure. What if Mamaw thought she was too curvy, too melanated, or too…*not* Kendall Chase? Would that change his feelings about her? Her thumbnail sliced into an already shredded cuticle as she tried to fix her face into a neutral position.

As she followed Jamie through the garden path toward the cottages, Brinton's hands were slicked with sweat. Her heart pounded in her chest. They stopped in front of a white cottage with gray shutters that was designed like a cozy farmhouse. When Jamie touched her shoulder, she jumped.

"Bee, you don't gotta be nervous," he said.

"I know, it's stupid…"

"It's not stupid. I get nervous every time I step foot on stage. It's normal. But she is gonna love you."

Brinton blew out a breath. "I'll picture her in her under-wear. That works, right?"

"Oh God. Please don't," Jamie barked through laughter.

He knocked on the door. Moments later, a woman appeared. She was tall, with skin so smooth and clear she looked far younger than someone in her 80s. She wore a baby blue cardigan and matching pants that brought out her aquamarine eyes. Brinton now knew where Jamie got them from. Her thick, silvery-gray hair was smoothed into a neat ponytail.

"It's about time you showed up," she said, her accent nectarine-sweet and prim.

"Are you kidding me? It's been a week," Jamie said.

She pulled him into a tight hug. "A week too long. And would it kill you to get a haircut? You look like a Beatle."

Brinton imagined him more like a surfer who'd traded his board for boots. He adjusted his hat over his tousled waves. She tried not to drool as his biceps jumped.

"The Beatles are iconic." Jamie grinned. "I wouldn't mind that."

Jamie's mamaw appraised Brinton and gasped. "Well, aren't you as pretty as a picture?"

"She is," Jamie affirmed. "Mamaw, this is Brinton. My girlfriend."

Jamie took Brinton's hand and squeezed. This was a good thing, because her heart stalled mid-thud. *Girlfriend.* She hadn't been someone's girlfriend in so long the word sounded foreign. But she liked the sound of it from his lips. He caught her eye, smiling like he'd won a medal. She beamed back like she knew she had.

"She's a journalist writing an article about me," he explained.

"Yes, I've heard all about it."

Jamie and Brinton exchanged confused looks.

"Oh, honey, it's a small town. People will talk about the color and shape of their you-know-what if it serves them." She turned to Brinton. "I'm Emma Lou, but you can call me Mamaw."

"I'm honored to meet you," Brinton said earnestly. By now, she knew better than to extend her hand. Instead, she stepped forward to hug her. Emma Lou embraced her firmly, enveloping her like a fuzzy robe. Another thing she must have passed on to Jamie.

Once Brinton left Emma Lou's cocoon, Jamie leaned down and whispered against her ear, "That's my girl."

Soon, they huddled at the round, wooden table in the middle of the kitchen. The room was cozy, teeming with the character and charm of a life well-lived, including a collection of flea market glasses and dishes on open shelves and a brigade of family photos in mismatched frames on the walls. Pink roses, fresh-cut from the garden, in tall glass vases dotted nearly every corner of the room.

Emma Lou had the head chef send over flaky buttermilk biscuits and gloriously tart strawberry jam. She also made the most luscious soft-scrambled eggs and buttery grits Brinton had ever tasted.

"More orange juice?" Emma Lou asked. She started pouring into Brinton's half-full glass before she could answer.

"Thank you, that would be great," Brinton said. She pitched an amused look Jamie's way.

Emma Lou retrieved a blue etched glass from the shelf, filled it to the brim, then set it before Jamie. "I know your daddy won't let you have this when you gotta sing, but he ain't here," she said, a satisfied grin on her face.

"Yes ma'am," Jamie said. He drained it in a flash.

"Brinton, how are you finding it here in Iris? I suspect my sweet boy has been hospitable?"

"I love it. I've met some amazing people. I also think sweet tea is officially running through my veins," she said, laughing. "And it's been incredible spending time with Jamie."

From across the table, he regarded her like he was admiring one of Earth's natural wonders, like everything she said was valuable and worth preserving. Blissfully, her cheeks warmed.

"Once Yeehaw Fest is done, I've got a few more places I wanna show you, if you're up for it?" Jamie asked.

"That would be great," she said.

Great was an understatement. After nearly two weeks in Iris, Brinton was more game for life than in the last two years. When she first arrived, she felt so miserably out of place, and she couldn't wait to finish the story and go home. But as the days passed, these serene moments with Jamie went by too quickly.

"And when will you be leaving us? I hope not too soon," Emma Lou said.

Brinton's optimism cracked under reality's crushing weight. "I'm finalizing the article now, then it's back to New York City on Monday."

That was two days from now. She felt confident about her work so far, but she'd also done it in a silo, insulated from the prying eyes and rampant criticism at work. At some point, she had to send the draft to Rich before it was published next Friday. It was a thought that kept needling its way into her subconscious, but in this peaceful moment, she tamped it back down.

For once, she wouldn't let fear fuck up her day.

Emma Lou clasped her hands together. "Well, that means we gotta make the most of every second."

Brinton genuinely smiled back at her. "I couldn't agree more."

"Mamaw, how about I play a new song for you and the girls?" Jamie asked. "I got my guitar out in the truck."

Brinton checked her phone. It was only eight. They had plenty of time before he was due in Nashville for the eleven o'clock soundcheck.

"Oh, I'd be pleased as punch." Emma Lou beamed, then turned to Brinton. "You know, Jamie has quite the fervent fan base. He plays for us in the garden every week—I have to beat those old biddies off with a stick. Especially Cheryl McClain. Don't be fooled by her smile. Her lips are as loose as her—"

"Mamaw," Jamie barked.

"I was going to say morals, but I suppose both work," she said, a sly smile on her face. "The sweet Lord can strike me down if I'm lying."

Emma Lou began clearing Jamie and Brinton's plates from the table, but he intercepted her and placed them inside the extra-deep white enamel sink.

She winked at Brinton, who giggled. "Cheryl likes her men old enough to shoot whiskey but young enough not to need a little pill, if you follow me."

"Wait—I found a new angle for my story," Brinton said, hand waving in front of her. "'Country's prince finds happy ending with sexy octogenarian.'"

"You'd like that," Jamie said, rolling his eyes before scrubbing calcified grits from a copper pot.

Emma Lou laughed, leaning close to her. "Oh, we're gonna get on famously."

# CHAPTER THIRTY-SIX

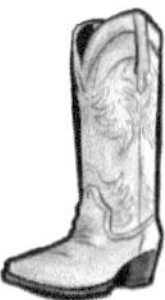

The garden felt like stepping inside a Monet painting. Iris Grove staff had lined up three rows of white, fold-down chairs on the lawn in front of the large redwood pergola. On either side, there were sweet bushes full of red tulips, African marigolds, white zinnias, and pink roses, all meticulously pruned and offset by a perimeter of tall, sharply angled hedges.

Brinton stood a few feet behind the last row of chairs as women in groups of twos and threes filed in, followed by a few grumpy grandpa-types she assumed were their husbands. She had planned to watch the performance from this vantage to avoid drawing too much attention to herself. After all, this concert was for Jamie's mamaw, not her.

Emma Lou was seated in the first row and motioned for Brinton to join her. Most of the seats were filled now, but Emma Lou patted the sole empty one beside hers. Brinton's anxious heart thawed a little. She couldn't say no.

Brinton snaked through the crowd, but as she was about to sit, another older woman plopped down instead. She wore a violently pink floral maxi dress, and her severe pixie haircut screamed "I would like to speak to the manager."

"Thanks for saving me a seat, Emma Lou," the woman quipped through a pert Tennessean accent. "I'd never miss Jamie play. Who knows, one day I might become your granddaughter." She unleashed a spiraling, wheezing laugh. The portly man beside her cringed.

"Good morning, Cheryl," Emma Lou said, her tone like honey with a little vinegar splashed in. "I do apologize, but this seat is taken."

"Oh, that's fine, Emma Lou," Brinton squeaked. "I'm good in the back—"

Emma Lou's palm floated over the chair. "Oh, no such thing. Your seat is right here."

"And who are *you?*" Cheryl asked, winded from all the self-indulgence. She twisted her thin red lips as she mused to herself. "Oh, my mistake. You must be staff. I heard we're getting some new girls in housekeeping. You're gonna need something to pull back all that—" Cheryl reached out to snatch one of Brinton's errant braids, which had slipped over her shoulder, but Brinton swiftly flicked it back.

*Ah, there's that Southern Hospitality I've been bracing for.*

The last thing Brinton wanted was to embarrass Emma Lou. But she didn't endure all that she had to be racially profiled in a rose garden on a Saturday morning.

Brinton started to speak, but Emma Lou grabbed her hand.

"Her name is Brinton, and she's writing a wonderful story about Jamie for *Landmark*. If you aren't otherwise engaged in indelicate conversation at the Piggly Wiggly, you should read it. And if you make one snide comment to or about Miss Brinton to anyone in this town, I'll ensure you're served nothing but pigeon peas and saltines until the New Year. I trust you know I'm friendly with Chef Roberts and all of our hardworking staff. Do you understand me clearly? Because if I have to repeat myself, I promise, I won't be so polite."

Cheryl's lips stretched into a pained yet obsequious grin. Slowly, she rose from the chair. "Well, I better take my seat. I see they've added a few more in the back. Nice meeting you, Brinton. And good to see you, Emma Lou."

"I'll see you at church tomorrow morning," Emma Lou said, her smile real and triumphant.

Brinton took her seat. When Cheryl was out of earshot, Emma Lou leaned in and whispered, "There are three Bs in this world I can't stand: bullies, busybodies, and bigots. Cheryl McClain found a way to be all three."

Emma Lou patted Brinton's knee, and gratefully, Brinton sandwiched her hand on top and squeezed. Moments later, Jamie stepped onto the pergola, an acoustic guitar strapped around his shoulders. He launched into the jangly opening chords of "Table for One."

The intimate crowd cheered as he sang, pitch-perfect and powerful despite no microphone or amplifiers. And when he hit the soaring chorus, Brinton could only marvel. She'd seen him perform in various social media posts, but watching Jamie in the flesh was simply electrifying. Her eyes refused to blink and lungs declined to exhale.

Brinton couldn't contain all the feelings he summoned in her. One day, she knew, they could swell into something more…permanent. Admittedly, that was a huge step. While she wasn't there yet, she longed for it just the same.

She already adored how he made her feel seen in a way she hadn't before. She adored that he made her feel safe enough to second-guess her fears. She adored that he graciously gave back to the people he cared about, including a discerning group of senior citizens.

She *adored* him.

"Thank y'all so much," Jamie said, politely motioning for

the rowdy seniors to simmer down. "I've got one more, a new one nobody's ever heard before…because I wrote it a few days ago."

Brinton beamed. That meant Jamie was sharing a song that he—not a ghostwriter—wrote. His fresh start. This was why he'd brought her there. Jamie looked nervous, which she certainly understood. She'd rather sacrifice herself to the 6 Train rats than unearth her most intimate feelings.

"This song is dedicated to the most important women in my life, my late mother, MaryBell Crawford. And my mamaw—who y'all know and love as much as I do—Emma Lou Chambers," he said.

His eyes once again locked on Brinton's. She swallowed hard.

"And another extraordinary woman who inspired me to be brave enough to put all this into words. Bee, you inspire me every day. This one's called 'Guiding Light.'"

Brinton melted right on the spot. Perceptively, Emma Lou tipped her head on her shoulder.

He strummed the opening chords, the sweetness of a lullaby, with storytelling enlivened by unspeakable loss and perseverance. His eyes latched onto Brinton's as he sang the buoyant chorus.

*When I look to the sky each night, you're my guiding light.*

As soon as Jamie finished, the crowd of old folks swarmed him. He was attentive to each person, took his time, making them feel like he was as lucky to have the experience. Brinton never saw herself being so open to the world, but watching him made her want to try.

"Let's head back for a drink," Emma Lou said. "Some tea? Or something stronger?"

Back in Emma Lou's living room, Brinton settled into the tufted blue plaid couch. Like the kitchen, family photos covered every inch of wall space. On the white rattan table beside her, Brinton recognized a picture of a young Jamie, still adorable while missing a front tooth, smiling with his parents on the dock at Crawford Lake. She picked up the silver frame, tracing a finger over Jamie's exuberant face. Emma Lou triumphantly strolled in with two ice-cold mimosas in champagne flutes.

"That has to be my favorite photo of them," Emma Lou said, handing Brinton a glass.

Brinton replaced the photo on the table. "I bet it's hard to choose one." They clinked their glasses and took a sip.

"You know, I'm so happy Jamie brought you today. You remind me of my daughter, God rest her soul."

"I am so sorry for your loss," Brinton said softly, hoping to show she meant it with every breath she took. "Jamie told me a little about her. Would you be open to talking about her for my article?"

Emma Lou nodded. Brinton retrieved her recorder from her purse, turned it on, and set it on the side table.

"She was a special woman. A little fiery—she was my daughter, after all—but so soulful. I think there's a lot of her in Jamie too. People think it's an easy road because of who his daddy is. But the more successful Jamie's daddy got, the harder it was for him to keep the family together. My daughter refused to raise her son on tour buses, or in airports, or hotel rooms. And bless him, but Jamie's daddy didn't fully understand what she was going through with her...mental health. Nobody knew what she felt in that big house, alone, save for a small child."

Emma Lou tightly clasped her hands in her lap. "My baby struggled, but she loved that boy until her last breath. I know Jamie and his daddy's relationship ain't perfect. A lot of it has to do with all the answers we'll never get about what happened that fateful night. But she lives on in Jamie. I see it every time he picks up that guitar."

# CHAPTER THIRTY-SEVEN

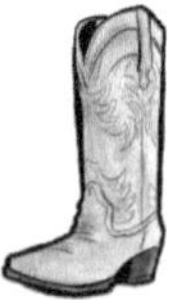

*A*fter snapping photos with everyone who asked, including the Grumpy Grandpas, Jamie had lost all feeling in his face from forcibly smiling. He ducked into the living room to the sound of Brinton and Emma Lou's laughter, as if they'd come up with a lifetime of inside jokes between them. His heart squeezed at the sight: his future and his past, colliding atoms that lit up his entire world. While Brinton wouldn't ever meet his mother, he felt her presence —her unwavering grace—in the room.

She'd be happy he found Brinton too.

On the coffee table, Emma Lou had pulled out her infamous album of drooly baby photos—him in the tub and the good Lord knew where else.

Clocking the empty champagne flutes, he chuckled. "Y'all throwing a party in here without me? Not very hospitable of you."

Brinton held up the album, open to a photo of him as a newborn. He was naked, wearing only a tiny blue cowboy hat as he lay on a white shag rug. "I think this should be your next album cover."

Emma Lou and Brinton broke into another fit of laughter, which didn't bother him at all. He knew, for a fact, he had a great ass.

"What time should we head back?" Brinton asked once she settled down.

Jamie grabbed his phone from his backpack. He almost had a heart attack.

It was 10:34 a.m. His scheduled soundcheck started in thirty minutes. They should have left an hour ago. With traffic, it'd be a miracle if they made it on time.

Worse yet, Sammi and Tex had left him dozens of voicemails and increasingly hostile texts. Sammi's spirited use of emojis alone belonged in a *Saw* film. Nothing from his father, thank God. Or was that a harbinger of shit-eating to come?

His shoulders seized, and he turned off his phone.

"Shit—I mean, shoot. Please excuse my language, Mamaw," he said, kissing her on the cheek and hoping to soften the stunned look on her face. "We're late getting to soundcheck for tonight's show. I'll call tomorrow and let you know how it went."

"Sure, sure. I love you," she called. "And promise me you'll drive safe."

"I love you too, and we will." He turned to Brinton, trying to stay calm despite the tightness in his chest, a Coke can crushed by a monster truck. "We gotta go right now."

Somehow, Jamie caught a break and traffic was cooperative enough to get them to the stadium at ten fifty-five. They pulled into a VIP entrance, flashed their all-access credentials to security, and motored to the artist check-in tent. Tex and Sammi were waiting by a narrow stairwell leading up to the main stage.

"Where the hell have you been?" Tex barked, the first time he had ever raised his voice at him.

Jamie rubbed the back of his aching neck. "I'm sorry, we got here as soon as we could. We went to see Mamaw and—"

"You don't answer your phone, you don't tell anyone where you are. I was scared you got kidnapped," Tex bellowed.

Sammi brandished her phone at Jamie. "With how mad your daddy is, you might consider making that happen," she said, her shrill voice cutting through the ambient backstage noise. "Or get a fake passport and flee to Mexico, because he's gonna be hotter than fish grease when he finds out."

Tex nodded to Brinton. "Did *she* talk you into this?"

Without thinking, Jamie stepped in front of her, shielding her with his body. He was fucking done being admonished. "It's my fault I was late, you hear me?"

"Well, the promoters are threatening to pull you from the show," Tex said, his voice lower but still tinged with ire.

"What? They can't—"

Sammi slid between the two men. "Yes, Jamie, they can. That's why we called you. Your father moved your rehearsal time up for ten o'clock to make room for an extra meet-and-greet scheduled for"—she checked her phone—"right now."

Jamie clenched a fist. "And you let him?"

Sammi's emerald eyes narrowed and her nostrils flared. "I don't *let* him do anything, you know that. And if you'd bothered to read the contract you signed for the show, you'd know the promoters stipulated that you—the headliner— must attend soundcheck. Or you forfeit your spot."

"There must be something we can—" Brinton started, but Sammi cut her off.

"Brinton, honey, I'm sorry. The three of us need to figure this out." Sammi waved over a passing staff member, a lanky twenty-something guy with a headset, who immediately brightened at her attention.

"Excuse me, could you please take my friend to Jamie's

greenroom?" Sammi asked, sweet enough that Jamie almost forgot she planned to whoop his ass.

The concert staffer nodded.

"I'll meet you there as soon as I can," Sammi told Brinton as she answered her buzzing cell phone.

Brinton peered up at Jamie for the answer. He nodded, rubbing slow circles on the small of her back. "Don't worry about me, Bee. I'll see you tonight at the show. Everything's gonna be fine."

He needed to believe it.

Jamie looked back at Tex, arms now crossed over his broad chest, and Sammi, who held her phone between them as they shout-talked to someone over speakerphone.

Brinton nodded, a little shell-shocked, and followed the guy.

Another artist's song blared over the loudspeaker. The show had gone on without him. It was strange because on one hand, Jamie knew he was only there because he'd successfully scammed his way into fame. He hadn't actually earned it. On the other, a tiny part of him longed for the chance to play such a prestigious show, as if he did.

Sammi hung up, then she and Tex watched him with the same expression: relief and a smidge of irritation.

"That was the promoter," Sammi said. "After what you pulled—"

Jamie slid his palm down his jaw. "Hell's bells, I said I was sorry. Am I playing this show or what? Because I've got plenty of other ways to spend the time if not, so stop jerking me around."

Sammi straightened her spine and raised both hands in defeat. "We deserved that. I was gonna say that you're a lucky son of a gun. They're gonna honor the contract, partially because I begged and partially because your father agreed to extend the meet-and-greet by an hour."

"Tonight, you're headlining a completely sold-out show," Tex said. He moved closer and outstretched his hand to Jamie, who took it. "I was worried about you, son. Didn't mean to blow a gasket."

"I appreciate that," Jamie said slowly, taking in that, in a few hours, he'd be performing for a hundred thousand people. He'd be happier if it weren't another moment signed, sealed, and delivered by his father.

"No more foolishness," Sammi said, signature grin returning. "The promoters are already cagey. Unfortunately, there aren't any more slots for you to rehearse before doors open, so when you walk out there tonight, you're flying blind."

"A broken clock is right twice a day," Jamie cracked.

Sammi smirked and nudged his shoulder with hers. "Bless your heart."

THE CONCERT STAFF guy led Brinton backstage through a series of interconnected hallways painted in the same corporate beige. Eventually, they reached a door with a red-and-white sign and Jamie's name thickly scrawled in black marker.

Inside, the makeshift greenroom was stocked with what Brinton assumed were items from Jamie's rider: high-end bottles of whiskey, multiple coolers overflowing with beer and wine, and every packaged junk food imaginable, lined up on two long tables against the walls. Two plush gray couches with matching weighted blankets anchored the middle of the room.

A pair of brand-new iPads and a few fancy-looking swag bags sat on the nondescript black coffee table. Next to a lighted vanity in the corner, in a display making any respectable It Girl swoon, there were two full clothing racks of designer T-shirts, jeans, sneakers, and boot options.

Brinton waited until the door shut behind her, then let the dam containing her tears falter. Back home, she called times like these "wet days." When something stressful or overwhelming happened, and she was on the verge of a panic attack but it hadn't quite materialized, the tears came more easily. She typically spent a wet day at home, rotting in bed, entombed in Cheeto dust and steeped in white wine. Certainly not in a crowd of tens of thousands of people.

The ground tilted beneath her feet. Her head felt like it was full of cotton. Why did she agree to visit Iris Grove with Jamie? She knew the concert was today. It was foolish to let him play so fast-and-loose with his schedule, presumably to impress her.

She roughly wiped her eyes with the back of her hand and peered into the lighted vanity mirror. Being in Iris—and being with Jamie—taught her that she was stronger than she thought.

She needed to believe it.

There was a knock at the door.

She expected Sammi, or better yet, Jamie. "Come in," she rasped.

Rich popped his head in first. His stretched eyes seemed surprised to see her. "Oh—hey…"

A grenade detonated in her belly. "What are you doing here?"

"Nice to see you too. And I'm here because *Landmark* is one of the festival's sponsors. Or did you forget with all the fun you're having down here?"

She stared at him blankly, wondering how he excelled at making a bad day astronomically worse. He closed the door and plopped down on the couch, slapping a cushion beside him. Begrudgingly, she followed.

"I'm here with the social team to make sure we get enough content to cross-promote on the homepage," he said. "But…I was hoping to run into you."

"Oh?"

"Yeah. I agreed to let you skip the daily pitch meetings to write, but you stopped answering my emails. I need to know we're on the same page, because I'm getting a lot of questions about the draft. I don't like not having an answer."

Brinton conjured a smile. "It's going great. Truly. This morning, I interviewed his grandmother, and she gave me an exclusive about his late mom. I think it'll—"

"I'd like to read something soon."

"We agreed my deadline is Tuesday. Three days from now."

"We did. But how about you send something by the end of today? I'll take a look and share feedback."

"But—"

"Look, I'm trying to fight for you here, give you a shot to prove yourself. Isn't that what you wanted?"

The tremors started in Brinton's hands, an emotional earthquake that radiated through her chest and down her arms and legs. But she had to hold it together. If not for herself, for Jamie.

"Because Agatha's got a killer pitch on deck. It's nothing for me to text her—"

Like hell he would.

"I'll have it for you tonight."

"Agatha's a beast on deadline." He laughed, rising from his seat. "It'll be good for you to be under the gun."

He plucked a frosty beer from the cooler, twisted off the cap, and took a long swig. "This could be a career-making piece. Oh, and don't forget to have fun out there tonight.

Sitting side-stage, and all this shit"—he gestured around the room with his free hand—"best perks of the job."

The door slammed behind him.

*Shit.*

Too distracted by Jamie's allure that morning, she'd stupidly left her laptop at the guest house. Was she being punished for daring to have it all—namely, being with someone who actually wanted that for her?

Brinton shakily texted Michael to come pick her up.

It was noon; she could transcribe Emma Lou's interview, update her draft, and get back to the stadium with plenty of time before Jamie went on at nine. Couldn't she?

She just needed to hold it together. Jamie's words echoed through her mind.

*Everything is gonna be fine.*

# CHAPTER THIRTY-EIGHT

*H*ours later, on Saturday night, Jamie enjoyed some much-deserved silence on the couch in his greenroom. He had eaten dinner—brown rice and grilled chicken, though he would've preferred a cheeseburger—and showered in the luxurious owners' suite.

He'd even changed into an exorbitantly expensive navy tee and dark-wash jeans Sammi had a stylist pull for the occasion, topped off with his University of Tennessee hat and his own scotch-brown cowhide boots.

After that morning with Brinton, they were his *new* favorite boots.

Pre-show, he usually prayed, journaled, had a whiskey, or let his mind go blank. But that was before he met Brinton. He hadn't seen her since that morning, and she hadn't responded to his texts. It worried him.

Had something happened? Should he try to find her? Unfortunately, he knew that was impossible. In a few minutes, he was due to rock the shit out of that stadium. Still, his whirring thoughts refused to settle.

A knock at the door snatched him back into the present.

"It's open."

A petite brunette with a clipboard and headset ducked her head in. "Mr. Crawford, they're ready for you."

He drained the last of his whiskey and followed her out.

A few minutes later, when Jamie stepped on stage, it felt like nothing he had experienced before. Not the Grammys or the other sizable shows he'd played over the years. This was, hands-down, the biggest crowd he'd ever seen.

The stadium lights and flashing phone screens looked more like oval diamonds strewn across a midnight sky. A sea of fervent faces in the crowd. He briefly took out his in-ear monitors—it was worth the residual buzzing he'd experience —and let the roar rip through every cell in his body. He was nervous, as always, but he was also exhilarated. Strapping on his guitar, he waved to the crowd. They went nuts.

When he glanced side-stage, Brinton was sandwiched between Tex and Sammi. She looked a little frazzled, eyes wide and darting around her. But she also looked beautiful in a flowy white dress. Under the lights, she glowed like an angel. He'd have to tell her that later.

He waved, but she stared at the ground, oblivious to everyone around her. Was she all right? There wasn't space to unpack that, because now, it was go time.

He nodded to his drummer, Lee, who counted the band off as they blasted into his latest single, "One More Heartbreak."

By the time Jamie rolled through the first two songs, his adrenaline had smoothed out. His voice was strong, despite missing soundcheck, and the crowd ate up every second. He reciprocated that love. Because connecting with his fans— bringing them a reprieve from their troubles, even for three minutes at a time—made every late night, every tough decision, and every crushing moment he'd experienced in his life worthwhile.

As he strummed the opening chords of his father's hit, "The Long Road," Brinton caught his eye again. She looked wobbly, crouched low to the ground in a shadowy corner.

Something was wrong.

His team didn't seem to notice. They were watching *him*. Jamie focused on singing the right words at the right time, praying somebody would step in. Yet, each time he stole a glance her way, nobody did.

Brinton's head bobbed between her knees.

Through the first chorus, his mother's smiling face, on the last morning she was alive, flashed in his mind. Nobody had *seen* her pain either. Jamie was a helpless kid then.

Now, he was a man.

His father would be pissed. The bad press from what Jamie was about to do may even put Brinton's article at risk. Could he survive the fallout? Would Brinton think he went rogue again?

*Fuck it.*

He couldn't let her suffer alone.

During the bridge, Jamie crossed to his guitarist, Garrett. He turned his back to the crowd. "Stretch out that solo as long as you can," Jamie shouted, leaning in.

Garrett nodded, his mop of dark hair swinging over his eyes. Yet, he couldn't mask his bewilderment—along with everyone else in that stadium—when Jamie stormed off stage.

BRINTON WAS HYPERVENTILATING, her face sticky with tears. She couldn't make them stop, couldn't breathe. Her chest clenched, a warning that if she didn't inhale soon, if she didn't *move*, the mounting pressure would crush her bones and squeeze her organs, until there was nothing left. That's what her panic felt like: a ravenous black hole.

Then, Jamie's guitar scraped against the pavement. She could barely make out his body's distinct lines, which she'd come to catalogue like a fingerprint. Still, she felt his presence beside her. He bent down on one knee.

"Brinton, honey, you're okay," he said slowly, cautiously, as if soothing a spooked horse. "I'm here with you."

"No—you can't," she yelped, surprised that her voice still worked. It came out mangled, the words compressed cement-tight, congesting her airways. "The show. You have to play," she gasped, hands gripping the back of her skull. "You can't be *here*."

Jamie projected confidence, doing what he loved. She couldn't help but admire him. And yet she was fucking everything up for him.

Gently, Jamie grasped one of her trembling hands, bringing it to his soft, smooth lips.

"I-I don't know what happened," Sammi told him, eyes wide and gripping her sides. "Said she needed some air."

Brinton had started spinning out that afternoon, during her confrontation with Rich. Then, she spent many more hours spinning out at the guest house, as she tried to piece together a workable draft to send him. Eventually, she did, and hightailed it back to the concert.

Brinton hated her misfiring brain. The lightning-hot stage lights, wall of screaming fans, and Rich's threats were a powder keg for another surprise panic attack.

She tried to ground herself with five things she could see. Four things she could touch. Three things she could hear. But her vision blurred and hands went numb.

It wasn't fucking working.

"Son, you gotta get back out there," Tex said, exasperated. "We'll take care of this."

"I'm not leaving her." Jamie's voice was like iron. He didn't shift his eyes from hers. "Sweetheart, keep your eyes on me. Don't worry about anything else going on. Can you do that for me, Bee? Take one deep breath, please?"

She did. The snarled knot in her throat unspooled. She could see, even faintly, that when Eli and everyone else had pushed her away, Jamie had run *to* her. He was a safety net, breaking her fall. Finally, she started to catch her breath.

He squeezed her hand and breathed right along with her, smoothing the tears away from her cheeks with his thumb. "Good, honey. You're doing so good. Keep your eyes on me and keep breathing."

"She all right?"

It was Jamie's father. Brinton hadn't noticed when he approached, but his disapproval clotted the air nonetheless. The volcanic heat of embarrassment and fear seized from the pit of her belly, but she followed Jamie's steady breathing. Let herself hold on to him.

"She will be," Jamie answered. "Give her some space. Please."

His father grunted, then stalked toward a flight of stairs leading backstage, where a trio of suited executives received him like loyal supplicants.

"Have Michael take her back home, will you?" Jamie asked Sammi.

"Yeah, sure. I'll go back with her."

"Thank you," Jamie said. He kissed Brinton's forehead. "I swear, you're gonna be okay, after some rest. I'm gonna be home soon to take care of you."

But what about all the commitments he had? All the hands to shake and self-righteous jackasses to play nice with, so he could continue doing the thing he loved most? He couldn't throw that away, not for *her*.

The waiting crowd, now a unified, jeering chorus, had turned on him. It was her fault.

"But—"

"Woman, that's not up for discussion." Sweetness emanated from his smile. "I said, I'm gonna take care of you."

Brinton nodded. He helped her to her feet.

An older man with a headset nervously tapped Jamie's shoulder. "Um—Mr. Crawford…" He nudged his black, thick-framed glasses up his nose. "The band don't know what to do next, and folks are getting rowdy out there. Are you…coming back?"

Jamie picked up his guitar. "Yeah, I'm coming."

"I got her, Jamie. Go on," Sammi said. Taking Brinton by the hand, she led them down a set of stairs and toward the VIP parking lot.

"I'm sorry about that, folks," Jamie said over the speakers, moments later. "I had to take care of a family emergency. I appreciate your patience; everyone is fine now. So, let's get back to it."

He had called her his family, something she had never expected when she thought back to their headline-making first meeting. And everything that had happened since.

But after tonight, he felt like family too.

# CHAPTER THIRTY-NINE

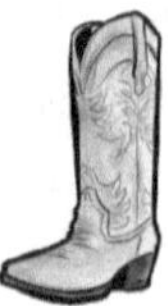

The rest of Jamie's set was a transcendent experience. Fans shouted every lyric, the band rallied behind him, and he sang his goddamn heart out. Yes, his little interlude meant that the show ran ten minutes over, which Tex informed meant a not-insignificant $20,000 production fine. That wasn't even on his radar.

All he cared about was getting home to Brinton.

So, he bypassed the afterparties and skipped his greenroom, where God-knew-who-wearing-God-knew-what waited with whiskey and a smile. He didn't even pose for pictures at the front barricade, where fans had gathered for hours to see him. He regretted that, but he'd find some way to make it up to them.

Post-show adrenaline propelling him, he drove faster down the highway than he should have, took the curves of those dirt roads a little too sharply. He couldn't bear another moment without Brinton wrapped in his arms.

When he pulled into the family compound, the driveway was empty, save for his father's GMC Sierra 1500 Denali.

The lights were on in his second-floor office. His father had waited up to properly flog Jamie following his seditious act.

He too would have to wait.

Jamie sprinted to the back of the main house. He didn't stop when the motion detector lights sprung on and made an Olympic leap over the sprinklers showering the zucchini patch.

When he reached the guest house, the front door was ajar. Something was off, he could feel it. It terrified him.

He shouldered the door open.

"Brinton?" he called out, breath lodged in his throat.

It was quiet and nearly pitch-black, with only the coffee table light flickering softly. Brinton's laptop, notebooks, and scratch paper littered the kitchen table. On the counter, there were two glasses, an empty bottle of Pinot Noir, and remnants of cheeseburgers and fries in takeout boxes. In the morning, he'd hug Sammi for looking after Brinton when he couldn't.

But he was there now.

"You came," Brinton rasped, voice thin as gossamer.

He scanned the living room, but he couldn't see her.

"Sweetheart, where are you?"

"Down here..."

He inched into the living room, heartbeat a grenade in his ears, and followed her voice. She lay on the floor, curved into the three feet of space between the couch and coffee table. He wasn't sure what he was walking into, so he waited.

His hand hovered over a switch by the stairs. "Can I turn on a light for you?"

She groaned. "Please don't. My head—I have a bad migraine. The lights will make it worse. Or the wine made it worse?" She laughed tepidly.

Relief power-washed his nerves. He could handle a migraine.

"Do you have any medicine? Tell me where, and I'll get it," he said, crouching down next to her on the floor.

"Upstairs in the bedroom, on the dresser," she whispered.

"It can't be comfortable on the floor. Can I please take you to bed?"

She made a strange sound: part sigh, part wail. Shit, she was sobbing. It crushed him to see her engulfed in pain. Once again, he felt powerless.

"I ruined everything tonight—this was such a huge opportunity for you," she choked out. "I'm so sorry…"

He blotted her cheeks with his thumbs. "Baby, please don't cry. That's not even close to true."

She tottered like a three-legged table but tried to lift herself. He caught her as she swayed, hugging her against his chest as he lowered himself to the floor.

"The best part of my night—hell, of this whole summer—is you," he murmured against her ear.

Turning her head, she gazed up at him through tear-slicked eyelashes and a faint smile.

"You're the best thing that's ever happened to me," she whispered.

He gave her the most tender kiss he could muster in his stage-weary body, moaning softly as one hand slid through her braids while the other clutched her back. She met each glide of his lips, though she trembled and gripped his shoulders like a life preserver ring.

He wanted to be that for her.

It pained him to do it, but finally, he broke their kiss.

His eyes were still closed, but he almost felt her smile against his lips. "Let's get you upstairs."

Jamie laid her on the bed and lit a few candles around the room so he could get to work. He retrieved her medication from the dresser, a small artillery of prescription bottles, pain patches, heating pads, ice rollers, and balms.

He brought her water and two ice-cold cans of Coke, which she shared had mystical healing powers for migraine attacks.

Brinton decided the pain was bad enough that he needed to administer an injectable dose of sumatriptan from a syringe that looked like an EpiPen. He balanced it between his fingers, eying it curiously.

"I hate how much it hurts to do this, but it works fast," she whispered.

He nodded.

"Do I stab it in your chest *Pulp Fiction*–style or…"

She laughed weakly. "I swear to God—"

"I'm messing with you," he said, smiling down at her. "Show me what to do."

She bunched up the hem of her dress to expose her mid-thigh. He ignored the black, lacy edge of her panties and focused on the top of her thigh, where she slid his hand.

He nodded to his bicep. "Squeeze as hard as you need to. Ready?"

She nodded. He applied light pressure with his leveraging hand, positioned the syringe, and released the spring-loaded trigger. She winced, gripping him hard.

Lord, he'd take all her pain if he could.

"Okay?" he asked.

She closed her eyes and exhaled, still gripping his arm. "I think I'll live to see another day."

"That's my girl, so strong."

She laughed, shaking her head. "Everyone thinks Black women are strong because we're born this way. But when you're constantly tested, undermined, or ignored altogether, you have no choice *but* to be strong."

His eyes grew glassy. "Oh, honey…"

She smiled earnestly. "It's fine. I've grown to live with it. I think…I want to be strong now, for us."

His lips brushed against her forehead, and she moaned gratefully.

"Can I run you a bath?" he murmured.

"Yeah, that would be amazing."

He lit a few more candles in the bathroom and added some fancy lavender Epsom salt he found in the medicine cabinet to the extra-deep clawfoot tub. He scooped her up from the bed and carried her into the bathroom.

"I'm gonna give you some privacy, but holler if you need me."

Her eyes dipped to the white marble floor. "Oh, I thought…well, it's a very big tub."

Despite the pain he knew she felt, she was blushing. It was almost too endearing.

"Mmm. That is tempting," he said, fully knowing that *tempting* didn't come close to the irrefutable longing he felt. "I have the same one at home, and it comfortably fits two."

She looked at him sideways.

"If I had to guess," he added quickly, suddenly feeling like he was digging himself out of quicksand with a plastic spoon.

She rolled her eyes. "Of course."

Before thoughts of her naked body overrode his last rational brain cell, he pulled out two plush, white towels from the linen closet. He set them on a small ledge next to the tub.

"But there will be plenty of time for us to test that theory," he said. "Very soon, I hope. Right now, I wanna help you feel better."

"I knew you were a prince, but you're also an angel." She smiled, hugging a towel to her chest.

"That's because I haven't told you all the dirty things I wanna do to you in that tub," he chucked over his shoulder.

#RIP to that last brain cell.

As he shut the bathroom door, her unmistakable giggle

floated into his long-term memory. That, combined with the spark of possibility in the air, made his heart swell like a hot air balloon.

After showering in one of the spare bathrooms, Jamie changed into a clean pair of basketball shorts and a T-shirt he kept in his truck. He brought her something to sleep in and waited for her on the bed while she changed.

Dramatically, Brinton flung open the bathroom door.

"You had to pick the most unflattering one from the pile?" she asked, shrieking with laughter through each word. She wore an oversized pink T-shirt dress that hit above the knee, which didn't deter Jamie from musing about how sexy her knees were.

Because apparently, that was a thing he did now.

"This is my binge-*Bridgerton*-and-instant-ramen look. Not at all suitable for cuddle-party-with-hot-country-star."

"So, you do think I'm hot, huh?"

"Shut up," she teased, sticking out her tongue. "You know what you look like. Though, I still haven't seen your…"

She let the wicked thought hang in the air.

He grinned, leaning back on his elbows. "Woman, I'm trying to behave myself, and you ain't making it easy."

She turned around and popped out her butt, unhurriedly smoothing her hands over telltale panty lines. "It's the granny panties, right?"

Jamie laughed so hard he tipped on his side, then gestured for her to join him. When he could breathe again, he said, "You're damn right."

Later, they lay together in bed, her head in his lap as he blotted her forehead with a cool washcloth. He marveled at how everything he thought he'd never have—stability, mutual respect, and contentment—was right there in his arms. And he was gratified to bathe in her healing light.

She laced her fingers through his and kissed his palm. "If

you weren't this huge country star, what would you do instead?"

It'd been so long since he'd thought about it. He spun his ring, suddenly self-conscious about his woefully unrealistic pipedream. Jamie chose to tell her anyway.

"Before I dropped out of college, I was a business major. Had a dream to start my own label and independently release my music. That meant I could shape the business from the inside and get out of my dad's shadow." He slid the cloth from her right temple to the left. "But everybody thought I should just sing. They said it was my destiny. Don't get me wrong; I love it. But sometimes, I wish I'd stuck with my plan. What about you?"

She sighed deeply enough that her shoulders bounced in his lap. "There's this book I've been trying to write since college."

"What's it about?"

Brinton squeezed her eyes shut, as if it were a still-tender bruise. "It's about an anxious Valedictorian who accidentally gets locked inside her high school with her free-spirited nemesis the night before graduation. The experience makes her question her perfectly curated future. Ultimately, she discovers there's more to life than straight-As and Ivy Leagues. Corny, I know."

"No, that sounds awesome. Is this about you?"

"It's inspired by my relationship with my sister. Shay never had to try hard at anything. All I did was try. But it's a vicious cycle: I work on it for a few months, and then trash it. I'd love to publish it one day and use my lit degree for once. Journalism was easier. Well, at least until it wasn't. And I became a joke."

"You're not a joke. You talk to people and tell their stories. Make them trust you—me included. That's brave as hell."

He rubbed his palms down her shoulders, and she sighed blissfully. He loved that his touch could melt away her pain.

"And why can't you quit *Landmark* and finish that book? You don't gotta be afraid to start over."

"Well, no offense, but I'm not a Grammy-winning music sensation, so I have to work. Those student loans won't repay themselves," she said, opening her eyes.

He nodded but didn't speak. Even if he wanted to pay off her debt—which he absolutely would—she wouldn't want that. She was the kind of woman who wanted to solve her own problems. He wanted that for himself too.

"But, Jamie, I believe in you. You could still start a label or put something out independently, without your dad. Everything you want is right there, waiting for you."

"I feel trapped too. No one takes me seriously—not unless he says so. I've felt it my whole life." Yet, he had no one else to blame. This was the cost of his Faustian bargain with his father.

She winced and rubbed her left temple.

"Well, you have so much more life ahead of you," she said. "I can't wait to see what you do next."

"That's incredibly sweet of you to say," he said, kissing the spot where her fingers lingered. "But now, I need you to relax and let me ice your head."

She exhaled, dropping her shoulders.

He grinned down at her. "Hey, we didn't talk about it earlier, but when I called you my girlfriend, I meant it. Even if there's still a lot to figure out, like handling how to go public."

"You mean, you *don't* want to soft launch on Iris After Dark?"

His heart sank like a feather tied to a boulder. "You saw that?" He expected her to be hurt, or worse, angry. Instead, her lush lips curved into a playful smirk.

"I did. I was doing some research for the article, and it came up in my feed. I don't know, it was kind of funny. I've been called many things, but a Yankee interloper was… refreshing."

"Well, I took care of it. Sammi had that post pulled down. It won't be like after the Grammys. I won't let that happen to you."

"You know you can't, like, control what people say, right?"

He shrugged his shoulders. "I don't want what's happening in the outside world to control who *we* are. I've lived through that enough in my life. I got a lot of regrets, but wanting you, and protecting what we have together, ain't one of them."

She reached up and caressed his jaw, smiling as he kissed her palm. "So…do you wanna read the article, now that it's done? I'll email it."

"Absolutely. I'd love that."

He slipped her phone into her palm. She quickly tapped the screen, rubbing her weary eyes with her free hand.

Jamie smiled down at her. "Now that's settled, how about I take you on a proper date tomorrow, after you've gotten some rest?"

She pulled him in for another languorous kiss, igniting a torch that chased away the fears in the dark recesses of his mind.

"So, I'll take that as a yes," he whispered.

"That's a hell yes," she breathed.

"Wanna watch something?"

"Mmm-hmm," she said, the promise of sleep coating her voice.

He pressed play on *10 Things I Hate About You*, which she had said was her favorite movie. Thankfully, it wasn't too bright or too loud for her over-sensitized body. When he ran his fingers through her braids, massaging her scalp the way she liked, she released a low, rumbling moan that enveloped him like a prayer.

After she fell asleep, her head resting on his chest, Jamie pulled out his phone. He opened Brinton's email. As he read each meticulously crafted word, a tapestry comprising *his* story, he radiated with awe. It was breathtaking. Exactly like her.

# CHAPTER FORTY

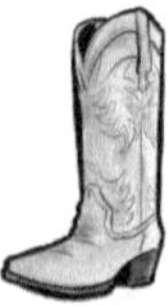

On Sunday, the next morning, Jamie was gratified to find Brinton's thigh hooked over his hip, her head buried on his bare chest. She smelled like her herbal-sweet hair oil mixed with lavender from the bath. He could have stayed enmeshed with her forever. But tomorrow, she was going back home. He intended to make use of every blissful second.

First, he had to eat the frog. Or rather, tame the beast that lived in the castle next door. He kissed a still-sleeping Brinton on the forehead and carefully slipped out of bed. After commandeering a spare toothbrush from the bathroom, he splashed cold water on his face and looked in the mirror. For the first time in his adult life, he was no longer willing to let the most important people in his life ignore that this was *his* life to live.

It was eight o'clock when he rapped on the double doors at his father's office. Jamie knew he'd be awake, likely drinking black coffee at his desk after his morning workout. Or plotting the course of the rest of Jamie's life, just for fun.

"Come in, son."

Cautiously, Jamie crossed the threshold. "You were expecting me?"

His father set his open newspaper on the desk. "Saw you sneak in late last night. How is she?"

"Better now," Jamie said, straightening his shoulders.

"I think you and I both know that's not true," his father said casually, sipping his coffee. "That girl needs some help. More than you can give her. I watched your mama break down like that for years. I couldn't be a hero to her, so don't think you can be one to Ms. Shaw either. Women like your mama—and Ms. Shaw—aren't built for this chaotic life. If I hadn't been so selfish to think I could protect her, that all the love I had could buffer all the ugly in this world, she'd still be on God's green Earth today."

"Daddy, respectfully—"

His father paused. "You sleeping with Ms. Shaw?"

Jamie's molars clenched along with his fist. "I don't see how that's any of your business."

"You're my namesake, boy. Everything you do is my business. That's why I set you up for another golden run with this record."

"What about what I want? For years, I went along with your plan because I was too scared to fail, but I'm tired of living this bullshit lie. She believes in me, and I believe in her."

"So you're throwing everything away—everything I've done for you—for a woman you barely even know?"

"I want her in my life." He matched his father's acerbic tone. "That's what I know."

Jamie Sr. slapped that morning's copy of *The Tennessean* on the desk, and slid it forward. "Well, I suppose you oughta see how that article comes out first. In the meantime, here's your latest glowing review."

On the front page, the first headline read: *Jamie Crawford Jr. Abandons Sold-Out Show for 'Family Emergency.'*

Jamie's heart was a free-falling elevator. The good press was fleeting, but the bad press never got easier to take.

Jamie Sr. half smiled and crossed his arms over his chest. "Yeah, it's all over the internet too. A lot of colorful rumors out there. Everything from you were drunk off your ass to you're on the verge of a meltdown. Don't worry though. Sammi's already on damage control. You're lucky if the label don't get cold feet and cancel the tour."

He rose from his seat, met his son where he stood. Even as an older man, he still had an inch on Jamie's six-foot-two frame. "And don't think I don't know about the production fine. I told Tex to cut it from every band member's check."

"Now wait a minute, that's not even remotely fair—"

"Somebody's gotta learn the consequences of your actions since, clearly, you haven't."

Jamie stepped forward, now nose-to-nose with his father. "Fine. I accept full responsibility for my actions last night and will pay everyone back myself. But I gotta tell you, Daddy, I don't regret it. I'd do it again. You, Tex, and Sammi…Y'all treat me like this ain't my life to live. And that's gotta change."

"You're choosing a journalist—an outsider—over your family? But then again, the way you've been acting, it's no real surprise."

"If that's how you see it, so be it. But for me, I'm finally choosing for myself."

His father smiled wryly. "What are you gonna do when it gets out that y'all were sneaking around when she was supposed to be working? You read what folks said about her after the Grammys? Not for the faint of heart."

Jamie's breaths were clipped as he considered this. He

hadn't read anything. One more regret he had about that time.

He wouldn't let those razored barbs hurt her again.

"That's in the past," Jamie said, even as the words fell flat from his lips.

His father's eyes narrowed. "You and I both know that ain't true. In fact, everything she does from now is gonna come back to you. She'll never have an identity outside your name. And if she fails, she'll blame you. She'll leave you. Did you think of that?"

Jamie shook his head. "I'm gonna support her because she's supporting me."

His father's wry smile dissolved. "What are you getting at?"

Jamie exhaled, dug deep for the strength he needed to say what he had to. Years of lies, rolled in shame and spiked with regret. It all came down to this moment.

"I told Brinton everything, and she wrote about it for *Landmark*. It's gonna be this month's cover story. Which means, that new deal you made me sign is *done*, because the truth is gonna be out there. So I want you to cancel the contract, make it official."

His father's lips parted, but he didn't speak. Instead, he strode toward one of the picture windows overlooking the guest house, his back turned to his son. "Fine. Clearly, you've made your mind up. Just know that all I've ever done was look out for you, even when you cut off your nose to spite your face. I tried to keep you from throwing your life away on a whim."

"I ain't that thirteen-year-old boy running away from my problems anymore." Jamie turned to leave, but his father's voice halted him like a concrete wall.

"When I was starting out, I didn't have a pot to piss in or a window to throw it out. I never wanted you, or your mama, to struggle like that." He scoffed. "My daddy split before I could even walk, and your grandmother, God rest her soul, folded boxes in that paper mill 'til her joints were stiff, and then the cancer spread…"

He waited a long moment, but didn't finish.

Jamie had never met either of his paternal grandparents, and his father rarely talked about them. Jamie, sadly, didn't even know where his grandmother was laid to rest. But he knew that his father's early life had been much harder than his own. Over time, with each personal loss, ruthless pragmatism had calcified his father's emotions. Jamie couldn't let himself suffer the same. He wouldn't waste the grace Brinton brought into his life.

"You're all I got left in this world, son."

Jamie spun around, meeting his father's unyielding stare. "I appreciate you, Daddy," he offered earnestly. "And everything you've done for me—for us. The thing is, there's more than one way to care about somebody. I hope one day, you'll see that."

Jamie didn't look back again.

# CHAPTER FORTY-ONE

When Brinton woke up, Jamie was gone, which made her feel way too sad for ten in the morning. Her headache had faded, and though she was groggy from the medication, she jumped out of bed. She brushed her teeth and dabbed on concealer, blush, and lip gloss, then changed into a familiar slinky, black midi dress from her closet that Shay had somehow snuck into her suitcase.

Shay had graciously removed the tags and tucked a note neatly into the halter neckline that read: *Warning: May Cause Immediate Erection. Proceed Like the Bad Bitch You Are.*

Brinton read it a few times and laughed. Shay was the most overbearing, obnoxious, lovable, and perfect little sister. After stepping into her cowboy boots and fastening her gold hoops, Brinton spritzed on another few pumps of vanilla perfume, including between her thighs, and bolted down the stairs.

To her disappointment, Jamie wasn't there. But there was a bouquet of pert, violet irises in a tall glass vase. Beside it, a still-hot French press pot of coffee and a white box tied with butcher string. She plucked a note from inside the bouquet and read it aloud:

> Bee,
> These flowers, the jewels of my town, are said to represent faith, hope, and wisdom. I feel every ounce of each when I look at you. Enjoy some blueberry coffee cake—Liza made it special for you. I'll be back to pick you up at four. Hope you're ready for an adventure.
> Yours,
> J

Brinton's knees buckled, hard enough that she braced her hands against the kitchen. Three months ago, she was a viral leper. Now, she was living in this storybook little town and receiving romantic gestures from the actual prince of a country music empire. This wasn't her life. This was the making of a '90s rom-com.

And why not? Last night was perfect. He was everything she ever wanted but didn't believe she deserved. While it was easier to live in perpetual fear, she wanted to believe that she deserved happiness, that she deserved *him*.

By a quarter to four, Brinton had packed and re-packed her suitcase, cleaned her room, eaten the entire coffee cake, and finished *Legendborn*, which she added to her approved reading list for the book club for the kids in her neighborhood. She pulled out her phone and FaceTimed Shay, who answered immediately.

"Does this call mean what I think it means?" Shay asked from their mom's cream sectional couch. Her eyes stretched in anticipation.

"It means I'm going on a date…with Jamie. I'm telling you this because I'm freaked the fuck out, and I need a pep talk."

"What are you wearing?"

Brinton rolled her eyes. "Don't be a creep—"

Shay took a long sip from a white coffee mug with *Will Honk for Pussy* in bold red text, complete with a cartoon cat driving a fire-engine red Corvette. "Seriously, show me."

When Brinton panned the phone down the length of her body, Shay gasped. "Baby, I don't think you'll have to do or say anything to that man. Let that dress be your guide. You look fucking hot."

"Don't wait up," Brinton chirped through an appropriately pleased grin.

"Of course I'm waiting up. And if I don't hear from you by tomorrow—"

"Then I'm calling the police," Athena interjected, popping into the frame behind Shay's head. She wore a white crop top and leggings that made the lines of her obliques pop. "I'm sure he's nice, but I don't know this man from Adam. He could drag you into a backwoods swamp."

"Mom," Brinton and Shay screeched in unison.

"I'm cutting you off from *Dateline*," Shay added, shaking her head.

The doorbell rang.

"Crap—it's him. I gotta go."

"Brinton Maxwell Shaw, if you hang up right now, I'm disowning you," Athena pleaded. "I want to meet him. Only for a minute."

"Ugh—fine. But be nice. And don't ask any weird sex questions, got it?"

"Deal," Athena conceded, satisfied.

Brinton opened the door. While Jamie generally wore the same combination of jeans and T-shirt when she saw him, nobody—dead or alive—deserved to look that good. She wanted to peel off that white shirt, gold chain, and tight, light-wash jeans with her teeth.

Maybe in a few minutes.

"Wow, you look…" he said, eyes taking in every inch of her. Then, he picked up on her contorted expression, raising a brow.

"I'm sorry, this is weird, but my mom wanted to say hi," she breathed. "So, Jamie, this is my mom, Athena."

Brinton flipped the phone around and leaned in closer to him on the porch.

"Oh, my…handsome. I-I mean, hello," Athena said, giggling.

Brinton couldn't help but snort. It was nice to know she wasn't the only person he had that effect on.

Jamie's cheeks turned a stunning rose shade, a rare but welcome sight. "Thank you, Miss Athena. I'm honored to meet you, finally."

Shay angled her head into frame. "I'm sorry, my older sister is so rude. I'm Shay, by the way. I'm a big fan of your ass—"

"Shay," Brinton hissed.

"Damn, Brinny. I was gonna say his *aspirational* music. You know, about love and stuff. Jamie, good luck getting this one to relax."

Jamie offered one of those megawatt grins that made Brinton's thighs crumple like a Capri-Sun.

"I've heard so much about you both. I hope we'll see each other in the flesh sometime soon. And, I promise, Miss Athena, I'll take good care of your daughter. Get her back home to you in one piece."

"I hope you two have fun. And, listen, if you have any single friends in their fifties—"

"Okay, Mom, see you later," Brinton blurted out before tapping the red button. "Bye, Shay."

Jamie didn't stop laughing for a good five minutes. "I like your family," he said.

"Good. I'll loan them to you sometime." She tried to swallow her smile, but it was impossible when his was blinding.

He stepped closer, wrapped his arms around her waist, and pulled her into him. He smelled as good as he always did. She let herself melt into the hard planes of his chest.

Tipping his head to her ear, Jamie whispered, "You look incredible in that dress. I don't know how I'm gonna concentrate."

"I was afraid it was...too much."

"Bee, I couldn't ever get enough," he said, kissing her softly on the cheek.

She thought about what might happen in the rom-com of her fantasies and skipped straight to the good part. She caught his lips, keeping his same gentle pressure, teasing his mouth open with her tongue. Jamie cradled the back of her head, pulling her closer with one hand so he could explore her deeper, his silken tongue flooding her with effervescent want. With his free hand, he caressed her bare back. She questioned how quickly she could get out of this dress.

After a few blissful minutes, he broke their kiss.

"I'm definitely not complaining," he said, breathing heavily, his cheeks stained a distinct shade of take-me-now. "But we should get going. Lots on the agenda." He gently sucked on her bottom lip, drawing out the tiniest whimper. He groaned in return.

"Can I get a hint?" she asked, equally breathless.

"Yeah. Hope you like cold beer."

Not long later, Jamie led Brinton into the Mockingbird Cafe, Iris's locals-beloved, drop-in-when-you-fancy listening room. He was ecstatic to show her where many country hopefuls played to their first crowds, including his father, and years later, himself. This was home. Jamie wanted Brinton to experience, in one place, all the reasons why he loved country music.

The venue was small and held only a few hundred people, with tables scattered around the modest stage and a battered, wood-topped bar along the back wall. The floors were always a little sticky, the amplifiers a little too loud. The smell of crispy fried chicken mingled with sweet-smokey whiskey. It wasn't fancy, but it was as real as it got.

A bouncer with a jet-black mullet and a septum piercing enthusiastically patted Jamie on the shoulder with a hand as big as Brinton's head, then led them to a small, roped-off table near the stage. The place was completely empty.

Brinton's eyes cut around the room. "Am I about to get pranked or something, because I feel like there should be more people here?"

Jamie nodded and grinned. "Yeah, typically it's standing-room only, no matter what time or day. I wanted us to have a little privacy, so I called in a favor."

Brinton's eyes narrowed knowingly. "Sammi?"

He laughed, shaking his head. "She's gonna make me wash her truck in a leopard thong, but you are beyond worth the pruney cheeks." Jamie then pulled out a stool for her as "Tennessee Whiskey" blanketed the cozy room.

"I recognize this song from your playlist," Brinton said, leaning close to him. "Chris Stapleton is amazing. I think I'm slowly becoming a country convert."

He squeezed her bare knee, a coy grin on his face. "That's my girl."

A waitress with pink cat-eye frames brought over two

bottles of beer. Jamie thanked her and waved to a man with thick blond corkscrews behind the bar.

"So, what's it like being so famous that people send you free drinks?"

"Hmm, exhausting," he said lightly. "But it'd be a crime to waste good whiskey and beer."

They clinked their bottles.

"Congress is working on a bill as we speak." She laughed, rolling her eyes.

He kissed her neck, lingering enough to breathe in her scent. She smelled as good as a first kiss or making love in the stillness of midnight. Sweet and addictive.

"I think you're gonna love this next singer, Kadidja Wilde," he said. "I recently discovered her music, so she's not on your playlist yet, but she's my new favorite. Her voice is so raw and powerful. And her storytelling…She's not afraid to call out how supremely fucked up and ugly the world can be. Still, she makes it feel like poetry."

Brinton tipped her head on his shoulder as he massaged her hand in between his.

"I love how passionately you talk about music. Like it's part of you on a vital, cellular level."

Jamie nuzzled her temple, desperate to get *closer*. "I think you bring it out of me."

She turned to face him, eyes ripe with sincerity. "I think you bring something out of me too." As they gazed at each other, lost in the headiness of the moment, it felt like theirs alone. She pulled his face to hers, kissing him like it was.

The house music died down, and Kadidja took the stage. Her natural curls were styled into a fierce crown. She wore a fringed, light pink leather jacket, matching dress shirt, and black slacks. Adjusting her acoustic guitar, she motored into a bluegrass-tinged opening chord.

Brinton's eyes widened as she took in the song, a

scorching manifesto about breaking free from the confines of oppression in an anti-Black world. She squeezed Jamie's bicep. He kissed her cheek. Watching Brinton experience his lifeblood—the bright lights, stripped-down emotion, and excitement of discovering a new artist—was as satisfying as playing his favorite six-string.

In between songs, she nudged his shoulder. "I almost feel bad for giving you a hard time about country music when we met."

"Almost?"

"All right, I feel bad! I'm eating my words. There's more to it than whiskey and pickup trucks. A lot more. Thank you."

He rubbed her back, his heart full. "Don't thank me yet. Our night's only beginning."

# CHAPTER FORTY-TWO

They parked on a gently sloped hill overlooking a field dotted with a kaleidoscope of wildflowers. In comparison, it made even the bucolic sights from *The Sound of Music* look like a Home Depot garden department.

"This is straight out of a fairytale," Brinton said, unable to believe what felt like a mirage. "You really are a prince."

He smirked that sexy-ass smirk. "Since I was little, I'd come here when I needed a break from…the king's reign."

Jamie toted the blankets and wicker picnic basket from the truck bed and set them on a low, long table beneath a sugar maple tree. "When my dad first purchased the land, he took my mom here. She loved it too."

He placed electric lanterns strategically around the table, flicking them on as he went. "Every so often, he talks about selling it. But I don't think he's got the heart."

"Hell of a date night spot, Crawford," she said, spreading a pillowy quilt on his side of the table.

This was indisputable: he had dated many, many women, meaning that while she'd never experienced this brand of affection, she accepted that there were very few firsts left for him.

He pulled a Michelin Star–worthy charcuterie plate from the picnic basket. "Well, I wouldn't know. Never brought anybody up here before."

"Oh," she whispered, attempting to sound casual as her stomach tumbled to her ankles.

"*Oh*." He'd done all of this for *her*.

"It's gorgeous," she added. "I thought—well, I assumed…"

He winked at her. "I know what you assumed."

Brinton knelt next to him at the table. "I…don't know what to say."

She was so grateful that her heart felt too big for her chest. Her adoration surged at hurricane strength. No man had ever made her feel so *acknowledged,* and *rare*. He must have seen it on her face, but he didn't seek validation or make it about himself.

Instead, he held a wine bottle in each hand, eyes glinting with anticipation. "How about we start here: You in the mood for red or white?"

Unsurprisingly, they were in the mood for more than wine.

They enjoyed one exceptional glass of Sancerre before she yanked him on top of her. They kissed fervently, if not sloppily. Greedy hands over needy, sun-warmed skin. Clinking teeth and hushed laughter until the promise of eye-crossing bliss sambaed alongside earthy-sweet notes of summer grass.

The sky was an arresting swirl of fuchsia, streaked with the deep purple of impending nightfall. Stars poked through stretched cotton wisps of clouds.

Brinton's phone pinged. Immediately, her senses dulled.

"You wanna get that?" Jamie asked, kissing the shallows of her throat and stroking her back. She didn't answer.

Without opening it, there was no way to know for sure, but the email notification had to be from Rich. The thought of it was a Doc Martens boot on her trachea. While Jamie's date had been a sedative for her nerves, she couldn't avoid Rich forever.

Yet, Jamie was there with her. In such a short time, he made her feel less alone. He was somebody she could confide in. She needed that now more than ever.

Her phone pinged again. She sat up, and Jamie followed.

"I couldn't tell you last night because I was way too stressed out, but I've been expecting this email from my editor, Rich," she said. Her throat bunched like a zip tie, making her voice shake.

"That's why I freaked out at your show. He wanted to read a draft of the article because, frankly, not many people back home take me seriously either. I think he wrote to tell me he hates it." She gripped her temples, shook her head. "If that happens, I have no plan. I'll be screwed."

Jamie's usual carefree smile grew more solemn. He wrapped his arm around her shoulders, which trembled under his weight. "Whatever it is, we'll get through it together."

She nodded and sucked in a deep breath, then retrieved her phone from her purse. Shit, she was right. There was a new email from Rich. Her hand shook as she tapped a few more times on the screen, opening the message.

She exhaled deeply, then read aloud: "'Great fucking work. I knew you had it in you. We'll run a teaser article online tomorrow, before the print issue drops next Friday. With your cover story.'"

She gasped. Her heart could have blasted through her chest. "I can't—oh my God…"

Jamie pulled her tight against his body, his warmth

bringing her back to Earth. "I knew you could do it. I swear, the article was perfect."

"You read it?"

He nodded, grinning. "Last night. Congratulations, honey."

She released a grateful breath. Unfortunately, there was more to Rich's email. Still shaking, Brinton squeezed Jamie's hand to anchor herself so she could keep reading. "'I can't lock this in without proof that Crawford is striking out on his own. Need something substantial for the fact-checking team ASAP. Send along with your coverage notes.'"

Somehow, Rich had found one last fucking hurdle to fling in her path. When would she ever be *enough*? Brinton dropped Jamie's hand and buried her face in her own, her ragged, hot breaths dampening her palms.

"Fuck," she croaked. "How am I supposed to do that without talking to your father? He'll never agree. It's impossible—this was a colossal waste of time."

When she looked up, desperate for air, her eyes burned from the pressure of holding back tears, regret. Everything.

Inexplicably, Jamie was smiling.

"Brinton," he breathed, his palm slowly circling her back. "The contract."

"What?"

"This morning, my father agreed to cancel my new songwriting deal. It'll be in writing. It's proof."

She grasped his shoulders. "What?" she exclaimed again.

"I got a copy at my place. You can send it to your editor," he explained, sincerity emanating from his body like a shimmering aura. "Bee, *you did it.*"

"Thank you, Jamie," she said. Burning hope spread across her cheeks and down her chest. She had *done it.*

There wasn't anything left to say, but she knew what to do. She flung her arms around his neck and pressed a searing kiss to his lips, euphoria stoking the flames. Her hands glided through his hair, and their tongues communed like a vow.

He caressed her jaw, barely touching her but making her feel both so cared for and hot, hot, hot all over. She angled her chest forward, showing him where she wanted his hands most. Instead, he moved his to her shoulders.

"Patience, Bee, we got all night," he murmured against her lips, his curved into a devastating smile. He slid next to her, flicking his signet ring around his pinky. "I wanted to talk to you about something too."

She watched his ring spin. He was nervous, which made her nervous. Was he breaking up with her, before they truly began?

"I know you're leaving tomorrow, but I couldn't let that happen without saying this."

Brinton picked at her cuticles to distract herself from her mounting panic. Was it his father or Kendall or any number of telltale signs she must have missed, proving that Jamie had grown tired of keeping track of all her nagging, inconsolable needs?

He blew out a long breath. "My mom's death ripped my family apart. It didn't matter how much my father and I loved her, she was gone. So I decided I wasn't ever gonna let myself feel that kind of pain again."

Jamie laughed bitterly as sweat beaded the small of her back.

"I thought I didn't wanna be vulnerable again, but the way I feel about you...I wanna give you all of me," Jamie continued, taking her hand. "I want us to have a real future together, no more hiding."

Finally, she exhaled.

"Yes," Brinton said, body humming with relief. "We should tell our families, friends. My mom will be happier than me." She laughed. "But maybe we still wait until after the article comes out to go public?"

"I'm gonna do everything in my power to protect you." He frowned, then shook his head. The words seemed too excruciating for him to vocalize. "No matter what people say."

Brinton squeezed his hand. Their new reality, outside this safe Iris bubble, was always lurking, waiting for its moment to leap from the shadows. She had to face it, even as the Grammys fallout had nearly destroyed her.

Jamie couldn't protect her from that heartbreak. She didn't need him to. Having him in her life was enough.

She exhaled, laughing to ease the discomfort. "I don't know if you're aware, but I'm a Black woman in a country that puts diminished value on my existence."

His dejected expression throttled Brinton's heart.

"But I'm stronger now," she went on, lifting his chin and meeting his sparkling eyes. "I think you helped make me stronger. My whole life, I molded myself into somebody else because I hated the things that I couldn't control. I didn't want to see those parts of myself, but even the scary shit—it makes me who I am. So I want to do this for us, and myself."

He smiled, pressing her so hard into his chest she was winded as she laughed. "Woman, you make me so damn happy."

Brushing her braids off her shoulder, he kissed her neck, setting off little sparks behind her eyes. His fingers marched down her hip to the top of her boots. "These look good on you. Even though I kinda miss the combat boots. Made you look like you stepped out of a Wes Anderson movie, in a good way."

"Mm, and what else do you miss?"

Their faces inches apart, he nipped at her bottom lip, prompting her sharp intake of breath. Jamie cradled her head, anchoring her and slipping his tongue between her parted lips. On contact, she moaned into his mouth.

"*That*. The way you moaned for me in that alley." His voice dropped an octave, making her stomach corkscrew. "Music to my fucking ears," he said, still cradling her head.

This was another first for her: a man she was crazy about, admitting his true intentions and making space for her in his life. And wanting nothing but her heart in return.

That, and a few kinky extras she was more than willing to supply.

"You can have me," she said, untying the halter straps around her neck.

Jamie's eyes followed the pooled fabric at her sides, then swept over her bare chest. "Goddamn, woman..."

That's all he got out before she pressed his hands onto her collarbone. She guided them down, down, down. Until he didn't need her help.

"What about our plan?" he asked between spiraled, lazy licks on each nipple, her moans eclipsing his. "Waiting until the article was published to—"

"I agreed to wait until it was *done*." She gasped at each supple lash, then smiled triumphantly. "I submitted it yesterday. So—"

Jamie guided her onto the soft quilt, one hand on her back, the other still shamelessly squeezing her breasts.

"Hell of a plan, huh?" He helped her drag the dress down her legs, then tossed it to the side. Jamie eyed her boots.

"Leave 'em on," he grunted, prompting a delicious swell between her thighs.

"Fine," she teased, "but if you scuff them—"

"Best believe, I plan on it."

One corner of his mouth quirked. She was so turned on, she decided to lick it. The sound he made would have brought her to her knees if she weren't already lying down.

His eyes worshiped her body, as they always seemed to when he looked at her. "You're a goddess, you know that?" Jamie rolled onto his side, next to her. "I can't even believe you're real."

After denying herself for so long, she felt the same. Brinton's hands sifted through his silken waves and tugged, earning each of his rumbling moans. "I need to make sure you're not some weird AI. There's some pretty good ones online."

He smiled back. "Satisfied?"

"Well, I remember you promised to fuck me six ways to Sunday."

"I told you, baby," he chuckled, the sound dark as obsidian. "I never miss the hole. Now, spread those pretty-ass legs for me."

Ecstatic, she propped herself onto her elbows and dug the heels of her boots into the quilt. Plucking a dandelion bloom from the sugar-soft soil, he traced the cottony puff over her underwear, sighing appreciatively as she rocked against his knuckles. Jamie brought the bloom, mostly intact despite her best efforts, up to her lips.

"Make a wish," he whispered, nose buried into the apex of her thighs. "Quick, 'cause I'm dying to taste you."

She blew, releasing the white wisps—seeds of their budding future—into the technicolor sky. "It already came true."

"Mine too."

His smile warmed her core, where, coincidentally, he was building more heat. Slowly, he dragged his thumb up and down her folds. Her thong was so damp it clung like second skin. She needed it off, and something else on her.

Him.

"Should I make you come like this?" he asked, aquamarine

eyes shifting cobalt in the lantern's glow. "You fuck my fingers so good."

"God, you're a pain." She laughed, breaths jagged and voice floaty.

"Then tell me what you want." The playfulness in his eyes morphed into pure, red-blooded want. "I wanna give you everything."

"Everything."

The only word she managed. She was a supernova of lust.

He slid her panties aside. Jamie pressed one thick finger inside her and then another, elongating her airy moans and making her half-lidded eyes squeeze shut.

*I wanna give you everything.*

His words echoed in her mind. She wanted that too, but it had been years since she'd come from sex with a man. Not even with Eli. These days, she was more of a vibrator-on-high kind of girl—a pragmatic solution for emotional burnout so severe, getting off felt like a chore.

Jamie pulled out his fingers, taking his time. He sucked indulgently. "Even better than I remembered. Can I lick you, baby?"

Tempting, but the stiff peaks of pleasure in her belly felt too right. She couldn't wait. "Later."

Brinton stroked his erection, which strained against his jeans. She keened at his throaty groan. "I need this right now."

It was stitched across his face: he was one nipped thread from coming undone. She dragged his T-shirt over his head, revealing more of his skin, which glowed in the lantern's light. He popped onto his feet, toed off his boots and socks. In one, seamless motion, he peeled off his jeans and boxer briefs, kicking them to the side with her dress.

When he straightened, Brinton was beyond words. Every distinct line of his chest, corded muscles on his forearms, and

Michelangelo-carved thighs were masterful. And not to mention what she discovered when her gaze dipped beneath his waist.

"Jamie, you're beautiful."

Her fingertips traced the deep grooves near his hip bones. She licked the creases forming his abs and the soft trail of hair leading to his crotch. She could have bottled his salty-sweet taste, lathered herself in it.

"I love when you look at me," he said, lust burning bright in his eyes. "Nobody sees me like you do."

Brinton needed him in a way words wouldn't satisfy. When he dragged her panties down her thighs, she whined at the shock of humid air on sensitized skin.

Finally, he pulled a strip of condoms from the picnic basket.

"Were you planning to bust those out after appetizers or before dessert? No, wait—an amuse-bouche?" She laughed until he planted plush kisses down her chest and belly, teasing out a low, rolling moan that dragged her to the edge of consciousness.

His tongue caught between his teeth. "I got no clue what an amuse-bouche is. But if it makes you sound like that, then yeah. It's an amuse-bouche."

Jamie rose on his knees, giving Brinton an extraordinary view of him. He was so wonderfully and unmistakably *hers*. She plucked the foil packet from his hand, set it beside her. Maybe she *could* wait a few more minutes.

"I'll give you a hint," she teased, sitting on her own knees. Brinton sucked him into her mouth, eager to be filled despite the sheer magnitude of his length.

*Damn.*

Blissfully, his eyes floated shut. He whimpered, soft and easy.

"My sweet girl—"

She'd previously sworn off blow jobs. Eli had a tendency to confuse the dangly thing in the back of her throat for a punching bag. But Jamie looked at her like she was imbued with magic, tenderly massaging her back between husky praise. He'd pull back if she momentarily gagged. She'd grab his ass and plunge him deeper. Open her mouth wider. Find new heights to reach.

She swallowed Jamie's short, hoarse groans as he tensed and vibrated in her mouth. It wasn't long until he gently cupped her jaw, brow furrowed with gratification.

"I love how you do that." He thumbed away the warm trail of saliva that had traveled down her chin. "But, baby, I'm desperate to be inside you."

He lowered Brinton onto her back, letting her thighs hug his sturdy hips. She rolled the condom on, guided him with one hand, and cradled his face with the other.

Slowly, he pushed.

Brinton's lips parted on a gasp. The sharp bite of pressure was punishing as it was glorious, but she clung to his warmth. Let him smooth her quivering breaths.

Their tangled moans rang out in the serene silence around them. He stilled his body and searched her eyes, waiting for something.

"Okay?" he asked, adoration painting his face.

"Yeah," she whispered, smiling up at him. "Please, don't stop."

His lips claimed hers again.

Jamie quickly found his tempo. His hips rocked back and forth, as steady as a sailboat. "Prettiest little thing," he rasped between determined pumps that made her breath catch in her throat.

She was gloriously dizzy. Fired up and spent, all at once.

He lifted both of her thighs higher, up near his shoulders, giving him more room to fuck her freely. Brinton's hands glided through his damp hair. Her body hummed each time he unlocked a new level of pleasure inside her.

"I could fuck you like this all damn day, Bee."

And she would like it. A lot.

As he moved, Jamie's gold chain crashed into her forehead or caught on her parted lips.

"Shit, baby—I'm sorry," Jamie stuttered, suddenly aware of what was happening. Clearly, he had been busy.

He slowed his pace and softened his eyes. "Let me take it off."

"Don't you dare," Brinton rasped, absolutely drunk on sensation. "I fucking love it."

Smiling wickedly, she caught the chain mid-swing between her teeth, held it for a few luscious thrusts, then let go. Beholding her, Jamie laughed darkly, his eyes a mix of hunger and wonder.

That is, until she palmed his heavy sack. Then, his eyes rolled back into his head.

She felt herself grow wetter at the ravenous sounds spilling from his mouth. The slick-slide of their bodies becoming one thundered through her ears and spiraled down to her pulsing center.

"The way you're gripping me…So fucking good," Jamie gritted out, teeth scraping his plump bottom lip. He punched his hips forward even harder, tunneled into her deeper, rewarding her.

Brinton's hands sank into his perfect ass, fusing his desire with hers, until her tightest contours bloomed and her belly clenched. His fervent praise emboldened her greed. She wanted to milk every exhilarating second.

"Let me ride you."

Still panting, he smiled. "Yes ma'am."

Without breaking their connection, he rolled her on top

of him. He regarded her like this new perspective took him to a higher plane of existence.

The ruthless stretch of him broke all rules of time and space. His fingertips kneaded the breadth of her hips. Angling his hips higher, he gifted her every ounce of him as he grunted and gasped and moaned her name.

She moved slowly at first, relishing all the ways his hardness melted into her softness.

"Use me, sweetheart," he whimpered, lacing his fingertips through hers. "Take what you need."

She did.

Finding that exquisite spot and heavenly pressure, she rocked her hips faster against him. To her absolute delight, he met her at every sharp thrust. When she flattened her palms against his damp chest, flushed pink beneath that golden tan, every muscle in his body clenched.

His head tipped back, exposing a fine vein running down the center of his throat. Her center fluttered as the vein pulsed.

Slowly, she leaned down and traced it with her tongue. He was so fucking beautiful.

"Shit," he hissed, equally dazed. "Lean back. Let me see you."

She anchored her hands on his thighs. He sighed appreciatively, gripping her hips to hold her steady. Taking his time getting a good look.

Slowly, his hands traversed her curves like a map. First, he cupped her breasts, pinching her pebbled nipples until she cried out. Then, he massaged the soft slope of her belly. She slipped her own hand beneath his. She was eager to feel his thickness, flexing and making space inside her.

"This view," he moaned. "I could die watching you. I'd be the happiest man."

Jamie reached between their bodies and made easy circles

where he knew she needed it most. He worked her slick, tender bud—sometimes quickly, sometimes infuriatingly slow—until she ached for release.

She sucked her bottom lip and bounced faster.

"Oh, fuck—"

*There.* So much pressure. So much *good.* Warm and pulsating and refusing to be ignored. Heat rushed from her belly and up to her throat.

"You can let go, Bee," he said, voice snagging on each breath. "Keep your eyes on me."

She rocketed through the atmosphere until she saw stars —not just the ones in the sky.

"Show off for me. You know I need it. I need you…"

"I need you too." She tossed her head back, letting endorphins drag her higher.

Brinton cried out again. It was, perhaps, the best perk of making love in the countryside. Her body was a drawstring, every muscle cinched at once. She begged to snap, reanimate, and snap again.

Firmly, his hands ground her hips into his as they rolled. "You gonna come for me?"

"Yes, I—"

"You feel like heaven. The best I've ever had, Brinton—"

"Jamie—"

Her vision went white, then electric blue. Finally, she *let go.*

She was free-falling into Earth's atmosphere as Jamie's hips punched higher, practically erratic. He pressed her into his chest, then surrendered to her completely in one long, desperate push.

He felt incredible. No—otherworldly. She'd never felt more alive than with his hot, raspy breaths splintering across her neck.

Brinton lay on his chest—legs tingly, his big hands still

squeezing her hips—and listened to his pitch-perfect heart-beat. A steady *lub-dub, lub-dub, lub-dub.* It was her new favorite song. After a few minutes, he brought her water and pulled a quilt over their sweaty, satisfyingly spent bodies. They lay on their backs, silently marveling at the stars, as if exclusively out for them.

Jamie rolled onto his side, facing her.

"Lordy, woman. That was…"

Beneath the blanket, he traced overlapping hearts onto her obliques.

"Mmm-hmm," she mused, lazily draping her thigh across his hip.

"If I knew that would happen, I would've taken you straight here two weeks ago."

They both laughed.

"But think of all the fun you would have missed. Like my ass in those shorts."

He palmed said ass and grinned. "Would have been a real travesty."

Before she could counter, he eased his tongue into her mouth, moaning softly when she reciprocated.

Slowly, he pulled away. "I could stay here with you all night, but the mosquitoes will tear us up. Let's get this packed so I can get you back home. And by home, I mean in my bed."

She gave him a prize-winning smile. "Ah, the grand finale?"

He grinned back, thumbing the curve of her bottom lip. "Bee, I hope there ain't nothing final about it."

<u>Verse #1</u>
I just wanna dance here with you
Wear out that old jukebox
Wear these boots down to their soles
I don't care who knows
I don't care who watches
Let them whisper in the shadows
Let them cut the house lights on
Baby, all I see is you

<u>Bridge</u>
Can you see me too?
Do you need me too?
Baby, if you do

<u>Chorus</u>
Keep your eyes on me
This dance floor is ours tonight

Keep your eyes on me
Just our heartbeats keeping time
Till my final breath
Till there's only love left
Just keep your eyes on me

<u>Verse #2</u>
I just wanna be where you are
One moment is all we need
One moment until we're free
All you gotta do is breathe
All you gotta do is be in my arms
Even if the ground ain't steady
Even if there's no ground
To stand on
I'll stand by you

<u>Bridge</u>
Can you see me too?
Do you need me too?
Baby, if you do

<u>Chorus</u>
Keep your eyes on me
This dance floor is ours tonight
Keep your eyes on me
Just our heartbeats keeping time
Till my final breath
Till there's only love left

Just keep your eyes on me

<u>Bridge #2</u>
I know you see me too
I know you need me too
Baby, I'll wait for you
I'll wait for you

<u>Chorus</u>
Keep your eyes on me
This dance floor is ours tonight
Keep your eyes on me
Just our heartbeats keeping time
Till my final breath
Till there's only love left
Just keep your eyes on me

 ot long later, after a hot bath that had turned into an even hotter makeout session, Jamie had to stop himself from going a few more rounds with Brinton. He needed to conserve energy for his last surprise.

He led her into his small recording studio downstairs and flipped a switch, triggering a set of dimmed lights in the ceiling. Custom foam soundproofing panels were built into the walls, and from the ceiling, silver moonlight spilled from two huge skylights onto a patchwork of patterned rugs. In the center of the room, there was a sleek black desk with an imposing computer setup that included two curved monitors and an intricately rigged microphone. And along the walls, more than a dozen mounted guitars of all shapes and colors.

"This, as they say, is where the magic happens," Jamie quipped. He strode toward the desk and sat down in the blue velvet wingback chair.

"Here I thought the bedroom had seductive powers," Brinton said, gleefully falling onto a matching blue couch across from his desk.

He shamelessly enjoyed the way her breasts jiggled underneath his orange University of Tennessee T-shirt.

It definitely looked better on her.

"I started putting together this space a while ago, mostly to work out ideas on my own. I didn't have the nerve to actually do it, until…"

He smiled shyly at her.

Knowingly, she grinned back at him. "Well, I'm happy to be of service. Every cowboy needs a muse."

He smirked, then leaned back in his chair. "You do realize I sing country music, but I'm not, like, a cowboy, right? Couldn't be more different."

She pouted her full lips. He wanted to graze them with his teeth, then suck away the sting.

"Yeah, I don't know about that. Cowboys and country boys both have an affinity for boots, wide-open spaces, and outlaw behavior. Oh, on occasion, honky-tonk badonkadonks. That's according to my thorough Wikipedia research."

"Ah, America's most trusted news source."

"It's basically the U.S. Constitution at this point."

"Can't argue with that."

She rolled onto her side, adorably propping her head against her bent arm. "How does it feel knowing that, this time next week, the album will be out? And you'll be on a new path?"

"It feels like the start of forever," he said, smiling fondly back at her.

"I like how that sounds." She beamed.

"Can I—um…"

He shook his head and laughed, then tapped a few strokes on his illuminated keyboard. "Do you wanna hear something?"

Jamie spoke slowly, carefully working through what he'd

practiced all day in his head. However, she'd never know it by how dramatically his brain glitched each time he opened his damn mouth.

"I wrote it…It's—um—about you," he stammered. "What you mean to me. It's very different from anything you've heard from me before. But this is who I really am as an artist."

"You…wrote a song about me?" she asked, sitting up now, her expression open and curious. His heart hummed at the sight.

He nodded. "It's pretty rough. Actually, I finished it this morning, after I left you. I think it has great bones, but if it's bad, you can tell me—"

"Jamie," Brinton said earnestly, looking straight at him, truly seeing him, as she always did. "Nothing you do—or write—could be bad. It's impossible."

How did he get so damn lucky to find her?

He nodded, injected with the courage to keep going. "All right, then. It's called 'Eyes on Me.'"

She tucked her legs beneath her, clasped her hands, and smiled at him like she'd waited for this moment her entire life. It felt like he had.

He pressed play.

The demo was raw but felt more real than anything he'd ever recorded. Her expression shifted from surprise to something more delicate as his stripped-down vocals and mewing guitar enveloped them.

He stared at one of the computer monitors to give off the illusion that he wasn't losing his damn mind, wondering if she liked it. Or hated it so much that she'd run out of his house in disgust. After what felt like the longest three minutes of his life, the music faded out.

He'd never written a song explicitly about a woman he was committed to, because this was the first time he'd committed. To make Brinton the exception felt right. More than right. It felt inevitable.

Jamie's attention shifted back to the couch, but she wasn't there. Now, she stood directly in front of him. She nudged a tear from her cheek, a little puffy and glossy in the low light, his shirt a little rumpled as it inched up her thighs. Her braids hung loose, tumbling over her shoulders and chest with reckless abandon.

She never looked more beautiful.

"Jamie…I love it," she whispered. "I can't believe you did this for me."

That's all she could get out before he pulled her into his lap. Her thighs straddled his hips. Jamie wrapped his arms around her, like he'd rather be struck down dead than ever let her go.

Angling his jaw toward her, she kissed him hard, scorching him to the core.

"I'd do a lot for you, Bee," he murmured through quick, desperate moans, unsatisfied with every second her taste wasn't on his lips. His hands gripped her upper back, and her nipples grazed his bare chest through the well-worn T-shirt.

"I know," she said urgently. When she tipped her head back, exposing her neck, he grazed the edge with his teeth until she rumbled against him.

Jamie was overwhelmed with gratitude. The song revealed to her, in the most intimate way he could, how she made him feel. How much he needed her in his life. And she had accepted him. He'd successfully carved out the rotten parts of himself.

He could still be a good man.

Pulling back, he cupped her face. "I wanna be yours. I wanna be so good to you."

"Yeah, Jamie, you're mine. Mine, mine, mine," she

affirmed, punctuating each word with a dizzying kiss. "And I'm yours."

It was all he needed to hear. He dipped his hands underneath that threadbare shirt. He was eager to feel her supple skin, up and down her torso, but stopped beneath her breasts. He reveled in her frustrated whine.

She bunched the shirt over her head and flung it across the room.

"That's my favorite T-shirt, you know," he said, generously laving one peaked nipple with his tongue and rolling the other between his fingertips, just how she liked.

"Collateral damage," she said, giggling.

She arched her chest forward, braced her hands against the arms of the chair behind her, and slowly rocked her body against the solid column in his shorts. Head tossed back and lips parted, she unleashed a succession of rolling moans. It made him shudder so hard that, for a second, he thought he'd come all over himself.

Apparently, old habits and such.

She pulled one of his hands from her ribs and slid it between her thighs.

His breath hitched.

"Oh, honey—fuck," he groaned, the scalding heat and effortless glide amounting to a sexy sledgehammer to his frontal lobe. He cupped her like she was the most precious gift he'd ever received. But not so precious that he wasn't eager to fuck her until there was nothing left but sensation.

Right in that ugly-ass armchair. His interior designer had once praised it like it was the Second Coming.

Her hips moved to their own soundtrack against him.

"I aim to please." She laughed.

"Yeah? Me too."

In about two seconds, he rolled her off his lap and onto the chair.

"Oh," she gasped through broken laughter.

Kneeling on the floor before her, he nudged her knees wide, hooking each over the arms of the chair. His cheeks flushed at the sight of her, so open to him, but Jamie embraced the magnetic desperation, as if he didn't have her a few hours ago. As if he might never again.

Entranced, he inched his pointer finger down her center and back up again, spreading her wetness as her hips rocketed forward.

He'd never witnessed a better sight in his life.

"Before I do this—and I can't fucking wait to do this—I need you to know that if you can't…" he stammered.

Shit, why was talking so hard?

Probably because her body, glistening and ripe for him, had hypnotic powers. He pressed both hands into her thighs, tried to focus on something other than twisting his tongue over her like a damn cyclone.

There was an unspoken question in her eyes.

"I don't need you to come if…it's hard. Or if you feel scared," he said, remembering how stressed Rich's email had made her earlier in the meadow. "Everybody's different. Every time we make love, it's different. If your anxiety means you need something else, I'll give it to you. Let me please you the way you need."

"You are incredible," she whispered, pulling him into a decadent kiss not meant for this world. Slowly, she pulled away. Brinton snaked her hands down his shoulders, chest, and stomach, leaving a blaze of tingles across his skin.

"But if you don't lick me or fuck me right now, I'm going to explode."

*Welp, that settles it.*

He smiled coyly then slid down her body, right where she wanted him. With one hand, he parted her, and with the other, he pressed a finger inside. He moved slowly, greedily exploring, adjusting for what made her teeth drag across her bottom lip or shudder against him.

She was so hot and supple it almost felt too good. But she begged for more, and he obliged like a good Southern gentleman. He flicked his tongue steadily and pressed another finger inside her, this time moving harder and curving his fingertips to stroke her deeper. Brinton's fingers sifted through his hair, and when she tugged, pleasure spiraled across his scalp and down his chest. All he could do was revel in her magic, licking firmly until her hips bucked against his face in a way he fucking loved. He pulled away only to lavish her with the downright filthiest praise he'd ever uttered.

And it didn't make him blush one bit.

It wasn't long before her low moans shifted into sharp screams. She tightened around his fingers. She gripped his hair so hard he was dazed from pleasure. Gloriously, he felt her all around him now.

As he glanced up to behold her, simultaneously thrusting with one hand and teasing out ecstasy with the other, her soft belly trembled, and her decadent thighs went stiff. She unspooled for him with melodic gasps that escaped from between luscious lips.

Her aftershocks sparkled like the Fourth of July. A unique, scintillating expression every time she breathed or shook. She lay back in the chair, body completely relaxed and skin glowing with the indulgent sheen of satisfaction.

"I think we ruined this chair." She laughed, stroking his hair.

He laid his head on her thigh and kissed the place where his lips met damp skin. "Disagree," he said, still catching his breath. "I think we improved on the old model."

After a while, he rose to his feet. Jamie extended his hands out to her.

"I should take care of that for you," she said, gripping his hands and letting him scoop her up. She dropped one down to palm the tightness in his shorts, which made him groan loudly enough to consider making an equally hot mess on his desk.

But he had other plans.

"Oh, I know you will," he practically growled. He picked her up, tossed her over his shoulder, and carried her toward the stairs.

"What—where are we going?" she shrieked playfully.

He slapped her ass. "I promised to take you to bed, remember?"

Brinton laughed and squeaked the whole way there.

SOME TIME LATER, after Jamie made her hoarse from screams of a more sensual origin, Brinton awoke with her head on Jamie's smooth, warm chest, his even breathing an entrancing meditation, his scent cloaking her skin. It was heaven—except that she desperately needed to pee. She kissed his chest and wriggled out from beneath his arm, hand lightly gripping her hip, and tiptoed to his bathroom.

As she washed her hands in the creamy white marble sink, she studied her naked body in the mirror. She was the same person, but she appreciated every curve, dip, and dimple with a newfound confidence. Jamie, and his patient, gracious affection, amplified it all. She thought about the song he had written for her and felt giddy all over again.

Jamie outstretched his arm, expecting the sleek contours of Brinton's body. Instead, he found a shock of cold sheets stretched across his king-sized bed. It was still dark out. Across the room, a faint breeze carried the chorus of cicadas and tree frogs through the open sliding glass doors. He sat up, eyes still glazed with sleep, instinctively searching for proof that Brinton hadn't escaped into the night.

What if she decided he wasn't worth the gossip—and erosion of her credibility—when the teaser article went live later that morning? He'd been trying to evade those poisonous thoughts, but like most did, they bared their fangs after midnight.

His pulse slowed as he spotted her cowboy boots and dress in a heap at the foot of the bed. He swung his legs over the edge and peered out at the lake. The moon shone like a spotlight, and he needed clarity.

Jamie reached for his phone on the nightstand. He knew he shouldn't; it would absolutely make him feel worse. But he had to see it for himself. Like his father had warned.

Jamie googled Brinton's name.

As he scrolled through the results, clicking into gossip websites rehashing their Grammys interview and scanning seedy comment threads, an icy wave of disgust crashed over him.

*She'd screw him on camera for five more seconds of fame.*

*Hideous! She should k*ll herself and save us the embarrassment.*

*Black girls are so nasty. There's your proof.*

Nausea and shame rooted in Jamie's gut. He'd been so self-absorbed to ignore this. Hell, Brinton had to tell him that he'd embarrassed her on the Grammys stage; it hadn't even occurred to him. All because he was blinded by his own optimism—no, his privilege—both as a white man and as someone who'd been insulated by wealth.

Someone who'd never weathered the storms of a real, committed relationship.

What if he couldn't comfort Brinton like she needed? She said she could handle the critics. Ultimately, despite being the most talented woman he knew, she would be judged—and defined—by who she slept with, for the rest of her career. Her character would be assassinated. It would be his fault.

His father was right.

Jamie ran both hands over his face and filled his lungs with as much oxygen as they'd take. If he did make new music, his own music, and it wasn't any good, he would have ruined her career—and her life—for nothing. What if she blamed him for that? He'd lose her.

His stomach seized. It reminded him of the tunneled loneliness of losing his mother. He fruitlessly tried to shake it away.

Brinton had saved him from his nightmarish future, but he couldn't guarantee he'd do the same for her. That worried him most. Somehow, he'd fuck it up. He couldn't take what hurting her again would do to him.

"Can't sleep?"

Jamie jumped as Brinton pressed her soft lips between his shoulder blades. He hadn't heard her come in.

"I can now," he said, clasping his hand over hers as it caressed his chest.

Her fingers danced along the hollows of his abs. "What if I'm not sleepy yet?"

Sleep-thick and husky, her tone was unambiguous. Ordinarily, it would have lit him up like a Roman candle. But now, he needed something more than her body. He was scared, and he needed to know that, at least for the next few hours, he was everything that she needed. Before everything between them changed.

He turned to face her, knees touching, and took her hands in his. "Can I hold you?"

Even in the dim moonlight, her caramel-brown eyes warmed. "Of course, Jamie."

He slipped his fingers through her braids and gently pulled her closer, letting his lips say everything he wasn't ready to yet. She lay on her side, and he fit his body tightly around hers. Jamie breathed in her sweet scent, one hand smoothing her hip, the other resting on her steadily beating heart as it lulled him to sleep.

# CHAPTER FORTY-FOUR

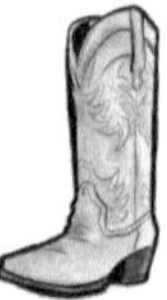

It might as well have been Christmas morning. At 6:59, Brinton's eyes flew open, eager to greet the day, and her future. The teaser for her article would be posted any minute now. She was slightly dismayed to find Jamie was already up. But soon, he'd be back to celebrate. Hopefully by making pancakes. Wasn't that what boyfriends did in all the movies? She'd be equally happy to let him press hickeys into her inner thighs until she screamed.

Her flight home to New York wasn't until that afternoon. Hopefully, he'd do both. She wet her lips and sank in the possibilities.

Brinton slipped his University of Tennessee T-shirt over her head, grabbed her phone, and bounded down the stairs. She wanted to be with him when she saw the headline for the first time.

Jamie was on the couch, his shirtless shoulders striped with the first beams of morning sun. Golden waves tousled and beautiful as ever.

She slowed her tempo, then slid next to him. "The article's out. Shall we pull it up?"

He didn't look up, but stared at his own phone in his hands.

"I saw it," he said, voice more distant than she'd ever heard it.

When her fingertips brushed his shoulder, he finally looked at her. His eyes were cloudy, like he hadn't slept. The corners of his lips lifted, but something drowned his attempt to commit.

"What's wrong?"

"You should pull it up."

She did. At the top of *Landmark*'s website, in bold black letters, read:

Preview: Jamie Crawford Jr. and Brinton Shaw, everyone's favorite Grammys couple, reunite for a groundbreaking confession.

Brinton blinked at her glowing phone screen to ensure it wasn't a mirage. Yes, the headline was a little click-baity. It wasn't what she had submitted to Rich, which focused on Jamie's fresh start, not *their* internet stardom. However, seeing the article, out in the world, meant *everything*.

She finally had something to show for all the years she had languished in the margins.

"Holy shit, Jamie." She kicked her feet and squealed. "We did it."

His smile had collapsed and body remained rigid. "Scroll down to the comments."

She did what he asked, reading in silence.

*Gobbling D for another headline?*

*Stop trying to make them happen. That bitch is nasty. #NotMyCouple*

*Jamie would never date a n—*

Brinton stopped reading. Even at seven in the goddamn

morning, the bigots were gonna bigot. But she knew this was coming, and she'd deal with it. Eventually. She closed her eyes, and swallowed it down, because it didn't matter.

It shouldn't matter.

"Ouch," she said lightly, hoping to make him smile that smile that lit up her entire world. "Good thing our website manager has a block button. He'll clear out all those comments and—"

Jamie turned to her, took her hands. "Brinton, honey. I—"

His voice cracked with emotion, like it pained him to keep going. Why wasn't he happy?

He exhaled, shoulders slumping from the force. "We can't do this."

SHE SQUEEZED HIS HANDS TIGHTER, her sincerity a pickax to his heart. "I don't—Jamie, what's going on?"

"Sweetheart, we can't be together," he continued, still unsure if he was in a nightmare.

But he had to do this.

"I can't let you be villainized again for my benefit. Look at that headline, look at those disgusting comments. Every amazing, beautiful thing you'll do in your career will be poisoned by me. They'll chew you up and spit you out. You don't deserve that."

His phone buzzed, but he ignored it.

She rubbed her thumbs across his knuckles. Slowly, he pulled away, even as he'd rather take a dagger to his abdomen than to let her go. "This is the only way you get the career of your dreams. I know how important that is to you."

"Jamie, please." Her eyes were stretched and her voice wavered. "Being with you is my choice. You promised me that you wouldn't make decisions on my behalf. We agreed—"

"I know. But baby, don't you see? This is my decision to make. I'm trying to help you, like you helped me."

She shot up from the couch, tightly wrapping her arms around her ribs, as if that were all that kept her from collapsing. "But—I thought you cared about me?"

He rose to meet her frantic eyes. His sprouted fresh tears, but he didn't wipe them away. It wouldn't change how the glorious thing that had saved him had to end.

"More than you can ever know, Bee. I think I lov—"

His voice was anemic, devoid of the confidence needed to say those three words. There was no doubt that he loved her, he finally knew, because he wouldn't be willing to let her go otherwise. So that she had a chance to live the full life she deserved, outside fame's punishing glare.

Jamie's mother never got that chance. She wasn't protected, and he still lived with that pain every day. Telling Brinton that he loved her would only muddy this disaster, which he dragged her into by asking for her help and selfishly falling for her.

"Are…you ashamed of me?" she asked, voice weakening by the second.

Jamie stumbled backward at the accusation. He didn't trust himself to be the man she needed, in a world hell-bent on tearing them apart. She deserved a clean break, even as he ached to press her trembling body into his.

"Honey, please—"

"Did you ever care about me?" she sputtered.

Ringing panic blared between his ears, making it difficult to fucking *think*. If he ignored his gut and they stayed together, it would only be a matter of time before the reality of being in a relationship with a musician set in: ruthless chatter and infinite late nights and unpredictable days.

Brinton, as strong as she was, would weather much of it alone, as his mom did, while he was God-knew-where making a name for himself. He couldn't risk repeating his father's mistakes.

But if Jamie let Brinton go—the *right* thing—he'd lose her forever too. There was no way to win.

"Were you using me?" she asked, breaths ragged.

He slumped back on the couch, hands cradling his forehead. It disgusted him, but the only way she'd choose herself was if she hated him. She'd never accept this if she didn't. Regret clawed up his spine as he did what he had to.

"I only needed you to tell my story."

More than his songwriting grift or that Heartbreak Prince ruse, this was his most unforgivable lie. "Michael should be outside to take you to the airport."

She shut her eyes, like she could burst from her resistance. "How could you lie to me, for all these days?"

Next to him, Jamie retrieved a thick stack of papers. His songwriting contract. "Take this, for your article."

She batted them away. "I don't want these."

"You have to, Brinton—"

Jamie's phone buzzed again, but he threw it across the room. It ricocheted off his mantle, sending his Grammy tumbling to the hardwood. Served it fucking right.

They both stared at the mangled statue, the gramophone cracked and severed from its base.

With a trembling hand, she snatched the packet from him.

Her chest was heaving by the time she raced upstairs to retrieve her things. He wanted to reach for her, but it was like sand slipping through an hourglass. Against what his heart demanded, he had to let her go. He stood idly on his porch, tears blurring his vision and stinging his throat, as she slammed Michael's SUV door.

Jamie was halfway upstairs when the front door swung open. His body throbbed with agony. If it were Brinton, seeing her beautiful face, especially after what he'd done, would kill him.

"Jamie?" It was Sammi. She sounded distressed.

He took the steps two-at-a-time and met her at the door. Her hair was pulled into a messy bun, her cheeks flushed. Her mascara was smudged.

"Sam, I already know about the *Landmark* article," Jamie croaked. "I can't get into this right now—"

"Jamie, it's your mamaw," she screeched. "She had a bad fall and is in the ICU. Nobody could get hold of you, so they called me. We gotta get to the hospital now."

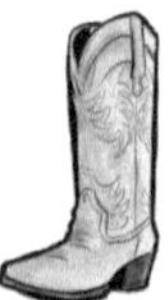

The next few hours were a blur, but Brinton vaguely remembered jamming what she could fit into her suitcase. Then escaping in an Uber perfumed with stale cigarettes and rotting takeout, made worse by her snot-bubbled sobs in the back seat. She refused to let Michael drive her, even at Jamie's behest. Her flight was delayed twice, but eventually, she made it back to New York City.

She collapsed into bed, still in her jeans and Jamie's T-shirt. The same pillows, same quilt, and the same stack of unread novels on the nightstand. Yet, it all felt unfamiliar.

It wasn't the room or the sounds or sights of the city that had changed. It was her. Jamie had left a nasty scar that would never heal.

He was ashamed of her. As she had always feared, she, a social pariah and anxious outcast, had been too much to keep him. Or perhaps, not enough to make him stay.

Eventually, the adrenaline subsided, and sheer exhaustion dragged her into a comatose-deep sleep. She didn't dream. Her splintered heart wouldn't allow it, lashing her for giving it to a man who couldn't keep it safe.

The next morning, Rich met Brinton in *Landmark's* conference room. Across the table, he beamed at her and held up a large framed document, which faced away from her.

She loathed a curtain reveal.

"So, big day," he said, with the enthusiasm of a man on his fourth double-espresso. He nodded to the frame.

"Sure," Brinton said. He'd called her in to reveal the final layout for her cover story, which, annoyingly, he was dragging out. She wanted to get this over with so she could return to her previously scheduled wailing in the dark.

"The Crawford teaser yesterday, thanks to your reporting in the field, was off the charts. The traffic alone nearly broke the site. Every major outlet in the country picked up the story."

"Oh. That's good, right?"

"That's fucking great." He tapped his pianist-thin fingers along the frame's top edge. "I got your email with his songwriting contract—holy shit, by the way—so the only thing left was to show you this. I even had it framed for you. Well, my assistant did it. And she picked the frame. But she used *my* company card."

He flipped it around. The gleaming black wood frame looked expensive, she'd give him that. On the left, there was Jamie's stunning *Landmark* cover photo. He was perched on a wooden fence that she recognized from his property, softly smiling as he held his lacquered black acoustic guitar. Above him, in white curved letters, the headline read: *Jamie Crawford Jr. Breaks Free.*

Her breath snagged on her ribs.

*Without me.*

Then, her heart dropped into her combat boots.

Mounted in the right side of the frame, her full article and her byline. Only, it wasn't *her* byline. In italicized black script: *By Agatha Cornwall, with Additional Reporting By Brinton Shaw.*

Brinton's neck jerked backward and both scapulae knit together. She was in an episode of Jordan Peele's *The Twilight Zone*, where an unassuming Black woman's emotional breakdown triggered a black hole that swallowed Manhattan, never to be seen again.

Yet, now was no time for swallowing her feelings or being *palatable*. She was fucking pissed. "'Additional reporting by Brinton Shaw'?"

His eyes bulged. "Something wrong?"

Brinton jabbed her pointer finger at the text. "Yeah, something's wrong. Why is Agatha credited for my story?"

"Oh, that," Rich said casually, blowing out a relieved breath. "That was me saving your ass. Look, I'm not an idiot —I read your copy, and it was great, but I couldn't shake the sense that something was going on between you and Crawford."

He counted aloud on his fingers. "You stayed at his father's mansion. Then, I found you waiting in his dressing room at Yeehaw Fest, not a handler in sight. Even if nothing happened, which, I'm not quite sure I buy, now you don't have to worry about anyone questioning your integrity. Agatha adds that extra credibility, free of charge. You're welcome."

Eyebrows raised, Brinton's scoff scraped against her teeth. "My credibility? You fueled questions about my integrity with that teaser article headline. You buried my integrity in service of getting clicks."

Brinton realized she was screaming when, from the corner of her eye, the entire office had huddled in front of the glass.

Naturally, Agatha waved from the front, recording with her phone.

Rich had pulled his hands from the table. She suspected he was reaching beneath the desk for a button to activate Angry Black Lady Protocol.

"I thought you'd be happy." He leaned in closer, trying to soften his eyes. He looked like he'd swallowed a fart, which might have been his brand of empathy. "I helped you out."

"*Helped me out?*" She shot up from her chair, snatched her purse from the table. "I gave everything to that story, to this job—"

"I think you're overreacting. You should see this as baby steps, training wheels for the next time. In a few years—"

"A few *years?*"

"—we can talk about getting your first solo byline."

At the conference room door, Brinton grimaced. Hopefully, it was the last time this asshat had the privilege of seeing her face. "That's the thing, Rich. I'm done waiting for the next time."

# CHAPTER FORTY-SIX

At the hospital, the electrocardiogram machine's persistent beep was Jamie's confidant. Emma Lou had hit her head after overshooting her serve on the tennis court. It had been touch-and-go, but the surgery was successful. Doctors expected her to recover, though it would be slow, given her age and risk factors. For now, she hadn't woken up.

Jamie had sent everyone else home hours ago, but he wasn't leaving her side. He'd been through enough trauma in the last twenty-four hours. He couldn't bear losing her too. There wasn't enough whiskey in the world to make him forget how it felt to have found serenity and to squander it.

The fallout from the *Landmark* teaser article had been swift. Tex relayed that the record label had canceled his current record deal, album release, and next month's tour. Which meant, in the eyes of the town, his career was dead.

Jamie wasn't exactly surprised. He made his choice when he agreed to hire Melvin, make two albums with him, and keep up the facade in front of an intrepid journalist, with whom he unwittingly fell in love.

Rightfully, Brinton hated him. He needed her to hate him so that she, at least, could be happy. Even still, the loneliness hacked at him.

When Jamie turned on his phone, it was flooded with missed calls and texts about the article, but he ignored them all. He leaned forward in the metal folding chair, which squeaked against the linoleum floor, and held his head in his hands.

The door creaked open, followed by familiar heavy footsteps.

"You should eat something."

Jamie looked up to see his father, his figure shadowy in the low light. He held out a Styrofoam cup filled with black coffee and a pack of Zebra Cakes. They were his favorite when he was a kid.

"You remembered?" Jamie asked. He took the cellophane package and the coffee.

"Mm-hmm. I remember your mama pitched a fit anytime I brought them home. 'Too much sugar,'" Jamie Sr. said, chuckling and shaking his head at the distant memory.

Perhaps it overwhelmed them both, because the next thing Jamie knew, thick tears had spilled down his cheeks.

"Sammi told me about Ms. Shaw," his father continued.

"I cared about her daddy," Jamie choked out, through ragged sobs. "But I had to let her go. You were right."

His father gripped his shaking shoulders, which soothed Jamie enough to catch his breath. He dragged his eyes across his T-shirt sleeve.

Jamie Sr. slid a metal folding chair beside his son's. "I think you and I are a little more alike than I'd hoped. I thought if I worked hard enough, stayed disciplined, I could give your mama this sterling life, and that would fix her problems," he continued. "That she'd be happy. All the money, resources, and doctors didn't give her what she needed. She *needed* me to show up for her in a way I couldn't. She *needed* me to stop trying to control every outcome and listen. But I didn't know how. I didn't come up in one of those 'feelings' households like on TV. So I was blinded by what *I* thought was best. Then, I lost her."

"We both did," Jamie said. His throat was raw from the exertion of speaking.

Jamie Sr.'s eyes darted to Emma Lou, whose chest faintly rose and fell in time with each damning beep. He sniffed and sighed deeply, then drug his palm against his own face.

*Was he crying too?*

Jamie had never seen it before, wasn't sure what else to do but sit in discomfort *with* his father, for once, quietly absorbing every wave of emotion. Together. His body ached with stress but somehow, the pang dulled with his father now beside him.

"Jesus, seeing her like this brings me back to that God-awful night," Jamie Sr. started. "First your mama, then I found you slumped over the steering wheel. They brought you into a room just like this. I swear, I thought I had lost you too."

He shook his head. "To think I put ambition over your happiness, what you wanted for your own life, for so long, I..."

As his father's voice broke off, Jamie felt like he was truly *seeing* him for the first time. Not as a man who ruled with an iron fist and a long memory. But as a man who'd made mistakes—maybe just as big as his own.

"I was so stupid and selfish the night I crashed your truck," Jamie cut in. "I was too overwhelmed to say it then, but I know it's why you had to be so hard on me. To shape me into a man who didn't let his emotions control him."

Jamie Sr. turned to his son. "No, son. You were just a boy. It wasn't your job to bury what hurt. It was my job to show you that it's all right to *feel* it, that you can *survive* it. I failed you."

"I wouldn't be in this mess if I'd listened," Jamie sputtered, gripping his knees.

"I pushed you to work with Melvin because I thought if I steered you right, I could protect you from the heartbreak that feeds this business. I pushed you away from Ms. Shaw because of how torn up you were after your mama…"

Jamie Sr. let his words drift into the ether.

"I was afraid that if something went wrong with Ms. Shaw, it'd destroy you all over again. I can see now how wrong I was, shoveling my insecurities onto you. Something's gotta change, and it's me. I wanna try, at least, if you'll offer me some patience. Old dog, new tricks and all."

"Okay," Jamie croaked. He meant it. "But what about Brinton? It's all my fault."

The wound was still so fresh, it almost didn't feel real. But, he knew, it absolutely was.

His father squeezed his shoulder. "You and me, we'll get through this too, you hear?"

Jamie nodded and let his father pull him close.

There was a distinct shuffling near Emma Lou's bed. She glanced back at them with a faint but sage grin. "I've waited nearly twenty years for y'all to say all that. Next time, don't make me wait until I'm strapped to a gurney."

She laughed. And so did Jamie and his father.

It was after two a.m. when Jamie left the hospital. A nurse —a friend of Emma Lou's—threatened to have him carried out by security if he didn't get some sleep in a bed and not stretched out across two metal folding chairs.

Thanks to the few extra cups of black coffee, Jamie was wide awake. After his father had left the hospital, Jamie jotted down ideas on his phone for the kind of album he'd make. Not a song here and there, as he had been, but a cohesive body of work that showed who he was as an artist.

Now, he had no obligation to anyone but himself.

In that hospital room, he realized that his whole life, he acted like he had to ask permission to be who he wanted to be. And he finally reconciled how much he'd masked his insecurities with meaningless sex and lies.

Of course, that didn't include Brinton. She was the best thing he'd ever called his. Rather than run from the heartbreak of losing her and the safety of his old life, he wanted to understand it.

Jamie flipped on his office lights, then sat in that wingback armchair. It smelled herbal-sweet, exactly like her. But he could use that.

He flipped on the monitors and desktop computer, then picked up an acoustic guitar.

# CHAPTER FORTY-SEVEN

## ONE MONTH LATER

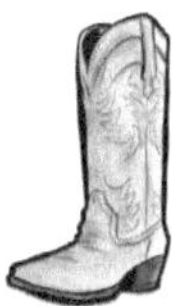

After quitting *Landmark*, Brinton had settled into a new routine: she woke up at a respectable two in the afternoon. Cold leftovers, eaten while standing over the kitchen sink, followed by a glass of tap water swished with a scoop of instant espresso, plopped directly into her mouth.

She spent the rest of the day in bed—wearing a T-shirt and cotton briefs ripped from the multi-pack her mom left by the door each week—binging comfort movies until her body forcibly shut down.

Lather. Rinse. Repeat.

"So, we're not even knocking anymore?" Brinton groused as Shay flung open her bedroom door, rudely interrupting her *Zenon: Girl of the 21st Century* triple-feature.

"Since Mom is out of town, I'm checking to make sure you're good."

Shay surveyed the staggered piles of clothes, crumpled baby wipes, and junk littering the floor and every surface. "Though it'd be hard to tell in this emo dungeon. This is a UFS crash site."

Brinton plucked a rogue spaghetti noodle from her Aaliyah T-shirt, slurped it into her mouth. "UFS?"

Shay pursed her lips. "Unidentified Freaking Shit. How do you live like this?"

"Feel free to leave at any point—"

"Relax, I'm kidding." She kicked an open package of golden Oreos with her chunky black loafer. "It's giving more Quantum of Sadness vibes."

Shay cautiously stepped through the minefield and cleared a small corner at the edge of Brinton's bed so she could sit. Immediately, her caramel eyes stretched open, and she pinched her button nose between her fingers. "Oh my God. Brinny, when was the last time you showered?"

In fairness, personal hygiene was the first thing to go when Brinton slipped into a depressive episode, which she was definitely in. It was somehow worse than the anxiety variety.

Brinton chucked up her shoulder. "I don't know. Sunday?"

"Bitch, today is Friday." Shay whipped her palms around the room. "I know you've been going through it for a few weeks, but you gotta get it together."

Brinton sat up, back aching from the slouch-induced curve in her spine. "Fine, pass me the baby wipes."

"No," Shay hissed. She slapped down Brinton's laptop screen. "You haven't left the house in a month. And you ditched Gael and the book club. I've been covering for you, but I'm done. That will make you wake the hell up."

Brinton wriggled to the edge of the bed and snatched the pack of baby wipes from the floor. "I'm awake, thanks to you. In case you forgot, I blew up my whole life. I got dumped by a man I should have known better than to trust. Forgive me if I hate myself so much I want to crawl out of my skin."

Shay smoothed her orange daisy-print maxi dress, eyes

narrowed contemplatively. "Well, at least you're not trending anymore."

Brinton flicked away an eye-boogie with a baby wipe. "Yeah, because Agatha is. She's getting praised for her *brave* storytelling in Jamie's profile. For stealing my fucking work, remember?" She collapsed back against the pillows. "And she got away with it."

"Yeah, that was shitty. It was so shitty I don't even have the words to properly sum up how shitty it was. But my question to you is, what are you going to do *now*?"

"Rot in peace. The universe skewered and roasted me extra-damn-crisp. I'm done, Shay."

"Why, because you're not perfect and need some help from time to time? I love you, but for years, I've watched you look everywhere but inside for validation. That only happens when you love and nurture yourself—and especially the hard stuff—first and foremost."

She flicked Brinton's toes. "You know I've struggled with my ADHD, but that's how I've managed it. Notice I didn't say that I've overcome, because neurodivergence isn't something to overcome. I will live with it for the rest of my life. It's the same with anxiety or depression or anything else. You can lie down and bleed for a minute, but you have to get back up. And you have to stop hiding from things that are uncomfortable."

Brinton scoffed. "Dad wouldn't."

"Uh-huh, and that's why Mom divorced him." Shay pulled a face. "And what about Jamie? You're going to pack all those feelings in a box and torch them, *Waiting to Exhale*-style?"

"Actually, yes."

Brinton had told Shay about her fight with Jamie. Only, she didn't have the heart to admit that he'd called and texted her for weeks. What was left to say? He didn't want to be associated with her. *She* didn't want to be associated with *herself*.

"He wanted his fresh start without me, and he got it. He used me."

Shay flung a dirty sock into the wicker laundry hamper. "Look, I thought about galloping down to Tennessee to slap some sense into him myself, but...I don't know, Brinny. People are like jigsaw puzzles with bent edges. The answer is never straightforward. His life was in shambles, even before you met him. That said, it's hard to believe that he woke up one morning and decided to stop caring about you. You need to talk to him. He *wants* to talk to you."

Brinton bolted upright. "How do you know I've been ignoring his calls?"

"Ha—I do now." Shay clapped her hands triumphantly. "Besides, I had a hunch. Your phone's been blowing up, and bitch, nobody calls you but me."

Brinton rolled her eyes. "Wow, thanks for that."

"What are sisters for?" Shay stuck out her tongue. "At the very least, now that some time has passed, it's worth getting some closure."

"What are you, a disciple for Mom's rules for well-adjusted living?"

"Whatever gets you out of those crusty-ass pajamas," Shay trilled. "Lie to me all you want—which, you're horrible at, by the way. I know you still care about that man. I also know you deserve to be happy. Aren't you tired of giving up on yourself?"

"I can't call him." Brinton's cheeks warmed with the looming threat of his rejection all over again.

"I didn't say you gotta call him. You're a brilliant writer. Use your words." Shay flipped open the laptop, where Zenon's smiling face was still paused. "Who's the white girl?"

"Zenon, Disney Channel Princess and the GOAT of space," Brinton said. "You are so uncultured."

"Ah, how uncouth of me," Shay snorted, sauntering to the door. "I really hope it works out for you two. I no longer dabble in the men, but Jamie's face was made for riding."

Brinton didn't want to smile, but the corners of her lips betrayed her.

When Shay was gone, Brinton closed out of the movie. On her home screen, her Photos app randomly generated a beaming Jamie on the pontoon boat. Golden sun kissing his face and chest. It felt like someone had taken a Louisville Slugger to her core.

What did that mean? That Shay was right? Brinton had lost, round for round, in bouts with her own self-doubt.

She rolled out of bed and crossed to the old wood dresser by her door. Opening the top drawer, she tore through the abandoned receipts, single socks, and maxi pads until she found the business card with the number of the psychiatrist her mother had suggested. Brinton had lived through this bad movie enough times to know the ending. She needed to rewrite the story.

She plucked her phone from her knotted bed sheets and dialed.

A few days later, outside an Upper West Side bar, Brinton considered her options: she could go home, where another season of *Insecure* awaited her. Or, she could do the exposure therapy homework Dr. Mensah, her new psychiatrist, had given her to help address her panic disorder. The idea was that gradually, the more she immersed herself in places and scenarios that triggered her, the less likely she was to experience severe panic attacks.

That's how she found herself in the crowded hellscape that was a professional networking mixer for Columbia alumni.

The bar had that old New York City feel, dimly lit with cracked leather booths and permanent rings on the tables from the many pint glasses of yore. This was the first time Brinton had been out since she left Iris. It was nothing like the Skylight's neon glow, but it would do.

She slipped into a booth with a glass of tap water and waited. The plan was to stay for twenty minutes, enough time not to feel like she completely lied when she reported back to Dr. Mensah tomorrow morning. She pulled out a copy of *Pleasure Activism* by Adrienne Maree Brown, but only got a few lines in before the seat across from her dimpled and the table lurched forward.

She looked up to find a woman with a crown of Bantu knots and violet lipstick that popped against ebony skin. Brinton learned that Aida was a literary agent who, on the side, was set to open her own YA Fantasy–themed bookstore in Brooklyn.

They bonded over their mutual distaste for forced networking and, surprisingly, Aida's admission of being a highly functioning Virgo with OCD. To her surprise, Brinton was drawn to Aida like a moth to a flame. It had been weeks since she'd smiled so hard.

A few hours later, Brinton hunched over her laptop in bed. She opened the manuscript for her would-be novel. It had been at least a year since she last touched it. Then, she thought about what Jamie had said weeks ago at the bar.

*You're an artist, like me.*

The draft was a mess of half-baked prose, but it was hers. That was part of the artistic process, as Aida reminded her when they had talked at the mixer.

Screw it, she *was* an artist.

Brinton massaged paragraphs and strung together lines of dialogue for hours. By the time she looked up, the sun had started to rise, shading the sky a spectacular shade of iris.

# CHAPTER FORTY-EIGHT

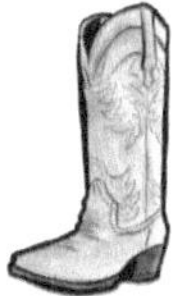

"*S*hit, man. You trying out for a remake of *The Life and Times of Grizzly Adams?*" Cory did a double take after popping his head into Jamie's home studio the following Monday. "I almost didn't recognize you with that beard."

Jamie had been so busy writing and recording *Honeybee*, a six-song EP, that apparently, he'd made enemies of his razor and can of Barbasol. He stroked the wild, dark-blond bush and smiled. "A worthy sacrifice for my art. Is everybody here?"

As Cory flopped down on the cobalt velvet couch, Jamie winced, remembering Brinton sitting there for the first time not too long ago. Watching him pour his heart out. He missed the hell out of her.

"I think your daddy's on the way back from picking up Mamaw, but I reckon they'll be here any minute. Are you gonna finally reveal why you assembled us all here? I love a good mystery, but the Braves play in an hour."

Jamie stood from the new ergonomic armchair at his desk. It didn't smell a thing like Brinton, which made things simpler and more devastating at the same time. But the reduced distractions had served him because a lot had changed in six weeks.

The circus of the *Landmark* ghostwriting article had died down, and while there was no shortage of trolls on the internet who called him a jackass-Nepo-baby-phony, the truth was out there. He had accepted that. That was, in part, thanks to a few sessions with his old therapist, who helped him sit with that discomfort.

A little whiskey under the silver moonlight didn't hurt either.

But today, Jamie decided it was time to share his plans with the people he loved most.

"I will—when everyone's here," Jamie called as he walked out the door.

Cory shot up behind him. "Why does this feel like a reverse intervention?"

A few minutes later, Jamie stood in his living room by the mantle. Across from him, Emma Lou, Tex, Cory, and Sammi sat on the couch while his father was posted in the tobacco leather armchair in the far corner.

Jamie cleared his throat. This had been a long time coming, and he was ready. "Y'all are the most important people in my life, and I would be nothing without you. I haven't always been easy to deal with"—Jamie looked directly at Tex and Sammi, who smiled back—"but I need all of you."

His gaze shifted to his father.

"But I acted like I didn't have a choice in how my story played out. I'm making the right choice now. Last night, I finished my first EP, which I wrote and performed...entirely. And I'm gonna release it soon. I hope I can have all your support."

"Of course, son, whatever you need," Tex said.

Sammi draped her arm around Tex's shoulder. "You're stuck with us until the end of the line."

The invisible anvil lifted from Jamie's shoulders. "Good. The EP's called *Honeybee*. I was thinking I could play it for you now?"

The room erupted in wolf-whistles and applause as Jamie pressed play.

Not long later, Jamie's living room buzzed with excitement. He felt good about what he'd made, but this response was exhilarating.

Emma Lou, who had recovered nicely from her accident, rose from the couch. "I think it's marvelous. But why stop with us? The whole world needs to hear this."

"Mamaw, please be careful," Jamie nearly shouted as he helped her back down to her seat. "You got out of the hospital, like, fifteen minutes ago."

"Oh, please. I'm fine," she said, playfully waving him away. "I'll be on the court in no time. Can't let those old birds think I've lost my edge."

Amused, Jamie rolled his eyes. He peered at his father, who hadn't said a word since he arrived.

"We can start shopping this EP for a new deal," Tex mused, rubbing his round chin.

Jamie sighed. He needed to get out ahead of this before history repeated itself. "I appreciate it, Tex, but I don't want to jump into a full project right away."

"Well, what do you wanna do?" Jamie's father asked, finally. The room fell silent, save for the rattling of ice in Jamie Sr.'s whiskey as he sipped.

Jamie swallowed the rising dread in his throat. "I wanna put the EP out but haven't figured out how."

His father shifted in his seat, took a long sip. "Then we'll put it out."

Jamie's heart felt like a sandbag. Ever since that night in

Emma Lou's hospital room, things had been better between them than they had been in years. He didn't want to go back to square one by agreeing to release his most personal work on his father's imprint.

"But not on my imprint, on your own label," his father said, as if reading his mind. "Go independent like you wanted. Tex and I can help set it up, but it will be yours creatively. We could have it done by the end of the week."

Jamie did a double take, Tex slapped his hands excitedly, and Sammi drew an emphatic whistle.

"I don't know what to say," Jamie said quietly, almost unable to process what had happened. "I would love that. And I'll make you proud, Daddy."

"You already have," he said.

"We're all proud of you," Cory added.

Now Sammi was standing, practically levitating in her flowy red dress. "We could do an EP release show on Friday. Livestream it? Stage it somewhere classy and traditional."

"Respectfully, forget about tradition," Jamie Sr. said. Everyone, even Jamie Sr. himself, erupted in laughter. Once they settled, Jamie Sr. stood and crossed the room. "Let's focus on him. Son, how do you wanna play this?"

He rested his hand on Jamie's shoulder. Surprisingly, it settled him.

"We should stream it from my website, but I wanna perform the concert here. Call it a bonfire session, and I'll play it all live on acoustic. We'll invite all our friends from town."

"Perfect," Cory shouted, slapping his knees and stomping his boots.

Tex shot up with clenched fists, like his home team was up in the game's final minutes. "I love it. I'll start making some calls."

"And I'm already on it," Sammi said, typing furiously on her phone. "Any requests for the guest list?"

Jamie hoped Sammi wouldn't ask him that. "I mean, the usual crowd."

"What about Brinton?" Emma Lou asked. "I was so fond of her, and you were too. You may have fallen out, but if I know nothing else, it's that life is short."

Jamie squeezed her hand. "We're not exactly on speaking terms. I don't blame her after what I said. And now she won't return my calls or texts."

Cory joined Jamie at Emma Lou's side. "She'll come around. No one is immune to that charm of yours. The beard, though, is questionable."

Jamie lightly jabbed Cory in the shoulder.

"I'll try talking to her too," Sammi said, her nails clicking on her screen.

"Just because you ain't in the same room, it don't mean you can't reach her. That's what the music's for," Jamie Sr. said.

Emma Lou looked at Jamie in that way all grandmothers did when they knew they were right. "I have a feeling all those songs you played for us are about her. Be sure to look after that heart of yours. She might want it back someday."

# CHAPTER FORTY-NINE

After Brinton's therapy session with Dr. Mensah on Friday, she stared into the abyss of the open blog post on her laptop. They'd agreed that productively questioning her scariest thoughts would help her better manage them.

While she didn't know why Jamie had said what he did, Brinton warmed up to believing that he had the best intentions. She learned in therapy that forgiveness was a gift, not for others, but for oneself.

The open letter that Brinton had written was the start.

Publicly telling her story, her own way, was the path to freedom. Brinton longed to shed the anger and sadness, a crackled snakeskin, so she could become anew.

Pausing Sade on her headphones, Brinton read the words aloud one last time.

# AN OPEN LETTER
# BY BRINTON SHAW

*You probably know me as the girl who threw up on an unsus-pecting country music star at the Grammys. I became a punching bag for keyboard warriors and trolls hell-bent on making me feel as small as possible. But joke's on them: I already felt small. Because that's how anxiety tells you to feel every waking moment of your life.*

*So, for the record, I was not drunk or high out of my mind during that livestream. I was experiencing a severe panic attack.*

*Then, a few months later, I found myself in a strange, new place. That place was Iris, Tennessee, where the people took me in and showed me a spectrum of warmth and kindness I'd never experienced. One of those people was Jamie Crawford Jr. I don't need to tell you who he is. But for the uninitiated, watch his excel-lent performance at this year's Yeehaw Fest. He is as hardworking, thoughtful, and soulful as they come. And yes, he's made a few mistakes. I'm sure you read about those too, in an article published with my (albeit buried) byline by Landmark.*

*And about that article: while it was sold to you as an intimate look into an overexposed persona, Landmark manipulated the circumstances so they could benefit from my poor reputation—as soiled as Jamie's Grammys boots, you could say—to drive clicks to the website and sell print issues. And so, I quit. I was not fired, as many have claimed, because I allegedly slept with Jamie. This allegation factoring into such dialogue crystalizes our society's unchecked subjugation of women. Do better.*

*I'm also aware of infinite speculation about my personal relationship with Jamie. And the truth is, that's none of anyone's damn business. Until one day, if we choose that it is. What I will say is that in the time that I knew him, he encouraged me to accept myself, crippling fear and all. I'll always be grateful to him for that. He is a remarkable man who deserves everything that he's working toward in this next chapter.*

*If you're wondering, the worst part about leaving Landmark was breaking what I'm sure was the longest tenure for a Black staff writer. Sending thoughts and prayers for who comes next—you'll need them. Because Landmark values inclusivity only if it doesn't hinder their bottom line.*

*You will be the hot sauce on the stringy, unseasoned chicken breast that is corporate America. You will feel the hypodermic prick of anxiety every time a pair of skeptical eyes look straight through you. But remember: you are so much more than a box to be checked. You're an artist.*

*Jamie taught me that too.*

*I may have gone viral during my most mortifying moment on Earth. But now, with this open letter, I'm taking back my power. And my reputation.*

*O*nce she finished reading, Brinton made sure she uploaded the accompanying images correctly. Then, she posted it. In truth, it was anticlimactic, since no one followed her Substack page. But it was the first step.

Sammi had agreed to spread the blog link to all her media contacts, which Brinton needed for this to work. They'd been in touch over the past few weeks, and Sammi had shared updates on Emma Lou's recovery.

Turning down Sammi's multiple invites for Brinton to return to Iris and watch Jamie perform his new songs was a necessary evil. It was a goodwill gesture, since Jamie had decimated her heart, but how would it feel to stand there and look at him again? To feel every spike of emotion when they couldn't possibly be together? The well was too poisoned.

The concert was later that night, which was an unfortunate coincidence, but it wouldn't deter her plan. She opened a new text message to Sammi.

Brinton: Here's the link. Let's do this.

> Sammi: Here's to changing the narrative, honey.

An hour later, Brinton's phone exploded with texts and calls, her email was over-run, and her social media mentions popped off.

Including a repost from none other than Kendall Chase, where she wrote: "Us girls gotta stick together." Immediately after, Brinton earned a thousand more subscribers on Substack. Steadily, the numbers climbed.

JAMIE COULDN'T BELIEVE his eyes. Sammi texted him all kinds of things he was supposed to pay attention to, which, yeah, he often ignored, but the words—Brinton's words—in that Substack post left an indelible mark, as she had. He labored over each one as he sat on the open tailgate of his truck at the top of the hill overlooking the meadow. Their meadow.

Brinton was right—in a few short months, she'd been forced into the role of both public laughingstock and pawn for *Landmark,* which succeeded in its goal of making money off her pain. And then there were the beautiful, candid photos of him that she had embedded, including one of them together, lying in the grass before sunset in this very meadow.

This emotional gut punch was probably the last thing he needed before performing the most important show he'd ever done. He needed to see her, to hold her. To tell her how stupid he'd been not to trust her, or himself.

That was out of the question now. Sammi couldn't convince Brinton to come to the concert. As much as he wanted to go to her, he couldn't abandon this commitment.

He needed this concert to move on, like she had with her letter.

That was that.

Jamie climbed into his truck and drove home for soundcheck.

BRINTON WAS FLYING HIGH. Her usual pad Thai order, which she ate straight out of the carton, tasted even better. *High School Musical 2*, blaring from the TV in her mom's living room, hit even harder. She was with her family, which made her soul hit a falsetto.

"I can't believe what you did. That letter was ballsy as hell," Shay said, waving a veggie spring roll like a wand. "And I couldn't be more proud."

"Likewise," Athena said. She leaned closer on the couch between them and kissed Brinton on the cheek. What she'd done *was* ballsy, not to mention terrifying. But now she knew what it meant to have agency in her own life.

It felt fucking fantastic.

Her phone buzzed. She ignored it. It had been going all day, and Troy was about to launch into "Bet On It." Obviously, the best part of the movie.

"So, this is what people born in the nineteen-hundreds did for fun? Lip sync poorly on a golf course?" her neighbor Gael asked, brown eyes gleaming against his yellow hoodie. From the comfy armchair, which swallowed his small frame, he grinned wide through a mouth full of shrimp shumai.

For a twelve-year-old, he was a savage. But she was glad that he was there, and that, after plying him with sugar and Robux, he'd forgiven her for ghosting the book club for all those weeks.

"Um, rude," Brinton teased. "You'll understand when you're older."

Gael flicked his chocolate curls from his eyes and laughed. "Whew, Y2K did a number on your people, huh?"

She cracked a smile as her phone kept buzzing.

"Honey, don't you want to get that?" Athena asked, rolling out her hamstrings with a massage ball.

"Nope."

Shay craned her neck toward the coffee table, looked at the screen, and shrieked. "It's from a Nashville number."

Brinton's heart dropped like a bowling ball. It couldn't be Jamie. Could it? She hadn't heard from him in a few weeks because, no doubt, he'd given up, because she had been too afraid to answer his calls.

But what if he hated the blog she posted? She'd learned in therapy how to stop catastrophizing through mindfulness, but she wasn't close to mastering it.

"You should answer," Athena said, pausing the movie. "I know how hard this has been, but what if he wants to talk?" She had the good sense not to say his name, like he was a sexy-ass Voldemort.

"No, I don't think—"

Shay didn't let her finish before she picked up and tapped the speaker button.

"Hello?" Shay purred like a cartoon villain.

"Is this Ms. Shaw?" The voice on the other end was deep and a little gruff, like he'd swallowed tumbleweed, and clipped, like he didn't have time to waste. Brinton knew that voice anywhere.

"Hi, yeah, it's me," Brinton breathed, suddenly unsteady.

"This is Jamie," the man said, then cleared his throat. "Jamie Sr., his father. Did I catch you at a good time?"

Shay dropped the phone, but Brinton scooped it at the last minute. "No, I can talk. Um, how can I help you?"

"That was a helluva blog you wrote."

"Oh," Brinton said, failing to temper the surprise in her voice. "Thank you."

"I'll cut straight to the chase. I'm calling for a favor. Not for me, but for Jamie. My son didn't deserve what I put him through, and frankly, neither did you. I'm truly sorry for getting you involved."

"I appreciate that," she said.

Jamie Sr. was silent, as if searching for the words. "And he'll never admit it because, like his daddy, he's as stubborn as a mule, but he's still torn up over you. That makes for incredible music. But it also makes for a miserable person—I would know. You should see this horrible beard he's grown."

He laughed softly. It was the first time Brinton had heard it, and it was strangely soothing.

"Listen, I know Sammi told you about his show tonight. He's pretty nervous about it, but I thought if you could talk to him…"

Brinton waited a few seconds to think, then answered. She'd vowed never to set foot in Iris again. The wound was still too fresh to probe, so she had to protect herself.

Didn't she?

"I'm sure he's going to do great," she said.

"I…think he needs you there. He needs you in his life. The show's at eight. It's a two-and-a-half-hour flight from New York, but you could still make it, if you leave now."

He needed her in his life? At what point would he have told her that? Then she remembered all his calls that she'd declined and winced. Still, this was all too much, too sudden. Brinton was starting to feel better, feet firmly rooted in herself. The last thing she needed was her world, once again, upended by this earthquake of a man.

Gael silently thrust his fists in the air while Shay and Athena clasped their hands together, hopeful. The premise was absolutely insane, even though Brinton knew, deep down, she wanted to see Jamie one last time. For closure.

Was she crazy? Or was this her chance to bet on herself, like Troy Bolton, and be happy? It didn't matter because there was no way she could pull this off.

"It's already three. I think that's cutting it close," she said. "Besides, I have plans with my family tonight, so—"

"Go!" Gael, Shay, and Athena shouted emphatically. It was heartwarming, if not for the whole betrayal of it all.

Brinton chewed the fleshy inside of her cheek. "Well, I can't afford a same-day flight. As you know from my blog, I'm unemployed. I'm sorry, Jamie, but unless you can pull off a miracle—"

He didn't let her finish. "Why do you think I'm calling?"

# CHAPTER FIFTY-ONE

*A*s sherbet sunlight melted into the horizon, Jamie slung a 1957 Gibson acoustic with sunburst paint, a twelfth birthday gift from his mother, over his shoulder. He peered through his bedroom window and down at the front yard.

Once again, Sammi and Tex had outdone themselves. Dozens of friends and family had gathered on rows of logs near the bonfire and small stage. There were enough steel coolers, packed with ice-cold beer, for a University of Tennessee tailgate.

It was perfect, save for one thing missing. One person.

"You ready?" Sammi asked from the doorway. She twirled in her cork heels, which made her orange sundress float around her knees. "We've already got two hundred thousand people in queue to access the livestream, and we're expecting that to double in the next ten minutes. The on-site producer reckons your fans are gonna break the server."

Jamie always had pre-show jitters, but this felt like something different. He was re-launching his career. The new beginning he'd craved—a fresh, clean start. The air was thick with pressure, especially sharing this EP as an independent artist.

It felt better than he could have ever imagined.

Jamie ran a hand over his now–neatly trimmed beard and smiled. "And that's a good thing?"

"That's a great thing," she said. She playfully pinched his cheek. "You ready to make history?"

"If the creek don't rise," he said.

Minutes later, Jamie peeled through the opening chords of "Guiding Light."

It felt as natural as breathing.

JAMIE SR. DID PULL off a miracle by way of a private jet. Brinton had made him promise to make a donation to half a dozen environmental conservation groups to ease her conscience.

Nonetheless, Jamie Sr.'s generosity was no match for Nashville-area traffic on a Friday night. Brinton had been watching Jamie's livestream since she hopped into Michael's waiting SUV. It was already 8:34. Jamie was playing a six-song EP, which, by her count, might go on for another few minutes.

He was already halfway through the fifth song.

By the time the SUV lurched into Jamie's driveway, he'd finished his set. The crowd was cheering, and he was taking a bow. The show was over. And she had missed it, probably the most important performance he'd ever given.

It was cruelly fitting, given the star-crossed quality of their relationship.

Frozen in her seat, she dropped her phone into her lap. Disappointment snaked around her heart, growing tighter each time she exhaled. Why had she waited so long to see him, to say what she needed to say?

Now, it was pointless. The moment—*their* moment—had passed. He had moved on.

"I'm sorry, Miss Brinton. I tried to get us here quick as I could," Michael said. The sadness in his big, brown eyes almost made tears spring to hers.

"It's okay, Michael. Probably for the best. Actually, um, can you take me back to the airport?" Her former bravery squandered, she was embarrassed and wanted to go home.

Then, Jamie started speaking into the microphone.

JAMIE PEERED ACROSS THE CROWD. Sammi was sitting with Rhett, Cory and Priyanka next to them. Tex and his wife, Loretta, a petite woman with a '50s beehive hairdo, waved from the front row. He waved back, almost too overcome with emotion to speak.

But he had one last song to play.

"I wanna thank y'all for coming and supporting me through what has easily been the biggest transition of my life. These songs and stories I shared with you tonight mark the beginning of an exciting road ahead. But I have one more for you. It's not on the EP. Hell, I only now decided to play it. But it's dedicated to someone incredibly special to me."

*Just because you ain't in the same room, it don't mean you can't reach her.*

Jamie Sr.'s words reverberated in his mind. He looked to his father, who sat next to Tex, for reassurance. He nodded back.

Jamie looked straight into the camera in front of him. "She's not here tonight, but I pray that she's watching. Brinton, I miss you something fierce, and I'm begging that one day, you'll come back home to me. I hope you'll give me another shot, so I can…"

His voice broke off as the emotion swelled in his throat. Even as supportive whistles and pops of clapping rang out from the crowd, he let himself cry. For himself, for Brinton, and for the past that he couldn't change.

He dried his eyes with the back of his hand and chuckled. "For the record, I didn't write this one."

He let the smattering of laughter pass. "This one's a cover of 'Cherish the Day,' originally performed by the incomparable Sade. Baby, I know it's your favorite song. I hope you love it."

BRINTON'S HEART fluttered in her chest.

*Holy shit.*

Only those words spiraled in her mind, because she was overtaken by Jamie's stirring rendition of her favorite song, a gripping story of the intertwining of souls between lovers.

Should she move? Should she stay there?

Her phone buzzed incessantly as Athena and Shay blew up their group chat.

> Shay: OMG you better open-mouth kiss him, or I'm gonna scream!

> Mom: Brinny, he loves you! How romantic

Brinton tried to catch her breath as she typed.

> Brinton: Ugh, mom, please don't use that emoji

Mom: What? They're tears of joy! I saw it on online

Brinton: Not in this context

Shay: I'm canceling your internet plan!

Michael cleared his throat, slingshotting Brinton back into the moment. "Ms. Brinton, I don't mean to be forward, but I've watched a lotta rom-coms. Go get your man. What the hell are you waiting for?"

Brinton laughed, a broken, exasperated thing she recognized as the deepest sigh of gratitude. "That's a great freaking question."

Yes, she should move. She should go to *him*.

She flung open her door.

# CHAPTER FIFTY-TWO

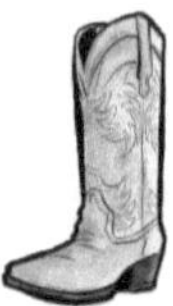

The driveway blurred by as Brinton sprinted toward the bonfire's red-orange aura, past the faint murmurs from the crowd. Finally, something in her told her to stop running. She was right in front of the stage.

He stopped playing, beholding her as an apparition that had come to life. In one motion, he pulled the guitar off his shoulders, set it on the stage.

"Hey," he said softly, voice trembling.

"Hey yourself," she said, so breathy she briefly worried if he'd heard her.

"You came."

"How could I not?" A coy smile spread across her lips. "You played my favorite song. You basically sent out the Bat-Signal."

He smiled, the one that reached his eyes. Jamie laughed as if he were still processing that what he'd done had worked. She held out her hand, and he lifted her onto the small platform. They watched each other, unsure if any of this was real or imagined, as the crowd whispered animatedly and recorded with their phones.

"I broke my promise to you," Jamie said, still holding her hands, eyes searching hers.

"Jamie—"

"Please, honey. I've waited so long to say this."

She nodded, biting her bottom lip, holding space for him to continue.

"I promised that I wouldn't make decisions for you, for us. But I was afraid. That don't absolve me, but the truth is, I thought if I couldn't control every outcome, that if all the noise that came with being linked to me got too loud, I'd disappoint you. And you'd leave me. I believed it because I've never been equipped to navigate any of this. Then, I let you believe a lie so you'd hate me. Thought it'd be easier that way. But dear God, Brinton, I couldn't ever be ashamed of you. I burn for you. You set me on fire with joy and peace I never thought imaginable."

He shook his head, squeezed his eyes shut. "You care for me so good, I wanna be a better man. So I can earn you. That's all I've wanted since the moment we met. I thought I was protecting you, but I was a damn fool."

Slowly, she dropped his hands so she could cradle his face, as warm and reassuring as she remembered. "I don't need you to protect me," she said, chest still heaving, "I want you to want me. I want you to want me even when I'm scared, and I can't find any light in the shadows. I want you to want me when my foundation is cracked, because I'm a work in progress, Jamie. But, little by little, I'm rebuilding myself. And I want you to want me anyway."

"Brinton, I don't want you," he said.

Her eyes stretched in disbelief, breaths rattling against her windpipe.

"I love you," Jamie continued, eyes softened. "I love you so much, I'd trade the last breath in my body to proclaim it. I should have told you that weeks ago, when I had the chance.

I'll say it 'til infinity: I love you. Bee, you are the love of my life."

Was she dreaming? No. This was happening, and she was ready. She loved him. She absolutely did.

"I love you too," she said, laughing, a release she felt like she'd waited years for. "I want a career that fulfills me, and I want to build that on my own merit. I want to be happy. And I want it all—with you."

It would have been a convenient coincidence that the bright lights caused the overflowing warmth behind her eyes. His own tears shimmered in the bonfire's glow.

Even the man's *tears* were stunning.

This moment, however, was anything but convenient; it was inevitable. Like him.

When he wrapped his arms around her waist and pulled her close, her stiff body melted into his tenderness. She draped her arms around his neck, delighting in his hypnotic scent. Neither of them gave a damn about the microphone and cameras.

Her lips curved into a playful smirk as she thumbed a tear from his cheek. "All this time, we could have been doing this instead of me watching *10 Things I Hate About You*, alone in my underwear."

Jamie tipped his forehead to hers. In his hickory baritone, he whispered, "Sounds like we got a lot to catch up on."

He pulled her into a slow kiss, and tingles zinged from her head to her toes. For a change, the good ones that signaled she was safe, loved, and exactly where she was supposed to be. She was so caught up that she almost didn't hear the chorus of applause and whistles. Gratefully, he smoothed his hands across her back.

"Well," she said, breaking their kiss but running her hands over his cheeks, relishing the soft bristles of his beard. "It looks like we gave the whole world quite the show. Again."

Eyes alight, he smiled down at her. "Mm, yeah. That sounds like us."

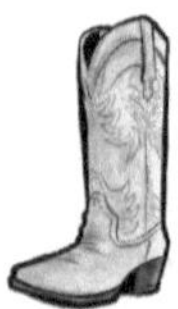

Brinton's cheeks flushed, and her heartbeat surged. Her thoughts blurred like paint on a spinning plate, and there was increasing certainty that she would pass out. Was it good that her lungs were an overfilled balloon, a single prick from obliteration?

But what followed—the electricity radiating through her body, prompting divine convulsions and making her scream unspeakable things—was well worth it.

Her body relaxed into the crisp white sheets of her bed. Well, *their* bed.

So they could split their time between Iris and New York City, Jamie purchased their charming Tribeca penthouse. Its exposed brick walls and floor-to-ceiling windows over-looking the Hudson River never ceased to make her gush.

Brinton exhaled comically loud. "Tell me, am I ever supposed to get tired of that?" Something about that beard made this part of her morning routine even better.

Jamie popped his head up from where he'd taken up resi-dence between her still-trembling thighs. And he was the best kind of roommate, as he generously proved every morning and night.

"Not if I can help it." He planted a soft kiss on her forehead and smoothed a hand down her thigh. "I think that performance deserves some coffee."

He climbed out of bed, an appropriately smug smile on his face.

"Yes, please," she mewed, still breathless. "But, um, don't you wanna put on some pants first?"

Unashamed, she dragged her eyes ever-so-slowly below his waist.

"Hey, eyes up here." He playfully used his pointer and middle fingers to guide her. "And for the record, no. When I get back, I'm gonna make you jump another octave."

She tightened the silk scarf tied around her head and laughed. "You're ridiculous. And you're gonna sweat out my silk press."

He winked. "Baby, I ain't doing my job if I don't."

After Jamie's *Honeybee* EP banked an astounding one million streams its first month, every label in Nashville clamored to sign him. He settled on a great deal, and his father and Tex helped negotiate terms that included creative control of his own imprint, ownership of his masters, and a brand new, full-length album. Sammi took over PR for Jamie's imprint and spearheaded an initiative to sign ten new country artists from diverse backgrounds each year.

Sometimes, late nights at the recording studio and grueling tour schedules forced them apart for longer than what felt comfortable. Sometimes, the paparazzi photos or venomous comments section burrowed beneath Brinton's skin. But Jamie was a faithful balm, as she was for him. It wasn't always easy to traverse newly unlocked levels as they built a life together. Yet, they made a promise to embrace each one, so that whatever darkness befell them, they'd always find their way back home.

Jamie kissed her left hand, admiring his mother's sparkling solitaire on her ring finger. "The only thing that looks better on you is me," he said, giving her a coy look that almost made her yank him back into bed.

Three months ago, at sunset, he proposed at their meadow. And when her thighs cradled his hips, her tears flowed from a place of all-consuming, immeasurable love. When they went Instagram-official the next day, Brinton stayed off Google to protect her damn peace.

After watching Jamie's fantastic, naked butt turn the corner, Brinton checked the clock on the nightstand. She had a few hours until she was due at Aida's wildly successful bookstore and smoothie bar, Pages and Potions, in Brooklyn, where Brinton was the head curator.

The store was five minutes from Shay and Miley's new condo and a few blocks from Athena's new favorite yoga studio, so Brinton could count on them to pop in and lovably annoy her almost daily.

It was also the new home of the monthly book club Gael now ran on his own, and it introduced her to a vibrant community of friends and colleagues who were equally passionate about stories. When Aida recently agreed to represent Brinton's finished manuscript, Brinton knew it was fate.

She couldn't have dreamed about this a year ago when she first met Jamie, and she was on the brink of falling apart. If what she went through taught her anything, it was that life would constantly shift unexpectedly. But the goal wasn't to hold on so tightly that she shattered in the process. The more open she was to possibility and taking the risks that felt rewarding, the more likely she was to survive the inevitable thrash.

But she wasn't surviving. Now, she was thriving, despite the occasional nausea from the anti-anxiety medication Dr. Mensah prescribed. But even that was worth it, because it meant Brinton was caring for herself. Because she now believed, with every fiber of her being, that she *deserved* to be cared for.

Jamie returned with two steaming mugs and handed her one, then he crawled back into bed beside her. His not-too-sweet vanilla latte was one of the many things she'd grown to love about him.

She took a decadent sip, let her eyes roll back, and groaned appreciatively. "God, this is perfect."

"How about that." Slowly, Jamie nuzzled her neck. "You just gave me an idea for my next song."

# OFFICIAL PLAYLIST - "ONE NIGHT IN IRIS"

Scan to listen to the official AMERICAN LOVE SONG playlist, "One Night in Iris," on Spotify:

# ACKNOWLEDGMENTS

*American Love Song* started as a whisper. Now, it's a fully realized dream. None of this would be possible without my parents, who encouraged my voracious reading habit (and even bigger *Babysitter's Club* collection). I love you with all of my heart. I must also tip my hat to James Crawford Middleton Sr., my late granddaddy, a true icon. Heaven got a good one.

To my fiancé, thank you for being the bumper guards for my daily crash-outs while writing this book, and through the ups-and-downs of life. Baby, look what we've built.

I am privileged to partner with my agent, Naomi Eisenbeiss, at InkWell Management. You empower me to dream bigger. This book wouldn't be what it is without you.

To my incredible mentors: Amy Spalding, the very first person to read a single word of this manuscript. I am in awe of your humor, wit, and generosity. To my SmoochPit fairy godmothers, Amy Buchanan and Alexandra Vasti: you believed in me—and this book—when I wasn't sure I believed in myself. I will never, ever forget how much your friendship means to me. Christine Cowan: thank you for making SmoochPit a safe space for romance authors of color. You changed my life. And to Dr. Jennifer Maritza McCauley: You are the best teacher I ever had.

The Dream Team: my cover illustrators Amanda Webb and Ali Shearer, and my copy editor, Britt Tayler. You made me the luckiest girl on Earth.

To my friends, my lifelines, who tirelessly uplifted me so I could reach this incredible milestone after three long years: Shane Tully, Tzywei Cheng, Cassie Ramoska, Michelle Mitchell, Greta Wolfe, Jasmine Ogunjimi, Hayley Todd, Dr. Shaina Thomas, Jacklyn Laryea, Sammi Minion, Lauren Porter, Catherine Morse, Ellie May, Iris Venturino, Mouna Coulibaly, Petra Lurch, and Michelle Kempner.

Thank you to every single beta reader and bookish creator who showed Brinton and Jamie so much love. I'll never stop making art that uplifts marginalized voices and pushes us toward a more compassionate consciousness.

Beyoncé, Hayley Williams, Shania Twain, and Taylor Swift. Your music was constantly on repeat, pushing me forward through many late nights. Let's go, girls.

And to you, dear reader, thank you for being here.

# ABOUT THE AUTHOR

Britt Middleton is a novelist, journalist and poet based in New York City. She writes sexy, conscious romances exploring self-identity. When she's not discussing current affairs with her cats, Coconut and Wakanda, she's probably baking sourdough. AMERICAN LOVE SONG is her romantic comedy debut. Connect with Britt at http://www.brittmiddleton.com

instagram.com/thebrittmiddleton
tiktok.com/@thebrittmiddleton